Dominic Ruggiero
b. 1903

—m—

Gina Cassella
b. 1907

Dominic Vechiarelli
b. 1930

—m—

Magdalena
b. 1935
(deceased)

Aunt Feen Ruggiero
b. 1932

Gianluca Vechiarelli
b. 1958

—m—

Mirella
b. 1957

Orsola
b. 1983

—m—

Matteo
b. 1981

Jaclyn
b. 1981

—m—

Tom
b. 1981

Valentine
b. 1975

Teodora
b. 2008

THE SUPREME MACARONI COMPANY

Also by Adriana Trigiani

FICTION

The Shoemaker's Wife

Brava, Valentine

Very Valentine

Home to Big Stone Gap

Rococo

The Queen of the Big Time

Lucia, Lucia

Milk Glass Moon

Big Cherry Holler

Big Stone Gap

YOUNG ADULT FICTION

Viola in Reel Life

Viola in the Spotlight

NONFICTION

Don't Sing at the Table

Cooking with My Sisters (coauthor)

THE

Supreme Macaroni Company

A Novel

Adriana Trigiani

HARPER

www.harpercollins.com

HarperCollins books may be purchased for educational, business, or sales promotional use. For information, please e-mail the Special Markets Department at SPsales@harpercollins.com.

FIRST EDITION

Designed by Jennifer Daddio/Bookmark Design & Media Inc.

Library of Congress Cataloging-in-Publication Data has been applied for.

ISBN: 978-0-06-213658-9

13 14 15 16 17   OV/RRD   10 9 8 7 6 5 4 3 2 1

In memory of Violet Ruggiero

THE SUPREME MACARONI COMPANY

1

The Hudson River lay flat and black like a lost evening glove. The clouds parted overhead as the distant moon threw a single, bright beam over lower Manhattan as though it were looking for its other half.

The big Christmas Eve moon appeared out of nowhere, like the diamond on my hand. From the roof of the Angelini Shoe Company, as far as I could see, it seemed the world had stopped spinning.

The opera of roaring engines and horns and screeching brakes on the West Side Highway was suddenly mute. Not even the turning of a page could be heard as the trucks came to a stop at the light. My fiancé and I were surrounded by sweet silence until the canopy over the door snapped in the winter wind, reminding me that this wasn't a dream. This moment was different from all the others that had come before it. I knew I would return to it in all its detail in the years to come, so I paid careful attention.

Gianluca Vechiarelli had asked me to marry him, and I had said yes to the man with the blue eyes, silver hair, and a full and complex past. But it was his future that I was invested in, that I would be a part of, and now he would be a part of mine.

A shoemaker would marry a tanner.

This could work.

Shoemakers and tanners form a symbiotic relationship out of necessity. One provides the leather while the other whips it into a glorious creation. At Vechiarelli & Son in Arezzo, Gianluca creates some of the most sumptuous leather, calfskin, and suede in Italy. He is also a meticulous artisan who monitors the silkworms in Prato as they spin glittering threads that are woven together to form their world-renowned fabrics.

Those Tuscan satins became our signature material used to build our family wedding shoes. My great-grandfather named his designs after memorable characters of the opera, so theatricality was as important to him as durability. For over a century, there has been and remains a shorthand between our families' shops. The Angelini Shoe Company in Greenwich Village has proudly used Vechiarelli & Son's goods for generations.

Gianluca is a master craftsman. He takes all kinds of leather and treats, dyes, presses, and buffs it so I might build the shoes I see in my imagination. The relationship is creative, but it's also a business. A savvy tanner knows which leather the major designers have chosen for the upcoming season and can guide the storefront shoemaker into the heart of current trends. When the designers swarm Italy like bees in search of the best goods, the tanner extracts their creative impulses like honey.

I met Gianluca for the first time on a buying trip a few years ago. His father and my grandmother had fallen in love, and I was the first to know about their love affair. As my widowed grandmother started over and went her way with Dominic, I was alone. When Roman Falconi, my boyfriend at the time (What is it about me and Italian men?), stood me up on the Isle of Capri, Gianluca, dispatched by my grandmother to check on me, arrived to make sure I was all right.

I didn't need or want a tour guide on the island where Augustus conducted his clandestine Bronze Age sexcapades, so our friendship had a rocky start. I thought Gianluca was handsome, but the observation was strictly superficial.

You can throw a wooden nickel into any crowd of men in Italy, and it will hit a great-looking guy. Gianluca is older than me, and I'd never dated someone in that particular category, so I didn't take his interest in me seriously. He had been married and had a grown daughter, so I had to drop a lot of my hard-and-fast rules to get to know him. I understand how a first impression is often just that, a quick snapshot that on its own merit is meaningless. After a vacation, in time, it gets lost in a shoe box full of them.

Gianluca is particular, exacting, and thorough when it comes to his work, a lot like me. We work well together, and now we'll partner at home as we build a family of our own. A chill goes through me when I realize that this moment almost didn't happen, and it would have been my fault.

Tonight began with a terrible mistake, a transgression that no other man or woman would overlook. But Gianluca forgave me. Sometimes redemption lands in your life like a bird and looks you straight in the eye, even when you believe you don't deserve forgiveness.

"It means everything to me that you asked me to marry you on this roof," I told him.

"I know how much you love your river. Whatever you love, I love."

"You just made everything so simple."

Gianluca lives and works in Tuscany, the creative heart of Italy. His only draw to New York City, Greenwich Village, and this roof is me. I wonder if he could be happy here.

Overhead, the sky was trying so hard to snow. The clouds moved over us like a silk canopy, and the two of us could have easily gotten lost beneath it, but Gianluca held me tight. It was as if he read my thoughts and wanted to reassure me. There was everything in his kiss, the glory of the moment, our high hopes for our future together, and forgiveness, the only proof of true love. I was ashamed that I had doubted him. After all, he still had faith in me, even when I had betrayed his trust.

"You know I love you," I told him.

Gianluca pulled me close.

"But you can cut your losses right now. Nobody ever has to know you asked me to marry you."

"But I did. And you said yes. And I want to marry you."

"Even after what happened tonight?"

"I don't care about that," Gianluca said firmly. "Forget it. Let's tell your family our news."

"Once we tell my mother we're getting married, it's iron-clad."

"Good."

"Full disclosure. I have serious—what I would call . . . flaws. And by the way, I'm getting worse as I get older."

"You'll never catch up to me in years."

"Or experience. Good point."

"You're perfect."

"Everyone seems perfect in the moonlight."

My truth seemed to take on a fever. I had to let him know every rotten thing about myself, right then, before he found out later and ran. "There are all sorts of predispositions to disease in my family tree."

"Should I be worried?"

"*Very.* We've got diabetes, heart disease, and dyspepsia. Less alarming but equally annoying are the onset of eye tics in our late thirties. I have middle-aged cousins who blink more than stare. There's a psoriasis that pops up after fifty. It attacks the elbows. Usually hits the women, but Cousin Toot got it on his head. No one knows why.

"Aunt Feen has suffered from depression and a lifelong bitterness that comes from low serotonin. Yeah, yeah, a pill could help, but nobody takes it. Bitterness is chronic, and it comes with cold sores when we're disappointed. Every now and then, there's the emotional jaundice."

"You turn orange?"

"In theory. Evidently we carry a glandular predisposition that prevents true happiness. It colors reality negatively, or at least that's what Dr. Oz says. He did a whole show on it. It's a mindset of certain Mediterranean DNA. Nothing can be good for long because it's already in a state of rot. That includes everything from mascara to baked goods to relationships. Oh, yeah. On the addiction side, we're sick."

"Drinking? Drugs?" Gianluca wondered.

"Gambling. We have bookies, cardsharps, and dice throwers on the Roncalli side, and they aren't necessarily talented. My uncle Peedee once lost everything including his shoes in a street game in Times Square and had to walk home to Queens barefoot. Luckily, he called it quits before he lost his pants. But now with Internet gambling, we can lose our shirts in the privacy of our own homes between courses at holiday meals. All bets are off."

"*Va bene.*"

"And there's the sugar. When you see any of the following surnames in any combination—Angelini, Roncalli, Bozzuto, or Fazzani—the confluence of those bloodlines creates a pancreatic nightmare that causes a glucose spike that gives way to a raging river of denial. We can't cope with reality, so we pretend everything away. Real problems carry the same weight as imagined anxiety. We press the panic button just *because.*"

"I've seen the panic."

"So you *know.* And you've observed the spiritual flailing firsthand. We pay mediums to connect to our dead ancestors, often just to remind them that they owe us money. Cousin Victoria is a coffee psychic who reads our espresso at the end of a meal. She saw my father's prostate cancer in my mother's cappuccino."

"Is that it?"

"I'd like to leave the list open-ended, if that's all right with you. Things will crop up as we go along."

"I'm sure." Gianluca smiled.

"By the way, and this is a big one . . . we aren't good with money."

"I am."

"That's a plus."

"Not that it would matter."

"Oh, it matters. I'm running a business here. We're making shoes in Argentina. Money matters."

"Whatever you say."

"If my family were made of porcelain, you'd be marrying into a bunch of crackpots. You should think long and hard about your future. You will be legally bound to our family forever. You should require a full workup by a team of physicians in advance and, at the very least, a consultation with a one-eight-hundred lawyer. I'm only a member of this club because I was born into it, but I worry about you. You have to be a little off yourself to choose me."

Gianluca threw his head back and laughed. "All families are crazy."

"Why is that?"

"People are involved."

"I've never seen a family as crazy as mine. Your family seems normal to me."

"Look again. My daughter married a strange family. They never speak in full voice. They whisper and are very remote. Professors."

"At least they have their keen intellects to hold them together. What have we got?"

Gianluca thought for a moment. Then he said, "You're shoe-makers. So, leather. Nails."

The penultimate romantic rooftop moment plummeted into ruination as Gianluca compared what we felt toward one another to the components of the common penny loafer. "Oh, and love," he said, catching himself. "Everlasting love."

"Oh, right. *That.*"

"If you have love, what more do you need?"

"Permission."

Gianluca laughed. "When I asked your father for your hand, he cried."

"He was disappointed you only requested the hand. He hoped you would take the entire kit."

"I want the kit."

Couldn't Gianluca see that my father's tears were not from joy but relief?

Ever since Dad got the radioactive seeds implanted for his bum prostate, he'd been an emotional wreck, worried about his children, fearing for our security, hoping that none of us would have to face the unknown of the future alone. (Never mind he also had to take female hormones and for a moment thought he'd permanently end up in a sports bra and tap pants instead of an old manly T-shirt and boxers.)

"You underestimate your father," Gianluca said.

Dutch Roncalli defined security as marriage, a regular paycheck, and a roof over our heads with a spouse who never hits us. But instead of admitting to that very practical but low bar, I said, "Dad trusts my judgment. He always has. If I choose you, that's good enough for him."

"I think his love for you is beautiful. It's every father's dilemma: You hope for your daughter's happiness, but you know no man is good enough."

"Your daughter married a great guy."

"A father doesn't see a good man. He only sees the flaws."

When I married Gianluca, I would have an instant family—his daughter, Orsola, and her husband, Matteo. This was where our age difference was most apparent. His daughter was the same age as Jaclyn, my baby sister. I hadn't even thought about being a stepmother. Dear God, more to worry about!

Gianluca continued, "Matteo is a good man, but it was the strangest thing. When he came over to ask for Orsola's hand in marriage, I thought I would be defensive. I wanted to make sure he knew what a treasure he had, that my daughter was so special, he should know it and I would be the one to tell him. Your father felt the same way. He confided that you were his favorite and that he would kill me if any harm ever came to you. Then he offered to take me for a drive."

"Did you go?"

"Of course."

"He took Charlie and Tom for a drive too."

"I see. It's a ritual."

"It's an excuse to get the suitor alone and scare him. Charlie was driven to Home Depot. Dad parked by the dumpsters to make his point. Turns out Dad didn't actually want to kill Charlie and dispose of his body, he wanted to test Charlie's home repair skills. He had Charlie change out all the storm windows on the house in Forest Hills."

"Did he pass the test?"

"Took him three Saturdays to install them, but he married Tess, didn't he? And when it was Jaclyn's turn to get married, we figured it would be another trip to the hardware store. Mom had been nagging Dad about putting a replica of the Trevi Fountain in the front yard, and rumor had it Tom has an uncle who owns a backhoe. But instead of fountain installation, Dad took Tom to the Queen of Martyrs cemetery, to find the grave of James Hurley, the only other Irishman who had married into our family. By the way, the symbolism was lost on Tom."

"As it would have been on me. Are you hungry?"

"Starving. Want to go to Valbella's? We could do the Feast of the One Fish. The crabmeat is unreal over there."

"Let's go to your sister's," Gianluca offered.

"Seriously?"

"You don't want to be with your family on Christmas Eve?"

"Did nothing I just said sink *in*?"

"I think you exaggerate."

"Going there would be a mistake."

"We should share our news with your family."

"The news can keep till tomorrow. You'll be their Christmas Day surprise. It's the Feast of the Seven Fishes. I'm freshly betrothed. I don't want to smell like fried clams on the happiest day of my life."

"This is the happiest day of your life?"

"Can't you tell?" I plastered the biggest smile on my face and stood up straight, because Mom taught me that good posture is always important when you're selling something. And I'm selling myself tonight. For a moment, I remembered my big mistake earlier that evening and wished I could erase it like a chalk mark on suede. But there were other things I was worried about too. Gianluca and I had a grand love affair that started in Italy, exploded in Argentina, and turned to marriage in America. We fell in love when we were apart, and when we were together, there was an urgency to express every feeling—and yet we didn't. He was in his fifties, so he had a long life story, and mine, even though it was shorter, was no less complicated. There was so much I wanted to know about him, but between small fires at work and the constant tug of my family obligations, we hadn't gotten around to sharing everything.

"I want to make you happy."

I threw myself into Gianluca's arms. "I can't believe this is happening!" I shouted so loudly my voice echoed through the Holland Tunnel and over into Jersey. I didn't want to pick the night apart, thread by thread, and leave it in a heap on the shop floor like linen slag. For once, I wanted to enjoy my good fortune and *choose* to be happy. There would be time to examine my conscience later.

"I told your father we'd be there. He's expecting us. But I asked him not to tell your mother or the rest of the family. I want to tell them our news."

"You really planned this out."

My fiancé smiled. And then he said the words that are sheer music to a city girl's ears, to those of us whose MetroCard is scanned more often than our Visas, to those of us who regularly take public transportation and long for a lift on four wheels and a bucket seat instead of twelve wheels and a plastic one.

"I rented a car."

"In that case—" I actually felt a surge in my sexual desire for this man.

"So, we drive to Montclair, New Jersey." Gianluca put his arm around me and turned to go downstairs.

"Wait." I grabbed his arm.

"What's the matter?"

"Please, give me one more minute on this roof, alone with you. Because when we walk in Tess's door, our wedding belongs to my sisters and my father and my mother and my grandmother and your father and Gabriel . . . and the bridal registry departments at Saks Fifth Avenue, Restoration Hardware, Costco, and Lou Filippo's Discount Crystal and More in Forest Hills. I want you to myself before my sisters lay claim to our wedding and go on crash diets so they can fit in sample-size bridesmaid gowns."

"You're serious."

"No worries. They'll do the cabbage diet and be down

to fighting weight in six weeks. They won't have the muscle strength to lift a fork, but they will be thin. It's the Roncalli girls' seesaw. When the teeter goes up, the totter must go down. It's all about the dress size."

"I have a daughter. I know all about it."

"Anything important that ever happened in the history of my family required a new outfit and therefore a diet to get *into* the outfit. You'll see. The first thing my mom will say is, What will I wear? And the second thing she'll say is, Have you set the date?

"For a woman who never worked in corporate America, she runs our family like the Ford Motor Company. This wedding will become her rollout of the new models. Or the old model, as it is."

"Do you want a big wedding?"

"God, no. But here's the problem: my cousins. I went to all their weddings, and now it's payback time. If I don't reciprocate, they'll stop speaking to me."

"Is that a bad thing?"

"Depends. You've got pluses and minuses either way. I really love some of them, but there will be a caravan of three buses from just Youngstown, Ohio, alone."

"If you want them to come, then we invite them."

"There will be negotiations."

"For what?"

"Who will run the show? Will it be Trish Meiser, the wedding planner, or Vincenza Napoli, the event coordinator? My mom will make a big deal out of choosing the best woman for the job and waste three legal pads making lists of why she should choose one over the other.

"Then there's the venue. That's always a tussle. What borough, do they have valet parking, and what is their version of the Venetian table? For the passed hors d'oeuvres, do we go with the mini cheeseburgers or chicken sate on sticks? What do you do with the sticks? Go with the burgers. Skip the sushi. Italians don't digest it well. Mini crab cakes? Yes. Eel roll? No.

"Then there's the parting gift. The souvenir. In the old days it was an embossed pack of matches with your choice of a cigar or cigarette case loaded with Lucky Strikes, but that was killing people, so we switched to the goody bag."

"What's in this bag?"

"Something to nosh on the way home. It's not enough that you just ate a nine-course meal, God forbid you drive three miles and have nothing to eat. Do we give a sack of hot doughnuts on the way out, or is there a sampler box of Godiva chocolate? Or do we get creative and give them the Sunday paper tied with a ribbon and a brioche? Come to think of it, I may get Hillary Clinton to do the negotiations. We need a big gun. My wedding planning committee will be one man short of a hostage situation. Do you have cookie trays in Italy?"

"I don't think so."

"Another Italian American institution. Every woman in the family bakes cookies, dozens of them. They box them up and meet at a disclosed location where they stack the cookies on trays lined with gold doilies. They wrap the pyramid of cookies in cellophane and tie it with curling ribbons that, once again, match the bridesmaids' dresses. As dessert is served, the flowers are removed from the tables and the cookie trays become the centerpieces. They're pretty and delicious, but never forget, it's also a competition, fig bar against fig bar, but no one sings the National Anthem and gets a medal in the end—you just get bragging rights."

"I see," Gianluca said as he pondered the insanity of our cookie competition.

"Dress gloves are not for style—they were invented in the third century in Italy to hide the burn marks from pulling five hundred hot cookie sheets out of the oven the week before a wedding. The women bake as though their lives depend on it. It's cookie-lookie! You got snowballs, pizzelles, amaretti, sesames, chocolate biscotti, mini cupcakes, jam-centered thumbprints, peanut butter rounds with a Hershey kiss hat, seven-layer cookies, coconut bonbons, and confetti—don't forget those candy-coated almonds. They're good luck, even when you crack a molar when you bite down on one."

"I'll avoid the confetti." Gianluca smiled.

"While you're at it, don't eat the coconut cookies. They put something in the frosting dye that could survive a nuclear winter."

"Frosting dye?"

I was beginning to lose patience with him, so I spoke slowly. "The frosting on the cookies is dyed to match the Barbie dolls dressed as the wedding party that become hood ornaments on the convertibles."

"Convertibles?"

"Borrowed cars that carry the wedding party from the church to Leonard's."

"Who is Leonard?"

I put my hand on Gianluca's face. He had the bone structure and profile of an emperor on a lucky Roman coin that turned up in my life and changed everything on a dime.

"I'm getting ahead of myself. Forget all this. Let's go to Tess and Charlie's. But step on it, or we'll miss the crab legs. They're always the first to go."

Montclair is a sweet village on the coastline of the Hudson River on the Jersey side. We laughed when Tess and Charlie moved to another state but still picked a place where they would be close enough to look across the river and find the Angelini Shoe Shop. It's a comfort to me that I can reach any of my immediate family by phone, car, or canoe.

Gianluca maneuvered deftly into a small space next to the driveway on Tess's lawn.

"God, I love Christmas," I told him.

My sister Tess knew how to throw around the merry. There was a big Christmas tree in the bay window clustered with tiny blue lights that twinkled like sapphires. She had settled a series of big red-and-white candy-cane decorations up the front walk. On the roof, Santa in his sleigh and Rudolph with a glowing red nose clung to the slates, fully lit and ready for takeoff. There was a wreath on the door with giant brass bells and red velvet ribbons. Two ceramic elves the size of my nephews flanked the door. This Santa Village was so elaborate, it needed its own zip code.

Gianluca turned off the car. I took a deep breath. He leaned across the seat and kissed me. "Shall we go inside?"

"No. Let's sit in the car all night and make out."

"Your father is watching."

I looked up at the bay window, and there, next to the tree, was my father's silhouette, with its big head and square, trim body.

As he turned, you could see the outline of the Roncalli schnoz I'd inherited, but which had somehow magically skipped my sisters.

The sight of my father alone in the window reminded me of all the times throughout my life that he'd waited for me.

I remembered him sitting alone on the bleachers of the Holy Agony gym when I didn't make the cut for JV basketball, at the foot of the sidewalk with the video camera when I emerged from our house in my First Communion dress and veil, and the night he came over to my studio apartment when I broke off my engagement with Bret Fitzpatrick, the perfect man for some-body else. Dad stood in the doorway, knowing that I was break-ing up with a wonderful man, but didn't stand in my way when I decided to take a different path.

No one in my family had wanted to speak to me back then, they were so furious. I had caught a big fish who happened to be my childhood sweetheart, but I threw him back into the river like an old shoe instead of the Wall Street wonder he became. It was typical of me to throw away something good without an al-ternate plan in mind. No one understood—no one but my father. Dad only wanted my happiness, whatever that meant.

When Bret pivoted a few months later and married a beauti-ful blonde named Mackenzie from East Eighty-First Street, hit it big on Wall Street, moved to Chatham, and had two children, my father was the only one who pulled me aside and told me I had done the right thing.

Bret and I remain friends—we even work together on the fi-nancials for my business—but on the personal side, my father understood why I chose learning to make shoes over becoming a Wall Street wife. My dad wanted me to make my own destiny, instead of helping Bret realize his. At the time I couldn't do both, but only my father understood.

Dutch Roncalli was the last of his breed, the strict Italian father with a heart made of mascarpone.

"Why are you crying?" Gianluca asked.

"In the very worst of times, or the very best, my dad has always been there for me. He may not have said anything, but he's always stood by me. He's been my witness. I never thought that I'd find someone who loved me as much as he does."

Gianluca and I walked up Candy Cane Lane. The air had the scent of freshly cut balsam and the oncoming snow. When we reached the porch, my father threw open the front door. The diamond on my finger was nestled inside my black suede glove like a secret. I was about to embrace my dad when he body-blocked us from entering.

"It's bad," he whispered. "Go."

Instead of the Dean Martin Christmas album playing, we heard shouting. "How bad is it?"

"I'd turn back if I were you."

"Dutch? Who is it?" my mother shouted over the fight. "We feel a breeze in here!"

I went up on my tiptoes and looked past Dad down the long hallway to the kitchen. I was suddenly famished as the scent of buttery broiled lobster wafted through from the kitchen. What's a little throw-down before lobster? My father tried to close the door, but I placed my hand on it.

I will always choose food over personal safety.

Gianluca tightened his grip on my arm as we heard yelling, followed by the banging of fists on the table. "What happened? Did Aunt Feen cheat at cards?" Aunt Feen is my grandmother's only sister, her baby sister. Feen has lived in my Teodora's shadow since she was born. It is not uncommon for Aunt Feen to attract attention by any means necessary, whether it's complaining the most or starting small fights that turn into brawls, triggered by her passive-aggressive comments. It isn't any help when she deliberately wears a muumuu and orthotics when the event is black-tie. "Did she pick a fight with Gram?"

"I wish. That's a bonfire you could contain. No, Tess and Jaclyn served the third fish, and all hell broke loose."

I could picture my sisters with steaming plates of fresh fish, clams, and oysters, navigating the small dining room like a military front, hoping to deflect a fight with good food.

"Your sisters served the shrimp while your sister-in-law Pamela followed them with the lemon wedges. Charlie was ejaculating—"

"Oh, Dad, you must mean gesticulating—talking with his hands?" My dad's malaprops get worse when he's nervous.

"Yeah, yeah, whatever the word is. The sauce went flying. Let's just say it looks like a crime scene in there."

"Okay, so we lost the sauce. But don't tell me she ran out of crab legs." I shouldn't have been thinking about food at a time like that, but I like to think about food, especially at a time like that. "I told her to order a crate from Sarasota. I made shoes for the guy who owns Joe's Crabs."

"There's enough fish. But there's more agita. Charlie had a couple of drinks and announced that he'd lost his job, and Aunt Feen called him a loser, and now it's all over but the weeping. Once Feen attacked Charlie, he came out of his corner like an animal, and your sister had to be restrained."

"Charlie lost his job?" My heart sank. Tess had married a

good working-class man who was solid and stable. He also had so much body hair that at the beach he looked like he was wearing a brown Slanket.

"Company is leaving New Jersey," Dad explained. "They left the building behind as well as Charlie and about thirty-two other people."

"Poor Charlie."

"He's soaking his sorrows like a gas rag in a nozzle."

"He's drinking?"

"Like he's parched. Your brother-in-law downed a bottle of prosecco like it was mother's milk and his name was Romulus. Now they're all screaming at each other, airing issues that go as far back as 1983." Dad cocked his head. "Uh-oh, they just climbed into the time machine. I heard 1979 mentioned."

"We're outta here," I said to Gianluca.

"Make it quick. They saw your headlights flash through the bay window." My father reached to close the door.

It was too late.

We heard the stamping of feet, the shoving of chairs, and the tinkling of glasses as my family got up from the table and headed to the foyer. On cue, as dramatized in the biblical epics, the Israelites came pouring out of the living room as they did during the parting of the Red Sea. In this sweet, small house, they appeared like a cast of thousands, except that unlike the people of peace, my family was arguing. They shouted. They shoved. They threw their hands in the air. Alfred tried to reason with Aunt Feen (mistake) while Tess tried to soothe Charlie (won't happen).

The children charged past the grown-ups.

My nieces Chiara and Charisma embraced me as my

nephews Rocco and Alfred Jr. fist-bumped Gianluca. They ran up the stairs to the playroom. Even they knew retreat was the best tactic when it came to a Roncalli family battle.

"Don't wake the baby!" my sister Jaclyn yelled after them, her volume certain to wake the baby.

My father raised his hands in the air like Moses without the tablets. "Silence!" he shouted.

The last thing I heard was the clickety-click of Pamela's stilettos against the wood floor as she joined the throng. I was so happy she'd decided to come for Christmas Eve. She and my brother were working on their marriage, for her sake, for his, and for their sons. Marital therapy was helping them, and tonight, I was jealous.

Had I gotten the psychotherapy I desperately needed all those years ago—instead of building the shoe business—I would have taken a deep breath, turned back down Candy Cane Lane, and said, "When things calm down, and you all decide to act like adults, Gianluca and I shall return," but instead I lost control, and so went my temper.

All my emotional trigger points jammed, and my gut spasmed. All I could think was that the happiest moment of my life was being ruined by these nut jobs. So instead of behaving with maturity, I sank to their level, buckled under the pressure like a hormone-enraged tween, and shouted at them in my highest soprano, "What the hell is going on here? What's wrong with you people? You're ruining *Christmas*?"

Tess actually put her hand on her heart. "Aunt Feen ruined it."

"Don't blame me that your husband lost his job. I didn't fire him," Feen said.

"*Downsized*. He was downsized!" Tess yelled.

"*Shit-canned*. We called it shit-canned in my day." Feen rapped her cane on the floor.

"Charlie, what happened?" I asked him quietly.

"I was laid off."

"So? This is a family where there have been layoffs. We've all been let go or fired or downsized. It's part of life. Okay, it's worse because it's Christmas, but that's on them, not on you. You were a great employee. Weren't you District King or something?"

"Best Salesman in Monmouth County," Tess corrected me.

"See that? You were on top. And now you're not. But you will be again. Come on. This is life. You're not alone in this family. We all have a story to tell. I was fired from Pizzeria Uno in college."

"I was let go from Macy's," Tess offered.

"The Parks Department took a powder on me for six months in '87," Dad remembered.

"I'm sure you have people on your side who were let go," my mother chimed in. She has spent a lifetime trying to be fair, but somehow, this wasn't her moment. Tess glared at her.

"Look, Charlie. It happens. Jobs come and go. We get laid off, and we figure something out. Come on, people." I threw my hands up.

"Valentine is right. We always figure it out." Alfred looked at Charlie.

My brother Alfred straightened his tie. It occurred to me that my brother is never out of a tie. He even wore one on a family picnic while roasting weenies on a hibachi. He's a tie guy. Most occasions are formal for him, and it suits him, as he has always been prim. His jet-black hair, now streaked with the occasional gray fleck, was slicked back with a side part that was so clean from years of combing, his hair actually grew in the right direction.

He gave Charlie a quick pat on the back. "It's going to be all right, Charlie."

"See there? All better. Thank you, Alfred. Now, let's all go back to the dining room and finish our meal and talk about something of a noninflammatory nature," my mother suggested as she tucked a loose strand of hair back into her upsweep. Her hair reminded me of a similar style worn by Joan Collins in 1985, when big hair meant big style. However, Mom made the look her own. She had embedded a rhinestone Christmas tree brooch in the braid around the bun.

Reason ruled for a moment until Aunt Feen pushed through the crowd with her cane. "Take me home!" she thundered.

"You're not going anywhere, Aunt Feen," my mother said as she yanked at the thigh-binding Spanx under her red velvet chemise. Michaela "Mike" Roncalli was decorated for the holidays, and by God the party would continue. My mother considered a party an utter failure if any person left it before the crystal was back in the cabinet. "You're not going home."

"I sure as hell am!"

Mom closed her eyes and simultaneously patted down her false eyelashes with her forefingers. "Well, you'll have to call Carmel. And they are not likely to have any drivers on Christmas Eve."

"Damn them!" Aunt Feen snapped.

"We're not taking you home until we've served the four remaining courses and the cannoli and espresso," Jaclyn said.

"And the sweet timbale!" Gabriel said from the back of the room. I could hear him but couldn't see him.

Gabriel Biondi, my best friend of a thousand years, is perfectly proportioned but petite. He's one of those Italian men who has the face of a gorgeous general but the stature of Jiminy Cricket. The entirety of the Biondi family but for him is dead, so we adopted Gabriel and he adopted us. My father calls him his second son.

Gabriel and I are so close we have no trouble living together and working together in the shop. He redecorated the apartment above the workroom, and for my Christmas gift this year he made the roof garden into a Shangri-La on the Hudson, complete with a sound system and awnings. "I dragged this timbale to New Jersey like a wagon wheel, and by God, we're going to eat it!"

"We'll eat it!" I hollered back.

"Yeah, like your brother-in-law eats failure," Feen mumbled.

"Aunt Feen, where's your filter? You shouldn't say everything you think! Boundaries!"

"Oh, boundaries. Big deal. I watch Dr. Phil, too. I know from boundaries. It's like those candy canes up the walk. They look like a railing, like they're sturdy, but they're cheap plastic. I leaned on one for support and almost keeled over and tasted cement."

"I caught you, Auntie," my father piped up.

"Yeah. So what."

"*So what* we're not at the hospital with your head sliced open like a kiwi," my father fired back.

Aunt Feen ignored him. "The fact is, your brother-in-law is not only unemployed, he's drunk."

"Oh, and you're sober?" Charlie countered.

"I can hold my liquor, Buster, and you can take *that* to Citibank and get a second mortgage, which you probably need, since you got shit-canned."

"Feen, your tone!" Gram interjected.

"I can't abide a drunk in this family." Feen banged her cane. "I won't have it!"

"Really, Aunt Feen? You're on your third tumbler of Maker's Mark. And I know because I'm pouring them," Jaclyn said. "You're tanked up too!"

"It takes one to know one," Feen shouted.

"Okay, now we're veering toward complete chaos here," I said evenly. "We're now agreeing with the disagreements."

"But Aunt Feen *is* hammered," Jaclyn said.

"It doesn't matter. Feen'll sober up. She always does." My grandmother put her arm around her sister. "She'll have some bread and butter and she'll be fine."

"In the meantime, I'll get the tarelli." Mom headed toward the kitchen for the tarelli, best described as bone-dry bagel-shaped crackers we make around the holidays that no one eats, so they languish in a ziplock bag until Easter, when they're fed to the ducks. "Tarellis sop up the alcohol like gravy."

"What the hell does that mean?" my father yelled at her.

"I don't know. I'm trying to make things nice." My mother's voice broke, and she looked as though she might cry. "I'm trying to get us through this party! It's like pulling a plow in ten feet of manure! Stop arguing with me!"

"You're the one who wants to be nonmandatory!" My father pointed his finger at her.

"Non*inflammatory*!" we corrected my father in a chorus.

"What the hell do you want from me? They're only words!" my father thundered.

"Take it down, Dutch. Take it down," Mom growled.

There was a momentary ceasefire where all that could be heard was the low buzz of Aunt Feen's hearing aid.

"Aunt Feen, you getting AM or FM over there?" My dad attempted humor to break the stronghold of family pain.

Gianluca sensed an opening and went for it.

"Valentina and I are getting married," he announced.

If you needed proof that the members of my family are, despite their flaws, supportive of one another, you'd just have to see how quickly they switched from all-out war to unification. My family rejoiced at the news as if they'd won the lottery in three states. After all, I'd beaten the odds. I was closer to forty than thirty, and I was engaged to be married. The scent of relief wafted through the house like the cinnamon in the sachets hanging from the chandelier.

I looked at Gianluca, the smartest man in the room. Here was a guy that understood how to handle my people. They acted like children, so they had to be treated as such. When a toddler throws a tantrum, the parent in charge must divert the child's attention to diffuse the rage.

Gianluca had made our engagement a bright orange squeeze toy.

What a tactic!

Sheer genius!

No sooner had I removed my glove than my left hand was grabbed as the diamond was ogled, assessed, and blessed. The comments ranged from, *Wow, big stone*, to *Flawless! No carbon.*

I love an emerald cut! The baguettes really sizzle. Nice. Better than yellow gold. Platinum goes with everything.

Gram kissed me. Dominic gave me a hug and then embraced his son.

"Sono tanto contento per te!" Dominic kissed both of Gianluca's cheeks.

My nieces came running down the stairs, jumping up and down, begging to be junior bridesmaids.

My mother pushed through the crowd, put her arms around me, and then pulled Gianluca close. "God bless you! Welcome to the . . ." Mom didn't want to use the word *family* in the current environment, so she said, "It's wonderful. What a perfect romantic note to end the year 2010! Now, *when* do you want to get married? What will I wear? Do you have a date?"

"However long it takes me to build a pair of shoes, Ma," I told her.

Gianluca looked at me and smiled. My future husband had just gotten the first bit of living proof that I never lie.

"We need a photograph. An official engagement picture!" My mother looked at my father, who hadn't leaped up to capture the moment on film. My mother would tell you that in all of our family history, my father is never ready with the camera unless she insists. "Damn it, Dutch. Get out your phone!"

"I'll take the picture!" Gabriel said, pushing through the crowd. He's been around my family for so long that he knows about my mother's photo obsession. My mother handed him my dad's phone. Soon my sisters, Gram, and Pamela handed their phones to Gabriel as we assumed our positions. The adults formed a long standing row in front of the tree, and then a kneeling row in front of the standing row. The children sat in

front of the kneelers. We looked like the Latin Club in the year-
book from Holy Agony. I watched as Gabriel backed down the
hallway, trying to get everyone into the shot. "Squeeze, people!
I need to see a squeeze."

"Wait! The baby!" Jaclyn got up from her kneeling spot and
sprinted up the stairs for the baby. We remained crammed.
The scent of Aqua Velva, Jean Naté, Coco cologne, and Ben-
Gay wafted up from my family like sauce on the stove. I turned
around to get a good look at them.

My sister Tess, the second eldest in the family after our
brother Alfred, looked pretty, her jet-black hair in a bun on
top of her head. She did the full Cleopatra with black eyeliner
to bring out her green eyes, which were bloodshot from the
crying jag she went on in defense of her husband. From the
neck up, she was a movie star. From the neck down, she was
dressed for kitchen duty, including a white apron splotched
with red gravy. She looked like a dancer in the musical version of *All Quiet on the Western Front*. Charlie, her burly bear
of a husband, had unbuttoned his shirt down to the pocket,
exposing more fur on his chest than went into making my
mother's mink jacket.

Jaclyn returned with the baby.

Jaclyn, the youngest of our family, mother of one, appar-
ently still had time to go for a blow-out at Fresh Cuts. Her chest-
nut brown hair had not a crimp, and she still could fit in her
pre-baby sweater dress. Her husband Tom still had the Irish
good looks of an innocent Kennedy. He's all freckles, thick light
brown hair, and white teeth.

Aunt Feen stood next to him in a Christmas sweater embroidered with two cats playing with two blue satin Christmas

balls. Her pink lipstick had worn off except for the ring around her lips, which matched the kittens' pink tongues perfectly. My sisters and I call her lipstick look "the plunger."

My gram, Teodora Angelini Vechiarelli, wore a white winter suit. Dominic looked very dapper in a white shirt, red tie, and forest green Tyrolean vest. Gram had her hair cut short in feathered white layers, while Dominic's silver hair was combed back neatly. It occurred to me that my grandmother and Dominic actually looked younger since they'd married. Maybe the slow pace of life in Tuscany kept them young. Whatever they were doing, I wanted some of that.

My sister-in-law Pamela's long blond hair looked white-hot against the simple turquoise wool sweater she wore with a black leather pencil skirt. She makes forty look like thirty-two. Her stilettos were laced with turquoise ribbons—I had to find out where she got them. My brother Alfred knelt dead center in the middle row, looking exactly like the photo from his basketball team at Holy Agony, aging aside. He'd been the captain then, and he was still the captain.

The children were decked out for the holidays in matching ensembles. Chiara and Charisma wore blue velvet party dresses. Tess had given them French braids in an upsweep with giant bows on the nape of their necks. Alfred Jr. and Rocco wore dress shirts with bow ties, miniature versions of my brother when he was eight and ten years old.

Gianluca and I stood at the center of the back row, his arm around me. I placed my head on his shoulder and closed my eyes, taking in the scent of his skin, fresh lemon and cedar, and imagining years of burying my face in his neck.

"Get a room, Val," Gabriel said as he snapped away.

"Here," Tess said, handing him her phone.

Soon Gabriel was juggling the phones, snapping the group shot for each of us. He handed the phones back as he finished. Finally, he snapped a final photo with Alfred's camera. "That's it! Francesco Scavullo is done. I need carbohydrates. We're all done here."

"I want you in a picture, Gabe."

"I have a thousand pictures with you."

"But you're my best man."

"I am? I'm too hungry to be excited." Gabriel lifted his phone to the best angle, put his cheek against mine, and snapped. "Got it."

"Everybody back to the table. We've got plenty of time to plan the wedding," Jaclyn said. "But two more minutes on the stove and the linguini will be gruel."

"Throw it out if it's not al dente," Aunt Feen ordered. I guessed she'd decided not to call Carmel after all.

"Nothing worsh than mushy homemades," Charlie slurred. He was definitely drunk, and there was no way to sober him up with the overdone pasta. Maybe the clams would cut the insulin spike. Here's hoping.

"Red or white sauce?" Tom asked.

"Both," Tess replied. "Everybody gets to have what they like on Christmas."

Mom and Gram grabbed Gianluca and herded him into the dining room. The remaining Israelites turned tail and returned to the far shore as though the Red Sea had never parted. So went the biblical Roncalli/Vechiarelli family epic on that night before Christmas. No loss of life, but no miracles, either.

I was about to join the family when I turned and saw my

father standing alone by the twinkling tree, which was en-crusted with more sequin crap ornaments than you could find in a January sale bin at the Dollar Store. He was checking his phone to make sure the photo was good enough. Satisfied, he turned off the phone and slipped it into his back pocket. He stood back and watched as the family took their places at the table. There was a small smile on his face, a look of near con-tentment. Dad is a man of peace, and for the time being, we had a sliver of it.

Dad buried his hands deep in the pockets of his winter-white Sansabelt trousers that he ordered from the ad in the back of the Sunday *Parade* magazine. A New Yorker through and through, in his black dress shirt and white Christmas tie he looked like the holiday version of a black-and-white cookie. The expression on his face was just as sweet. No matter what, as long as I was making my own choices, my father was happy for me. What more could I ask for?

2

The family was crammed around Tess and Charlie's dining room table, extended to the max with three leaves, covered in white damask, and lit with tiny blue tea lights. Tess had hung Christmas ornaments from the chandelier. The glass angels shimmered over the holiday table as though it were an altar.

My sisters and I, as always, took the worst seats near the kitchen—we'd be up and down, serving the food and clearing the dishes between courses. The seat levels of the extra chairs around the table varied wildly from piano stool to lawn chair, making my family look like a row of mismatched tombstones. There's an email chain amongst my sisters before every holiday about the possibility of renting a proper table and chairs from a party supply place, but we never do. Somehow, this weird mash-up of furniture is part of our holiday tradition just like Gram's ricotta cake.

Gianluca was wedged between his father and Aunt Feen in

the chairs that actually went with the Ethan Allen classic six suite of formal dining room furniture. In proper chairs, they loomed over the rest of us like a billboard. Tess had set the table using every piece of her wedding crystal, so for most of the meal, from my low-flow ottoman seat, I was looking at my family through goblets that distorted their features like an abstract landscape by Wassily Kandinsky.

"Are we on a clam diet around here?" Aunt Feen swished the noodles on her plate. "I can't find any clams in this linguini."

"That's because they're *shrimp*," Tess said as she swirled the ladle at the bottom of the pasta bowl and dumped a school of shrimp swimming in butter sauce onto Aunt Feen's plate.

"You didn't toss. You have to toss, otherwise all the chunks sink to the bottom," Feen said.

Tess shot me a look like she'd like to toss Aunt Feen out the window.

"We should call the cousins in Youngstown with the news," Mom offered.

"Maybe the Pipinos are having a peaceful holiday and we should hold all calls," Jaclyn offered.

"Good idea," Dad said.

"How's Cousin Don?" Gram asked.

"We're planning a cruise to nowhere in the spring," Dad said.

"Where are you going?" Alfred asked.

"Nowhere." Dad laughed at his own joke, but no one else did. "Don is still working. I told him we need to take a few days off and have some fun. So he came up with the idea of a boat that goes from Miami and does a loop out in the ocean."

"It's a floating crap game." Mom smoothed the linen napkin

on her lap. "They go out on the ocean, drop anchor, play cards, and lose their shirts."

"You only see water?" Aunt Feen asked.

"And the top of a green felt card table." Dad sighed. "It's bliss."

"I'd kill myself," Aunt Feen said.

"I hear cruises are very relaxing," Pamela said, speaking up for the first time that evening. That third glass of wine really turned my sister-in-law into a conversationalist.

Pamela almost walked out on my brother when he had a brief affair last fall. Somehow she'd found a way to forgive him, and in so doing, forgave all of us for being lousy in-laws. Pamela had never forgotten that we'd given her the nickname Clickety-Click behind her back because of the sound she made when she walked in high heels.

My sisters and I went to a priest to discuss how we could better build trust with Pamela. The first thing he said was, "Stop calling her names behind her back." The bulb blew in that lightbulb moment. We don't always acknowledge the obvious. Since then, we've poured love all over her like an alfredo sauce, thick and heavy. My sisters and I leaned forward toward Pam with big smiles of support on our faces. We wanted her to know we were on her side.

"Maybe we'll go on a cruise sometime," Alfred said, placing his hand over his wife's.

"Why would you waste a cruise on Pamela?" Aunt Feen barked. "That's an *eating* vacation. Look at her. When was the last time you had a meal? She looks like a breadstick."

My sisters, mother, grandmother, and I quickly blew a chorus of compliments Pamela's way to compensate for Aunt

Feen's rudeness. Pamela flipped her long blond hair and plastered a smile on her face. Tess wasn't the only one who would like to throw Aunt Feen out the window.

"No vacations for me until after the wedding. We have a lot of planning to do," Mom said. "The last Roncalli to marry is an excuse to pull out all the stops." She suddenly sounded out of breath, like she'd just finished the final meter of the New York City marathon. "We have to make this the best wedding ever."

"No, we don't. We need a priest and a cake," I told her. "You know. Simple."

"Simplicity is not my thing," Mom said. Through the years she had announced a list of things that were not her "thing," including household budgets, driving moccasins, black diamonds, and skinny margaritas.

"Whatever you decide, don't invite your cousins Candy and Sandy to dance at the reception," Pamela advised. "I cleared them to lead the Electric Slide, and instead they appeared in crop tops and did a belly dance."

Perhaps had our cousins been better dancers, the number wouldn't have come off as lewd. A table of nuns were so offended they put their dinner napkins over their eyes as though they were in a dust storm in a spaghetti western. That's the last time we saw the Salesians at a family party.

"No worse than Cousins Sophia and Vivianna doing ballet en pointe at the rehearsal dinner," Jaclyn remembered.

"At least that was tasteful," Mom said. "Ballet is elegant."

"Anything French is elegant," Aunt Feen said as she chewed with her mouth open.

"There will be no entertainment at either the wedding reception or the rehearsal dinner. No standup routines or magic acts." I laid down the law. "No spontaneous comedy, no Tricky Tray, and no door prizes."

"You're no fun. Sometimes the entertainment is good," Jaclyn said, remembering Rose Lena Littlefield's tap-dance routine at her own rehearsal dinner.

"If people want to be entertained, they can go on the TKTS line and see actual professionals in a Broadway show. My wedding is not going to be a circus." I instantly felt guilty because Tess had had a circus theme at her wedding shower. "I like pups in skirts and a clown car, just not on this go-round."

"Look at your fiancé," Tess said as she peeked through the door to the dining room. "He's flirting with Aunt Feen."

"How touching," I said as I washed the salad plates.

"I think Aunt Feen has dementia."

"Then she's had it since she was eight years old," Gram said, dropping an empty manicotti tray on the counter. Tess followed her with the empty salad bowl.

"Is Charlie okay?" Gram asked.

"Luckily, he won't remember any of this in the morning," Tess said as she picked up a dish towel.

Gram gave me a hug and looked at my ring while Tess peered over my shoulder.

"What do you think?" Tess asked, squinting at the ring. "Two carats?"

"One and a half," Jaclyn guessed.

"It doesn't matter," Gram said. "It's beautiful."

"He could have put a cigar band on my hand, and I would've been fine with it."

"You say that until you realize that you have to wear that ring every day for the rest of your life. Why should you have a puny stone? You're worth a decent center stone *and* the extra baguettes," Tess said.

"Thanks. But you get what you get, and you don't get upset."

"You're a bigger person than me."

"Three and a half inches in flats," I reminded her.

"Don't rub it in."

Gram picked up a tray of cookies and took them into the dining room. Jaclyn followed her out with the coffeepot.

Tess dried the salad plates. "Thanks for what you said about Charlie and his job."

"He's a good guy. It's not the end of the world."

"It sure feels like it."

"Does Charlie know what he wants to do?"

"He said he'll find something in sales."

"He's good at it."

"We have a little saved. We'll be all right. ADT already called him when they heard he was let go. I guess when the economy is bad, people buy alarms to protect what they already own."

Gabriel burst into the kitchen, juggling a stack of dinner dishes that dipped to one side like the Leaning Tower of Pisa. "Hands. I need hands!"

Tess helped Gabriel safely deliver the dishes onto the butcher-block island. "I work less at my job," he said as he straightened the ruby red velvet vest under his black wool sport coat. He smoothed back his thick black hair. "Shall I slice the timbale?"

"Why not?" I handed him a big knife.

"You're a guest. You shouldn't be working the party," Tess said.

"I'm happy to join you girls in scullery. The chitchat in there is getting on my nerves. Clickety-Click regaled me with a half-hour tutorial on face fillers. I told her the only face fillers Italians believe in are cannolis."

"You don't get to pick *where* you gain weight," Tess said. "I put on ten pounds, and it all went to my rear end. It's like somebody dropped a TV set down my pants."

"It'll come right off, Tess." Gabriel forced a smile before turning away from my sister and rolling his eyes. "Diets are a discussion for another night. This is a night for cabernet and calories. Congratulations, Val." Gabriel gave me a kiss on the cheek. "I'm happy for you." Gabriel put his hand on his heart. "He's gorgeous. You had to cross an ocean and a generation to find him, but it was worth it."

"Thanks, bud. What's a holiday without a backhanded compliment?"

"Sicilian DNA. Sorry." Gabriel shrugged.

Jaclyn pushed the kitchen door open with her hip. She carried the empty artichoke fondue bowl. "Well, this was popular. If I didn't know better, I would think that you'd already washed the bowl. Thank you, Nigella Lawson. Did I interrupt something?"

"We were just being happy for your sister."

"He's a good guy, Val," Jaclyn agreed. "And tall."

"So tall," Tess agreed.

"I can't believe that everyone likes him. I mean, are there no negatives whatsoever?"

"His age," Tess said bluntly. "He'll die before you."

"Nice, Tess." Gabriel glared at her.

"I'm just being realistic. Besides, she asked."

"I'm not worried about death, I worry about when he's eighty and you're sixty. Dominic looks good in his early eighties, so I guess you're all right," Jaclyn said.

"Ladies, Gianluca is a knockout," Gabriel said. "And let's face it. Valentine is at that age where all that's left is the scrap heap. You got the divorced ones with the little kids who need to do homework, or you got the weird singletons who never married, and the three gay guys that are still in the closet but marry a woman to create a bigger closet, but at forty, if they're still single, they have problems. Gianluca is older, but he's primo, so let's take him. Twenty years is not that big an age difference."

"Eighteen," I corrected them.

"Over fifty, two years is like a day and a half."

"Do I look a lot younger than he does?"

"No," Tess and Gabriel and Jaclyn said in unison.

"Great."

"You don't look like you're in your fifties. You look around forty," Gabriel said.

"I'm thirty-five!" I reminded him.

"What does it matter? Everybody gets old," Gabriel said as he checked his reflection in the microwave door. "And if you're worried about your looks, forget it. Women end up two ways by the age of seventy. If you're thin, you wind up looking like Granny Clampett from *The Beverly Hillbillies*, and if you're heavyset, you end up like Aunt Bee on *Mayberry*."

"Those are our choices?" Tess said with wonderment.

"You either get etched with the lines of wisdom, or you balloon as you careen toward death. Flinty or fat. Take your pick."

"I don't think age matters," Jaclyn said. "Gianluca loves you, and that's what's important."

Tess and Gabriel stared at her.

"Are you married?" Tess asked Jaclyn.

"Yes."

"And you can actually say that and mean it?"

"Love is a . . . lot," Jaclyn said defensively.

"Come on," Tess said impatiently. "Love is one ingredient in a good marriage. By that, I mean it's not the whole cake—it's the eggs in the batter. It sort of holds everything else together. But you need the other ingredients. Without them, you're out there without a life plan, goals, dreams, money. Money is as important as love. I love my husband, but right now I'm more worried about the money than I am soothed by the fact that he loves me."

"But love sustains you through the hard times," Jaclyn insisted.

"I'm going with Tess on this one. Love doesn't fix anything. You don't want to put on a teddy when he's online filing for unemployment," Gabriel reasoned. "Nothing takes the starch out of sex like a lack of self-confidence."

"I'm not talking about sex, I'm talking about love."

"Love as in forgiveness, mutual support, honoring his dreams. Right?" I asked Tess.

"Yeah. Those things. Once you have children, the marriage comes dead last. The kids and their needs are above Charlie's and mine. Sure, we have a date night here and there, but it's really about the family as a whole now."

"Spoken like a woman who traded her subscription to *Fit & Trim* for *Fat & Sassless*," Gabriel told her. "Your husband is going through a rough time. Now I'm not saying you haven't been a peach through the whole thing, but he drank a lot of dessert wine tonight on his return trips to the bar at O'Fazzani's. You should recognize the signs of a man in crisis."

"I know he's had a few drinks. But I'm not going to yell at him on Christmas Eve. So what he has a nip or two or a gallon? He's entertaining my family, and frankly, had there been a second bottle, I would've been swigging it."

"Are we that bad?" Jaclyn asked meekly.

"Yes!" Tess and I insisted.

"At least there are no police on your doorstep," Gabriel said. "There was always a Christmas Eve bust at the Biondis. That was the night when the cops thought they'd catch my father and uncles unaware and break up their gambling ring for good. Bookies get sloppy during the holidays. They leave their bet sheets next to their children's letters to Santa. I remember our *Buon Natale*s like it was yesterday. We'd flip on the tree lights, put out the *baccalà*, and ding-dong, the doorbell would ring. 'We're here to see Gus Biondi,' the detective would say. We'd invite him in. My mother prepared for the bust in advance and had filled Tupperware with linguini in clam sauce. I rolled the paper Santa napkins with plastic forks and spoons for the to-go meal to be eaten in the police car. She always included a cookie tray for the cops down at the precinct. Sweet memories. My mother. May she rest in peace. What an angel."

Mom poked her head in the kitchen and said, "Valentine, Daddy wants to make a toast."

We threw down our moppeens and joined the family in the dining room. My dad stood at the head of the table holding a flute of champagne.

"I'd like to make a toast," he said.

I tried to maneuver my way around the table to join Gianluca.

He met me halfway, squeezing past the chairs filled with relatives.

"Gianluca, we're happy to have you join our family. We've enjoyed getting to know Dom. He's been nothing but an asset, and as the saying goes, figs from the same tree taste the same, so you're probably as good a guy as your father."

"He is," Gram said.

"I'd like to say a few words about my daughter. When Valentine was born, she looked about forty-two."

"Thanks, Dad." I downed a swig of prosecco.

Dad continued, "She got her mother's eyes and my bugle—that's a nose by the way—but look how she grew into it. A beautiful smile, thank you Dr. Berger, and height—she's almost taller than me."

"I *am* taller than you, Dad."

"Anyhow, she was different and she was special. We always told Valentine we named her after the saint, but that's not true." Dad reached into his pocket and pulled out his wallet. He began to go through its contents, shuffling credit cards and paper business cards scribbled with his notes.

"Dear God, do the Roncallis run numbers on Christmas Eve too?" Gabriel asked. "I'm feeling nostalgic."

"No, no." Dad found a small square from a newspaper. "Your ma had a long labor with you. It took so long I read the paper cover to cover—and even the ads. Here's where I found your name.

Valentine
An angel from heaven
I love you forever
Your husband Kevin

"I don't know. It made me smile and then I laughed. It was a silly little poem but it meant something to me. And tonight I know why. I'll be damned if it didn't come true. You have made me smile and laugh all of your life. And now, another man will know that joy. Take care of my Valentine, Gianluca." Dad raised his glass.

"Or he'll make you replace his gutters in Forest Hills," Tom said.

"*Salute!*" As my family toasted us, I felt my past meet my future. I was drunk with happiness, but then again, it could have been the Asti Spumante.

You would think after the Feast of Seven Fishes, sweet timbale, cannolis, and cookies that we wouldn't have any more room to stuff down one more bite. But our family wasn't done eating until the overflowing nut bowls, nutcrackers, and silver picks had been placed on the dining room table. Somehow, there was always room for nuts.

"I'm going to have to cut off this dress with pinking shears," my mother said. "I always say I'm not going to overindulge, but then I just can't resist." She daintily unwrapped another Baci kiss from the dessert tray before taking a bite.

Aunt Feen pulled a nut bowl toward her. She picked through until she'd found the walnuts, lined them up on the tablecloth in front of her, and commenced cracking them. "So you think this will be your only marriage?"

"My one and only," I assured her.

"Uh-huh." Aunt Feen cracked a Brazil nut. "Italian Stallion here is already on wife number two, so don't count on it."

"Aunt Feen!"

"Go on. Be indignant. Giancarlo, how many times you been married?"

"*Luca*," Mom corrected her. "Gian*luca*."

"This will be my second marriage." Gianluca actually blushed.

"At your age, I guess we should count ourselves lucky that you only have one under your belt. But I never liked sloppy seconds, not for myself or my grandniece. You're besmirched."

"He is not!" Tess rushed to defend him and me.

"Tell it to the bishop. How you gonna get married in church with a divorce on your record?"

"I have an annulment. My ex-wife remarried in the church."

"Oh, so you have connections. Cut a check for your freedom. That's what it takes. *Soldi*. Let's not forget the *soldi*. You pay mother church, and mother church sets you free. What a racket."

"Aunt Feen, we're not that kind of Catholic," my father said.

"He is." Feen snapped her nutcracker in Gianluca's direction. "Wake up, Dutch."

Before my father could respond, my fiancé spoke up. "I'm not perfect, Aunt Feen."

"You got that right, *mammone*. You know what a *mammone* is? That's a kid who lives with his parents when he's old enough to be one himself."

"It's true. I was a *bamboccione*." Gianluca took one of Feen's walnuts and cracked it open.

"You understand that over here in America, you're only forty and living at home if you're feeble."

"Aunt Feen!" My mother was horrified.

"In Italy, it's different," Gianluca explained. "It helped me to be with my father when I went through a terrible time. I was married for many years and lived with my father after the divorce. The only thing I know for sure about marriage is that what was right when I was twenty-one wasn't so great at forty. Can you understand that?"

"The man I love was killed in the war, so I wouldn't know. I never knew happiness after that. I was robbed, and the purse has remained empty ever since. I have a barren heart."

"You had a second chance at happiness. You loved Tony when you married him," Gram reminded her.

"I faked it because he had a nice car."

"Could we change the subject? I actually liked Uncle Tony," Mom said.

"You would." Feen cracked a nut. "I liked his Bel Air town car. That wound up being his best feature."

"At least you came up with one nice thing to say about him," Mom said drily.

"It was hard. He was a real bargain, that one. The secret to happiness? Never marry an Italian. Never. Ever. If you can find any ambulatory gentleman on two legs who is not Italian and has never visited the Boot, marry him instead. But an Italian? Never."

"Ridiculous," Gram said.

"Never marry someone from the other side. That's what Mama said."

"Mama was wrong," Gram said.

"Ignore our mother at your own peril." Feen shrugged. "She told me to brush my teeth with salt and baking soda, and to this day, I have all my choppers."

"You make it sound like my grandmother disapproved of all Italians. I think she was referring to opportunists from the other side . . . ," Mom said carefully.

"Carpetbaggers," Gabriel said.

Mom continued, "Opportunists who wanted to marry an American to come over for a better life. Sometimes there were men looking for a hardworking woman here, and so all Italian men from the other side got a bad reputation."

"Whatever my mother said, she had her reasons."

"Well, she wasn't always right about this one. I married Dominic, and we are very happy."

"Keep telling yourself that," Feen said.

"I don't have to. It's true."

Feen turned sideways in her seat and flung her arm over the back of the chair. "Giancarlo, what the hell, I'll call you Johnny. Johnny, you watch stories?"

"I don't know what you mean."

"Soap operas."

"No, I don't."

"I know you got bad scripts, cheap sets, and crap acting on those shows, but I've been watching them since 1962, and despite the schmaltz and corn, I've learned a lot from tuning in. One of the big lessons is family relations. Do you realize that when you marry Valentine, she will not only be your wife but your niece?"

"I didn't think about it." Gianluca blushed again.

"You wouldn't. You'd have to be a soap fan to sketch a family tree. These are the kinds of things that occupy my mind. My mind is filled with scenarios."

"Oh, *that*'s it," Gabriel said, cracking a nut.

"Scenarios large and small." Aunt Feen waved her hand over the table as though she was imagining them.

"Whose idea was it to serve the Irish coffee?" Tess asked accusingly.

"Sorry," Tom McAdoo said. "Wanted to bring a little of my culture to the holiday."

"Thanks," Dad said. "Maybe next time you'll bring a shillelagh and play a tune instead of getting Aunt Feen drunk."

"A shillelagh is a walking stick," Tom said softly. "It isn't a musical instrument."

"What do you want from me? I'm Italian. Both sides," said Dad.

"Anyhow, what you learn from soap operas is that you have to be careful when you get married, because you could be marrying a relative."

"Aunt Feen, please," my mother implored her.

"And then you marry that relative, and the children—dear God, the children."

"We have no blood ties, Aunt Feen," I assured her.

"If this was *General Hospital*, and we're pretty close since we got divorced people marrying in, somebody would marry their uncle accidentally and wind up in a mental institution, that's all I'm saying." Aunt Feen snapped her neck and looked at Gianluca intently.

"It's just a story, Aunt Feen," Tess said calmly. "Pure fiction. It's important to accept a happy life when it's presented to you. The only time you can go wrong is when you make a decision to please others and not yourself."

"What? You over your Charlie?" Aunt Feen cackled.

"No, I love him more than I ever did. I'm saying that even

though it's a little odd that Gram's stepson is marrying my sister, it's wonderful that she has found a good man who loves her."

"You mean to tell me out of all the billions of available men in the world, we had to find two in the same tannery?" Aunt Feen cracked a nut.

"What's wrong with that?" Jaclyn asked.

"Path of least resistance." Feen shrugged.

Gianluca and I looked at each other. We were being discussed as though we weren't there.

"Or the only path," Gram said as she stood in the kitchen door, holding a tray of linen napkins that she'd collected from the table. "Love has a funny way of showing up when you aren't looking for it and didn't plan on it. I think it's wonderful."

"You would. You always looked out for number one," Feen said. "But I always admired that in you. You always did what you wanted to do."

"And you could have."

"That's a matter of speculation." Feen smiled.

"The only time people get in trouble," Gabriel said, "is when they live their lives for someone else. It never works. You end up living a bitter life that's not your own. And the very people you gave up everything for never acknowledge all you sacrificed for them."

"That was a mouthful, but not the kind I was hoping for." Aunt Feen frowned at her sister. "Are you going to serve that ricotta cake, or are we saving it?"

"How do you like it?" Gram asked.

"Shot of whipped cream." Feen shrugged. "That should do it."

3

There's the famous Legoland, known for its plastics, and during the holidays, we Roncallis build our own version, Tupperware Land. After the table is cleared, the dishes are done, the silver is carefully placed into its chamois sleeves, and the piles of shells from the nuts are swept off the tablecloth, we disburse the leftovers in various plastic containers, which are handed out as guests, three to five pounds heavier than when they arrived, depart.

Our family never leaves a dinner party without providing a full takeout meal to reheat and serve the following day. For the ride home, you can count on our additional to-go snacks: a napkin shaped like a cone and filled with cookies, or a slab of cake in a sheet of tinfoil, or a paper sack filled with dinner rolls, just a little something to tide us over until the next food tsunami.

I went home with a tray of manicotti to freeze and a bag of

biscotti for breakfast. Aunt Feen asked for cannoli, so she got a container of shells dipped in chocolate and nuts, with another snap lid bowl with the extra filling.

"Are you sure you don't mind driving Aunt Feen home?" Tess asked, handing me a stack of containers, her bun askew, her lipstick worn off, and her kitchen apron splotched with gravy.

"I think she already said every mean thing she could think of."

"I think you're right," Tess said.

I followed Gianluca and Aunt Feen down Candy Cane Lane. I looked back at my sister. "Go back inside. It's freezing."

Tess went back into the house and joined the remaining family members in the bay window. One of the hallmarks of our family life is that we gather at the door to greet you when you enter and also to say good-bye when it's time to go.

My hands were full, so I nodded good-bye with a head bob as Gianluca navigated Aunt Feen into the front seat of his rental car. He reached around her and buckled her seat belt. For a moment, Feen looked like a kid at Coney Island getting strapped into the roller coaster. I climbed in behind the driver's seat. Gianluca tapped the horn as we turned down the street.

The delicate scent of fried smelts lingered on our clothing and filled the car. Aunt Feen had been sitting in Tess's house for hours. Her holiday sweater and wool skirt had picked up the scent of the seven fishes like a sponge.

"That was nice," Aunt Feen said.

Gianluca shot me a look in the rearview.

"Another Christmas Eve for the history books," I said.

"It's important for families to share holidays," Gianluca said.

"You think so? Then where's your kid?" Aunt Feen asked. "Don't you have a kid?"

"A daughter. Orsola. She's grown up now. She's in Florence with her husband's family and my ex-wife and her new husband."

"Cozy for a divorced bunch. Yours, mine, ours, and *them*," Feen said. "We don't believe in divorce."

"I don't either," Gianluca said.

"But you're divorced."

"Sometimes we learn from our mistakes."

"She dumped you?"

"In a way." Gianluca smiled.

"Seriously. What happened?" Aunt Feen demanded.

"I'd rather not talk about it," Gianluca said.

It was fine with me that Gianluca avoided an autopsy on his first marriage with Aunt Feen, but I wanted to know what had happened. He had always been vague about his divorce, and when pressed, had said the distance that led to their split was about geography not emotions. She wanted to live in Florence, and he wanted to stay in Arezzo. But as much as I wanted to believe him, I wondered if that was the truth. I wondered what went wrong.

The GPS lady said, "Turn right onto Watchung Avenue." Gianluca took the curve quickly.

"Whoa there, Mario Andretti." Aunt Feen steadied herself by placing her hands on the dashboard. She chuckled. "I guess I hit a nerve. How do you say that in Italian?" The spaces between Aunt Feen's dentures whistled as she exhaled.

"*Che vecchia ottusa*," Gianluca mumbled.

"I'm sure you did your best with what Fate, God, and your first wife handed you. No matter what you do, sometimes you can't avoid failure. There's no way to protect yourself. You can't duck from the asteroid or hide from the bomb. Heartbreak will rain down on you as sure as you live and breathe free in the United States of America. Or Italy, Giancarlo."

"Gian*luca*," I corrected her softly.

Aunt Feen didn't hear me. She kept talking. "Someday, and you will not know the day or the hour, heartache will return. It's a bastard. It always comes back. It shows up unannounced like our cousins from Jersey."

"Auntie, do you mind? I just got engaged, and I'd like to end the evening on a happy note."

Feen was undeterred. "You can't count on people. You fall in love, you take a shot, you hope for the best. But the truth is, you never *really* know what the other person is thinking. There is no wall between you and certain trauma. There is no way to stay safe. You try to dodge the bullet, but just like in the cartoons, it follows you around sharp corners and through doors until it lands like a bull's-eye in your heart and kills your joy."

"Continue onto Bloomfield Avenue," the GPS lady said.

"I got a black cloud over me. And it has a stench. I stored the crèche from Italy in the basement—and it flooded. I put the family photo albums in the attic, and an electrical fire torched them. Everything ever given to me that was supposed to last forever hasn't. Dollhouse, Christmas 1939: dry rot. Timex wristwatch, June 1950: stopped. Evidently I was given the only one in America that could *not* keep on ticking. I hid cash in books, and they went to the yard sale by accident. I had mammograms every year and missed the lump by one day. I fell in love for real on a Tuesday, and by the following Thursday he was shipped off to fight, and four months later he died in a blow-up raft in the Pacific Ocean. Can't find him or his remains. Gone, baby. *Gone.*"

"But you bounced back," I reminded her.

"Not really. It was all an act. I got no support. The things that were said to me in my darkest hours. 'Take it on the chin, Feen,' and 'Don't cry. Look at Nancy Lou down the street, who lost three sons and her daughter in the war. You lost one man. Buck up. You're young. Love will come your way again, if it even was love.' Oh yeah, cruel and stupid things were said, as if I didn't know what I felt. 'Stop crying,' they said. 'You're wearing out your tear glands.' Yeah, yeah, that's the kind of sympathy I got in my hour of need. Those were the things said to me in my bleak nights of agony. So if you want to know about life, if you're looking for the truth, you ask *me*. Remain unaware. Stay stupid. Pretend the worst isn't happening even when it is. Don't turn on the lights. It's your own damn fault if you open that door and find the burglar with the kitchen knife."

"Merge onto NJ Three E."

"I have ADT, Aunt Feen."

"There's no burglar alarm that can keep you from being robbed of the important things. If you're lucky, you get a dollop of happiness here and there, random moments of unintended joy that land in your lap like an old cat. It feels warm, but remember, it's just a cat. You won't be missing much when you're my age and your brain is fried from dementia and Alzheimer's."

"You don't have dementia or Alzheimer's."

"Not yet."

"You appear to be very intelligent and alert," Gianluca said.

"That's because I exercise my mind. I play cards. Word search. Crossword puzzles. I'm a sudoku person."

"Continue onto Lincoln Tunnel," the GPS lady said.

Aunt Feen continued, "I try and stay alert so I can feel a

tingle when something nice happens. I want to be ready to embrace those moments of bliss, those lucky breaks when the coat comes back from the cleaner and you reach inside the pocket and there's Nonna's ring you thought you lost. You can't remember putting it there and you're shocked that the bastards at the dry cleaners didn't steal it, but you got it back so you can't complain. You think to yourself, Oh, goody. But that's not the norm. It's an accident when a happy surprise rises up to meet you. When something you lost was found. When something you dreamed of comes true, and then just as quickly you lose him so you go ahead and marry another numb-nut anyway to ease the pain. You think it's a balm on a burn, but it only aggravates the wound. Your great-uncle Tony was a horse's ass and a poor substitute for the love of my life. There it is. The truth."

"I'm so sorry," I told her.

"Ah, don't worry about it. When you get old and the Grim Reaper scratches your back, it feels good and you know it. Nothing but death will relieve you from the disappointments and endless purgatory of this life on earth. Whenever the Lord wants me, I'm ready to go."

"Dear God." I cracked the window, suddenly needing air.

Aunt Feen tried to turn around to face me, but the seat belt held her in place like a parachuter before he pulls the cord to jump. "Oh yeah, Val. The golden years are made of tin. Your body, *Madonne*! You just wait. Rashes, lumps, migraines, and varicosities. Hair grows in places it shouldn't and falls out where you need it. Everything shifts, freezes up, and plummets. Last Tuesday my foot was pronated for three hours, and nothing I did would release it. I walked around on one heel for the good part of an afternoon. This morning I woke up on my side and found one of my breasts under my arm. You'll see."

"I hope not," I told her.

"Your home takes a dive too: dust, peeling paint, termites, and mold. Who you are, you can't remember, who you loved, all dead, where you live gets gamy and smells like canned corn. The world turns from fine silk to burlap overnight. You can't see, you can't hear, you remember sex but would rather kill yourself than attempt it because any jostling would snap your brittle skeleton in two like kindling. A moment of release for a lifetime in traction, no thank you. But it doesn't matter anyway. What you once craved, you no longer desire. It's all . . . all smoke."

"You must believe in something beyond this life." Gianluca looked over at Aunt Feen.

"Not really. Only death awaits me. I'll wind up on the scrap heap like a broken toy. In the end, whatever remains of me and my contribution to this world will disintegrate in the valley of regret like the bones of a dead dingo. It will just be me, my immortal soul, and the memory of nothing. But I'm happy for your engagement. I'm going to give you money for the wedding, if that's okay."

"That's wonderful, Aunt Feen, thank you, but you don't have to give us anything."

"You make a good point. What the hell do you need? He's an old fox, and you're almost middle aged. If you don't have a nice set of dishes by now, you probably never will."

"We have plenty of dishes. Mom is giving me the Lady Carlyle."

"Those pink dishes? I hate pink."

"I like them for the sentimental value," I insisted.

"So, enjoy them. But you'll still get cash from me. I can't walk around Queens Plaza mall hunting for a food processor or candle holders without wanting to kill somebody."

"I get it. No problem."

"Giancarlo, I'm the next left," Aunt Feen said.

This time neither Gian*luca* nor I bothered to correct her.

Gianluca helped Aunt Feen out of the car. The brown and white Tudor street-level apartments looked like a stack of Tootsie Rolls in the dark. I took Aunt Feen's keys, went up the sidewalk, and unlocked her front door. I flipped on lights. The apartment was neat and clean.

Her Regency dining table was polished, and the plaid sofa's chenille pillows were plumped. Her coffee table was neatly arranged with puzzle books, cards, and a carnival glass candy dish with a lid, the decor mainstays of every senior citizen in my family. She was right, her apartment smelled like canned corn, but the top note was Gold Bond foot powder. I would have to get her a basket of pungent potpourri or a candle or something for her birthday. That, or I'd bring in the Reiki healer Angela Stern and have her wave a bundle of burning sage around to smoke out the negativity. Come to think of it, she'd need to build a bonfire.

Gianluca guided Aunt Feen into the living room. She threw down her purse and gloves, and for the first time that night, she smiled. I understood. She liked to be home, where she controlled the thermostat, the remote, and the refills.

"I hope I wasn't too rough tonight. I can be a little opinionated," Feen said in a rare moment of self-examination. "You know I live alone and don't have anybody to talk to day in and day out, so when I get an audience, I don't modulate."

Gianluca and I insisted that it was fine. We didn't want her to feel worse. After all, it was Christmas Eve and she was alone.

"You know me," Aunt Feen sighed. "I'm a negative Nellie. Every time I burp, I taste bitter."

After saying good-bye, Gianluca returned to start the car so it would be warm for the trip home to Manhattan. I loaded Aunt Feen's fridge with the leftovers, brought the box of Baci chocolates into the living room, refilled her candy dish, and handed her the remote control.

"Good night, Aunt Feen. Jaclyn will swing by and pick you up for Christmas dinner at my mom's. Around three?"

"So early."

"You want her to come and get you at four?"

"What time is dinner served?"

"Five."

"We gonna nosh hors d'oeuvres for two hours? How much clams casino can I consume before it ruins my dinner? Besides, the filling repeats on me. The garlic."

I gave up. I kissed Aunt Feen on the cheek. "Merry Christmas, Auntie."

"Merry Christmas," she said with a big smile. Aunt Feen was actually pretty when she smiled. She looked like the girl she was in 1946 when she had sausage roll curls and wore bright red lipstick.

As I turned to go, she grabbed my hand. "Congratulations, kid."

I gave Aunt Feen a hug.

"Be careful on the road. A lot of loonies out there," she said, breaking my embrace and pushing me away.

She closed the door behind me. I heard the dead bolt snap into place.

"She is impossible." I slipped into the front seat next to Gianluca.

"That's a very stubborn woman."

"Had I been behind the wheel, I would have driven us into the Hudson River. She drives me crazy, but it makes me sad that she's alone. I want to leave her and yet I want to take her home."

"She loves her apartment. Her mood lifted the minute she was home."

"True, but God help us if we don't check on her every day or forget to invite her to a birthday party or a holiday dinner. She gets livid. And yet when you get her to the party, she hates it. She complains, she sends back food, she insults the in-laws. Please don't let me turn eighty and not know what I need."

"Some people prefer to be alone. You have to respect that." Gianluca turned on the radio. I pushed the seat back, stretched out my legs, and watched the night sky ripple past through the window.

Gianluca was right. I was like Aunt Feen in the solitude department. I love Saturdays in an empty house with no work to do. Hadn't had one of those in years, and with the new business, I doubted I'd have one anytime soon. I had a wedding to plan and a business to run, hardly the profile of a woman who prefers to be alone.

When I was single, I imagined shaking things up and doing something new at Christmas time, maybe going someplace warm by myself, but there was always an excuse not to break with tradition. My nieces and nephews would only be little for a short window of time. I didn't want to miss them opening their gifts or singing in their school pageants. My grandmother and parents were getting older. How many more Christmases would they have? Would it kill me to give up my holidays for them? It didn't, so I stayed. But I had to wonder when my life would begin.

I held up my hand and let the beams from the headlights behind us illuminate the facets of the diamond. "The tectonic plates of my family structure shifted tonight."

"How so?"

"I'm legitimate."

"You weren't before?"

"Not really. You made me legit. I'm going to be a wife."

Gianluca smiled. "That's all it took?"

"A little velvet box. See, in my family, they believe married people have real lives. Single people are in a holding pattern until they become night nurses for the older generation."

"We may have to do that anyway. My father. Your grandmother."

"I won't mind because I won't be alone on the shift. This ring changed everything. I will no longer be the single daughter with time on her hands. I'm not going to get that call from Mom on a Saturday morning asking me to come home and help her clean out the garage.

"Dad won't send a replacement part for his car to Perry Street because it saves him on the shipping. From now on, he'll pick it up himself. I won't be the aunt who is happy to be the extra pair of hands at Great Adventure on opening weekend. I won't take Rocco on the Tilt-A-Whirl because his father throws up on carnival rides.

"I won't be the sister-in-law who gives up a Sunday afternoon to pour cement when Pamela gets a yen for a new patio in Jersey. I won't be asked to drop everything and take Aunt Feen to her doctor appointments. You will be my excuse. I have a fiancé now. You're the love of my life, but you're also my get-out-of-jail-free card."

Christmas Eve is the one night in Greenwich Village when you can find parking on the street. Gianluca pulled into an empty spot on Perry Street close to our front door. He got out and opened the door, lifting the tower of Tupperware out of the car.

The scent of the fresh Christmas tree upstairs greeted us in the foyer below. I looked up the landing and could see the soft blur of the twinkling white lights on the tree.

"I'll see you in the morning," Gianluca said.

"No, come up. You can stay here."

He smiled. "You have a roommate."

"So I'll come to the hotel."

"No, my father and stepmother will be here in the morning. We have lots of time. The rest of our lives." Gianluca pulled me close.

"Years and years and years."

Gianluca kissed me good night. He turned to go through the door, and I threw my arms around him from behind. I closed my eyes and held him. He laughed and turned around to face me.

"Merry Christmas Eve," I told him.

Gianluca kissed me again, and this kiss would be the one I would always remember. It was like the last button fastened on a topcoat against the cold.

"Took you long enough. Did you walk back from Queens?"

Gabriel asked as I made my way to the kitchen with the leftovers. He was already wearing his bathrobe. "Where's Gianluca?"

"He went to the hotel."

"Too awkward with me here?"

"No, not at all."

"Liar." Gabriel poured water from the kettle into a mug. "I'm not going to feel bad. You have the rest of your lives to spend together."

"That's what he said."

"Want a cup of tea? Laci Le Beau's Super Dieter's Tea. After that meal, my liver needs an intervention. While I'm at it, I'm cleansing my colon and resting my pancreas."

"Make me a cup, too. Now I have to worry about looking good in a wedding dress."

My cell phone buzzed in my purse. I fished it out. "Hi, Ma."

"Did you get Auntie home all right?"

"Yes. And that was our good deed for the year."

"Hon, I know it's too soon to talk dates—"

"Ma, seriously. After that meal, you want to talk about a wedding date?"

"Well, it's never too soon. At your age, you shouldn't have a long engagement."

"We're not *that* old."

"You're not particularly *young* either. You don't have a decade to spare like a twenty-something couple. Let's face it. You need to bust a move here."

When my mother uses phrases that she overheard on the crosstown bus in 1985, like "bust a move," it makes me want to do the opposite. "Let's talk after the New Year."

"I gave Carol Kall a jingle."

"It's *Christmas Eve!*"

"She picked up. They're Jewish."

"It doesn't matter. It's still a holiday."

"She didn't mind at all. I have her home number from the breast cancer benefit. She had the kids in bed, and she and her husband had ordered in Chinese."

"I don't believe you."

"Well, somebody has to take the bull by the horns."

"I got engaged at eight p.m. There's no bull, there's no horns, and the ring isn't even warm on my hand yet."

"You have to be strategic if you want to book Leonard's."

"We don't want Leonard's."

"Carol offered the Venetian Room."

"God, Ma. Seriously?"

"I know. Is luck on your side or what? And get this. She has an open date in February."

"A year from now is too far off."

"No, no. *This* February."

"Six weeks from now?" I pulled my stomach in. I couldn't possibly get down to a size 8 in six weeks. Well, maybe I could with the cabbage diet. "You can't be serious."

"I am! She has a runaway bride who just canceled out on February fourteenth. *Valentine's Day*—okay? If this isn't God coming down off a cloud and offering you a gift on your feast day, I don't know what is. This is fate at work. We should grab it and run like the wind. She's got a waiting list you know."

"I have to talk to Gianluca. We may want to elope." A few seconds went by. "Ma, are you there?"

"I always have problems when I call Queens," Gabriel said as he thumbed through a magazine.

A few more seconds of silence. I was about to hang up, and I said, "Ma? Are you there?"

"Not for long. I just had a stroke. Do not say the word *elope* to me ever again! You might as well slap me in the face with a shovel!"

"I can't take histrionics. I just drove through two states with Aunt Feen."

"Valentine, you listen to me. You're going to have a proper wedding. No running off. That's not even *real*. Catholics do not go to city hall. We marry in cathedrals. You get a white carpet from the foyer to the altar. Pews marked with ribbons. For the love of Mary, we festoon. We make a sacrament. It's holy! We get blessed and re-up our baptismal promises. Besides, we need to welcome Gianluca into the fold."

"He's seen our fold."

"All the more reason to put this planning period on frappé. You want to marry Gianluca before he goes on social security, don't you? Or do they even have that in Italy? You know, you ought to check. For down the line. What kind of coverage does he have? Your father's meds practically put us in hock every month."

"I give up. Book it."

"Fabulous! I already put a deposit down."

"Of course you did." I almost threw the phone across the room.

My mother was elated. "It's a little breezy in February, but so what? You'd never go strapless, and I'd never go sleeveless, so February is perfect. Silk shantung for you, and a bouclé bolero for me."

"As long as you're covered, Ma."

"As long as my *arms* are covered. I've still got the cleavage. Gonna show it with the big jewels."

I threw down the phone and sipped the bitter cup of Super Dieter's Tea slowly, like I was Juliet and it was poison.

"What was that all about?" Gabriel asked.

"Mom booked Leonard's."

Gabriel made a face. "How retro. That's like going to the Poconos for your honeymoon."

"Don't say that. Carol Kall will have me booked at Mount Airy Lodge in the bridal suite with the bathtub shaped like a champagne glass. I'll get my leg stuck in the stem like my cousin Violet Ruggiero did on her wedding night, and my first night of married life will end up with a stay in the emergency room."

"You know, instead of getting upset, why don't you just go with whatever your mother wants?"

"Why would I do that?"

"You're busy. You have a business to run. Plus there's something very seventies kitsch about all this. Leonard's. The Poconos. Your sisters can wear palazzo pants—hides a multitude of sins, and believe me, Tess won't be able to drop ten pounds in six weeks. I say, hand your mother your wedding on a silver platter."

I texted Gianluca. "Do you want to get married on February 14, 2011? Valentine's Day."

Gianluca texted me back. "Yes."

"How do you feel about a big wedding?" I texted.

"As long as you're the prize at the end of the carnival, I don't care."

I read Gianluca's text aloud to Gabriel.

Gabriel's eyes welled with tears. "I don't know if I'm emotionally moved or if the tea has formed a firewall in my colon around the cannolis I ate at your sister's, but what a wonderful man you're marrying. God bless us everyone."

I texted Gianluca, "I love you."

"I love you," he texted me back.

"You realize you could have an entire marriage on your phones," Gabriel said. "That's my dream, a mutually satisfying committed relationship that takes place over iPhone. Just odd symbols and snippets of thoughts and feelings punched into the phone with my thumbs and no one in my face bugging me for actual conversation. That, I could sustain. I could do that. A text-y marriage."

"I need air." I grabbed the tin of biscotti. "Come on. Let's go up to the roof."

"No, thanks. It's cold up there."

"I need to show you something."

We grabbed our coats, and Gabriel followed me up the steps to the roof. I pushed the door open and inhaled the cold air deep into my lungs.

"Okay, what do you want to show me?"

"Something bad happened tonight."

"I know. Aunt Feen put Charlie's manhood in a Tupperware container and burped it."

"No, not that. It happened here. On this roof. Tonight. Before we came out to Jersey."

"Oh boy. Did it have something to do with Bret? He sort of blew past me before he left tonight." Gabriel dragged two chaise longues to the center of the roof. He placed my cup of hot tea in the holding cup, and his in the other. He plopped down in his coat and folded his arms.

I stretched out on the chaise next to Gabriel. "He was upset about Mackenzie. She wants a divorce."

"She thinks she can do better than him?"

"She already has. Met another guy at church."

"Oh the piety!"

"And the pity. Look, Bret signed on for that life. That fancy life. And she wants out. So he came over here."

"You're his best friend, Val."

"What happened up here was a little more than friendship."

"What do you mean?"

"Bret was so upset he cried. I've never seen him cry. Ever. So I hugged him, and then he kissed me."

"Where?"

"Here."

"No, I meant cheek or lips."

"Both. Gianluca came out onto the roof and saw everything."

"I knew something was up when I was packing up the timbale. Gianluca came down to the kitchen and went to the windows and stood there."

"Did he say anything?"

"I tried to make small talk, but he didn't hear me. Or he was ignoring me. Then Bret came through and went down the stairs without saying anything to Gianluca."

"I wish they would have spoken."

"Why?"

"Because I love them both. I mean, I really love Gianluca, you know, as a wife, but I've known Bret since we were kids, and he was devastated."

"So now two men are devastated on your behalf."

"No, everything is fine with Gianluca."

"I'll bet."

"Don't make me feel worse."

"What you ought to feel is lucky. Gianluca still asked you to marry him after he caught you kissing another man? He's a man of steel, that one."

"He said he understood. You see, that's why I have to marry him."

"You make it sound like an ultimatum."

"No, no, I didn't mean it like that. I love him and I want to marry him. I can see myself getting old with him."

Gabriel let out a long sigh. "Are you going to have children?"

"I'd like one."

"One? The man is Italian. They have a farm mentality. He'll want six."

"He's a tanner, not a farmer."

"Where do you think leather comes from? You need cows. And a cow lives on a farm. Besides, he's a man. He'll place the order, and you'll deliver. Trust me. He'll want a few."

"But he only has Orsola."

"Fluke."

"Can you believe I'm going to be a stepmother?"

"I hope you turn evil. They're the only interesting ones. You ever met the first wife?"

"No."

"I bet she's a piece of work."

"I have no idea." Actually, when I agreed to marry Gianluca earlier this evening, the farthest thing from my mind had been that I was going to be his second wife. Clearly his first wife was not a keeper, and here I was, attempting to be the one who would last. I wondered if I had the goods or if he did.

"How are you going to do this?" Gabriel looked up at the sky.

"Do what?" Now Gabriel had me nervous, like I might have to actually address the situation with Mirella, the ex.

"Marriage and the shop and the shoes and Roberta and Argentina and me."

"I'm getting married, I'm not dying."

"Are you going to live in New York?"

"Of course."

"You discussed it?"

"No, but he knows the deal."

"Oh, you sad, naive girl. Men never know anything. They have to be told."

"Seriously?"

"He's probably got ideas of his own about where he wants to live."

"I can't live in Italy."

"You might have to, at least part-time."

"I can't! I took my brother on as a partner to hold on to this business and this building."

"I'm not the one you need to negotiate with. You have to talk to Gianluca."

Gabriel has a funny way of going round and round with me and getting to the pith suddenly and without intention. I hadn't asked Gianluca any of the hard questions, so I really didn't know why I thought my marriage with him would work more than, say, his marriage with his first wife. I know that these were the things I should have focused on, how to proceed with my creative life while also taking on the new role of *wife*. But that night wasn't a typical night. It was Christmas Eve. There was a big family party and a whopper family fight. There was no long, intense conversation where we shared our dreams for the future. I washed dishes, we drove Aunt Feen home, and he dropped me off. It was a night full of revelations and strange surprises and not necessarily the good kind.

My phone buzzed. I fished it out of my coat pocket.

"Who is it?" Gabriel lay back in the lawn chair.

"Bret." He texted, "I'm sorry. Hope you're okay."

"I'm fine. Sorry about everything," I texted back.

"Are you going to tell him that you got engaged?" Gabriel asked.

"I can't text that."

"I would."

"Why?"

"Otherwise he's going to think that kiss was something other than friendship."

"It *was* friendship."

"He doesn't know that."

"I think he does."

"You better write a disclaimer then. Say something about Gianluca without saying anything too specific."

I texted, "Went to Jersey with Gianluca."

Bret texted, "I am at my parents'. Kids are with Mac in the city."

I texted, "Hang in there."

"'Hang in there'? After what the man has been through, you act like he lost his wallet?" Gabriel sipped his tea.

"What am I supposed to say?"

"I don't know, but not *that*. That's a platitude you find on a poster at Denny's."

"It's all so bizarre. All of it."

"You can't change history. You were once engaged to Bret. And now you're engaged to Gianluca. All these threads tie together."

"What are you saying?"

"You're not being clear. You have a diamond ring on your hand, and you didn't discuss the conditions of the agreement to wed. You kissed one guy and got engaged to another in the time it took your sister to boil a lobster."

"What do you recommend I do?"

"I don't know. I can only identify problems. I don't solve them."

"Gianluca forgave me for the kiss. He didn't assume the worst about me. He figured I had my reasons."

"And what would those reasons be?"

"History."

"You should erase your history, if you ask me."

"No, it's the opposite. When you marry someone who's been married, or someone like me, who's been engaged, the history part is a gift."

"Or a constant reminder of past mistakes."

"Maybe, but what's wrong with that? I bring a lot of what I've learned to our life together. One of the things I love about Gianluca is that he's already seen and done so much, and yet he's not jaded."

"Well, Val, one thing's for sure, you're marrying an optimist. He has a few years under his belt, and he still sees the possibilities in the world and wants to start over with you. Good for him."

"I'm lucky."

"Poor Bret. He's ending as you are beginning."

"He'll bounce back."

"I never liked Mackenzie, and she never liked you. She always thought Bret carried a torch for you."

"Bret came here to see me because he had nowhere else to go. There's no romance between us."

"What about the kiss?"

"It was a lifeline kiss. He wanted to be reassured that everything would be all right. It wasn't about any feelings he had for me. He was scared about being alone."

"I know those kisses. They come around closing time."

"Right. A closing-time kiss. That's all it was."

"Would you have been as forgiving had you caught Gianluca kissing his ex-wife?"

"Probably not."

"Probably? Most definitely not! Fidelity has always been your big issue, and isn't it ironic that you went and did the very thing you're most afraid of someone doing to you?"

"Are you trying to make me feel worse?" I asked.

"I want you to think about how amazing it is that you're going to marry a man who really loves you and who didn't let a kiss with an ex ten minutes before he proposed marriage ruin everything."

"I get it, Gabriel. I really do."

"We've got another problem. A different complication. You know we *work* with Bret, right?"

"Yeah, I'm going to have to have a conversation with him."

"I hope you straighten everything out. He's our banker. He gets us our loans. He gets along with Alfred. We need him."

Gabriel was thinking about the shop, but I was worried about the rest of my life.

I looked up at the sky. A smattering of stars appeared in the distance over the water. I thought about what needed to be done. There were issues to sort out, feathers to unruffle, and plans to be made. Everything was going to change in my life, even the aspects that were already working.

"It's going to snow," Gabriel observed. "I hate snow."

Gabriel dragged the lawn chairs back to the edge of the roof, where he folded and stored them.

"Come on, it's been a long day." Gabriel held the door open. "And I need my rest. I have to close out 2010, and I have to find a place to live."

"I wish you could stay."

"No, thanks. Three of anything never works. It's two by two or nothing."

Gabriel and I had our routine in the apartment above the workroom on Perry Street. It was a kind of marriage. He took care of the cooking, and I did the cleaning. He'd taken my old bedroom after I moved into Gram's old room. The extra bedroom was for company, and we used it a lot. New York City funnels people on their way to most other places in the world, and having the extra bedroom gave old friends and relatives a place to stay when they were passing through.

Gabriel had fixed up the roof, upgrading it from rustic Italian to Village Rococo. He installed a washer and dryer upstairs, painted the walls, and refinished the wood floors. He always had a project going, a stack of wallpaper samples by his side. As I look back on our time together, I realize I was one of those projects.

I looked into the bathroom mirror as I brushed my teeth. Gabriel had artfully placed a dimmer switch for the lighting fixture over the medicine cabinet. The softened light diffused all my flaws, as there is nothing worse than being over thirty and looking into the glare of headlights first thing in the morning (or the last thing at night, for that matter). I held my hand up against the mirror, taking in the white-hot diamond on my hand.

One little ring changes everything.

As I slipped down the dark hallway to my bedroom, I saw that Gabriel's light was out. He's one of those people who goes to sleep quickly and wakes up five hours later, refreshed. I'm an insomniac who tosses and turns until I surrender to sleep. As soon as I got under the covers and sank beneath my down blanket, my mind began to race.

I began to list the changes that would come in the weeks ahead. I bundled the fears, beginning with my living situation. I knew Gabriel and I would share a work life going forward and our friendship as we always had, but we wouldn't be living together anymore. I was sad about that transition. Leaving Gabriel was a bit like choosing a new pair of shoes over the old, comfortable loafers. I would still see him in the shop every day, because he had become our pattern cutter after June died, but he wouldn't be there at breakfast, and he wouldn't be there at dinner. I was trading my best friend for a husband.

Husband! My heart filled to the brim with love when I thought of Gianluca. I'd found my partner in him. There were so many things we needed to talk about. I wanted to make Gianluca comfortable in his new home. For starters, he'd need a desk and a workspace. Closets. What else? We were going to be married in a matter of weeks. The idea of *that* seemed daunting, but it might be better to move quickly and begin our new life together instead of having one of those long engagements to buy time to make everything perfect. I punched the pillow and turned over.

Whenever I couldn't sleep, my thoughts would turn back to the ladies who nurtured my spiritual life when I was a girl. The nuns at Holy Agony taught us to examine our conscience at the end of every day. We were told to replay the events honestly and assess what we had learned, what we would change, and whom we should ask for forgiveness. I had a list as long as the Westside Highway.

I had hurt Gianluca. My worst moment (comforting Bret) gave way to the best moment (agreeing to marry Gianluca). I could not have had one without the other. I promised myself I would never knowingly hurt Gianluca again. Whenever I tripped up in a romantic relationship in the past, it was the end. Now, I loved a man who loved me enough not to walk away.

It is no small thing to be understood. For Gianluca to have assumed the best about my character in the worst possible moment must mean that he really loved me. He wasn't jealous or unkind, impatient or judgmental when I was at my worst; he assumed I had my reasons, and trusted that even if I made a mistake, I had the strength of character to make it right.

I don't know any other man who could give me the gift of trust when I hadn't earned it. I've looked for trust all my life, brought my hopes out into the world, and taken a few risks here and there, including imagining a life alone instead of settling for less. I even pretended that a pale version of a decent man's loyalty was enough, and that only led to a dark place where I ended up disappointed in myself for assigning integrity to a man who didn't have it.

In a world where time is precious, I spent too much of it working through problems in makeshift relationships, attempting to build something lasting with weak materials instead of insisting on excellence when building my life. The best components are the most durable. "If you want shoes to last, choose the best leather," Gram used to say. My grandmother taught me this, but I had forgotten the deeper meaning.

I texted Gianluca. "Thank you for loving me."

"Go to sleep," he texted back.

I laughed. Of all the things I loved about this man, the best trait was that he didn't agonize. I did enough of that for both of us. Gianluca showed me that when you're certain that forgiveness is yours, you're free to choose love. When the channels of the heart are open, a kind of wondrous beauty flows through. That is the power of true love, and that is why I agreed to marry Gianluca Vechiarelli.

Leonard's, here we come.

4

I swept a thin dusting of snow off the steps outside the entry-
way of our shop on Perry Street. Underneath the powder, glassy
ice peeked through on the concrete. Even the cobblestones had
a sheen, and the sidewalks, shiny patches where the puddles
had frozen like lost mirrors.

I took the broom, reached up, and swept the snow off the
Angelini Shoes sign over the door. I sprinkled salt on the steps
and threw a handful onto the sidewalk like fairy dust, though
in reality the white granules landed in a clump like a scoop of
laundry detergent.

The week between Christmas Day and New Year's is one of
my most productive in the shop. We close out the accounts for
the past year and send the books to the accountant. After the
holiday blitz, I have free time to think ahead and imagine what
direction I'd like to take the shoes.

The spring and summer lines had been designed and were

now in production in Argentina. My long-lost cousin Roberta was meeting production in her factory in Buenos Aires. Soon the spring line would be shipped to our vendors. It was time to create the designs for the autumn line and for winter 2011, and figure out what my customers might want to wear a year from now.

I removed my gloves and placed them on the radiator in the foyer, hung up my coat, and flipped the stone on my engagement ring back to the front of my finger before I pushed open the glass door of the shop.

The drafty shop, every cupboard and shelf, filled with the history of our family, has provided me with a sense of wonder and security. From the time I was little, this shop meant everything to me. Inside, I was fascinated by the craft of shoemaking while the big windows gave me a view of the world outside. Greenwich Village had it all: funny characters, winding cobblestone streets, and a big river.

As I flipped on the lights, the shop was serene, the mood almost reverent, reminding me of church. Creativity is born in silence. The quiet rustle of the pattern paper as it was pinned to fabric sounded like pages turning in a hymnal. The low hum of the machines sounded like the drone of prayers said in unison. The rhythmic chuff of the steam iron and the smooth staccato of the needle on the sewing machine made a kind of music.

The Angelini Shoe Company is where dreams are born in the name of style. We revere our process and our customers. There's a higher purpose in all we do; we create beauty through a sense of service. The high ceilings and low work lamps over the cutting table remind me of the pools of light over the altar at Our Lady of Pompeii on Carmine Street.

Maybe I was so attached to this shop because I knew I could

find my grandparents here seven days a week. That's what it took to make a profit back then, and it isn't so different today. We run the place like my great-grandfather and my grandparents. What worked a hundred years ago still sustains us.

What had been my childhood wonderland became my creative space. It hasn't changed much over the years, but it has changed me.

Every element a good shoemaker needs to make a pair of shoes is available in this room. I opened the floor-to-ceiling supply closets and marveled at the dowels of raw silk and duchesse satin, dyed in pristine shades of eggshell white, beige, and wheat. The shelves were filled with neatly stacked sheets of fine leather and suede, stored between layers of clean chamois cloth. Gianluca instinctively knows what materials I like and provides them.

The notions closet, a series of floor-to-ceiling drawers filled with small compartments of embellishments including shiny grommets, snippets of ribbon, mesh wire rosettes, all sizes, shapes, and styles of buttons, loose faux jewels and elegant seed pearls, was a giant jewelry box, and I spent hours sorting through the treasures. I still have the same thrill when I hunt for the perfect accent to finish a shoe.

I inherited my great-grandfather's original patterns for wedding shoes inspired by the opera. His creations were infused with the passion, drama, and colors of the theater. He even named the prototypes of his designs after the great roles sung by women. In his own hand, he wrote their names with a flourish, then he specified their dimensions in mathematical terms. Pinned to those sketches are bits of fabric and leather so the customer might imagine the finished product.

There is a shelf of wooden lasts, sleek model forms in various foot sizes that are over a hundred years old, which Michel Angelini carved himself in Italy. When he and his brother emigrated to the United States, they had no money or prospects, just a change of clothes and these lasts. The shop was Angelini owned and operated but whenever an outsider was hired, they became family.

I learned how to cut a pattern from June Lawton, who was trained by my grandfather. She answered an ad, looking to make extra money to pay her rent, while training as a dancer, not knowing that once inside the workshop, a different artistic enchantment would take over. June was a Greenwich Village institution. She moved to New York City in her youth to become a modern dancer in experimental theater. She danced for Alvin Ailey and jetéd onstage in the nude. She lived for years in a rent-stabilized apartment in the East Village. When her dancing didn't turn her into Margot Fonteyn, she, like so many artists, turned to the world of day jobs to make a living.

My grandparents saw that June had artistic talent beyond the dance, and trained her as a pattern cutter. She stayed at the shop after Grandpop died and Gram took over. When Gram handed the reins to Alfred and me, June stayed on long enough to convince Gabriel to learn how to cut patterns. He took June's place, even when I believed no one could. I miss her in the shop, but I also miss her in my life.

When June died, I thought we would lose our way. Gram had moved to Italy and June was the final thread that remained from the years my grandfather ran the shop. Gabriel gave up his job running the cabaret at the Carlyle Hotel and took on the work in the shop, full time. He made the transition his own. He hung a signed photograph of Keely Smith over the buffing machine, to remind him of where he came from. Keely's Gram's favorite singer, so when I look at her, I think of my grandmother, but when I watch Gabriel cutting a pattern with precision, I think of June.

Gram handed the business over to Alfred and me when she married Dominic Vechiarelli. I had already spent six years as my grandmother's apprentice. Artistically, she felt I was ready to take over the shop, but she believed I needed help on the business side. She brought my brother Alfred in to run the numbers. He had lost his job at a big bank, and Gram convinced him to switch gears and join the family business. Again, I thought this move would close the shop entirely, as I have never gotten along with my brother. But shoes mean the world to me, and finances to him, so we put aside our differences for the sake of the family brand.

Gram knew that it would take time, experience, trial and error, all the givens on the frustrating path of artistic creation, to turn me into a master craftsman. She also knew that everything I needed was right here.

I use the simple tools handed down from my grandfather, who inherited them from his father who had brought them from Italy. I like to think that their skills live in the awl, hammer, and knife as they do in me. We've added modern equipment through the years, including the roller, presser, steamer, and motorized blade over the cutting table. I'm careful when blending in any new technology, but if it makes the process better, I'm all for it. I often sketch on my laptop while Gabriel takes my designs and makes the patterns.

I was taught to maintain the tools and equipment, to treat them respectfully, to clean and service them. A shoemaker must also be a bit of a mechanic. Whenever a machine broke down in the shop, my grandfather would take it apart and analyze the problem like a surgeon in an operating room. I remember ceramic cups filled with tiny screws, nuts, and bolts, which he used as he figured out how to fix the glitch.

I grabbed the ring of keys, unlocked the safety shutters on the windows, and rolled them aside. The sun threw a triangle of bright gold on the worktable. Fresh coffee brewing on the counter signaled the start of a long workday, along with the scent of leather, lemon wax, and the last gasp of the fresh holiday wreath on the door. I was in my little corner of heaven.

I rubbed my hands together to warm them. I tapped the radiator and sat down at the desk that Alfred kept neat and orderly. The ledger, files, and sample book were all within reach on a shelf over the desk. A few bills I needed to look at were resting under the statue of Saint Crispin, the patron of shoemakers. Gram had begun leaving bills under him years ago, so as not to lose them, and now we do too.

I sipped a cup of coffee and flipped on my computer. There was an e-mail from my cousin Roberta, who wanted to check the lot numbers on the shipment of the *Bella Rosa*, our summer flats, made of pastel leathers inspired by a tin of saltwater taffy from the Jersey shore. I sent her a quick e-mail with the specifics, but I signed it:

VR, soon to be . . . Gianluca Vechiarelli's bride

Roberta e-mailed me back instantly.

How wonderful for you and even more for him to choose you! Intelligent man! Let me know the date. I'll dance at your wedding.

I unrolled butcher paper across the top of the cutting table, taping it down on both ends. I flipped open the box of tubes of oil paint and began mixing them on a palette. I swept a deep cobalt blue across the paper, switched brushes, and outlined the blue in a clean, white stripe. I picked up a small brush and made small stripes of black on the blue. It was fun to return to deep blues after months of playing with pastels.

When I painted the blue and black without the white stripe, the saturated tones read "evening couture" instantly. I took a photo of the colors on my phone and downloaded them into the computer. I'm able to work more efficiently electronically, when I can layer colors and test them on sketches that I've drawn to scale.

In the old days, shoemakers used to break down patterns mathematically on paper. Now I use stock measurements on my pattern program on the computer, invented by Joe Miele, the great mechanical engineer. I still have to dream and engage ideas in my imagination—these artistic drives have not changed over the last century and most likely never will—but we recently added some new software to help us realize the dream more efficiently.

When we were a strictly couture shop, we would sit with the customer, look at her gown, and match the shoe to the bride. Now that we've branched out into the retail market, we're serving a wider audience, so we consider trends. We study women in their ordinary day-to-day activities, and think about what they watch in the theater, at the movies, and on television. What does she like? What does she think? What does she need? We play a kind of guessing game. We analyze the times, what women are buying, and their moods. Sometimes the color of a popular cocktail inspires the suede of the moment. What becomes courant often begins with something ordinary like the color of candy or textural, like like pattern of a cobblestone street. What a woman is *feeling* translates into what she chooses to buy.

There is also a synergy among the creative impulses of all the other shoe designers in the world and the elements I choose. Somehow, themes emerge even though we don't officially consult the competition. It is as if we hear the same music in the air, walk the same streets, eat the same food, and interpret the same moment en masse. Our observations as we live in our times shapes the landscape of what we design.

I wrote words around the swirls of blue on the butcher paper. Over the course of the next several weeks, the paper would be filled with my scribbles, stream-of-consciousness thoughts and ideas, varied, unedited, and without censure. This crazy collage of layers of ideas would become the template for the next collection. I would spend weeks winnowing down the broad ideas into the specificity of the message.

A rapping on the window on the Hudson River side interrupted my thoughts. Bret waved to me from the sidewalk. As I motioned for him to come around, I wondered how long he had been standing there. I was happy to see him, despite what happened on Christmas Eve. He moved quickly to the entrance. His strong Irish profile, upright posture, and carriage showed total self-confidence, a far cry from the vulnerable person he was a few nights ago.

I wasn't surprised. Resilience was Bret's way; he invented the bounce-back. He didn't hold on to sadness or its sister, failure, for very long. Stability was one of his best traits, and the one that worried me the most. If there is ever a time to dig deep and find answers, it's when someone you love leaves you.

By the time Bret made it inside the store, I'd poured him a cup of coffee with a dash of milk in it, just as he likes.

"There's going to be more snow," he said, removing his coat as I handed him the mug of coffee. He wore a beautifully cut navy pinstripe Brooks Brothers suit with a white shirt and green silk tie that brought out his eyes. The stripes made him appear leaner and taller, if that was even possible. "How was the rest of your Christmas?"

"The kids had fun. Went out to Mom and Dad's Christmas Day. Gram and Dominic stayed with them so they could be with the grandkids."

"Seven Fishes at Tess's house on Christmas Eve? I remember the hoopla."

"Oh yeah. It was even bigger this year, a very special night." I held up my hand and showed Bret my engagement ring. "This is why I wanted to see you."

He grinned and took my hand. "You're getting married."

"I am."

"Well, it's about time."

"Only you could say that to me and it doesn't hurt my feelings. For the record, there have been, in the history of mankind, older brides than me."

"Who?" Bret teased.

"For starters, my grandmother. And, according to Gabriel, Ethel Merman was older than me when she married Ernest Borgnine."

"I have no idea who they are but I wish you every happiness." Bret embraced me, and as quickly as he had his arms around me, he removed them and stepped back.

"I don't want it to be weird between us," I told him. "You can still hug me." I gave Bret a quick hug again to prove it.

"I'm sorry. The other night was the worst of my life, and you're my best friend. You always have been. And in that state, I really needed to see you, so I barged over here, not thinking about your plans, or your out-of-town guests, or anything but my own misery."

"It's fine."

"I'm not worried about you. I'm worried about Gianluca. You know how they are about their women. He's Italian."

"So am I."

"You're Italian American—he's Italian *Italian*. I think we know the difference."

"We use a little sugar in our gravy, and they don't."

"For starters." Bret sat down on the work stool. "How could we possibly expect him to understand our history?"

"He has some wisdom. That helps."

"As long as you're happy."

"I am. And that's exactly what I want for you. Did you and Mackenzie work it out?"

"No. She wants a divorce."

"Wait a second. A divorce? How did you get there so fast?"

"We had a dramatic Christmas Eve, and by the afternoon of Christmas Day, I calmed down, and she got her bearings, and her folks took the kids to Central Park and we had a chance to talk. We were okay together with the kids, but as the day went on, it was apparent that we needed to clear the air."

"What did she say? About the future, I mean."

"She's fallen in love with someone else, and doesn't want to hurt me. She didn't mean for it to happen, but it did."

"If she didn't mean for it to happen, then how did it happen?"

"I wasn't around, and he was."

Bret had gotten a studio apartment in the city where he would crash after late nights at work. I thought it was a bad idea at the time, but he insisted he only had so many years to become a mogul, and every second counted. "Who is this guy?" I asked.

"She met him at church."

"Dear God. Do you know him?"

"No. You know I go to Saint Michael's and she goes to the Episcopal church. I didn't want to convert, and neither did she. I should have gone to church with her. That might have helped."

"Or maybe it wouldn't have."

"She told me it started as a friendship, and then they realized that they were meant to be together."

"How? When? She's married to you."

"I know. She said she made her decision after she talked to her parents. They want her to be happy and they'll stand by her no matter what she chooses to do. Funny, they didn't put up a fight to keep us together."

"Why would they? They never approved of you. They didn't like that you were from Queens."

"As if that's a negative." Bret smiled.

"I put Astoria up there with Athens, Sunnyside with Old Havana, and Forest Hills with Rome. We have an international flair in Queens that is not appreciated by those Upper East Siders. They still check the *Social Register* blue book for their Mayflower connections. We have our own blue book, but we use it to sell our used cars when we're ready to trade them in."

"I know that blue book well." Bret nodded.

"The only one that counts. What about the girls?"

"We're going to share custody. There are a lot of practical things we need to work out. She wants to move out of Chatham, and I don't want to stay in the house, so we'll have to sell it. We said we'd live close to one another and whatever school the girls attend, so that's what we're going to do. She wants to move back into the city." He exhaled.

"Just like that?"

"I can't believe it either. I asked for time. I begged her to reconsider. But there's no fighting it. Her mind is made up, and you know how she is."

"Well, you have your studio apartment."

"I'll need a bigger place with a bedroom for the girls."

"This is crazy."

"Tell me about it. I can't figure out how she fell in love with someone else while she was married to me. She was as busy as I was. But I have to figure out a way to make peace with this guy, because she intends to marry him once we're divorced."

Bret looked momentarily lost. I had never seen him this way. He was his practical old self when he was telling the story, but after sharing it, the weight of the situation hit him hard again. He'd always been cool in a crisis, including his own. But this state of calm was not going to last. When he realized the extent of what had happened to him, he would break and there wouldn't be anyone there for him. This made me sad, but it also frustrated me. What are the chances that I would become engaged just as his wife left him? Through the years, I had thought about what would have happened to me had I married Bret in the first place. Would he have moved to Perry Street and supported me in my creative life? Could he have walked to work every morning on the Hudson River and returned home at night the same way? I was surprised when he chose the traditional Wall Street life, with a big house in Chatham, two beautiful daughters, and a wife who gave up everything for him. It seemed a different Bret chose a life I did not recognize.

"Are you okay?" I asked him.

"The nights are awful. I can't sleep. I just think about my kids and how they're going to grow up without their mother and me together. You remember how it was at your house and mine when we were kids. Our parents were solid. All the parents on our block looked after the neighbors' kids like their own. I want that life, that feeling of security, for my girls. And now they'll never have it."

"They still have you."

"I should've seen the signs before I married her. I was so madly in love with her that I didn't see that she hadn't figured out what she wanted to do with her life. When you're planning a wedding, you have a job, and once you're married, you need a new one. She decorated the house and threw herself into motherhood, but I guess all that and me wasn't enough."

"She probably thought she'd get back into the workforce eventually. You never know what someone else is thinking." I twisted the engagement ring on my hand.

Bret smiled. "This is all your fault. If you had married me, I wouldn't have gotten myself in a jam."

"Oh, please. I would have driven you crazy. I wasn't ready for anything when I was twenty-five. I needed a good nine years to grow up. And one more to let the fear of being alone for the rest of my life force me to make hard decisions."

"You're going to do just fine."

"We'll see. Isn't every bride full of hope?"

"I wish I could go back and catch those small things that became big things. Address every problem head-on. Don't be afraid to admit when things aren't working. I saw the problems and tried to ignore them. You know they say that a relationship is work—well, I just assigned the problems to a to-do file. I figured we'd deal with things when we had time to deal with them and eventually come to some sort of agreement. But she basically accused me of living my life and leaving her out of it. She said a maid could do what I needed, that I didn't need a wife."

"You needed a wife."

"I needed *her*. I just didn't show it. And now I find out she wasn't getting what she needed the whole time we were married. Whatever you do, don't give up working when you marry Gianluca."

"No chance of that happening. This shop is my life," I assured him.

"If you're happy, your marriage will be happy."

"Did you suggest therapy?"

"She said it was too late. God, I hate that phrase, 'too late.' I believed that it's never too late if two people love each other."

"You still love her?"

"I do. Isn't that sad? Even when I know she doesn't love me. I'm either loyal or a fool. I can't help it. There's so much of her in our girls."

"Your daughters will be all right. She's a good mom. It's not like there isn't a fifty percent divorce rate, so they won't be oddballs. You have a big, extended family, and everyone will pitch in to make the kids feel connected. You can also bring them over here more often. I'd love it. And I'll get my sisters to bring the kids so they can all play together."

"You always find the positive in everything."

"I'm not saying it's going to be easy. But you can do it. You learn from your mistakes. That's not true of everyone. That's really what it comes down to. And if you didn't put her first and you regret it, well, next time you'll do better. That's all you can do, Bret."

"You know what my wife said to me as I was leaving on Christmas Eve? Go see Valentine. That's who you really want."

"Oh, please. That's just a dramatic good-bye at the end of a sad scene. She never got our friendship. She didn't like me, but I thought it was because I didn't wear Tory Burch. I guess it was something more."

He smiled. "You were my first fiancée. Mackenzie did not like that she was second, friend or not."

"I know. So *more* than a childhood friendship, but so what? I thought she was perfect for you—and, except for the leaving part, she was."

Bret sipped his coffee. I lifted a can of biscotti off the shelf, opened it, and handed him one. He dipped it in the coffee. I smiled because I'd taught Bret how to dip his biscotti in coffee when we were teenagers. In fact, I served him his first biscotti and taught him how to say the word in Italian. We had the perfect Irish-Italian relationship. I baked, and he poured me my first beer.

"Do you remember that sign in Sister Theresa's office at Holy Agony?" I asked him.

"Pay your library fines or you won't get your diploma?"

"No, the other one. It was a white card with light blue letters. It had been there for a hundred years. It said, 'Everything is a grace.' "

"You think so? Even breaking up a home, breaking my children's hearts, and getting a divorce?"

"Everything."

"Well, I don't believe it."

"You will. That will be your mission. Someday, you'll see it all as a grace."

The doorbells jingled.

"We're home!" Gram shouted. Gram and Dominic came in, laughing, carrying Tupperware containers from my mother's Christmas spread. "Hon, you have to spread the salt around out there. I almost ruined my shoes."

"Sorry. The only salt you and Dominic will have to worry about in Florida will be on the rims of your margarita glasses."

"Hi, Gram." Bret kissed her on the cheek. "You're going to Florida?"

"My cousin invited us down. We're going to stay until Valentine's wedding, then come back up for it."

"You set a date already?" Bret was surprised.

As Gram introduced Dominic to Bret, Gianluca came in, carrying a large dress box tied with a red satin bow. "From your mother," he said as he placed the box on the table.

"Congratulations, Gianluca," Bret said and extended his hand.

"Let's take the food upstairs, Dominic," Gram said.

"Grazie," Gianluca said without shaking Bret's hand.

"I want to show Valentine the leather samples," Dominic said as he placed a box on the desk.

"Time for that later." Gram handed Dominic a stack of Tupperware.

Gram and Dom made their way up the stairs, balancing

two leaning towers of Tupperware. I would have liked to follow them, but I didn't dare leave Bret and Gianluca alone. The shop was oddly quiet except for the clang of the radiator.

"I owe you an apology," Bret said, breaking the tension. "And you too, Valentine. I'm sorry about what happened the other night."

"I've had some difficulties in my life, and I understand why you needed someone to talk to," Gianluca said. "But if it happens again, I'll throw you off the building."

"And I would deserve it," Bret said as he pulled on his coat. "I'll check in with Alfred about the annual report."

Bret, who usually gave me a quick kiss on the cheek when saying good-bye, didn't this morning. He simply gathered his briefcase and left.

"I don't like that you work together," Gianluca said.

"He mostly works with Alfred."

"I don't see Alfred here."

I wanted to argue the point, but instead I pushed the box of leather samples across the work table.

Gianluca opened the box and began to shuffle through the squares. Soon the large squares filled the table like a mosaic of tiles. There were tone-on-tone striae in the leather, damask-style cutwork on one of the suedes, and soft stripes woven out of calfskin. There was a pearlized pink calfskin that I couldn't resist.

"I knew you would like that one," Gianluca said.

"It's like velvet."

"You want velvet?" Gianluca flipped through the box until he found a sheet of cream-colored suede. "Look." He brushed his hand over the surface, turning the grain in a different direction. It gave the suede a different hue entirely, one that appeared more soft blue than white. Gianluca's hands were magical. I may have fallen in love with him because of them. I watched as he rolled the end of the suede expertly until it was one sleek cylinder. He handed it to me. "Order it."

Gianluca took me in his arms and kissed me. I knew how rare it was for love and work to dovetail together seamlessly in a woman's life. I was going to marry a man who understood my work and therefore understood me. I thought of Mackenzie and Pamela, the women I knew who didn't have the luxury of marrying men who got *them*.

How many signs did I need from the universe that Gianluca was not only the dream, but the facilitator of all dreams to come? I hadn't given up anything to be with him, and choosing him felt as if it was shoring up my creative life, not draining it. I wasn't going to wake up on some random Tuesday morning ten years from now and find myself unrecognizable in the mirror. I wouldn't wander into church or a bodega and find a new man that understood me because the one at home was unavailable or too busy to notice that I was unhappy. Life would only become more rich, and thicken like a good sauce. I would not be a watered-down version of the person I was today, as long as I remembered that my life had a purpose that was well in place before I ever met Gianluca. I wasn't giving up anything. I reminded myself I was only adding to a purposeful life.

"I really love what you do," I told him. "I mean, when you cut leather, it's a master craftsman at work at the top of his game."

"Why do you watch me so closely?"

"I don't know. Maybe because I couldn't do what I do without you. If it weren't for you, I wouldn't have what I need to make shoes."

"I have a feeling you would find a way." He smiled.

"When are you taking Gram and your dad to the airport?"

"In a couple of hours."

"Did you check out of the hotel?"

"I can."

"You should. Gabriel is staying at the Carlyle tonight. The manager gave him the room for New Year's."

"You're all alone here?"

"Just me and my big old diamond ring."

Gianluca kissed me. "And me."

I untied the enormous red ribbon on the dress box. There was a tag hanging from it:

Merry Christmas Ma, Love Tess

Mom had scribbled over it:

Do not wear this dress!!!

I smiled and ripped off the tag. My mother never met a ribbon or a gift tag she didn't save and reuse.

I opened the box and removed tufts of fresh tissue paper. I lifted out my mother's wedding gown from 1970.

The gown was of its era, conjuring the mod early 1970s, the days of Lauren Hutton, Marisa Berenson, and Priscilla Presley when she married Elvis. It was a simple, straight A-line gown with a round collar. It was made of open antique cream-colored lace over a silk charmeuse lining. The lace of the trumpet sleeves was unlined, giving the gown a very fresh and courant look.

Clusters of tiny seed pearls were sewn into the flowers on the lace. The glints of milky beading gave the dress a classic finish. At the bottom of the box, folded neatly, was a long, wide shawl that I remembered from the wedding photographs. My mother liked dramatic emphasis around her face, and this shawl provided it. She had draped the shawl over her shoulders and thrown it over the back of her dress, giving a capelike effect.

I slipped behind the dressing screen and removed my jeans and work shirt. I slipped the dress over my head. It glided over me. I pulled a box of size 8 sample shoes off the shelf. I slipped out of my loafers and into the pumps. I crossed to the three-way mirror and stepped up onto the riser. I adjusted the mirrors.

The dress fit, but it was five inches too short. I examined it from all sides. I liked the neckline, the antique lace, and the silhouette. It needed something, and I wasn't sure what, so I went to the notions closet and found a wide grosgrain ribbon in lavender. I cut a piece and wrapped it around my waist. The pop of color changed the look of the old lace. The round cutouts of roses and daisies in the lace were offset by the straight lines of the grosgrain ribbon. The mix of textures did something to the dress. I went to the notions closet and picked out a chunky rhinestone buckle. I threaded the ribbon through the buckle.

There was a knock on the door. "I'm busy!" I called out.

"It's Gram."

"Are you alone?"

"Yes!" she called out.

"Come on in."

"We're all packed for the airport," she said, stopping when she saw me in the dress.

"What do you think?" I modeled the dress.

"Are you going to cut it off to the knee?"

"No, I was thinking of altering it." I picked up the shawl and unfurled it. "There might be enough fabric. I would add the lace at the bodice and waist and drop the hem to the floor."

"You really like it?" Gram asked carefully.

"You don't?"

"I loved it the first time around." Gram smiled.

"Mom tried to act like she lost it. I told her exactly where it was in the attic so she had to send it over. Why the resistance?"

"Because your mother is a drama queen."

"You raised her."

"So I speak the truth. Your mother has never liked anything old, including being old. She wants to buy you a new dress."

"I don't want a new dress."

"Why?"

"I don't want to make a big deal out of this wedding." I caught myself, but not before my grandmother saw through me.

"It *is* a big deal."

"I just want to get married and start a new life with Gianluca. I don't really care about the ceremony and the party."

Gram sat down on one of the work stools and faced me. "You're the most traditional person I know. You never wanted me to sell this building because of the history. So what's going on with you? Are you sure you want to get married?"

"Yes! I love Gianluca. But I don't care about the dress and the hors d'oeuvres and the band. I just don't. Maybe years of making wedding shoes for people has turned me off to the entire enterprise. To tell you the truth, I would be happy going down to city hall."

"That would kill your parents."

"They'd recover."

"I don't mean to cause trouble, but you need to get real here. Your mother needs this wedding, and just because you've always helped with your customers' weddings doesn't mean you give your own short shrift. It's a sacrament, after all. Why are you treating it like it's less than that?"

"Is that what I'm doing?"

Gram nodded.

"I don't like being the center of attention. In fact, it makes me a little sick. I don't like to broadcast my feelings or stand in front of a crowd. It's just not me."

"I understand. But a wedding isn't just about you and Gianluca. It's about family. All of us show up in our best clothes and promise to be there for you in the years to come. You need the people you love to make a vow to you, as much as you need to make one to each other."

"My family can't agree on manicotti or risotto for dinner—how is my wedding supposed to pull us all together?"

Gram smiled. "I don't know how to explain it, but it does. You have to welcome him into your family, and he has to welcome you into his. There are no lone wolves in the family structure—there shouldn't be. It's the community of your heart, your allies. You need them even though you think you might not. You don't know what the future holds, but your family will be there to hold you when you need them. Unless, of course, you don't think that's important."

I went behind the screen and slipped out of the gown and back into my clothes. Gram made sense, but the truth was, I was tired of thinking about what everything meant, and how to please my family.

"Is everything okay with you and Gianluca?"

I came out from behind the screen. "Did he say something to you?"

"No, he was just quiet. I saw Bret here earlier," Gram said casually.

"We straightened everything out. Christmas Eve was a sad night for him, and he needed a friend."

"Bret kissed you."

"A mistake."

"But you kissed him back."

"Another mistake. I felt sorry for him."

"Pity is the ruination of women. When we feel sorry for a man, we get into trouble."

"I did a dumb thing."

"When you're young and you marry, it's so simple." Gram sighed. "You have a blank slate. You have some ideas for the future. You're pretty certain you'll always be happy, and you hope for children and a nice home and a good life. But when you're older, it's more complicated."

"I know, Gram."

"I met his ex-wife, Mirella."

"What's she like?"

"Tough."

"Great."

"But you know how to deal with tough women."

"No kidding. I have a PhD in Aunt Feen."

"I'm talking about your stepdaughter. Orsola is very close to her mother."

"I see where this is going."

"I think you'll have a great life with Gianluca, but you'll have to deal with his first family, just like Dominic had to deal with mine, and I had to with his. It's not always easy. There's no shorthand. You don't have years of observation to fall back on. Now, sometimes that's a good thing, a little distance. But sometimes it's not."

"Gram, I get it. And I wonder, with all I know, and all I've seen, why I'm choosing to take a chance on a man who already has a family. He's from another country. My Italian is lousy. I'm in debt. Why would he want me with my baggage before he unpacks his own? I don't have an answer for you. I know love is not enough, and that the passion cools, and that when a man is in his fifties, he's different from a man who is my age."

"It's wise to anticipate."

"I do. I can even see down the road when he's older and he'll need me in a different way, and I'm worried if I'm up for the task, or if I'll even be good at it. I figure Gianluca will have a fabulous old age like his father. I mean, look at what you've built, and the chance you took marrying Dominic. Aren't you glad you did?"

"I'm so lucky. I had a fresh start when everyone I know was winding down. The golden years are better than I ever thought they could be. I can tell you something about the Vechiarelli men that might be of some use to you. Don't keep anything from them. They like to know everything. They don't like secrets."

"Well, that's easy. I don't have any. And if he has any, I'll deal with it. I'll even handle his ex-wife. I plan to make Mirella my friend."

"Bring your ice chipper."

I would remember Gram's words when I finally met Mirella Vechiarelli Delfina, the elegant, refined Italian glacier. I would need not only an ice chipper but patience, a blowtorch, and a therapist to sort it all out.

I fired up the new grill on the roof, placed the old iron skillet filled with glassy brown chestnuts on the flames, and put a lid over them. Soon the air was filled with the woodsy, sweet scent of roasting chestnuts. I gave the pan a shake. I could hear the muffled pops as the heat cracked the shells open.

"Bella?" Gianluca said from the door.

"That was quick."

"Newark is so close. I dropped them off without any problems." Gianluca stood behind me and put his arms around me. "What are you making?"

"I'm roasting chestnuts. Do you like them?"

"No."

I laughed. "That's honest."

"I ate so many when I was a boy, I vowed I would never eat them when I grew up."

"I guess we don't have to like the same things." I emptied the pan of chestnuts on to a platter.

"But we do."

"How do you feel about fighting?"

"I've done plenty of it in my life, so that's something I could give up."

"Well, I hate conflict. I don't like to fight."

"Why would we argue? Is something wrong?"

"I don't always say what I'm thinking. Today, I almost got in a fight with you."

"Why didn't you?"

"Didn't think I'd win."

"Oh, so you'll fight if you win."

"Maybe. Wouldn't you?"

"I think we should talk about Bret," Gianluca said, taking a seat on the old bench next to the fountain of Saint Francis.

I turned the grill off and sat down next to Gianluca.

"Bret's been my friend since I was a little girl."

"Childhood playmates are one thing, but you fell in love and were engaged to marry him."

"But I didn't marry him."

"Maybe he still loves you."

"Not like you do."

"How do you know?"

"Because you don't love Mirella in that way anymore."

Gianluca smiled. "I see."

"We remained good friends even though he married someone else and had children. We work well together. He helped save this company. He's really smart and works well with Alfred. He keeps my brother calm and represents my point of view to him."

"You can't do that yourself?"

"No. It's biblical with Alfred and me. You know that."

"I can help with Alfred," Gianluca said.

"I don't know if that's a good idea."

"We're getting married, we're sharing everything, no?"

"That's the definition of marriage, Gianluca."

"So we agree? I can manage Bret's workload."

"But, you're my tanner."

"I know how to run a business."

"Obviously. You've done very well. But we're okay here. We have enough profit to pay the salaries, maintain the building, and develop the line going forward. Why would you want to get involved with Alfred?"

"I don't care about Alfred and the business, I care about you. Unless you think I should stay out of your business?"

"No, I'd love your input."

"What can I do for you?"

"I don't know. I haven't thought about that yet."

Gianluca took a deep breath. "He'll be in the shop. You'll be in the shop. And you will still turn to Bret when you need help."

"It's not like that. I don't turn to him, exactly. He's a money guy. I don't have any romantic interest in him. I trust him with the big picture finances, but not with my heart. I love you, and I'm marrying *you*. There is no other man in the world for me."

"Maybe he thinks differently."

"Bret doesn't love me in that way."

"You understand why I feel the way I do."

"Of course. And Christmas Eve didn't help. You have a right to be concerned, but I'm telling you that you shouldn't be. I'd feel the same way about your ex-wife—and I'm sure I'll see her when we do things with Orsola and Matteo. But we won't have to have this conversation, because I trust you."

"This isn't about trust. I trust you, too."

"Then what is it about?"

"Time."

"I don't spend a lot of time with Bret."

"The past. He had years with you that I never will. He's

known you for thirty years. We don't have thirty years ahead of us to share."

"You're so morbid!"

"I'm practical."

"How do you know how long our marriage will last? Did you stop in at Madame Chantal's on Eighth Street and she slipped you the tragic love card?"

He laughed. "I don't need the tarot when I can do basic arithmetic. You're almost twenty years younger than me."

"*Eighteen*," I corrected him. "Why does everybody round up? I guarantee that no one does that when they weigh themselves."

"When it comes to age, any number over ten, you might as well round up. Now, I plan to fill every day of the time we're given, but we only have so many years, Valentina."

"You're really bringing me down. Didn't you hear me on Christmas Eve when I told you I come from a family of deniers? Cousin Albie's colon had to fall out on the kitchen floor before he'd go and see a doctor. We'd rather die than face the truth. And sometimes we have. I don't want to hear another word about our age difference. It's ridiculous."

"So I can't go around bragging about my young wife."

"*That* you can do." I put my arms around him. "You liked Bret just fine before the other night. And he just told you that it would never happen again. Other than Christmas Eve, what don't you like about him?"

Gianluca didn't answer.

"He's not a threat. He grew up down the block from me. We went to school together—we thought that meant we *had* to get married. All our friends were getting married, and we decided we should too. But I eventually figured out it was a bad idea. He is not my fiancé, or my lover, or the father of my future children. You are."

"Oh, you want children?" he asked.

"Don't you?"

"I asked you first."

"Yes," I answered him honestly.

"I'm surprised."

My heart sank. "You don't think I'd be a good mother?"

"You'd be a wonderful mother if you chose it."

"Oh God, this is the moment when I find out you're a traditional man who doesn't want his wife to work."

"I love that you work."

"Then what's the problem?"

"I've noticed that in America you think you can have everything your heart desires on your own terms."

"Isn't that the definition of happiness?"

"In Italy, we look at things with a little more common sense. A sense of reality, if you want to call it that. When the baby is crying, and you're under deadline, what do you do?"

"Take care of the baby, of course."

"What happens to the deadline?"

I was beginning to get frustrated with this conversation. "You'll help me with the baby."

"Of course I would. It's my baby too."

"We approach everything like a team," I suggested.

"I would like that."

"Gianluca, do you want children?" My stomach turned. I was afraid he didn't.

"I have Orsola."

My voice broke when I asked, "Do you want more?"

"I am open to whatever life brings."

Gianluca closed the lid on the grill and carried the pan to the door as if the conversation that had just taken place was about what color to paint the kitchen and not the dilemma of all dilemmas for every woman ever born.

I was fully American. My aesthetic roots were in the land of my heritage, but I didn't see myself as an Italian wife. And what is an Italian wife exactly? All I knew came from my limited observations. During my travels in Italy, the Italian wives seemed practical and a little removed. There appeared in them a resignation to the order and roles established in life as it had been for generations. How was I going to continue to be the woman I was, split between these two cultures, who had little in common when it came to a woman's ambition and drive? I was in for it. What, I didn't know. But I loved Gianluca and figured it had to go my way. This is also the hallmark of an American sensibility. Things naturally work out for the best when the intention is clear. Or do they?

A wave of concern tore through me, and I wasn't sure why. Were these bridal jitters? Did I feel rushed by the holidays and now the New Year? Should I call my mother and tell her that February 14 was coming too soon? I had shoes to design. Instead of giving in to the panic, I took a deep breath. I picked up the pan of chestnuts that only I would eat and followed Gianluca back inside. I wanted to be near him. I had more questions, but I knew him well enough to know that some things would have to wait.

5

I flipped the 2010 Our Lady of Fatima calendar to the next to last day of the year. I only had two days left to say that I was getting married *next year.* The countdown was real after January 1, 2011 and so was the knot in my stomach.

I washed my hands at the workstation sink, drying them carefully. I pinned the fabric for my wedding shoes to the thin pattern paper. I stood back and squinted at my work. It was harder to create a pair of wedding shoes for me than any customer that came before. All I could see were the flaws.

Alfred pushed the shop door open. He carried, as he always had, all three metropolitan newspapers. You could describe a person by the paper they read in New York City. Gabriel was strictly a Page Six junkie, so he read the *New York Post*, which provided the most hilarious wallpaper in our powder room, ripped from the headlines. I liked the *New York Times* because I liked my news serious. My brother Alfred was a *Daily News* guy—

he liked the sports and business section. He also read the *Wall Street Journal* on the commute, which Gabriel and I never read. It was about a world so foreign to us we needed a translator. I would mourn the end of newspapers as I would all of the institutions of life as a New Yorker. It seemed everything was changing—no more corner candy stores, bookshops, or Mom and Pop restaurants. More changes I tried to put out of my mind.

Alfred hung his coat on the hook.

"I need the file for supplies. I'm heading to midtown to place some orders."

"They're on the desk."

Alfred thumbed through the file folders. "What are we going to do about Charlie?"

"We have to do something, or our sister is going to jump out her window in Montclair. Tess is a nervous wreck. I called her and she's panicking about college. The girls are nine and ten. I told her she had time. But I guess that's what happens when you have children."

"Someday you'll find out," Alfred assured me.

"Charlie needs a job. Can we help him?"

"He was a manager at the alarm company." Alfred poured himself a cup of coffee. "He may not want to work with us. Besides, he's not going to take the first thing that comes along. He already turned his father down. Wanted Charlie to come into the landscaping business."

I don't know how long I was standing there pondering Charlie's future, while Alfred gathered the files, when my mother blew into the shop carrying two cups of coffee and a small pastry to share. If we weren't in pre-wedding deprivation/fit-in-the-dress mode, she would have brought me my own half dozen.

"Oh, my son and daughter hard at work. Alfred, I only have one cream puff."

"That's all right, Ma, I'm on Lipitor."

"When did you get high cholesterol?"

"When I turned forty. Remember? You threw me a party."

"Dear God, what's to become of us?"

"We become vegetarians and give up pasta." I shrugged.

"No, I mean now that I have a son who's forty."

"Ladies, I have a meeting in midtown with a button salesman. Not the one you dated back in the day, Val."

"He was a real bargain. If you notice, I only have zippers on my clothes now."

"It might have been painful, but you learned from the experience. I choose to be grateful to that button salesman. He kept you off the front burner so you'd be ready to cook with Gianluca," my mother said as Alfred rolled his eyes.

"No, Ma, you're confusing the button salesman with Roman Falconi, the chef."

"How's he doing?" my mother asked innocently.

"He's down to one and a half stars."

Alfred gave Mom a kiss on the cheek and left with the files.

Mom was dressed for shopping in a perfect ensemble for trying on clothes. She wore a simple, long-sleeved microfiber dress in navy blue stripes with matching tights and suede shooties. The wool cape over the dress was easy to get in and out of. The dress itself was easy to unzip, and underneath, she was cinched in by spandex shapewear that was so tight it dropped her down half a size if she didn't exhale. Perched on her head were her signature Jackie O sunglasses. Mom wears them inside stores so the saleslady can't read her mood. My mother does not appreciate any input from sales professionals. She feels she knows best when it comes to her own body and the message her body sends in clothes.

"I went to Kleinfeld's with your sisters," Mom announced.

"Anything interesting?"

"A few styles. Let me just say that planning a wedding that's taking place in six weeks is a physical, mental, and emotional impossibility. That said, we're making it happen. I'm fine until the thirty-first of December. When it's officially 2011, I'll kill myself."

"Mom."

"I know, despite appearances to the contrary, I'm keeping a tight grip on my emotions. Your father is no help whatsoever. He thinks the timing is nothing. He told me to *cut corners*! I don't do that. You'd think he would've noticed *that* after all these years. Leave the food to Carol and the invitations to *e-mail.* Can you imagine? You'd be the first woman in our family who did not have engraved invitations."

"We don't need engraved invitations."

"Queen Elizabeth would never have a formal event without an engraved invitation."

"Oh, right. How many times have we been invited to Buckingham Palace?"

"Never. But we can poach from the royal template. Etiquette is not dead, and I don't want your wedding to be the thing that kills it. Good manners never go out of style. Years from now, you'll want a permanent record of your wedding. An invitation is the bride's Dead Sea scroll at the bottom of her hope chest. An invitation is historical proof. We *must* have an engraved invitation. Besides, we have an intergenerational conundrum. Even if I agreed to send the wedding invitations via e-mail, and I'm not, what about people like Aunt Feen who have no Internet access?"

"Hire a yodeler."

Mom ignored me. "I'll have the invitations printed up. You don't even have to look at them. I want the Youngstown cousins to have proper invitations. When Chrissy Pipino got married, she had a fold-out card with tissue, and if you remember, it was gold-leafed. She even had a pop-up angel. You yanked a satin ribbon and the little cherub went over and down like a windshield wiper. We don't have time for a pop-up, but we will have our version of Caravaggio angels. The invites will be addressed with Olde English calligraphy. It costs a fortune, but I don't want to look cheap."

"They won't care."

When I disagree with my mother, she changes topics. "I approved the raw bar. Malpeque oysters. The seafood station with shrimp, lobster, and crab. Oh, and they added in a crepe guy since Jaclyn got married. He fills them with your choice of savory or sweet. Can you stand it? Oh, and I agreed to a risotto bar. Can you imagine? Somebody's biceps will be getting a workout stirring the rice. And, *hola!* we're having a make-your-own-quesadilla stand, mostly for our Latina cousins. I'm hoping that Roberta will come up from Argentina."

"Mom, she's very busy at the factory making our shoes."

"I know, but she's your business partner, and she's family. You know how I like to have everyone important to us at a wedding. Don't worry about it. I'll e-mail her."

"Did Pamela go with you to try on dresses?"

"Gave us fifteen minutes."

"Really."

"Said she had things to do. What could she possibly have scheduled during a holiday week?"

"She leads a Zumba class in Sea Girt."

"Oh, big deal. Call in a substitute."

"Did she like the dresses?"

"She can fit into absolutely anything. Her body is a sample size. She's so small she could wear your pants from fourth grade."

"Thanks."

"The point is: she's *tiny*. But let's face it, people *that* thin have brain fog, they can't focus. A couple of meatballs, and she'd be Albert Einstein. She's so wishy-washy. I want to shake her sometimes. Have an opinion, would you, *please*?"

"Ma, the meek inherit the earth."

"Well, then, she's coming into some prime oceanfront real estate. Jaclyn found a couple of gorgeous gowns for *you* to try. A Christos and a Reem Acra—"

"I'm not going shopping. I found the perfect dress. Ma, I love your wedding gown."

"You would."

"I'm wearing your gown. So stop looking. Don't put anything on hold. Don't leave bridal magazines around here with Post-its on dresses you like. I won't look. I won't surf the net. I have my dress."

"I just don't understand you, Valentine. We live in the fashion mecca of the planet. We could go to Kleinfeld's and cut a deal, or Saks and get a custom gown, and you want to wear my old thing. For Godsakes, I ran into Diane von Fürstenberg at Dag's, and she was so nice. Her store is around the corner. I want to march right over there and see if she has wedding gowns. You could wear a brand-new D.V.F. Instead you want to wear my old D.U.D. *Why*, if you could wear something *new*, would you ever wear something *old*?"

"Tradition."

"You want something old? You already have it. My Lady Carlyle china. It's in a crate in my garage. I have the complete service for twelve. Finger bowls. Cheese plate with lid. I even have the soup tureen. Please, let's go to Vera Wang and get you something *courant*."

"I don't want courant. I want to wear your dress."

"How did this happen under my watch? You're a . . . a . . . hippie. You know, all those girls my age"—my mother choked, then coughed at the mention of age—"you know who I'm referring to, people like my friend Jan Lampe, who lived and died by any lyric Joni Mitchell put out. Almost changed her name to Blue once. Blue Lampe. Imagine that. Anyhow, Jan would wear a secondhand *schmatte* on her wedding day and be happy with it. The peasant look."

"I like the peasant look."

"Dear God, our people fled Italy to get *away* from the peasant look. Who in their right mind wants to look poor? We emigrated to escape those patchwork prints, feedsack paisleys, those horrifying embroidered blouses. You scare me. You're just like Jan."

"Mom, it's not about the dress."

"Are you sure you're my daughter?"

"I'm going to make a beautiful pair of new shoes. I'll have your gown restored. The lace is still beautiful."

"It came from Florence. Mom picked it up on a buying trip."

"I'll probably do a couple of fresh accents to reinvent it a little bit. By the time I'm done with your old *schmatte*, you'll love it."

"You're my last daughter to marry. I wanted something more for you than a redone Halloween costume."

"Nobody wore it as a Halloween costume."

"Tess wanted to be Princess Diana. Remember?"

"It didn't happen. We went as a box of crayons."

"Whatever! It doesn't matter! You're wearing my old dress. This doesn't feel like the right choice, the fashionable choice. It feels like a real crappy do-over."

"Ma, look at it this way. It gives you more time for you to shop for *your* dress."

"Indulge me. Will you please think about wearing a veil?"

"I'm not a veil type."

"But they're so festive and flowy. Don't you want a little movement around the face?"

"I'll have movement around my face. I get a tic when I get nervous. Remember? Besides, veils have no purpose. I have nothing to hide. Gianluca's already seen my nose, and evidently he likes it."

"Are you going to hold it against me for the rest of your life that I brought you for that consultation years ago?"

"You took Tess for the nose job. I had the acne. You took me to a dermatologist."

"There's oil on your dad's side of the family."

"Right. The plastic surgeon said my nose was fine. Remember?"

"And your nose *is* fine. You inherited my old nose, and I just wanted to make sure you could live ninety years with it. It suits you. But I'd still like you to wear a traditional veil."

"Ma, women wore veils a thousand years ago to hide from the man they'd never met and were forced to marry. I chose Gianluca."

"Sure you did. And we like him, honey. We will love him as soon as the ring is on your hand."

I modeled the diamond. "This doesn't count?"

"Not quite. An engagement ring is all well and good, but the deal isn't a deal until you place a thin platinum band next to it, locking the future into place with a 24-K LoJack. Once you have the blessed band, you're golden."

"Did you talk to Father Drake at Queen of Martyrs?"

"I left him a message. God, I wish we were better Catholics and had some decent connections. If we did, we could climb up the food chain for an *officiante*. Our monsignor retired, and the one bishop we knew left for Scranton to live with his sister at the Mercy Home. He's a hundred and fifty years old if he's a day. I just couldn't ask him to travel to marry you. It might kill him. I suppose we could've done it on-site at Leonard's, but I don't like getting a judge to officiate. It seems tacky to take your vows standing in front of the ziti station. Frankly, those off-site weddings feel one level above processing a parking ticket. Judge Jane Marum Roush volunteered to come up from Virginia—"

"You called a judge in Virginia?"

"E-mail. Hey, we're in crunch time. I needed a plan B. When your back is against the wall, you have to reach out to anyone and everyone you know. If I taught you anything—"

"It's *who* you know."

"Right. Anyhow, Jane went to school with Alfred, but I told her to put a hold on the bus ticket. Remember her? She's the girl who got hammered on sangria at Alfred's graduation party and did cartwheels to the 'Thong Song.' I can't believe she's a judge! Lucky for her that she came up before the Internet. Oh, here's the number at the rectory. Call him to set up your pre-Cana."

"We have to do pre-Cana?"

"You can't get married in church without it. Besides, it's good for you. A little retreat with other couples who are going through what you're going through. Daddy and I led the discussion one time. We weren't asked back, because, well, we're not sure. Maybe because we got into a spat about home budgets during the financial portion. You know your father, he can be tight with the blades."

"Blades?"

"The cash. The green. You'll love pre-Cana . . . a spiritual discussion about the solemnity of the occasion and practical advice about day-to-day living with one another. That's not going to hurt you."

"If we survive it."

"I'm sure you and Gianluca have discussed all the big issues, and this is good for the small ones. Oh, he'll need his annulment paperwork."

"He carries it on his person like a passport."

"Do not mistake my anxiety for disapproval. I am thrilled you're getting married. I'm so happy for you. I want to make your life easier, not harder. I want you to enjoy this special day. I really do."

"Then can you be a little happy that I'm wearing your dress?"

"Not really. Years ago I had a yen to cut it up and make doilies, and now I'm sorry I didn't."

"But this gown is blessed."

"No, honey, I had it historically cleaned and hermetically sealed in plastic, but not blessed."

"I mean, it's lucky. Look at the good fortune you and Dad have enjoyed. You've really done very well."

Her eyes misted with tears. "Forty-one years. We were broke, then we got cocky, we got cocky and Daddy strayed, then Daddy repented and returned, then I went whack-a-doodle, then I calmed down, and then Daddy got the prostate, and ever since, we've been good."

"It helped when he took the estrogen therapy. I think he understood you better."

"Understood me? He practically *became* me."

"Ma, when did you go whack-a-doodle?"

"Don't you remember my yoga retreat in the Catskills?"

"Vaguely."

"You were in college. I was turning thirty-seven—"

"Forty-eight."

"Whatever. Don't correct me. I don't need my children pointing out my flaws. I'm bad with math."

"Only when it comes to your age."

Mom ignored me. "Well, I went to a couple of yoga classes, then a prayer meeting in a sweat lodge outside of Albany. I got impetigo, came home, and had to soak my foot in white vinegar for a month. My one journey to enlightenment gave me a rash. Go figure.

"Anyhow, my point is that even when you don't make a plan of it, you will change. You will want different things at different points in your life, just as he will. Circumstances will hit you with some whammies, and you'll fight back, and sometimes you'll just give in to it and choose to lie down in the river and glide. Whatever you do, know that there's a long line of us that came before you who walked in your shoes." Mom looked around the shop. "It always comes back to shoes with us, doesn't it?"

The Chelsea Market, a couple of blocks from our shop, had grown from a local food mall with bakeries, wine vaults, fresh seafood, and a soup stand to a tourist attraction with all the old guard shops dwarfed by a television studio, fancy restaurants, clothes shop, and a bookstore.

Buon Italia remained my favorite destination, with food imported from Italy and a fresh pasta department that tricked Gianluca into thinking he'd never left Tuscany.

I had planned a romantic dinner of tortellini in puttanesca sauce, fresh bread, and an arugula salad. I was studying the olive oil selections when I felt what I can only describe as a familiar presence next to me.

"I like Lucini. Tuscan. It's buttery."

I looked up at Roman Falconi and as if by habit, I blushed. "Roman."

He wasted no time and put his arms around me and kissed both my cheeks. The only thing between us was a small block of parmesan cheese. It wasn't a good buffer. Roman took the cheese and placed it in the cart, then stood back and looked at me.

"You look good," he decided.

"So do you." And it was true. He did. Obviously, he was working out because he was in better physical shape than I remembered. He was as handsome as ever, and he had cropped his hair short. He smiled at me, moving his head from side to side, squinting a bit as if he was studying a painting.

"What are you making?" He began to go through my cart.

"Something simple. Tortellini."

"Do you ever make the pork shoulder?"

"No, but I ordered it at Babbo. Does that count?"

He put his hand on his heart. "You go to Batali? You're killing me." He smiled. When he smiled, I remembered why I fell in love with him. "Why don't you come over later? I'll make you dinner."

"I can't."

"Right. You're cooking."

"And I'm getting married."

Roman's face fell. He looked slightly seasick, but quickly recovered as only a man who is used to juggling complex recipes, hungry customers, and beautiful women can do. It's the face of a man who always thinks he is missing something even when he isn't sure he wants it.

"I miss you," he said.

"Thank you." I didn't know what else to say.

"Do you miss me?" he asked.

"I miss that pork shoulder."

He laughed. "Who you gonna marry?"

"A tanner."

"You hate the beach."

"No. I hate bathing suits. I love the beach. Besides, he's not that kind of tanner. He works in leather."

"How old is he?"

This was exactly the kind of question that unnerved me when I dated Roman. He's a mind reader.

"Around your age," I lied. As soon as I did, I was ashamed. I didn't have a problem with the age difference, did I? "Why do you ask?"

"I like to have as many facts as I can about the competition."

"How about you? You serious with anyone?"

"Not really. And I'm not looking."

"That's a first."

"Why don't you just put a nutcracker in your cart?"

This time, I laughed. "I'm sorry. You know, Roman, you're like an institution—a big building with a fountain out front. Important. Impressive. I like knowing you're there because everything on earth changes except for you."

"Is that a compliment?" he wondered.

"Absolutely," I assured him. Roman followed me around as I finished my shopping. He helped me choose the best crushed and peeled tomatoes in the store. He stayed with me as I chose a bottle of wine. We laughed as we had in the beginning, but this time there was no anxiety. We knew exactly who we were and how the story ended. It meant we could be honest.

"Are you happy with the chump?"

I looked at him.

"Chump is a term of endearment." He smiled.

"Maybe it is in Chicago but it's not in Queens."

"So let me put it this way—are you happy?"

"Yes, I am."

"Then I'm happy for you," he said, not meaning it. "But if anything changes, you know the way to Mott Street."

"You're serious."

"Very."

Roman was, first and foremost, a cook. He thought that if he added new and interesting ingredients to an old recipe that it would somehow turn out differently.

"Don't you believe in fate, Valentine?" he asked.

"You think because I needed fresh tortellini that's a sign we should get back together?"

"Why not?" He beamed that glorious smile and I swear it lit up the room, causing every woman in Buon Italia to look into the light.

I shook my head and laughed.

"You think I'm joking," he said. "But I'm not. You still on Perry Street?"

"For a hundred years."

"Maybe I'll stop by sometime." Roman kissed me on the cheek and left. I stood there for a moment as though I'd been hit by a hammer.

"Baby, that man likes you," a lovely African American woman said to me as she picked up a can of olives near my cart.

"It's too late for him."

"People change," she said, pushing her cart past me. "I like a tall man."

"Me too." I smiled.

Alfred, Charlie, and I met for lunch at Valbella's, our favorite Italian restaurant in the meatpacking district. David, the owner, always rolls out the red carpet and the best sopressata this side of Naples. He sees me coming and starts cracking crab legs for my appetizer. I need to eat a lot of fish for the next month so I'm at fighting weight for the wedding pictures.

Charlie (I'm sure Tess is behind this) is wearing a three-piece suit. Never mind that I haven't seen a three-piece suit on anyone since I watched *Scarface* with Gianluca, but it looks nice on my brother-in-law. Alfred wears a tie with a white shirt and his jeans and cardigan. I feel like I'm out with a couple of rejects from Boys Nation.

"Charlie, do you have any idea why we've called you here today?" Alfred began.

"I'm guessing you want to save my family from financial and emotional ruin," he joked.

"Stop that. You're a winner. Would you like a glass of wine?" I asked him.

"My liver is still processing Christmas Eve," Charlie said. "I'll have a glass of seltzer."

"You know, Charlie, Alfred and I have been thinking about you. We'd like to have you come and work with us."

"We want to give you a job that uses your skills," Alfred added, looking at me. "We have some ideas, but we'd like to hear yours."

"I'm not wild about shipping," Charlie said.

I look at Alfred. I could kill Tess for tipping Charlie off about the position before our lunch. "Okay, what do you think you'd like to do?"

"I don't know. But I'm open."

"To anything but shipping," I thought aloud.

"I know this sounds a little nuts, but I'm not sure what you're good at," Alfred said. "I'm sure you're brilliant at what you do, but what is it exactly?"

"I managed a team of salesmen at the alarm company. I had to teach them how to sell, and I also oversaw operations. I was in charge of the team that checked the alarms before they were installed."

"Quality control?" I asked.

"Bigger than that. I had to make sure that the alarms worked mechanically."

Alfred looked at me. "Mechanics?"

"Yeah, I mean, I pretty much can take apart any machine and put it back together."

"Tess always said that you knew how to handle a remote, but I had no idea you had skills beyond that."

"I do." Charlie smiled confidently. "And I speak Spanish."

I grabbed Alfred's arm. "You do?"

"Fluent."

"Why didn't I know this?" I threw my hands in the air.

"When was the last time Spanish was spoken in the Roncalli household?"

"Never," I admitted.

"I minored in Spanish at Villanova."

"I had no idea," Alfred said.

"I almost got on *Who Wants to Be a Millionaire* in 2007. I think that's it for my secrets," Charlie said.

"Well, our shoes are made in Argentina."

"I'm aware of that," Charlie said.

"And now that I'm getting married, I'm not going to be able to run down to Buenos Aires—you could be our guy. Our operations guy."

"Make me an offer," Charlie said.

The waiter arrived with a silver tray filled with surf and turf for southern Italians. There were hunks of Parmesan cheese, delicate rolls of salami, and glistening yellow peppers stuffed with anchovies.

"First we eat," I said to Charlie and Alfred. "Then we make a deal."

The night before my wedding, I finished my new shoes.

I carefully snipped the threads around the shank of the heel. I had made a pair of formal pumps in off-white raw silk with a cutwork around the vamp that matched the lace on my mother's wedding gown. I cut three-inch Cinderella heels out of Lucite, stacked for comfort and all-night dancing. When I lifted the hem of my gown, the shoes looked like wings and my feet looked like they were floating a few inches off the ground.

Gabriel came in with a gift wrapped in white. He placed it on the cutting table.

"I told you I could finish up. I sent the patterns to Charlie via e-mail. He's going to forward them to Roberta."

"Great. I'm going to get married without a single worry about the shop."

"Val, are you sure I can't help?"

"I like the finishing. I zen right out," I told him as I clipped one last thread.

"Are you nervous?"

"Yeah."

"Everything will come off without a hitch."

"My mother is the hitch queen. She'll handle any problems."

"She lives for it."

I looked at Gabriel, who had hoisted himself up on the worktable. He dangled his feet nervously. "Are you okay?"

"I hate change," he said.

"Not as much as me."

"But you're the one getting married. The very definition of that is change."

"It is, and it isn't. I can't tell you what I'm going to feel on the other side of commitment, but so far, I haven't had to change anything about myself for Gianluca. I'm assertive, and I do what I think is best. I mean, he comes first, of course, but I'm my own person."

Gabriel looked at me quizzically. "You seem to have it all figured out."

"I don't know about that. I just want to be married on my own terms."

"Is there such a thing?"

"What do you mean?"

"You're joining your lives together. Two makes one. It's the only time math is fuzzy—when there's a marriage."

"I prefer two separate but equal people in love unite in marriage."

"Val, seriously?"

"What?"

"How does feminism play with a traditional Italian man?"

"He's the father of a very independent daughter. He gets it."

"Whatever you say." Gabriel got up and handed me the gift. "Want to open your present?"

"Shouldn't I wait for Gianluca?"

"It doesn't involve him."

"Nice. And you're coming down on me about joining lives together?"

"What do you want from me? I'm very torn."

I ripped into the package. I pulled off the bubble wrap. In an elaborate gold-leafed frame, Gabriel had mounted my final sketch of my wedding shoes. "Do you like it?" he asked.

"I love it. And I love you." I gave Gabriel a kiss.

"I was going to get you a salad spinner, and went with the art instead."

"It's a good rule to always go with the art."

"It's your work," Gabriel said. My wedding shoe, drawn with a light pencil, then painted with watercolor, highlighted in shimmering gold and pools of powder blue, in fact looked like that slipper Cinderella lost, if in fact Cinderella had been Italian.

"You're really good, Val."

"I have help."

"No, I mean it. You're a really good designer, and I think Gianluca gets it. He gets *you*. And believe me, as I wander the world like it's a giant desert and I'm looking for an oasis, I want you to understand how rare that is."

"Don't you think I know? I learn everything the hard way. When I dated the chef, I learned how to chop onions so I could help him prep in the kitchen. Then I got smart. Marry the man who helps you in *your* shop. I'm marrying my tanner."

"Now that I'm a pattern cutter, I'm going to be on the lookout for a scissor manufacturer. "

"Now you're talking." I lifted the shoe off the table and checked the heel. "I saw Roman."

"When?"

"A few weeks ago."

"Why didn't you tell me?"

"Because when I mention the man's name, he appears."

"How'd he look?"

"Good."

"Did you get a tingle?"

"I'd be dead if I didn't."

"That's good. Wow."

"I lied to him."

"You didn't tell him you were engaged."

"No, I said Gianluca was young. Like Roman."

"Why did you do that?"

"You're my best friend. You tell me."

"It's ridiculous."

"I know!"

"Gianluca looks amazing."

"I know! What's my problem?"

"Did you volunteer the lie?"

"No, he asked me how old he was."

"That Roman is like one of those metal detectors at the beach. He always finds the needle and then he sticks you with it."

"I didn't tell Gianluca I saw him."

"I wish you would've. There would have been a duel on the grass at Pier 44."

"No. Roman wouldn't have shown up."

"And that's why you're marrying Gianluca. He will always show up. You can count on him."

On the morning of my wedding, I stood on the roof in my parka, long johns, and boots and watched the sun rise. I should have been wrapped in a tinfoil cape, like a marathon runner after the race. In six weeks, we had achieved the impossible. We had planned an Italian American wedding. Every person that was still alive in my family was coming, from as close as Queens Boulevard and as far away as Argentina. They received engraved invitations. And yes, there was an angel embossed on the linen paper.

It wasn't just my wedding, it was a family reunion.

One of the best parts of getting married at my age was that anticipation of the actual event was insignificant. My sisters had long engagements in their twenties, and they needed them. They had to save up for all the things I already have, a place to live and the stuff that fills that place.

I had other issues on my mind. I wasn't worried about getting an Electrolux vacuum cleaner or a fondue pot for my new apartment. It was the marriage afterward that I was looking forward to. I would finally be alone with my husband, away from the lists, Post-its, tiffs, arguments, brawls about flowers, passed hors d'oeuvres, and veils. "Eye on the prize," I chanted to myself like it was May Day and I was going for the world record for reciting Hail Marys.

"Come inside, Valentina," Gianluca said from the roof door.

"Honey, what are you doing here?" I didn't "have my face on" (my mother's term), but I didn't care. Gianluca pushed the door open. I ran to him and put my arms around his neck.

"Your mother has been up for an hour already with the makeup artist."

"It takes a good forty minutes to draw on her eyebrows. She overplucked the left one in the sixties and has to fake symmetry."

"Women and their eyebrows. I don't know a man in the world that notices them."

"So you fled Forest Hills?"

"There was no room for me at your mother's house. There were so many hot rollers plugged in, I was afraid to recharge my electric razor for fear the Long Island transformer would blow."

"You stayed in my old room, didn't you?"

"I gave it to Orsola and Matteo. Your mother put me in the spare room."

"No! You were in the twin bed? How could she? Nobody sleeps in that bed. It's for show. When we were little, Cousin Gootch slept there. He was a bed wetter. Table fifteen. We sat him with Dad's surgical team from LIJ. No worries. Gootch got over it, and Mom put a Mylar sheet on the old mattress."

"It doesn't matter. I couldn't fit on the mattress, so I stretched out on the floor."

"I'm so sorry. Where did she put Roberta?"

"Roberta got the den."

"With the bathroom."

"Your mother thought that was important."

"Look." I pointed to the winter sky in the east. Gray clouds floated overhead like chiffon.

"The sunrise." He smiled. "The light can barely make it over the buildings."

"My grandfather told me that if you make it a point to get up and see the sun rise every day, you will eventually know the secret of life."

"And what is that?"

"That no matter what happens, the sun always comes up in the morning."

"How did you sleep, Valentina?"

"I had crazy dreams. I was an old lady. And you were an old man."

"Too late for that. I wish I was younger, so we could see the world in the same way."

"Well, get over it. You are looking at the end of my youth. I'm warning you, I'm going to let myself go, get cranky, and wear sweatpants. And if I look anything like I did in the dream, I don't want any mirrors in the house."

"You will always be beautiful to me."

"Will you say that to me every morning for the rest of my life?"

"Of course."

"You know that today will be a circus," I promised him.

"A circus with a bakery. I just walked through your living room. Every surface was covered with a cookie tray."

"Twenty-five cookie trays strong. My cousins are bringing them to Leonard's this morning. I was able to buck a few traditions, but not that one. Thirty-one different kinds of cookies. This is some kind of world record, I'm not kidding."

"We have traditions too, you know."

"Really. The native Italians. Who knew? I thought you only had vendettas, *malocchio*, and cigarettes."

"Among other things."

Gianluca reached into his coat pocket and gave me a blue velvet box.

"In Italy, every groom gives his bride a gift to wear on their wedding day."

I opened the box, stamped *La Perla Cultivada, Capri*. A stunning necklace, a string of glistening pearls separated by delicate shards of red coral, was nestled on a bed of cobalt blue velvet.

"This necklace belonged to my mother. When she was a girl, she spent her summers on Capri. The jeweler, Costanzo Fiore, made this for her from the coral in the caves of the Blue Grotto. His father, Pasquale, mined this coral himself. It was Mama's favorite piece of jewelry."

I lifted the necklace out of the box. The light caught the shimmer of the pearls.

"When I was a boy I was fascinated with these colors. I thought the coral looked like flames and the pearls like stars. When she died, my father gave it to me and I put it in a drawer. When I missed her, I'd open the box and look at it, remembering how beautiful she was when she wore it. Somehow, those thoughts made me feel less alone. And I remember when I was sent to Capri to check on you—"

"I was horrible to you! I'm still sorry about that."

"You had good reason. Your boyfriend hadn't shown up. You were by yourself, and I couldn't understand how any man could leave you alone in Italy. I couldn't understand how anything could be more important than you. We went to dinner, and I fell in love with you that night."

"I'm so glad I put on my best dress that evening."

"You could have worn a dishrag, I didn't care. I want you to have something of my mother's and also something to remind you of the memories we share. When I think of you, I imagine you high in the hills of Anacapri. I see you swimming in the Blue Grotto. And on the day I die, that's the image of you that I will take with me."

I closed my eyes and buried my face in Gianluca's neck. I remembered the grotto, and how we swam there. He seemed so serious. I was certain I was annoying him with questions about the Grotto. He seemed put off by my questions as I nagged him. It was like being a girl again, when a boy who liked me was mean to get my attention. Gianluca was trying to get my attention all right, but I didn't see it.

When we swam through the warm blue water to the walls of

the cave, he showed me the veins of coral clinging to the rock wall, glistening ruby red against the deep blue water. I had never seen anything so beautiful, the exact point where earth and water meet, where one holds the other and an eternal connection is made.

Sometimes before I fall asleep, I imagine the way the water felt against my skin and the way the smooth, glassy coral felt against my fingers. How could he know what I dreamed about when I had never told him? That was the knowingness of a man who truly loved me. I didn't have to tell him because he already knew.

"I'm going to leave you to get dressed, Signora Vechiarelli."

I lifted my face from his neck. "Gianluca? I meant to discuss the name change."

"Is there a problem?"

"Well, I'm in my thirties, and I'm a Roncalli. Everyone in the business knows me as a Roncalli."

"So?"

"I'd like to keep my name."

Gianluca's face fell. His expression was a combination of hurt with a confusion chaser. "I'd like you to take my name."

I thought quickly. "How about I keep Roncalli in business and use Vechiarelli at home?"

"I know who you are at home."

Gabriel pushed through the screen door. When he observed this private moment between Gianluca and me, he pivoted to go back inside.

"Gabriel?" Gianluca called out when he heard the door creak.

"I didn't mean to interrupt. But we've got a looming disaster with the cookie trays. They sent your geriatric cousins from Ohio to transport them to Leonard's. One of them is on a walker. Does the name Mary Conti ring a bell? She couldn't carry a single baba au rhum down a flight of stairs without breaking her neck, let alone a tray of them."

"I'll be right down," I told him.

"No, no. I'll get the cookie trays where they need to go. I'll see you in church." Gianluca kissed me.

I'd marked every important moment of my life on this roof. I'd made every major decision, and all the small ones, right here. Air and sky and space, a luxury in this city, were mine anytime I wanted to climb the rickety old stairs and claim them.

In all those years, I never had the same view twice. The sky has turned every shade of blue from the deepest sapphire to the palest aqua. I've learned how to predict oncoming snow, and been able to pinpoint the exact moment rain would stop before crossing the Jersey side into lower Manhattan.

The mood of the Hudson River shifts constantly with the drift of the cloud cover, the rising and setting of the sun, and the wind as it propels the waves as they ripple toward the sea. Sometimes the surf is choppy. Foamy whitecaps rise and lap against the shore like ruffles of lace. Other times, the water is as still and smooth as the surface of lapis. But on this morning, something new. The sun peeked over the buildings behind me and my river turned gold in the light.

The waterway was empty, barely a ripple rolling out in the distance toward Staten Island and out to sea. It was just me and my old friend, dressed up for my wedding day. The Hudson River was still and bright and clear, as if I could walk on it. It looked like a road, a simple gold path to somewhere.

"Okay, I love the necklace, but now the belt doesn't work," Gabriel said as I stood on the stool in front of the three-way mirror. "Couldn't he have given you amethysts?" Gabriel loosened the lavender ribbon belt from around my waist.

"There aren't any amethysts in the Blue Grotto."

"All right, all right. Let me think." Gabriel went to the notions closet and opened the door wide. He pulled several wheels of ribbons out. He brought them to me. He held them up against the lace. "Green, ick. White, you look like Helen Hayes in *The White Nurse.* Good movie. Lousy palette. Pink, no. Coral? Too on the nose."

"How about no belt?"

"You have to be cinched."

I studied the gown in the mirror. "I guess."

"No guess. You have to drape and shape. I want you to look like a woman in that dress, not the box it came in."

Gabriel stood next to me in his tuxedo and squinted at the image of me in the mirror. My hair was half up and half down. The loose side ponytail was very Claudia Cardinale. The curls looked like ribbons.

The gown was so simple, exactly what I'd hoped for. The delicate lace had a texture like frosted glass. The coral and pearl necklace hugged the neckline as though it were part of the dress.

"When in doubt, go with Chanel."

"I don't own any Chanel."

"You don't have to. We're knocking her off."

Gabriel went to the notions cabinet and unfurled a wide, black grosgrain ribbon from a spool. He dug around in the embellishment bin until he found an antique pearl shoe clip. He tied the ribbon around my waist, anchoring it in the back with the shoe clip.

"Now we got pearls coming and going." He stood back. "What do you think?"

I squinted at the mirror. Then I lifted the hem of my gown, revealing my wedding shoes. "It works with the shoes. With the Lucite, it's kind of deco."

"We knew it all along." Gabriel shook his head. "Black and white. Cecil Beaton knew what he was doing. Whatever possessed you to go with the lavender belt?"

"It was the first one I reached for—and you know how I feel about original impulses."

"I know. You live by them. But not today. This is the ticket, sister. Now *you* are the pop of color, not the belt."

My family opened the outside door. It sounded like the gate opening on the Circus Maximus when they let the lions out into the arena.

"In here, people!" Gabriel shouted over the din.

Tess entered first, in a ballet-length red velvet dress. Jaclyn followed her in a red satin A-line gown. My mother pulled a full-out Nancy Reagan in a long-sleeved red silk gown with a panel of red sequins draping from her shoulder and down her back. Pamela was in an adorable red sheath with a plunging neckline.

"It's the invasion of the candy boxes!" Gabriel said. "You look like a pack of Valentines."

"Forget us. Look at her," Tess said.

My mother held her false eyelashes up with her pinkies as her eyes filled with tears. "You're gorgeous, Valentine. The dress doesn't look like an immigrant tablecloth. Somehow you took my old schmatte and made it your own."

"You look like Audrey Hepburn," Pamela marveled.

"The gratitude goes to me. An hour ago we switched things up. We went from the Fashion Bug to rue Chambon with the snip of a ribbon," Gabriel said proudly.

"I don't even miss the veil," Mom said. "That necklace!"

"It belonged to Gianluca's mother."

"It's spectacular," Tess said.

"You ladies look amazing. Pamela, I'm in love with your dress." I tried to single out my sister-in-law so she felt a part of things.

"Thanks. Your mom found it."

"It's a sample. All we had to do was finish the hem."

"Well, it's gorgeous."

"Can we get some light on the subject?" Mom asked Gabriel.

Gabriel unfurled the security gates on the window. The bright winter sun warmed the room. "Hey, the window gates don't squeak anymore."

"Gianluca replaced the old track," I told him.

"Wow. Smooth as ice." Gabriel was impressed.

"I love a handy man." My mother sighed. "A woman can design her life when she's married to a handy guy. You want a new porch? He pours the concrete. A fountain? He can rig a water line. Bookshelves? He can build them. Wallpaper? He can glue it up without any buckling. A man who can build things is a problem solver. Really, when I think of it, handy is the new sexy." Mom stepped up on the fitting stool and checked her gown from the rear. "For *me*, at least. You're all young, so you still enjoy the old sexy. Even though your dad and I, even with prostate—"

"Ma! Please," Tess shrieked. "Don't ruin Valentine's wedding day with that image."

My dad appeared in the doorway, handsome in his tuxedo. "Can we please let one day of my life go by without talking about my prostrate?"

Usually someone corrected him when he mispronounced *prostate*, but we had bigger issues that morning, so we let it go. Dad pushed through the flock of women in his life, the bright red birds who filled his world with color when they weren't pecking him to death. When he saw me, Dad put his hand on his heart. "Now that's class."

"I taught you everything you know, Dutch. And you're right. She is pure elegance," Mom agreed.

"May I have a moment with my daughter, please?"

"Let's go, girls." Gabriel led them to the door. "I feel like I'm in the dugout with the Saint Louis Cardinals. Move it, ladies. We got the Carmel fleet outside."

"Happy Valentine's Day." Dad kissed me on the cheek. "It's your feast day."

"My feast day and my wedding day. Am I blessed or what?"

"You're blessed. Always have been. When you were little, I told your mother that there was something about you that was different from my other kids. Alfred is my only son and my namesake, so that's one thing. Tess is a sweetheart, and Jaclyn is a doll, but you, you've always been special. I'm not so good with words. But this morning, I wanted to tell you what you mean to me. You know, plain and simple."

"I know how you feel, Dad." I blushed because I didn't want Dad to tell me his feelings. They're too big. I've known every day of my life how he feels about me and we've gone thirty-six years without articulating it.

"Indulge me, would ya, please? You know, when I was a boy,

my grandparents were off the boat. They spoke Italian and they had the thick accents and the old-world ideas. Every Sunday we had a family dinner in the garage in Brooklyn. I used to hose the floors down and set up the tables on Saturday afternoon. Nothing like the scent of fresh manicotti and motor oil when you sit down to eat. But anyway, it was a good life.

"All the cousins came over and we had a ball. We'd play stickball in the street, and when it was hot, we'd open a fire hydrant and run in the water. We played bocce in a backyard the size of a postage stamp. We'd yank figs off the trees and eat 'em right there.

"All the old guys would sit around and smoke cigars and talk about women. The women would gather around a picnic table and yak for hours about whatever women talk about. This big extended family was what I knew. We were close, sometimes too close. We'd get into business with one another, fall out, and then have to find our way back to where we were before the deal went sour. There were a lot of lost years where we didn't speak to certain relatives, and I never approved of that. I never thought money was more important than family. But I was often alone in that belief."

"Alfred and I are getting along just fine."

"I see that, and I'm proud of you. I was sick when you left teaching to come here and learn how to make shoes, but now I see you have a talent. It's in you, like it was in your grandfather and your grandmother. Sometimes we forget that talent is a gift and we take it for granted. But it's important. You have a gift, and you should always be a guardian of your art."

I nodded because I couldn't speak.

"Now, I was raised a certain way. And one of the things that

got in"—Dad tapped his head—"was something I'm not particularly proud of. It's a bias against my own people. My grandparents were against any of their kids, their American kids,
marrying someone from the other side. I guess, in the Roncalli
family, there were some problems with those marriages, and
they caused permanent rifts. And I imagine that to my grandparents, marrying someone from Italy was going backward."

"I don't think you have to worry about Gianluca."

"I'm not worried about him. He seems like a stand-up guy.
I'm worried about you. I don't want you to give up everything
for him. He has a family already—a grown daughter and a son-
in-law. And you have everything ahead of you. Are you sure you
want a life where you're Act Two instead of Act One?"

"I don't look at it like that, Dad."

"Well, you wouldn't. Because that's the kind of person you
are. You always assume the best in people. And I hope you're
right. But if you're wrong, it's okay by me. I will be there for
you no matter what. If this thing doesn't work out, it's not a reflection on you, but on your hope in all situations. I never saw
you look down. You are always looking up, and I don't want that
to change about you. I mean, a person who can build a pair of
shoes can do just about anything. You know what I'm saying?"

I nodded.

"When you can make something, you have a certain power.
It means you can always survive by the labor of your own hands.
Don't forget that."

I took my father's arm, but before we left, we stood before
the mirror.

"We look like piano keys, Val," Dad said as he squinted at
the mirror. "Black and white. Always a classic."

"It's your signature look, Dad. It always works for you."

No one would have ever used the word *noble* to describe my father. Southern Italians were considered hard workers, but their reputations were made building the walls of the palazzo, not residing within them.

My father's gentle Calabrian roots and strong Sicilian ways might have been at war within him when he was young, but now they have etched him with character based upon loyalty and truth that sustains our family. I'm so happy that my parents stayed together when they went through the worst. It makes me think that maybe I could too.

I didn't know it then, but that lesson was the best gift I'd receive on my wedding day, so it was only right to give my father one. "Dad?"

"Yeah?"

"I'm going to keep my name."

"You are?"

"Because it's the first gift you ever gave me."

Dad took my arm and opened the shop door for me. I walked through it on my way to a whole new life.

6

My father took my arm as we crossed the piazza of Our Lady Queen of Martyrs Church in Forest Hills. The blustery February wind cut through me. No wonder people get married in June. I pulled my mother's borrowed winter-white cape closely around me.

The empty buses from Ohio were parked caravan-style in front of the church as though it was a tour stop at Howard Johnson's on the L.I.E. They had already loaded in for the fried clam special.

I paused before going up the stairs and remembered riding my bike on Queens Boulevard to go to the candy store when I was ten years old. My brother would watch from this vantage point on the church steps. I turned to see that the old neighborhood had changed, but I bet I could still find the candy store. I would always end my candy run with an Evel Knievel–style jump off the wheelchair ramp at the side entrance of the church. Funny the things I remembered while wearing my wedding gown.

Dad opened the door for me. I was immediately ushered in by Gabriel, who pulled me into a room in the back of the church. I looked over my shoulder and saw that the church was full of our guests.

"I've held your stepdaughter hostage in the cry room," Gabriel whispered.

Orsola was waiting for me. Tall, willowy, and classically beautiful, she had a serene countenance like Gianluca. She was her father's daughter in every way. She wore a pale silver dress and matching shoes. We embraced.

"I'm so happy you're here."

"Me too," she said.

"I'm sorry the rehearsal dinner went so late last night."

"We had so much fun. Matteo loved meeting everyone."

"I have something for you." I reached into my purse and gave her a gold gift box with a ribbon tied around it. "I wanted you to have something from me."

Orsola opened the package and lifted out a simple gold bangle bracelet. It had been engraved with the words *daughter* and *friend*. Orsola slipped it onto her wrist.

"Thank you. I love it!" she said.

"You have a wonderful mother, so you don't need an extra one. But I will be here for you whenever you need me. I'll always be your friend."

"Valentina?" Orsola seemed nervous.

"Yes?"

"How do you feel about being a grandmother?" Orsola took my hands. "I'm having a baby!"

I was stunned. I figured that Orsola and Matteo would have a baby someday, but I didn't think it would happen this soon. I'm barely a wife, and now I'm almost a grandmother. What kind of a hayride is this life?

"Congratulations! Does your father know?"

She shook her head. "I'll tell him after the honeymoon."

"You will not. He'll be thrilled! This is wonderful news! We should go and tell him right now!"

"No, no. This is your moment, and it won't come again. You go get married, and then we'll tell Papa."

Gabriel poked his head in and motioned for me to join him. Orsola slipped out and up the aisle to join her husband.

"We could've used her legs in the bridal party. We need the height," Gabriel said. "We got a low flow in the canoe with your crew."

"She didn't want to be a bridesmaid."

"Good call. Maybe she didn't want to get lung cancer from the hair spray."

Gabriel guided me into the sacristy, where baptisms were performed years ago. Mom and my sisters had taken over the holy space, turning it into a dressing room at a beauty pageant.

There was a curling iron heating in a plug under a stained glass window. There were makeup kits with open trays of lipstick, brushes, eyeliner palettes, and mascara tubes. Michelangelo used less pigment to paint the Sistine Chapel. There were last-minute beauty preps happening all around me. Whoever wasn't rubbing rouge was powdering down, and whoever wasn't spraying her updo was pulling tendril curls down for some drama around the face.

This wasn't a wedding. This was an opening night.

The only person who wasn't beautifying was Aunt Feen, who sat on a bench by the baptismal font leaning on the crook of her cane. Even in a room filled with heavenly light pouring through the stained glass windows, Aunt Feen managed to suck the air right out of it.

"Mike, Father wants to speak to you," Gabriel said to my mother.

My mother put down her compact mirror. "You know what your father always says to me. At a certain point, too much futzing results in diminishing returns." Mom gave me a quick kiss and followed Gabriel into the foyer.

When my mother returned, she had a look of panic on her face, which she tried to mask with a smile so broad it reminded me of the sample choppers dentists use to demonstrate proper flossing. "Val, we thought we had Father Drake."

"Who do we have?"

"Father Nikako."

"Who is Father Nikako?"

"He's a sub." Mom kept the Mr. Sardonicus smile going as though nothing was wrong.

"What happened to Father Drake?" Tess asked.

"He's giving last rites at Queens County Hospital," Mom explained.

"There's a full-time job for you," Aunt Feen piped up. "You better be bleeding like an animal when you go over there, otherwise you got a nine-hour wait. I saw a man holding his liver over there when I went for my flu shot."

"Why didn't they send the sub over to the hospital?" Jaclyn wondered.

"Because they didn't." Mom gritted her teeth. "It's not the end of the world. A priest is a priest."

"Yeah. But Nikako? Jesus. I can't understand a word he says," Aunt Feen groused.

Gabriel came in and closed the door behind him. "Where'd you get the priest?"

"He's from Nigeria," Mom snapped.

"Don Cheadle could play him in the movie," Gabriel said.

"I like Don Cheadle," Jaclyn said as she pumped her mascara wand. "He's a great actor."

"This is his first wedding," Gabriel said.

"Who invited Don Cheadle to the wedding?" Pamela asked.

"Not Don Cheadle—the *priest*."

"What?" Tess blurted. "What do you mean, it's his *first* wedding?"

"He's never done this before." Gabriel shrugged. "He just got ordained."

"Don't they practice in the seminary?"

"I have no idea what they do in the seminary." Gabriel put his hands in the air.

"I don't care that he's never done this, I care about being able to understand him," Tess said.

"Well, you won't. I come over for daily mass, and I fall asleep as soon as my ass hits the pew. He is incomprehensible. Where do they find these people?" Aunt Feen complained. "And he's a baby. How old is he? Nineteen? Twenty?"

"Black people look younger." Tess checked her lipstick.

"I know. Cousin Roberta is in her forties, and she looks, like, twenty-five," Jaclyn said.

"Father Cheadle is at least thirty," Gabriel said.

"How can you tell?"

"He has a very mature look of stultified anxiety on his face that only comes when you know for certain that you're in over your head."

"Great." I pulled my bouquet of red roses from the florist's box.

"I'll call Father Drake's cell and see if he can't hurry the last rites along." Mom fished for her cell phone in her purse. "I'll hunt him down."

"Don't. Never pull a priest from a deathbed. At the very least, it's rude. At the most, it's horrific karma," I told her.

"What's the difference if we have a young black African priest instead of an old white Irish one? We got black people in the family," Tess said.

"The Brazilians." Aunt Feen's dentures clicked on the Z sound.

"Argentinian," I corrected her.

My father poked his head in the door. "We're up!" he said.

The wedding party filed out. Aunt Feen rose with her cane. "I guess we're going with the black guy."

Gram entered the room. "There you are," she said to Feen.

"You found me," Feen said. "I've been sitting in here with the Real Housewives of Nowhere. My left lung is filled with goo from the hair spray. I'm lucky I can still draw a breath."

"You'll sit with Dominic and me. We'll process in together."

"Whatever you say. Just as long as I have a seat." Aunt Feen brushed past me. "Good luck, kid."

Gram took my hands now that we were alone. "You look magnificent. The dress is perfect."

"Gram, you know we're *double* family now. You're about to be a great-grandmother."

"Are you pregnant?"

"Not me. Orsola."

"How wonderful! Does Gianluca know?"

"Not yet."

"Life is crazy, isn't it?"

I followed the bridal party up the aisle on the arm of my father. I took a moment to look at the guests, faces from my days as a teacher, cousins from Brooklyn and Jersey, cousins from Ohio who clustered together in the same configuration they'd formed on the bus, customers who'd become friends, and even Bret, who winked at me from the end of a pew. My old fiancé and lifelong friend was there for the small stuff, but came through in the major moments too.

I thought of June Lawton as my heels tapped against the marble. She liked shoes that made noise. She fought for embellishments that jingled and liked metal taps on the sole for whimsy. From her years as a dancer, she liked anything that moved. I wondered if she would have been surprised that Gianluca and I married. She would have been there, in one of her dance skirts and a cashmere bolero sweater. She'd have worn a secondhand fur and a new hat.

When I eventually made it to the altar on my father's arm after Chiara and Charisma littered the aisle with rose petals, I saw Gianluca. He was breathtaking in his tuxedo. It's a good thing I like old movies, because today, he's my William Powell.

The light from the rose window bathed Gianluca and Saint Michael on his pedestal in the alcove with a single gold beam. Everyone else, including the priest, the bridal party, and his best man, his father, fell into shadow. The crisp white shirt and the black tie framed his blue eyes and gray hair so beautifully that I almost couldn't take it all in.

My father held me tight before letting me go. He wiped away his tears with a handkerchief that had been pressed and starched so stiffly, I was afraid it would cut his eye. My mother believed in a hard crease. He dabbed his tears and joined her in the pew.

Gianluca took my hand and whispered, *"Ti amo."*

Instantly, the moment, planned from afar and quickly, was real.

Father Don Cheadle was not only young and inexperienced, he was a nervous wreck. He gripped the prayer book firmly, but the satin ribbon that marked the pages shook.

I leaned forward and whispered, "Father, don't worry. You'll be fine. This is my first time too."

He seemed slightly relieved, but I can never tell about these things with holy people, so I whispered, "Now him"—I indicated my husband to be—"not so much." Father Nikako smiled at me. Now that he was certain we were not the perfect couple, he could let go of having it be a perfect ceremony.

As Father began the mass, the familiar words fell away. I wouldn't remember the sound of the music, the drone of the prayers, or Father Nikako's thick accent.

All I would remember were Gianluca's polished black wing-tips as he stood in a puddle of red rose petals.

When we pulled up to Leonard's in Great Neck, Gianluca looked at the grandeur of the wedding hall with the same sense of awe a visitor might feel when he first happens upon the strip in Las Vegas. His refined Tuscan sensibility had never been barraged by the likes of the Romanesque Leonard's. When you're from the place with the original antiquities, the plaster versions can be overwhelming. At first Gianluca was in awe, and moments later, he went numb.

My husband grew up on streets paved with stones that were over a thousand years old, and here at Leonard's, they are painted to look that old. Every element of the facade—the white marble stairs with their hand-painted gold veins, the columns with their crackled marble veneers, the palazzo-style windows—is a copy of the real thing, without chips, cracks, or faded metals. Every aspect of Leonard's is old-looking but in fact brand-new.

There is no history, just the dazzling patina of the stucco that resembles white teeth. Even the tiered fountain looks as though it has been dipped in Polident. As we pulled up the circular drive to the entrance, we were temporarily blinded by the bright lights nestled in the flower beds, throwing streams of white-hot klieg light on the entrance.

The last of the buses had unloaded.

We saw the defensive line of women, our Jersey cousins, going up the stairs in full-length fur coats. They conjured the glamour of old Hollywood or poker night in Bigfoot's Cave.

I kissed Gianluca. "Forgive me in advance."

"Why?"

"You're about to enter the set of a Fellini movie, except we speak English."

Carol Kall had outdone herself. Every possible extra had been thrown in for my wedding. I know every tier of what Leonard's offers, and we're talking first class all the way.

The food stations were a version of International Food Day on Ninth Avenue. The stations featured every nation and cuisine. She packed them into the Venetian cocktail lobby like stands in downtown Marrakesh. I was surprised there wasn't a pig on a spit or roasted duck hanging from the chandeliers Chinatown style, because there was everything else. There was even a free-flowing fondue fountain that made a river of cheese, with fresh rolls shaped like gondolas for dipping.

Gianluca was amazed and befuddled. I forgot he had never been to a world's fair or even knew what one was. Ours was the world's fair of weddings.

"What do you think?" Mom said.

"Mom, I didn't know Leonard had it in him."

"I know! Carol really rallied. She understood when I said last child, last wedding. I don't think there's a steam table left in Great Neck," Mom said proudly as she adjusted her bra strap.

"It's insane. We didn't need the sit-down dinner."

"Oh, we say that every time, but believe me, they'll eat the prime rib, and the Venetian table will be nothing but crumbs in ten minutes. Come on. Come see the ballroom."

Mom snuck me into the ballroom, where the tables had been set in red, with giant hearts dangling overhead. The band was tuning up.

"I can't believe I got the Mario Geritano Orchestra. They've got William Richard, who does his salute to Sinatra. He sounds just like him. And he wears a palmetto! And then, Lisa Puglise, you know, the bombshell from upstate? She does a salute to Nancy Sinatra. She's going to lead the line dance to 'These Boots Are Made for Walking.' "

"The crowd will go wild."

"I know! I just wanted it all to be perfect for you."

"It is, Mom." My mother's idea of a great wedding was unfolding before our eyes. She has to have her serious sacrament, but afterward, she goes for Talent Night at Grossinger's. We'll have everything but a plate-spinning juggler.

Gabriel poked his head in the door. "Everybody's looking for you, Val. They want pictures."

I followed Gabriel to the bridal room. The moment I could, I slipped out of my shoes and sat down on the sofa. I thought of Gianluca, stood, and slipped them back on.

"Where are you going?"

"I can't leave Gianluca alone out there."

"Your mother had a cigar bar set up in the garden room. He's fine. He's in there puffing away with the Ohio Players and having a scotch. He's with his father and your dad."

I slipped out of my shoes and sat back down on the couch.

"I'm very proud of you."

"Why?" I asked.

"You pretended to understand every word Father Nikako said."

"I sort of did understand him," I admitted.

"You're being kind. No one could understand him."

"I don't remember much of the ceremony."

"The mind has a way of shielding us from disaster."

Tess pushed the door open, followed by Jaclyn. Tess handed me a plate of fried things. They could have been vegetables, or mozzarella or ravioli, but whatever they were at the center, they'd been dipped in batter and fried.

"What is this?"

"It's from the Morocco station."

"Yum."

"I think they're stuffed with chickpea," Jaclyn guessed. "Don't you want it? Then hand it over." Jaclyn bit and chewed as Tess sampled a piece.

"If I could be a superhero, I'd be one who could eat anything and not gain weight," Tess said.

"No such thing, so watch your carbs," said Gabriel.

"You're cruel!"

"No, I know what it's like to overeat and have to walk around with my pants unzipped for a week."

"So you'd be the superhero who doesn't wear pants."

"Okay, then if I can't be the eater who stays skinny, I'd want to be invisible, so I could eat whatever I want and no one would look at me," Tess said.

"That's called marriage," Gabriel said. He looked at me. "I didn't mean that."

"You'd get married too if you saw the loot that Gianluca and Val got for their wedding," said Tess.

"Yep, I organized it in the storeroom at the shop. There's a list for the thank-you notes, and a little system I like to call the dot technique. You have repeat gifts, and when you do, they get a dot in the same color, so that the returns are organized. Of course, you have to see the gift to send the thank-you, but once you have, we take the dot boxes and return them to the stores." Jaclyn smiled proudly.

"Why don't we hire you girls to do the shipping at the shop?" I wondered.

Tess looked at Jaclyn. "I don't know, why don't you?"

"Let me get through the wedding and I'll talk to Alfred."

"I could commute into the city with Charlie!" Tess said.

"Oh, I wish you had something for Tom," Jaclyn said. "My husband is too humble to ask."

"Does he speak Chinese?" Gabriel asked.

"Not that I know of," Jaclyn said.

"If we expand to China for production, we'll need somebody who can speak the language." Gabriel looked at me.

"We're fine with Argentina," I assured them. "And Charlie's Spanish."

There was a tapping at the door. Gianluca pushed the door open.

"They're looking for us," he said.

"Get in here. I'm hiding."

The room filled with the scent of cigar smoke. I waved my hand in front of my face. "I guess Mom didn't go for the fine Cuban cigars. What are you smoking out there? Cornsilk?"

"What a lovely combo," Gabriel said. "Fried chickpeas and cigar smoke. What happens next? I get sold into white slavery?"

Jaclyn and Tess stood up. "We gotta go. Come on, guys. It's 'Oh Marie.' "

The guests had drifted into the dining room, and sure enough, Mario Geritano was cranking out "Oh Marie," a family favorite. Lisa Puglise, in a gold lamé jumpsuit, was doing her best Keely Smith impression while Mario did the full-tilt Louis Prima. The band's main attribute was volume.

"Valentine!" Don Pipino threw his arms around me. Don is my father's favorite cousin. They grew up like brothers with the same sense of humor and the same head of thick hair. "You are the most beautiful bride ever. But don't tell Chrissy and Mary."

"They were both gorgeous on their wedding days."

"You can't go wrong. Italian girls look good in white. You

know, there's only two ways to go for women. You're either a Cinderella or a Snow White. The blond-haired, blue-eyed thing not so much with the Italians. But the black hair and pale skin? We're Snow Whites. That's our bailiwick."

I introduced Don to my husband. They fell into a conversation like a couple of old friends. Cousin Don is one of those people who never makes someone feel like a stranger. If I didn't know better, I would have said that Gianluca was having the time of his life.

My brother Alfred pulled me onto the dance floor. "Are you having fun?"

"Absolutely. How about you?"

"Pamela is having a ball with the cousins."

"Sorry to leave you with all the work at the shop."

"Don't even think about it. Enjoy your honeymoon."

"I'll get winter sketches to you when I get home."

"We've got time. Don't worry."

"I worry about everything."

"Why? You're marrying a tanner. At the very least, he knows where we can get the best leather at the best price."

"I know. I just don't want anything to change."

"Val, get real. Everything changes when you get married."

"It does?"

"Usually the change is good. But you can't live like you did before you were married."

"Why not?"

"Because you have a husband now. He'll need you to be a wife."

"I can't get up and wander around in the middle of the night and draw and paint?"

"You'll work that stuff out. But that changes too. I'm just starting to win Pam's trust back, but I've learned that I messed up because I wasn't in my marriage. You gotta stay in your marriage."

The band played "Something Stupid." Mario and Lisa sang a duet just like Frank and Nancy. I had no idea what my brother was talking about. I couldn't grasp the notion of staying in a marriage. Is that akin to staying in your lane on the freeway, or inside the lines when you color? I decided to think about it as Gianluca cut in and we waltzed to the faux Sinatras.

The reception exploded into high Vegas gear when Gabriel took the floor, loosened his tie, grabbed the microphone, and called the wedding party to the dance floor. You know a Roncalli party is in full tilt when the floor show commences.

On cue, to up the drama, a flank of waiters entered from the kitchen, carrying the cookie trays high in the air. Soon the ballroom filled with the scent of vanilla, anisette, and sweet butter. The rustle of the cellophane sounded like applause as the guests dove into the thirty-one varieties.

Two waiters placed seats behind Gianluca and me. We sat and watched Gabriel, Tess, Jaclyn, and Pamela perform "Route 66." It wasn't one lyric into the second stanza when my dad and Cousin Don formed a line to bunny-hop/choo-choo through the reception hall. Even Aunt Feen got up and joined the line, grinding her arm like she was hand-cranking the starter on a Duesenberg.

Pamela slipped into the seat next to me. "What a wedding."

"Is it too much?"

"Way," Pamela said, making us both laugh.

I placed my hand on hers. I'd had just enough champagne so I said, "I'm so happy you stayed with Alfred."

"Well, we'll see how it goes. I can't predict the future, but so far, it's going okay. He agreed to some changes."

"*My* brother?"

"Your brother. He wasn't happy, but neither was I. I'm going back to school to study marketing. I'm a writer, and I want to write. You know. Business writing."

"That's fantastic."

"I got lost, Valentine. Really lost," Pam said as she watched the conga line in the distance. "Hold on to your own life. I got married, and it was all about Alfred and then the boys. I lost *me*. And I blame myself for what happened."

"It wasn't your fault."

"In a way it was. I never let Alfred know what I would and wouldn't tolerate. I just tried to please him and make him happy. It was all about keeping him from going into a rage. I'm raging myself in a whole different way. I have work to do. Now it's my turn."

"You deserve it."

"We all do."

Rocco grabbed his mother and dragged her toward the Venetian table. I watched Pamela as she clicked across the dance floor to the festival of desserts, my nephew leading her like he was a dog on a leash. I was getting a lot of advice on my wedding day, and all of it seemed to be about holding on. That day, I thought I had a pretty good grip, but of course, only time would tell if I did.

As the band played "Violets for Your Fur," my father-in-law/grandfather-in-law Dominic invited me to dance. The photographer snapped us from every angle.

"I'm so happy for you, Valentina. And happy for my son. I want you to come and live in Italy."

"Dom, I have the shop."

"I know, but don't you want to live in Tuscany?"

"You can come and live in Greenwich Village."

"No, no, I'm not a city person."

"We'll come and visit," I promised.

"It's not the same."

"We'll figure something out."

"My son is everything to me. When his wife left him, he was hurt, but I hurt more. I can't help it."

"I understand, Dominic." It occurred to me that I had spent a good part of my wedding day reassuring other people about how life would be the same going forward, and that I wouldn't get in the way of their long-standing relationships with Gianluca. I wonder if my family was telling Gianluca the same thing.

Gianluca and Orsola danced over to us. I put my arms around my stepdaughter and my father-in-law.

"Shall we tell them?" Orsola looked at me.

"Don't wait another second."

"Matteo and I are having a baby," Orsola announced.

Gianluca's face broke into a grin I'd never seen before. He took his daughter in his arms and held her. Dominic fumbled for his handkerchief. It would be his first great-grandchild. He was beside himself with joy.

Gram joined us and put her arms around Dominic. She was elated for her husband. There is no better news in our family than the announcement that one of us is having a baby. It trumps all the other great moments in life, because suddenly everything is new again. We start over.

The news of Orsola's baby spread quickly. As Gianluca and I made the rounds at the tables, and my satin purse filled with envelopes for La Boost (the wedding gifts of cash), we told everyone about the new baby.

Mom had really planned the tables beautifully. My sisters were seated with cousins they adore, the kids had their own table, and as I looked out over the crowd, everyone seemed to be having a great time.

"Your stepdaughter is having a baby," Aunt Feen said. "Takes the pressure off of you, doesn't it?" She tapped her fork on the table. "Tickety-tick tick-tock."

"I'm happy for her." And I was. Leave it to Aunt Feen to wind the gears on my biological clock until they broke off. "Very happy."

"Sure you are. As someone who has had her own thunder stolen all of her life, I understand. Here you are, a bride, and you're upstaged by your stepdaughter's news. Some of us are destined to be bit players, never the star. Welcome to the background, Valentine. There's room for you in the kickline, on the end out of the spotlight."

"Aunt Feen, I said I'm happy for her."

"All right, all right. I'm just glad you got married before you had a baby. I am sick and tired of people having babies out of wedlock and then throwing their kids into the wedding party like a pack of afterthoughts. I'm embarrassed for them. You do things out of order in your life, and you pay the price. Don't forget it."

I looked closely at Aunt Feen's face and realized that I wasn't having a conversation with a sober person. She was having another Bailey's on the rocks, and she was about to hit them hard like an old dinghy.

Mom passed Aunt Feen the bread and shot me a look. I've seen that look. My mother's face had that same expression when Aunt Feen ruined Gram's wedding in Tuscany.

Across the dance floor, Gianluca was in a huddle with Alfred and Roberta. Whatever they were discussing seemed important. I excused myself from the table and joined them.

"Is everything okay?" I asked them.

"Fine, fine," Albert said. "We were talking shop. Roberta was bringing us up to speed on production."

"Oh, okay." I acted as if it didn't matter that I had been excluded, but it did. We should be able to enjoy my wedding without discussing our work, but we can't. This is the very definition of a family-owned business. There is no sign on the door, no key in the lock, weekend off, or holiday free of trouble-shooting.

Gianluca sensed my feelings and put his arm around me. "There's nothing to worry about."

"It's a beautiful wedding, Valentine," Roberta assured me.

Mom flagged us down. They were serving another course, and Mom knew that the diehards wouldn't eat until Gianluca and I were seated. We made our way back to our tables.

Aunt Feen filled her wineglass. She was tipsy during the cocktail hour, and now, it appeared she had tipped. "The reception is better than the ceremony," she said loudly. "At least I can understand what people are saying here. Even the Russian servers. Of course, they're near our people. Near Europe. You know Shush-uh and Italy."

Cousin Don looked at my mother, who looked at my father.

"Aunt Feen," my mom said firmly. "Have some bread. I insist."

"Father got the job done. That's all that matters," Gabriel said.

"He had a very thick accent," Roberta agreed.

"I thought you of all people would understand him," Feen said, buttering the bread with her soupspoon.

"Because I'm black?" Roberta smiled.

"Hey, he is way blacker than you. You're mocha-chino. Caramel. The color. Not the car service."

"That's *Carmel*," my mother said slowly.

"Whatever. Now, Father Nigeria—"

"Father *Nikako*," my mother and I said in unison.

"Nikako. Now that man is as black as his cassock."

Gabriel leaned over me and took a sip from my wineglass.

"Aunt Feen, Abraham Lincoln just called. He wants his Civil War back," Gabriel toasted her.

A honeymoon in New Orleans the week after Fat Tuesday is a bit like walking Fifth Avenue at 3:00 a.m. the morning after a ticker-tape parade. The streets are quiet, except for a lone saxophone heard through the open door of a band bar. Some laughter floats through the air and fades away like the smoke from a cigarette.

The sidewalks are carpeted with a shimmering patina of confetti and shards of ribbon that stick to the cement. The street gutters have an occasional glint of gold or purple or green from a lost bead that makes your heart race momentarily when you imagine you've found a lost treasure. What is real and what is faux is intertwined in New Orleans. You cannot tell the huckster from a duke.

By day, chicory and cinnamon and the pungent scent of something slow-roasting meets you at every corner. At night, it's as if the city slips on her evening gloves. Fragrant freesia hangs in the air, and except for the booze, New Orleans has the scent of an elegant lady.

When I remember my honeymoon, I think of Gianluca and me walking in a city that doesn't seem to have a country. You can't say it's American (even though it is), but it isn't European either. It is its own universe with its own sense of time. New Orleans should be surrounded by a scrim of velvet curtains, because what happens within these city limits is pure theater.

The architecture is ornate, and in keeping with a city surrounded by water, aspects of old ships are used in the design. A face from the prow of an old ship is used as a finial on a porch lamp. Doors bound with hemp trim seem transported from another place, some banana republic to the south. Old steamer trunks are used as coffee tables on porches. This isn't a destination, but a glorious stop on some grand adventure. Like everyone else, we are passing through.

There is languid beauty in the design and movement of the city—brick facades dripping with old branches loaded with purple morning glories, banisters intricately carved to look like lace, latticework screens separating porches from the street, and windows heavily lidded from within by grand layered draperies, to keep whatever happens inside private.

If New York is about walking and moving and doing, New Orleans is about stopping, resting, and reclining. Gianluca couldn't have picked a better place to start our marriage. The city might be new to us, but we felt welcome. Here, Gianluca's accent and our age difference was of no consequence. In

New Orleans, what is on the surface doesn't matter much. It's the depths beneath that are celebrated here. Adventure, storytelling, cons, and danger make the atmosphere sweet and thick.

On the last night of our honeymoon, after a week of eating beignets for breakfast and jambalaya and beer, cornbread and crab cakes, Gianluca was enjoying a cigar on the terrace.

I was packing and thinking about the trip home, which made me think about work.

For the first time in years (and a honeymoon is a good work detox, by the way) I hadn't checked e-mail or called anyone about the shop. Gabriel said he'd keep everything running smoothly, so I didn't need to worry. So when I typed in the password to check the work e-mail, my heart sank when I saw 131 unanswered messages.

I scrolled through and saw a few from my vendors, with message lines that read "Italian suede," "Spanish patent," and "Kidskin from Brazil." Those would wait. It was the slew of e-mails from Roberta that concerned me. I opened the oldest one, in which Gianluca was cc'd, dated the morning after our wedding day.

> Dear Valentine and Gianluca,
>
> The wedding was beautiful. I now can say with assurance that Italian American weddings are the best anywhere in the world!
>
> It was a special treat to get to spend so much time with you, Gianluca. The Hotel Roncalli in Queens was full-service, but the best part was being able to talk through business matters. Your assurance that you would find a smooth transition

*between the closing of my factory and the end of my contract
with Angelini Shoes makes everything on my end less painful.*

 *It was a difficult decision to sell the factory, but I think it
will be best for me and my family. The auction on the equipment will take place later this summer, and I will forward the
information to you, should you know anyone who wants to get
into the shoe business.*

 *My father gave his life to the factory, and it occurred to
me that maybe this isn't all life has to offer. I look forward to
further discussion and correspondence.*

Love,

Cousin Roberta

I became so angry I threw the phone down on the bed. I
went to the terrace and confronted Gianluca with such fury it
caught him by surprise.

"Roberta is selling the factory?"

"Yes."

"When were you going to tell me?"

"Tomorrow, when we arrived in New York."

"How could you keep this from me?"

"She told me after the rehearsal dinner. Was I going to call
you up on the night before our wedding and ruin it with the
news?"

My mind raced as I remembered Gianluca, Alfred, and Roberta at the reception in a huddle and at the rehearsal dinner,
heads together, evidently figuring out a way to drop me as a
client. I felt betrayed. I could deal with Alfred later, but right
now I wanted to address my husband, who I felt had been dis-
loyal, and—worse—protective of me as a businesswoman. "I

built this business. It was my idea to design shoes for mass production. I found Roberta. She can't just close down the factory on whim! We have accounts! Obligations! Loans! What the hell were you thinking?"

"I was thinking that your life is more important than your work."

"My work *is* my life."

"Oh, so you married a pair of shoes at Queen of Martyrs?"

"I married a tanner."

"Ah, I'm a tanner now."

"Well, aren't you?"

"I'm your husband. And, I believed, your partner."

"Partners don't keep secrets from one another."

"I didn't tell you because I knew you would react this way."

"Oh, now you're a mind reader? The keeper of all information. And you know best?"

"In this situation, yes. We had a wonderful week together."

"Now it's ruined."

"Oh, that's how it works. One problem, and everything is ruined?"

"This is a big-ass problem."

"You're a child."

"And you're not my boss. I ran a business without you. You've made the situation worse. I could've convinced her to stay open. I don't have a manufacturer anymore. Not one I can trust."

"I was planning on helping you replace Roberta—"

"Stay out of it! This is not your concern!"

Gianluca was furious. He stood up and faced me. "What do you think a marriage is? Do you think it's going out to dinner and getting dressed up and making love in every room of the house, and then you go your way and I go mine and we meet in the kitchen for dinner and talk about whether it rained that day?

"If that's what you want, then leave me now. I don't want to be your butler, or your cook, or your tanner. I want to be your husband. For me, that means that I guard what you hold precious, I stand with you, I work with you, I make sure you have rest when you need it, I open the books and we figure out the finances, I build a space where you can create and I can help you get your creations out into the world."

"I don't need your help! And by the way, work doesn't consume my life—I'm here with you now, aren't I?"

"And it's such a pleasure."

I ignored his comment because I wanted him to understand. "Gianluca, you might as well know this tonight. I'm an artist. I can't turn it on and off. It's not just what I do, it's who I am."

"Let me help make your life easy. With two of us working at the business, the business will not consume our lives. It's not worth it, Valentina. There isn't a prize at the end of a hard day's work that can compare to the happiness you feel when you sleep with your lover in your arms—the lover you chose, the lover you married."

"You went behind my back."

"I protected you."

"I don't need protection!"

"Yes, you do. And if you think you don't, you're a fool. Letting me love you and letting me protect you is not a weakness—it takes courage. It means that I take your well-being and safety as seriously as my own—as Orsola's—as that of anyone that I love. But it's more than that. You're my wife. We are one now."

"We're one, all right. You're number one."

"I don't want to be king. I asked to be your husband. What you love, I love. What worries you, worries me. What you dream of, I will try and make come true. That's all it is, Valentina. I have no other agenda."

"You betrayed me."

"You choose that word to describe me? That's crazy!"

"Now I'm crazy for looking out for myself and the business I built."

"I didn't betray you. I wanted you to have a few days of peace. Your American ambition controls everything about you."

"I like my American ambition! I'm proud of it!"

"At the expense of everything else? Your ambition loves you back, gives you a peaceful home? Makes you feel complete?"

"Yes, it makes me feel useful and important and necessary. I make beautiful shoes just like my great-grandfather, just like Gram, my grandfather. This is history I'm living here. This is a legacy that I have to maintain. Why should I apologize for my high standards? The standards I set? I have something to show for my hard work. I'm doing something special with my shoes. I married tradition and style."

"Now we have it! Now I hear you! Now I know what you're married to—you're married to some idea, a notion that what you produce is more important than anything else in your life. I'm Italian. We don't eat ambition three times a day to sustain ourselves. We work hard, but it doesn't fill us up. Only love can do that. Only love. And here I am, in love with you, and you don't see my purpose in your life. Why don't you decide what's important to you? And when you do, let me know."

Gianluca grabbed a room key and left.

I will not stay married to this man. He's ridiculous. Pompous. Patronizing. A know-it-all. To think he wanted me to take his name. Thank God I drew the line. That would have been one more thing that I'd given up to become his wife, and one more thing I'd have to try and replace once he left me! What made me think I could make this work? Why hadn't I seen this before I married him?

And why had I been blindsided by Roberta's announcement? We talked every week, and yes, we'd complain about problems with the business. But I'd believed she was in it for the long haul like me.

Had I misread her? Her passion? Intent? She had a sign over her factory in Buenos Aires that read "Since 1925," and I have the same sign on Perry Street. We came from the same origins. We had the same roots.

I believed Roberta and I were more than cousins. We were simpatico artists who'd found each other after a long family estrangement, determined to resurrect the Angelini brand on two continents and change the world one beautiful pair of shoes at a time. But it would be no longer. I was in the shoe business for life. For Roberta, it was a means to an end, a path on the way to a new chapter in her work life.

I didn't know if my heart was breaking because I felt abandoned by Roberta, or misunderstood by Gianluca. What is true: I didn't see either scenario coming.

I sat and stewed. My big, *fast* Italian wedding had done the thing I was most afraid of—it had taken my attention off my work. I resented every moment wasted on or around my wedding.

I grabbed the laptop and sat in a chair and began reading

all of Roberta's e-mails in chronological order. She was selling the factory because she'd gotten an offer on the building and the complex behind it. They were building apartment houses in Buenos Aires. Roberta wanted to go back to school to study political science. What? Shoe manufacturer to politician?

Gabriel picked up his cell when I called him. "Are you all right?"

"I'm getting a divorce."

"What?"

"Roberta's selling the factory, and Gianluca knew about it."

"How is that Gianluca's fault?"

"He kept it from me." I began to cry.

"Maybe he wanted you to have a honeymoon. A vacation. You haven't been on one in years."

"I don't need a vacation! I need to be home in my shop, making shoes."

"No, everybody needs a vacation."

"He says I'm obsessed."

"You are. Who plans a wedding and builds her staff at work at the same time? You hired Charlie, then Jaclyn, then Tess. Who's next? Your mother?"

I didn't care about the staff. I was angry, and I wanted to revel in my righteousness. I wanted Gabriel to understand that I was right and Gianluca was a judgmental meddler. "He says I put my work before my life."

"You do," Gabriel said calmly.

"I don't know how else to do it. He says he's my partner now."

"Did you think you were going to get married, and he was going to roll leather in one room and you'd build shoes in the other? Are you kidding?"

"I thought I'd have my work, and he'd have his. Yes."

"Val, this is why shotgun weddings never work. You didn't think this through."

"No, I didn't. I'm going to get an annulment. Call that priest."

"He might be able to give you one, but we wouldn't understand it."

"I don't care. I want out."

"Oh, honey, stop it. You love Gianluca."

"I don't want to love him. I want to come home and have my life back."

"You'll have your life. It will just be different. It will be better."

"How?"

"You have a man that loves you. Every person that ever lived has a dream. To be loved. To have someone in your corner. He didn't do anything to hurt you. He was trying to help."

"But I need to know things," I wailed.

"You need a plan. You two need to sort things out."

"I don't want to."

"You say that, but you don't mean it."

"I mean it."

"No, you don't, Val. I know when you don't mean things. And you don't mean it. This man is the love of your life. He's a good guy, and he's got your back. Now you have to sit down and reason with him. No crying or histrionics. I know that's hard for you. But you have to do it."

"Or what?"

"Or you end up like Aunt Feen. Bitter and alone with a rum and Coke in one hand and a remote in the other, having sexual fantasies about Alex Trebek."

"That doesn't sound so bad right now."

"Come on. It's hell on earth. Talk to Gianluca. He's smart. He'll listen."

"I don't know where he went."

"He's probably downstairs at the bar. That's where I go when you get on my nerves. I have a stool at Automatic Slim's on Washington. Why don't you go look for him?"

"What will I say when I find him?"

"Tell him you need to make a plan. A life plan. The two of you."

"But I don't know what to ask for."

"Start with how you want to live, and then talk about the Angelini Shoe Company. Don't dive into business. Ask him what he wants first."

"He wanted me."

"And he still does."

"You think so?"

"Honey, only a man that loves you would move to Greenwich Village and build a new life when his old one was perfectly fine. May I point out that he left Tuscany for you? That's the one place on earth everyone wants to go and never wants to leave. And yet, he did it for *you*. It's you that he wants. It's you that he married. Stop acting like you still have a choice here. You love him too. Now go and find him and make this right."

I hung up the phone and looked in the mirror. I looked awful, and slightly crazy, not unlike my great-aunt after a few cocktails. I sat down on the edge of the bed and breathed. When tears would come to my eyes, I blinked until they stopped. I was doing everything within myself to get to a place where I could face Gianluca. I grabbed my coat and went out the door.

✑ **7** ✑

New Orleans is nothing like New York City, but I'm an urban girl born and raised, so I can find my way around any city in the world if there's a grid and I can walk it. I realized, as I walked through the French Quarter, that I really hadn't paid a lot of attention to where we went. I'd been content to follow Gianluca wherever he wanted to go. As I walked through the same streets alone, the haunted beauty of the city was lost on me. It was no longer lush and romantic. It was strange and confusing.

My feet were beginning to hurt. I'd run out of the room in a pair of mules, leather slides I take on trips so I'm never barefoot on hotel room floors. They're meant to get me from the bed to the bathroom, not walking around on pavement. It seemed all my decisions, great and small, were misguided. I couldn't even choose the right shoes.

I passed a small, crowded bistro next to Café Du Monde, our regular breakfast place. Something told me to stop and slow down at Ilaria's. It reminded me of a trattoria in Arezzo. It wasn't just a restaurant. There was a party going on. The crowd spilled out onto the sidewalk. The outdoor café was packed with customers eating crocks of gumbo and cracking the shells of crawfish while downing mimosas. I could have used a Gin Fizz myself right about then.

Going up on tiptoe to look inside, I saw the back of Gianluca's head at the bar. I squeezed my way through the crowd until I got to him. He was puffing on a cigarette, the open pack lying on the bar, and drinking a glass of bourbon.

"You smoke?"

"Sometimes."

"I mean, I knew you had a cigar now and then."

"And now and then I have a cigarette." He looked at the rows of liquor on the shelf behind the bar, not at me.

It was noisy, and I found myself getting angry all over again. Maybe if he had embraced me and said, "Why don't we go somewhere where we can talk?" I would've forgiven him on the spot. But instead, he put me on ice like Kentucky bourbon. He took a slow drag off the cigarette as if I were not there. I became furious all over again. I raised my voice. "Do you want a divorce?"

"We haven't been married yet."

"It's best to catch a mistake sooner rather than later."

"And how do you know this?"

"Common sense."

He nodded. "You're very calm." Finally, he looked at me. "You've thought this through."

I broke his gaze and looked off. "I'm holding it together."

"I can see that."

"You said some awful things to me."

"I'm capable of saying awful things, just as you are capable of doing them."

"Whoa right there. You're the one who kept a secret from me."

"It wasn't a secret. You could have read your e-mails all week."

"I didn't because you didn't want me to."

"Oh, so you do listen to me."

"I respected your wishes."

Gianluca turned and faced me. I couldn't help it. I wanted to be angry with him, but he might have been the most beautiful man I had ever seen. No, he *was* the most beautiful man I had ever seen. If I looked at his blue eyes for a hundred years, I would never be able to describe their color. I looked away because I didn't want to make this about his eyes. I was tired and my feet hurt and anger exhausts me.

"You look tired," he said.

"I've been crying."

"I can see that."

"What are we going to do?"

"I think we need a plan," he said.

"Do I need to call a lawyer?"

"Why would you do that?"

"Don't you want to get rid of me?"

Gianluca put out his cigarette. "No. Do you want to get rid of me?"

I felt my eyes fill with tears, and instead of trying to hide them, I just cried. "I don't know how to be married."

"Neither do I."

"I know. You're divorced! Whose brilliant idea was it to marry a divorced man? There's a reason things don't work out."

"Maybe Aunt Feen was right. Maybe I am befuddled."

"*Besmirched*. I don't think it's just you. It's me too. Maybe it's *all* me, and you're just reacting to the weirdness. I think I am incapable of being a wife. I don't want to change anything about my life, and yet I wanted to marry you."

Gianluca put some cash on the bar. He took my hand and guided me through the crowd to the street. I would miss the security of his hand in mine when he divorced me and jumped on the first plane back to Tuscany.

"I can find my way back to the hotel," I told him. I felt the crush of defeat in my heart and then, suddenly, all around me. This whole thing seemed impossible, and I didn't have a clue how to communicate what was wrong. I was wrong. That much I knew.

"We need to talk," he said. "You build shoes. Would you ever build a pair without a pattern?"

"I couldn't."

"Well, then, how can we expect to stay married if we don't have a plan?"

"I don't know."

"I have an idea, Valentina." Gianluca put his arm around me, and we walked back toward our hotel.

"You do?"

"I think we give this marriage one more shot. Just tonight. One more night. You may still want a divorce in the morning, and I will give you one if you still want one tomorrow."

"What magic thing is going to happen tonight to change our minds?"

"If it's magic, we won't know in advance."

We walked back to the hotel without saying much. If I saw

an antique urn, or he saw a stone wall that captured his attention, we'd stop and observe its beauty without commenting on it. We were avoiding returning to our hotel room where our anger hung in the air like a fog. Gianluca had made it clear that I should think of this as our last night together. As we climbed the stairs to our room, I felt like Anne Boleyn on the way to the tower. At least she knew why she was banished. There was within me an urgency to show him it hadn't all been a giant mistake. I loved him. I had wanted to marry him. And I wanted to show him exactly what he meant to me before we were over.

He pulled the drapes on the terrace closed and turned to face me. I unbuttoned his shirt because I wanted to be close to his heart. If this was our last night, I thought of all the things I wanted him to know, so that he might pack them up and take them with him wherever he went. As we made love, it was as if we were in water, immersed in an ocean beyond the gulf as blue as a night sky. How could two people connect like this and yet have so much trouble communicating? Maybe I needed to learn Italian, because I felt he had studied me in all my American detail.

He kissed me a thousand times. If his kisses were rose petals, I could have scattered them all the way home. It was as if he was storing them up, making certain I'd have enough to last in the years to come. He wrapped me in the blanket and pulled me close.

"It isn't enough to love you, but I do," I told him.

"Love *is* enough."

"I have to put you first."

"Do you want to?"

I had to think. I held up my hand so he wouldn't take it as a no. Plus, I'm the kind of woman who agrees to anything after romance. I can't help it. It's when I'm the most grateful. "I need something from you."

"Okay."

"I want you to tell me when I'm not putting you first. Will you do that?"

"I can do that," Gianluca said. "Will you tell me when I fail you?"

"Yes, I will."

"Then we agree."

"We have a plan."

I kissed him to seal The New Deal.

I wouldn't look back on New Orleans and think of it as the Big Easy. After our argument, I'd think of it as the Big Impossible. So in the same place that Hurricane Katrina came and ruined homes and lives, destroyed beauty and art, I had my first real fight with Gianluca.

I'd assumed that I would continue to live my life as I always had, wedding ring or not. Why would I change what had worked for me? Why should I compromise when I already had the best solution? Or does having a husband mean that I am required to defer to him, and therefore he speaks for me?

This was what my father warned me about. There were big differences between Gianluca and me. Some were small cracks, others fissures, and one was a deep chasm. The obvious one: our ages. He had lived longer and raised a child to adulthood. I couldn't imagine that breadth of experience.

The subtle difference between us: the way we did business. When one partner wants to rule the world, and the other wants to be happy and quiet in a corner of it, there's conflict. My ambition was fueled by a drive to be the best, his, by a gentle energy to do your best but not worry about the reaction.

The stealth difference: we're both Italian, but I was an American first and he was truly an Italian first. All the vowels in the world that we had in common couldn't make up for the disparity in our points of view.

The deepest divide was the one that was almost impossible to overcome. He was a traditional man, raised in a typical Mediterranean patriarchy. I was raised under the same label, but it was a fake. My mother made all the decisions. She just *pretended* that my father made them. And the kicker: she was content with the charade, but more importantly, so was my father.

Gianluca was very determined. This was a man who fought for what he wanted—including defying all convention and marrying the granddaughter of his stepmother. But in all the hoopla, we hadn't stopped to figure out how to drive the bus. We didn't know how because we hadn't made it a priority.

Maybe this is why a long engagement is a good idea. Those couples who take years to plan a beef tenderloin dinner learn how to talk things through. We sped through pre-Cana like we were going through a yellow light, hoping not to hit anything. But then we did hit something, and it was no speed bump—it was the Grand Canyon, and we couldn't cross it. We disagreed about how we saw the world.

I woke up alone in the hotel room the next morning. A wave of panic rolled over me. Maybe he'd left me and gone back to Italy, just as he had when we were in Buenos Aires.

I heard the key in the lock. Gianluca pushed the door open. He carried a sack of beignets, the round puffs of fried dough doused in powdered sugar that I had grown to love. He also carried two cups of chicory coffee. He placed them on the night-stand and came and sat beside me. He kissed me.

"We'll be all right, Valentina."

"I know." But did I?

Gianluca kissed me again. As he did, I released all my prob-lems: the closing of Roberta's factory, the loans due to the bank, and the search for a new manufacturer. I was not going to worry about where the money would come from, who the investors would be if it came or if it didn't. Even if I had all the answers, it couldn't be solved that minute, and in that moment, I needed to pay attention to Gianluca.

So I took my husband's advice on our last morning in New Orleans. I let go of all of it. He took me in his arms, and we made love as we said good-bye to our honeymoon and started our marriage all over again. We made peace and we made a pact. We promised to listen to one another. And we sealed the promise with a feast of beignets.

Someday I would look back on this fight and know for cer-tain that there is only one fight in a marriage, the first one. And as much as you might try, the fight is never solved. Over time, it becomes a conundrum, the immovable thing, the in-explicable conflict that forms a wall between you. It grows higher and higher, and then the vines come, and when the wall is grown over in bramble and weed, there's no getting over it. You cannot see past it, get around it, or blow through it. It takes up the space between you, and no amount of love can bring that wall down.

I knew I would look back on that fight and wish I could take back every word and the terrible thoughts behind them. In time, I hoped to understand Gianluca's point of view. He wasn't fighting to keep me from working. He was fighting to show me how to live.

Alfred and Bret sat at the cutting table in the shop sipping coffee. Alfred had made the coffee so it tasted like mulch. No amount of cream would dilute the bitter brew to drinkable. Gianluca joined us with his laptop. I opened a folder with the production schedule from Roberta's factory.

Gianluca was very secure within himself, and as he worked in the shop and observed our operation, he began to see Bret's knowledge as invaluable. Alfred was controlled, and rarely showed emotion in business. As a former banker, he wore a poker face, so it was hard to know when we were in crisis mode or in the deep, delicious, and profitable black. I was the wild card. I threw myself into the financial decisions as I had the designs. Sometimes I was emotional about how to bring a design to fruition. Other times, you would think I was working on an assembly line, focused but not emotionally engaged.

When I went off the rails, Alfred pulled me back on track. We had grown to understand each other, so I let him. I guess Gram knew what she was doing when she made this unholy alliance.

The short history of the partnership of the Caminito Shoe Company and Angelini Shoes was laid out on the spreadsheets in detail. It was a profitable deal for both of us. I didn't know where in the world we would find another manufacturer who wouldn't sacrifice quality for cost.

"The last of Roberta's obligations will be completed by early summer," Bret told us.

"So we need a new manufacturer in place by then," Alfred said. "Nice when your family gives you the heave-ho."

"Well, if you had told me about it, I might have been able to convince her to stay in the business."

"Val, it doesn't do any good to rehash what might have been. Roberta is out, Buenos Aires is out, and we have to find a new factory," Bret said calmly. "And if you want to stay on schedule for the fall line, we need to be up and running somewhere by the first week of June."

"I could speak to some of my friends in Italy," Gianluca offered.

"Thank you," Bret said. "The problem will be that most of the Italian factories are booked through next year."

"That's true," Gianluca admitted. "But it doesn't hurt to ask. I know manufacturers in Barcelona."

"I'm done with the Spanish," I complained.

"How about China?" Alfred wondered.

"We'd be starting from scratch," Bret said.

"We're going to be starting from scratch no matter what," I told them. "But you know, this is an Italian company. It started with our great-grandparents in Italy, and they came over here and built this business. I feel we should try to stay close to their vision. We could go anywhere we want in the world, but why would we if we could make the shoes here or in Italy? I know it might not be possible, but I'd like to try."

"I hear you, Val," Bret said. "But we have to think about cost."

"And you need an experienced workforce," Alfred offered. "Your shoes are not always simple. We need excellent machine operators who can also do any extra hand work. You designed a line with lots of embellishments—and one shoe with a tricky ankle strap with buckles. It's going to take some time on the line to build it."

"Valentina has worked with some factories in Naples that make the embellishments. We might be able to order the straps from them directly. That will save production time."

"Would you look into that for us, Gianluca?" Alfred asked.

"Of course."

"What about America?"

"What about it?" Alfred asked me.

"Is there a factory that makes shoes in the United States?"

"Sure, there are a few left. But they make men's shoes, and they have lug soles, and they use glue," Alfred said.

"Why don't we put up our own factory?" I asked. "People need jobs, and we need somebody to make our shoes."

"You'd have to cut a special deal on real estate, and you'd have to train the workforce."

"So we train them." I looked at Gianluca.

"We can't afford to put up a factory in Manhattan. I already talked to a guy in Brooklyn who used to make shoes for Kenneth Cole. Those factories went to China."

"We're not mass producing," I reminded them.

"Not yet." Bret smiled.

"How about Jersey?" Alfred asked.

"Expensive. Their real estate is high. And you're taxed up the wazoo."

"What about Youngstown?" Alfred wondered.

"Why would we go to the midwest?" I asked him.

"I was talking with Cousin Don. He is always on the look-out for new business opportunities. They have a workforce there that is familiar with piece-good construction. They had a couple of garment mills there."

"Where is Youngstown, exactly?" Bret asked.

"It's about six hundred miles away—halfway between New York and Chicago. It's the town that 'Boom Boom' Mancini came from. Made it famous," Alfred explained.

"It's close to Pittsburgh."

"So you're near a major airport."

"It's worth a look," Bret said. "If it makes financial sense."

"I haven't been on a road trip since 1979," my father said as he loaded his suitcase into the trunk of his car. "University of Michigan versus the University of Ohio. Lansing campus. It was a real head-knocker."

Dad handed me a separate Mylar bag filled with snap-lid containers of cookies, biscotti, ham and butter panini, and for good health, crudités, carrots and celery.

I put the bag of food on the backseat. "You know we can stop to eat along the way. This isn't 1812, when 7-Elevens didn't exist."

Dad lifted a giant cooler and placed it in the trunk.

"That cooler isn't for you. It's sausage from Faicco's on Bleecker Street. Don has a yen for it."

My mother came running down the sidewalk in front of her compact Tudor, the house I grew up in, wearing the exact color palette of the cross-timber trim: strictly black and white. She carried a bag of tarelles.

"Really, Ma?"

"They never go bad."

"But no one eats them."

"Then it's good for them that they never go bad."

Mom was wearing her housekeeping ensemble: black slacks, a crisp white T-shirt, gold hoop earrings, and a black-and-white bandana in her hair. She wore her "knock-around" shoes, brushed black suede mules with a kitten heel.

It occurred to me that I'd never seen my mother without her lipstick, including two weeks in 1988 when she had the swine flu. She is of another era when women dressed before leaving the house. There was never a dirty dish in her sink or a dead flower in her vase. She may be old fashioned but she lives to be mod and in the moment. The result of having grown up with a camera-ready mother is that I always think something is about to happen, even when it isn't.

"What are you going to do while we're in Youngstown?" I asked Mom.

"I don't know. Watch some movies. Light the gardenia candles, because they make your father sneeze and I happen to love them. I'll probably call some girlfriends and take a ride to the Short Hills Mall. I don't know. I'll fill up the hours."

I gave my mother a kiss. "Have fun without him."

"Not a difficult assignment," she said. "Did you pack a business suit?"

"For Gianluca?"

"For you."

"Ma, it's Cousin Don."

"You should be your professional best, even if you played Trotta Trotta Cava-lee with Don when you were five."

"There will be no bouncing on the knee. We're looking for a factory, Mom. It's not like I'm having a meeting at Bergdorf's. I'll look good enough for Ohio. I promise."

Gianluca came out of the house with a couple bottles of water. He handed them to me. "Thanks, honey." I gave him a quick kiss.

Dad was already in the front seat with his seat belt fastened. "Come on, G. L. You're driving the first leg. I'll take over in Pennsylvania."

The last thing we heard as we pulled out of Queens was the gentle hum of the front passenger seat as my father put it in recline. He pulled the brim of his baseball cap over his eyes and promptly fell asleep.

The hills of Pennsylvania gave way to the low, rolling flats of Ohio on Route 65. The first buds of spring turned the gray landscape into a green pointillist painting. The sky, wide and blue, had no edges. It extended as far as my eye could see.

Along the highway, we saw the abandoned steel mills obscured by overgrown brush, looking like lost toys in high weeds. I remembered when the rust belt was in full operation. I had cousins who worked in the steel mills and the auto plants on school breaks. Their fathers retired with pensions and dreams of travel beyond these fields. A few lived long enough to enjoy those years, but most weren't so lucky. The plants closed before retirement and pension plans dried up. There was a mad scramble to make a living.

The work began to dwindle in earnest when I was growing up.

And just as Don Pipino had moved west to work in Youngstown in the 1950s, now my generation did the same, moving in the opposite direction, away from steel towns like

Bethlehem and Allentown and on to opportunities in Chicago and Atlanta and Charlotte. Italian Americans who had never been south of DC were suddenly moving to places like Georgia and Tennessee and Florida to find work.

The manufacturing jobs in the small towns where they were born were gone. It was time to look for other ways to make a living in new places. Cousins my age went to college and came out and went into computer programming, pharmaceutical sales, and teaching. This new reality left us with the conundrum of building our own families away from our family of origin. The drive to Youngstown had me thinking about my brother and sisters, our family and our future. We had made a full circle, locking arms at work, just as our great-grandfather and his brother had at the turn of the last century.

Once we arrived in Youngstown, we followed the directions Don had e-mailed us. We found Bears Den Road with the help of the GPS, and turned off the main highway onto a dirt road.

I called Cousin Don's cell and told him we were moments away.

In the distance, through a clearing of trees, we saw a large rectangular box building with dull gray aluminum siding. There was a row of windows along the main floor and a double entrance door.

The parking lot had grown over with weeds, but I could see where once at least a hundred parking spots had been marked for the workers.

We pulled up. Cousin Don was waiting for us outside in a

University of Michigan baseball hat and matching jacket. He wore aviator sunglasses and chewed on an unlit cigar.

"Jesus, Don, you look like Banacek from the TV show." My dad gave him a hug.

"Did he have a good head of hair?"

"Yeah, good and thick like yours. U of M?"

"This is my go-see jacket. I like to wear a winning team when I'm about to lose my shirt."

"You won't lose your shirt, Cousin Don," I assured him as he gave Gianluca a slap on the back. In our family, "Cousin" is a title of honor. When I was a girl, I thought "Cousin" was Don's first name.

Don unlocked the door and took us inside the old mill. The large, empty room had a thirty-foot ceiling and a concrete floor. It was as cold as a meat locker and it had the scent of motor oil and crushed metal. I could almost hear the sounds of this steel mill in its heyday, the hum of the electrics, the sawing of the metal, and the hiss from the torches.

"It's a big space," Don said.

"You have a lot of room here," Dad said. "But you need it. You need the assembly space, room for the sewing machines, the buffer, the polisher, the presser."

"You could put up a wall and do packing and shipping over here." I pointed. "You have the loading dock outside this door."

"That door rolls up like a shade," Don said. "You pull the truck right into the building. And when you're dealing in high-end shoes, you don't want those boxes getting wet. Perfect for dry load-ins."

"You're thinking of everything."

"Ohio gets a wet spring. Think ahead. That's the Pipino way. No stone unturned. No rock unthrown."

"It needs work, Don," Dad said as he walked the floor.

"Look, we can't occupy the space tomorrow. But give me a couple of months, I get the water on, I rewire. I gravel the pavement out front. I put in the industrial lights, the HVAC. I mean, we could do this thing."

We spent the next day looking at more spaces. Don showed us everything Youngstown had to offer. An old dairy farm. The Weatherbee coat factory. A restaurant supply warehouse. If it was for sale, Don knew about it. But Gianluca and I couldn't shake the thought of the old steel mill on Bears Den Road. It was too perfect. It felt right.

Dad stayed with Cousin Don at his house. I imagined one widower, one temporary bachelor, and some colorful locals engaging in all-night card games played through a fog of cigar smoke over a plate of soppressata and Parmesan cheese washed down with grappa. However it played out, they would have a ball.

Gianluca and I checked into the Marriott, where I set up camp in the room with a coffeemaker and a cooler, just as my mother had on every family trip we ever made. Gianluca was propped up in bed, watching a soccer match, as I went through the particulars of the properties we had visited.

I organized my notes of potential factory buildings from best to worst, separating out my favorites. I tried to imagine the spaces accommodating the operations I had seen in Buenos Aires. I was concerned about ceiling height, an area for shipping, and enough space for cutting and finishing.

"It's not like buying a house," Gianluca said, flipping off the television.

"I know, honey."

"Are you sure about putting up a factory here?"

"Why? Are you?"

"Why would you choose this town over Italy?"

"Didn't you say that the factories in Italy are booked?"

"We could put off the manufacturing until next year."

"That's not an option. I have orders to fill." I took a deep breath, hoping I wouldn't snap. "I like the idea of Youngstown because the raw space is cheap, it's close enough to New York City, and they have a workforce here that needs jobs. Most of these families are like mine—they've worked in factories or run their own small businesses. They would understand the mission."

"Your father said things had changed over the years," Gianluca said. "The workforce isn't what it was."

"We'll revive it."

"So you're going to find the space, renovate it—"

"Gianluca, there are no shoe factories here."

"So you have to renovate. How will you pay for it?"

"We'll get a loan."

Gianluca picked up the file and began leafing through the circulars.

"You don't want to open a factory at all, do you?"

"I want you to have what you need to do your work."

"I need a little support from you."

"I'm here, Valentina."

"Are you? Or did you get roped into this because I was enthusiastic about it? Cousin Don is a great salesman—maybe you feel we played you."

"I don't understand."

"Tricked you into coming out here and looking at the real estate."

"What is your tie to this place besides your cousins?"

"I have memories of this town as a girl. I remember the boom years when the steel mills operated double shifts, and the small factories couldn't accept all the work that was offered them. I remember meeting middlemen traveling through from New York. They went from town to town making deals. There used to be a system. There were jobs and if you needed one, all you had to do was work hard and you'd be all right. You could take care of your family. If I'm going to manufacture shoes in a factory, then I want to make them in America."

"Because?"

I felt my face getting hot. "Because it's the right thing to do! Because American-made means quality."

"That's why manufacturing left this country."

"God, Gianluca, it was the North Atlantic Free Trade Agreement that killed it. Other countries like China made what we made more cheaply, and our factories couldn't compete."

"What happened to American quality then?"

"The standards were lowered. Customers started to accept cheaper construction and materials," I said softly. I knew when I was licked.

"And you, a custom shoemaker, are going to bring it all back."

"I want to try in my small way to do *something*."

"What if we went to Italy and worked from there?"

"Oh, man, you totally set me up. Do you want to live in Italy?"

"I want to live with you, wherever that is," he said.

"It sounds like you want to go back and take me and my work with you."

"Would that be so terrible?"

"No."

"Add that to the long list of things on that pad that you're thinking about."

"I need to be honest."

"Ah." Gianluca smiles, knowing that I haven't been.

"Italy is a dream to me, but I love my country. I love Greenwich Village. I love Youngstown. I love all those small towns between the two. I like the giant hot dog on a bun on the side of the road and that inappropriate four-story Indian outside the gas station when we crossed the state line. It might be kitsch, but it reminds me of the car trips we made when we were kids and how we marked the distance by the hot dog and the Indian. You'd only find those things in America."

"You can have that in Italy. We have the giant wheel of cheese."

"But you don't have a twenty-four-hour news cycle and buying in bulk. I like a deal. I enjoy making something out of nothing and selling it. I like that I can go from a custom shoemaker to a designer for the masses and still give the customer paying sixty dollars a lot of the same elements that the custom customer gets. I like home shopping on TV. I like the idea of someday showing what I've made on television, sold by a perky host wearing false eyelashes. I like the con and I like the sale. I love all of it. That makes me an American. But I'm an American married to an Italian, and what you want is as important as what I want."

"Is it?"

"Yes! If Roberta hadn't decided to close the factory, we wouldn't even be here."

"We'd be fighting somewhere else about something else."

"I don't think so."

"I told you how I feel and you disagreed and that's the end of the discussion."

"Not true!"

"It happened in the shop last Monday, Valentina. Whenever I suggest something regarding the business, you dismiss it."

"Am I supposed to agree to make you happy?"

"No. But consider it. That's the nature of a partnership. One shows the other the flaw. One handles one operation, and the other another. You see."

"I get it!"

"*Va bene.*"

"No, no *va bene*. Listen to me. There's a lot involved here. And I need you to be on board with what we're doing."

Gianluca nodded again.

"Would you please say something?"

"You won't like what I have to say."

"I can take it."

"It's not medicine or poison. It's the facts. You have no experience in running a factory. Roberta had a system in place, and you got into business with her. Don is a good man, and he's very smart, but he's seventy years old, and this is a lark for him. Is this a lark for you?"

"No."

"Be aware. Now, I'm not going to convince you not to put up a factory here, because you have good instincts. But I will tell you to be cautious and to make sure that what you build is what you need to make the shoes you want to sell. I think you should seriously consider the properties that Don has shown you—but I also think you shouldn't dismiss Italian manufacturing as a possibility. They know what they're doing at home."

There. He said it. Italy was *home*. Not Perry Street, not Youngstown's Main Street—but Arezzo in Tuscany. He couldn't tell me how much he missed being in Italy, but he didn't have to—I could see it, I could feel it. My husband wanted to take Angelini shoes back to Italy, but he wanted it to be my idea.

I went to the bathroom and changed for bed. As I brushed my teeth, I looked in the mirror over the sink. Then I turned and looked at myself in the full length mirror inside the bathroom door. I turned sideways. There was a softening to my edges that could only mean one thing. I already had the other indicator, I just was in denial about it. I joined Gianluca in bed.

"Well, you know how you say life is full of surprises?" I put my head on his chest. He pulled me close.

"I'm sure we'll find your perfect factory tomorrow."

"I'm not talking about work."

"No?"

"No. I think we're having a baby."

Gianluca sat bolt upright in bed.

"I think it was the night you landed in New York. You really landed in New York."

"Did you take a test?"

"No. But I'm one of those students who didn't have to take a test to access what I know. I just know it."

"I'd like you to take a test."

I laughed. "Of course. I'll be happy to." I took my husband's face into my hands, "If I am, are you happy about it?"

"Of course."

"Maybe we should go back to Italy, and I'll make shoes by hand. Our baby will grow up speaking Italian. You'll teach him how to cut leather."

"You're crazy."

"Isn't that what you want?"

"I'm not an expert on pregnancy, but I have been through the experience before. Anything you think, say, or do cannot be trusted. You are building a baby, and everything in you surrenders to that process."

"I'm a raging vat of hormones."

"To start."

"But we didn't plan this."

"Babies can't be planned. I've heard that they show up when they want to."

"You just threw out six years of sex education and my subscription to the *Our Bodies Ourselves* Web site and my doctor's advice."

"What did he have to say?"

"She. She said I'm at my peak fertility. Well, she was right about that."

Gianluca and I held one another. We were exhausted. Cousin Don had traipsed us through Youngstown like Lewis and Clark, and now we were facing an entirely new terrain, but this time, there was no guide to show us the real estate. We were on our own. I put my arms around my husband and for the first time, surrendered everything to him. After all, when it came to parenthood, he was the expert.

Don took us to dinner at the Lake Club on our last night in Youngstown. The elegant club, built on a crystal lake and hemmed by bright green rolling hills, was in full bloom.

I imagined bringing buyers from all over the country to the

club. We'd court Neiman's and Saks and Macy's. We'd fly their reps out and wine and dine them. I had to think about how to market the shoes once we made them. I was beginning to believe everything I envisioned was possible.

"I have an idea, Don," Gianluca said. "I know the equipment is expensive. Even in Italy, it takes months to make a good presser. Rollers, the best quality, are hard to find. These machines are not mass-produced. They're custom-built. They're like violins now—you need a master to make the equipment, because there isn't a great demand for it."

"A Stradivarius ain't cheap." Don nodded.

"I think you know that Cousin Roberta is selling her factory in Buenos Aires. She didn't sell it to a shoe manufacturing group, she sold the space to a developer."

"Condos and a beef processing plant."

"Beef is big in Argentina," Dad said. "So I'm told."

"She has the equipment and is going to sell it. I'd like to call her and offer her a deal."

"I like what I'm hearing." Don nodded. "The old-timey equipment is the best. You can't find steel rollers and copper gears anymore. Lots of shoe factories have turned to lesser metals and plastics in their machinery. We'd be better off with the tried and true."

"That's what I think. Alfred and I hired my brother-in-law Charlie to go down and take a look."

"Then I'd better get to work on the deal to lease this place. It's just sitting here rotting. Maybe I can negotiate a five-year lease with the first year free."

"Do you know guys who do this kind of refurnishing?" Dad asked.

I didn't bother to correct my father, but we were all thinking, *Refurbishing*.

"About a hundred guys. You could throw a rock on Main Street and hit somebody looking for a job. Everybody is looking for work."

"What about start-up money?" my father asked.

"I'll go to the bank. If we get a plant going with seventy-five employees to start, that's a lot of moolah flowing through the veins of the Y bank. It's a return to glory over there, believe me," Cousin Don said. "They'll look like a pack of heroes instead of suspicious financiers. So send Alfred out in full confidence that I can deliver the manpower to make your shoes."

"We may have him come out with Bret Fitzpatrick."

"Do I know him?" Cousin Don asked.

"You met him at my high school graduation." I looked at Gianluca, who didn't react.

"So send the boys out and we'll make the plan. The sooner we get this thing going, the sooner my Midas touch starts making us all some coin."

"But what if the bank doesn't come through?" my husband asked.

"I'll make sure they do."

"But if they don't?"

"We go the private investor route."

Gianluca smiled. "Just so you have an alternate plan."

"Oh, yeah, yeah, I got plans for every letter of the alphabet—I start with A and then on to B, and if that don't work, and so on and so on."

"This all sounds good to me," I told him. "Because baby needs new shoes."

"What the hell, you can make yourself as many shoes as you need."

"No, I mean real baby shoes." I took Gianluca's hand. "Go ahead, honey."

"We're having a baby," Gianluca announced.

My father's eyes filled with tears. "Really and truly? God bless you."

I gave my father a big hug. He shook hands with Gianluca.

"I thought you were looking a little thick, Val," Don said.

"A little? My face looks like a clock."

"Holy Mother of God. You know this is good luck." Cousin Don beamed. "Yeah, it goes way back to the Greeks."

"Do tell." My father smiled.

"Oh yeah. A woman with child brings good luck to anything she touches. It applies to everything from baking a cake to stock offerings. I used to put them under Ann's pillow at night. I sold my Wrather Corporation stock at a thirty-percent profit in 1965 when Chrissy was born. This factory is gonna work. I feel it."

The ride back to New York City flew. I was consumed with thoughts of the baby and the new factory. I guess that Mother Nature wanted me to become a juggler sooner than later. All this circus act needed was a trapeze. As I lay in the backseat, watching a small patch of blue sky underlined with black wires zoom past, I imagined myself walking along the electrical cables that stretched across Ohio, never flinching on the tightrope.

The notion that the equipment my great-great uncle invented would return to the United States, where he and his brother had founded their shoe company, made the transaction seem fated.

There is something so satisfying about taking a century-old rift in my family and healing it so all the parties involved feel a sense of closure. My great-grandfather and his brother never had the benefit of working out their differences, and here we were healing the hurt, laying the past to rest for good. We could not go back and bring my grandfather and his brother together again, but we could harness the spirit of their dream to make beautiful American-made shoes for women.

So what if there weren't a lot of shoe factories in the United States? Would we be better served by e-mailing our designs to China and hoping for the best? The Italian factories were booked years in advance by designers who had middlemen, logos, and contacts at *Vogue*. Could we wait and hope that another company would fall on hard times and we would sweep in and take advantage?

Youngstown was *on*.

When I was a girl and we visited our cousins, I never thought I'd be back and engaging the workforce. And the best part: Don Pipino was determined to make our factory the greatest business success of his career. It seemed to be a win-win.

I would trust Bret, Alfred, and Gianluca to figure out the finances. I had my own responsibilities in this new venture. I had to design beautiful shoes. And I could see them. I could see them in full in my imagination.

Gabriel unfurled the bolt of duchesse satin, nipped the corner with his scissors, and tore the yardage in a clean line. I helped him drape the fabric on the cutting table. He pinned the pattern pieces to the material.

Charlie came into the shop with a box of doughnuts. When he was courting my sister, his idea of winning us over had been to show up every Saturday morning with a box of fresh doughnuts from Sam's in Queens. It worked. Somewhere in the back of my mind, I remembered Tess telling me how Charlie used to win over new accounts with doughnuts. Gabriel looked up from his work and noticed Charlie's business attire. "Who died?"

"I dress for success," Charlie said. "And your best friend."

"You look good, brother," I assured him.

Bret, Alfred, and Gianluca came down the stairs into the shop. They greeted Charlie, who seemed nervous. We're a tough bunch; even twelve years legally wed into our family assures you of nothing.

"I'm going to bring up Don Pipino on Skype," Alfred said as he turned his laptop to face us. We gathered around the worktable, each of us taking a seat.

"There he is," Alfred said, pointing to the screen.

"How are you, Cousin Don?"

"Folks. I know this meeting is about welcoming Charlie into the club, but we have a problem here in Y-town. Let's just address this downer off the bat. We lost the building."

"What?" I shouted.

"Yep. Lost it. The owner won't lease. He's selling. He's gonna put a bowling alley in there."

"Well, that's that," Alfred said. "What else have you got for us, Don?"

"In terms of real estate?"

"In terms of everything." Bret looked at Alfred.

"Well, I can't very well go out and get a loan on nothing. We need to find another space."

"Do you want me to come out and help you?" Charlie offered.

"I think I can procure a temporary place to store the equipment in Pittsburgh."

"Why would we do that, Don? We'll be spending money we don't have to store equipment we don't need for a factory we haven't leased," said Alfred.

"I hear you. But I don't think you want to lose the equipment, do you?"

"No, we don't," I assured him.

"We priced out new equipment, and it's prohibitive," Bret said. "Valentine doesn't want the new stuff, she wants the old equipment her family used."

"I get that. So I really need to zero in on another building," Don deduced.

Gianluca put on his glasses and looked down at the spreadsheet. "Don, what about the old movie theater?"

"The Wilson Theater? It's pricey. But I could go over there and chisel."

"How do you feel about the Wilson Theater?" Gianluca asked me.

"I worry there's not enough space. And the floor has to be repitched."

"Don't worry about floors—I can redo them," Don said.

"I think I'll come out and do the tour with you, Don," Alfred said.

"I can go with you," Bret said to Alfred.

"I have an order to get out. Why don't you guys move on this quickly, and we'll send Charlie down to Buenos Aires to get a sense of how long it will take to ship the equipment and how we're going to get it here," I offered.

"Sounds good," Don said as he signed off.

"That's a blow." I closed the lid of the laptop.

"There are plenty of empty buildings out there, Val," Alfred assured me.

"That Bears Den factory was perfect."

"We'll find another place." Gianluca rubbed my shoulders.

"In the meantime, I think we should look at New Jersey again. And Pennsylvania. We shouldn't put all our hopes on Youngstown." Alfred looked at me.

"Hey, I'm open to all possibilities," I told my brother.

"It'll work out," Charlie said. "It always does."

Charlie tried to reassure me, but I wasn't buying it. I had a feeling of dread about the entire operation. Maybe I was taking on something that was bigger than I could handle. I'd been confident before the trip to Youngstown, when the factory lived in my imagination in a dream state. But just as in building a pair of shoes, I had to be practical and find the best components to make what I saw in my mind's eye. I had serious doubts that we could pull off our first American factory.

8

The view from my mother's kitchen window in Forest Hills is pure enchantment. She and my father took their patch of grass and turned it into the most ornate English garden this side of the Atlantic. There was a gazebo, a rock garden, a trellis, and wrought iron furniture to go with the English country feel of the Tudor. Mom decorated every shrub, surface, and branch. There were tiny lights in the Japanese maples and a new, moving wall of water where the fence met the property line. If you kept looking at my mother's backyard, you'd find things, like a ceramic turtle or a gnome. You would hear things, too, since she also collected wind chimes.

"Look. It's clear you need me," my mother said as she sliced me a giant piece of her chocolate cake.

"Ma, it's fine. Don't worry," I assured her as I poured cream into my coffee. If I was going to eat the cake, and I was, I might as well spring for the heavy cream.

"I studied to get my real estate license back in the eighties. Granted, I never got my certificate, but I still have a nose for property."

"Ma, you studied in Queens. You don't know anything about Ohio."

"How hard could it be? I learn a few things, drive around, get acquainted with the locals, and ba-boom, you have a new factory."

"If it were so easy, we would've already done it."

"Let's see what Bret and Alfred come up with. And I'm sure Gianluca has an opinion."

"I have to get Gianluca back to Italy before the baby is due. He's like a blowfish. He can only take so much New York City before he hits a wall and explodes."

"He hasn't adjusted to the city, has he?"

"Well, he doesn't love it. But he loves me, so he puts up with it."

"It's not like you can pull up stakes and move to Italy," Mom said nervously.

"Not until we put up a factory and make a mint."

"I can find you a factory!" Mom insisted.

"Cousin Don is all over it. And it's not just about finding the factory. It's about training the workforce."

"Who's going to do that?"

"We're sending Charlie down to Roberta's, and he's going to learn the ropes. Then he can be in charge of training the workers."

"You did a good thing hiring your brother-in-law."

"It was a no-brainer. He's mechanical. He's easy to work with, and he speaks Spanish."

"I have long supported learning a second language. And I had no idea that our Charlie had command of one."

"What's yours?"

"French, of course, for retail shopping purposes."

"Gianluca is going to speak Italian to the baby, and I'll speak English."

"I love a bilingual child! How was your doctor's appointment?"

"Fine. Except the doctor wrote *elderly primigravida* on my chart."

"How rude!"

"I'm over thirty-five so they consider me an older mother."

"No kidding."

"They have all these tests now. And Dr. DeBrady asked Gianluca a bunch of questions, since he's an older dad."

"Oh, they make such a big deal out of age in the medical community."

"Ma, it's all they've got. It's like raising cattle. You cordon them off by age and weight." I rubbed my growing stomach.

"What's Gianluca supposed to do? A stress test for fatherhood?"

"No, they worry about chromosome damage—that sort of thing."

"How pleasant. Ruin the happiest days of a woman's life with what-ifs."

"I'm not going to let anything ruin my happiness. Including *me*."

"There's nothing wrong with our gene pool."

"Not anything a little therapy can't fix."

"We've been reproducing for centuries. Look at us. I'd take our bunch over anybody else's!"

"Loyalty is your middle name."

"You got that right. I'd kill for my children. And you will too."

"Do you think I'll be a good mother?"

"Honey, what a thing to say. You'll be the best mother you can be."

"That didn't answer my question."

"Oh, the dirty little secret of motherhood—our children love us no matter what. So don't agonize. It will be just fine. You turned your marriage around. Give yourself some credit. You were a mess at first, and now, a few months later, you're in a groove."

My next thought was interrupted by my phone vibrating.

"Hi, Alfred," I said, picking up. "Say hello to Ma." I put the phone on speaker. There's nothing worse than repeating everything Alfred says to our mother, so I just looped her in, instead.

"Hi, Ma."

"How's Youngstown?"

"Promising."

"Where are you staying?"

"I think it's always a good sign when the first scent you get in a hotel lobby is bleach."

"It must be clean."

"Oh, it's clean."

"Did you find something?"

"There's a building in Smokey Hollow. The old Italian section, oddly enough."

"That sounds promising."

"We need you to come out and see it. Don is doing a number on the owner. A lease-to-buy deal. I think we should go for it."

"Gianluca and I will jump in the car."

"You should fly out. And bring Dad."

"Why?"

"Cousin Don thinks he's a good-luck charm."

"What about me?" Mom asked. "I'm good for some luck."

"You can come too, Ma."

"What's the weather like in Youngstown this time of year?"

"Just like it is in New York."

"Not a challenge. I can be ready in half an hour."

Gianluca loaded the luggage into the back of Tess's Suburban on the way to pick up our parents in Queens before going to the airport. Tess threw my husband the keys.

"Do you mind?"

"Of course not."

"It'll give us a chance to visit," Tess explained. "I'm a nervous driver."

Tess and I pulled our seat belts around us. "Precious cargo." Tess patted my stomach. "How much have you gained?"

"I don't know. Five pounds."

"Good for you. Three months in, I'd already gained fifteen pounds. Of course I was eating green olive and cream cheese sandwiches four times a day."

"Not me. I like caramel popcorn. How many calories could it have?"

"Oh, popcorn is light," she lied. "Charlie is all set for Argentina."

"I'm glad it's worked out. You'll be okay without him for a few weeks?"

"As long as he's working and he's happy. Thank you for taking him on."

"We're lucky to have him."

"You would say that."

"It's true. And we're lucky to have you and Jaclyn."

"As soon as you give us something to ship, we're all over it."

When we pulled up in front of my parents' house in Queens, it looked like a farewell scene at a train station from *Downton Abbey*, complete with steamer trunks and a hatbox. My mother packed for a trip around the world when all she needed was a pair of pajamas and a change of underwear. She came out of the house first, wearing a leopard trench coat and a pencil skirt, followed by my father, who wore an expression of exasperation.

I rolled down the window. "Ma, why all the suitcases?"

"I'm unsure about the weather."

"She thinks there's a nightlife in Youngstown," my father chimed in.

"There is. Three fingers of scotch and a sleeping pill," I joked.

"See, I needed a cocktail dress," Mom said as Dad hauled the luggage down the sidewalk with Gianluca's help.

"Why did you invite her?" Tess asked softly.

"She wanted to come. I think she's a little bored."

"You think?" Tess rolled her eyes. "She's been bored since 'Ice Ice Baby' was number one on the charts. She needs a job."

"She *has* a job. Daddy Incorporated."

"Girls . . ." Mom rolled back the door and climbed in between Tess and me. The car filled with the scent of Coco, her traveling cologne. "What are you whispering about?"

"How we hope we look as good as you when we're your age," Tess piped up.

"And how old is that?" my mother asked.

"Younger than Goldie Hawn and older than Brooke Shields."

"Thank you," Mom chirped.

Dad climbed into the front seat. "Mike, I don't know what I'm going to do with you."

"Dutch, not now. I have to be focused to travel."

Gianluca winked at me in the rearview mirror.

Don picked us up at the airport in Pittsburgh. We had to sit with Mom's luggage on our laps on the drive to Youngstown because the rest of our bags had filled the trunk. I imagined that this was how our immigrant forefathers and mothers felt in steerage when they made the crossing with everything they owned.

Bret and Alfred were waiting on the street in Smokey Hollow, which had an old-fashioned main street hemmed by modern apartments and townhouses.

Don led us down the street to an old storefront in the old Italian section. I stepped back and could see that the building was deep and about three stories high. There was one entrance door on the front and no windows. I looked at Alfred.

"Wait," he said.

We went inside. There was a small foyer, with an open electrical grid on the wall where there had once been a clock-punching machine. Bret and Alfred pushed the doors open.

The first thing I noticed was the scent of flour. This must have been a bakery of some kind, because there was a dusty sheen of powder on the floorboards. The ceilings were twenty feet high.

"It's awfully dark," my mother said as she pulled the belt on her trench coat tight. "It's drafty, too."

"There's no power on," my father told her. "That's typical in a building for sale."

"Dutch, I didn't get that far in my real estate studies."

Gianluca and Alfred cranked a large wheel at the far side of the room. Light began to pour in from the ceiling as a canvas tarp pulled back to reveal a series of skylights.

The double doors burst open. The light from the vestibule threw a bright beam of sunlight down the center of the room. A tall man in a cowboy hat stood in the blaze of light.

"What's happening?" I asked Cousin Don.

"Say hello to Carl McAfee. He's my lawyer."

"How we doin', Don?" Carl asked.

"Better now that you're here. We need a negotiator."

"Well, you got you one."

"Where are you from? That's a charming accent," my mother said.

"Norton, Virginia."

"Where is that?"

"It's in the mountains of southwest Virginia, close to East Tennessee."

"Oh. There." Mom pretended to know where that was.

"I brought Carl in because we need a big gun. I lost the Bears Den building because I approached the owner with sweetness instead of fear. Carl knows exactly how to handle the owner of this place."

"And why is that?" I asked.

"I've done business with him. He owns most of the buildings in Smokey Hollow. He has interest in steel mills in Pittsburgh, and I got to know him because he bought up a few coal mines in my area. He's what you call a speculator."

"Couldn't you have picked up the phone and called him?" I suggested.

"That's no fun, darling." Carl laughed. "You got to work the dirt to make the corn grow."

"Should we make an offer?"

"The owner doesn't want to break this building out of the bundle to sell. He wants us to buy everything on Pine Street," Alfred explained.

"We can't afford that."

"Unless the bank is willing to take a chance on us," Bret said.

"We could lease this building and, in time, expand," Alfred explained.

"I'm not sure that's what we should do," I said. I looked at Gianluca.

"Here are the pluses of leasing this building. It's in the center of things. It's the right size. There's an incentive program with the state to revitalize this area. We need that. And there are incentives for hiring local people."

"And Don, don't forget the most important element of all," Carl added.

"And what would that be?"

"I may be able to get the first year for free. Now, I'm saying 'may' because it's a maybe. But I think I can do that for you."

"If we can get the first year free, it would give us the head start we need," Alfred said.

"Free anything is always good," my mother, a true scion of family business, said.

"We're going to need all the upfront money to move the equipment from Argentina. Once it's here, we can get started."

"How do we get in touch with this man?" I asked.

"You just did," Carl said.

"You're the man?"

"I'm the man."

"I thought you were the negotiator."

"I am. I represent myself."

"Why would you want to get into the shoe business?"

"I like shoes. I especially like them sleek high heels on a woman with long legs."

"That's as good a reason as any to invest." Don nodded.

"And I like Don," Carl added.

"What are we going to call it?" Bret asked.

"The Angelini Shoe Factory."

"I advise against that," Don said. "As a general rule. It's best never to name a business after yourself, in case of . . . you know, failure. You can't go back and buy your good name once it's gone."

"What kind of factory was this?" I asked.

"They made pasta. It was called the Supreme Macaroni Company."

"I like it," I said.

"But you're not making macaroni, Valentine."

"It doesn't matter. It's a place, not a product. Besides, I like macaroni."

Orsola was due to give birth in Florence sometime in the middle of July. I tried not to think about my stepdaughter having my grandchild while I was pregnant with my first baby. Gianluca and I made plans to be in Italy, making it a family vacation as well as a buying trip. It seemed like this was our way. We didn't travel to relax. We always had a greater purpose, whether it was to find a piece of equipment or to negotiate a better price on leather goods. It was as if our work and our marriage were one, and hopefully they were, as this was by design and part of The Plan.

Don was busy renovating the Supreme Macaroni Company to prep it for the equipment that would arrive by the time we returned from Italy. Bret and Alfred were working on the loans from the bank and cutting a deal with "cowboy" Carl McAfee of Norton, Virginia. Alfred was hoping to cut a better deal than we would have had on Bear Den Road.

Gabriel was manning the shop on Perry Street, which always has a lull after the month of June. There was nothing to worry about. We'd had an uneventful flight to Italy, and now, it was time to relax.

As we pulled up to the Vechiarelli homestead in Arezzo, Gianluca relaxed. He was not a high-strung person, but New York City made him tense. I often found him on the roof or taking a long walk on the promenade on the Hudson River. He needed space to think. Even though we were blessed to live in a place with an expansive view of the river, Staten Island and the Atlantic Ocean beyond, it was still not enough for my husband.

"Valentine!" Gram threw her arms around me. "How far along are you?"

"Five months. Doesn't it look like eight?"

"No, you're right on schedule!" she said, looking me over from head to toe.

"Gram, this is all so new for me. I was sitting reading the paper, and I watched my fingers swell. It's like those time-release movies they used to show in science class, except it's not a frog laying eggs, it's me expanding to fill whatever space I'm in."

"She's beautiful," Gianluca said. "Tell her, Teodora."

Dominic and Gianluca embraced. I could see how much Dominic missed his son. I wished they could come and live with us in New York.

"Have you heard from Orsola?"

"Any day now, we're told. Dominic spoke with Mirella. She's there with her now."

Even though Gianluca and I had met each other long after his divorce, any mention of his first wife gave me a chill. I was sure she was a good person, and her daughter was certainly magnificent, but whenever Gianluca heard her name, his mood changed.

Having only been married once, I have no idea what it must feel like to have built a life with someone, only to have it end. I can understand how it happens, but the truth is, no matter how much two people want to stay married, you never really know what the other one is thinking.

Gianluca once told me that he was surprised when Mirella asked for a divorce. There wasn't an ongoing fight. They had slipped into a routine, and the routine of being apart, living separate lives, began to feel better than the marriage itself. At least, that's how he explained it.

It's a big deal for Italians to divorce, and I imagine that Mirella had an idea of what she wanted next while she was still married. She remarried a doctor about six months after the divorce was final.

Of course, when I got angry with my husband, I imagined that was why his first marriage ended. He could be very controlling, but so could I. He made decisions and consulted me later.

I did the same, but I felt I had an excuse. Marriage was new for me. I was beginning to understand the art of compromise.

We were doing plenty of that. We decided to raise our baby on Perry Street because we needed to keep the custom business going while we built the factory in Youngstown. Our goal was to spend time in Italy, but keep our base in New York.

Dominic and Gianluca went into the shop, where Dominic showed Gianluca the inventory. The first time I met them, they had been arguing over leather, and now I saw that it was a lifelong battle. A friendly battle, but it remained one.

Gram and I headed to the back, where she had put out a spread of local delicacies. My pregnant body craved mozzarella, fresh tomatoes, and bread. She had all three for me on a silver platter.

"How are you feeling?"

"Besides huge?"

Gram laughed. "It's an experience, isn't it?"

"Oh, a real hayride. Gianluca couldn't wait to get here. I haven't been easy to deal with."

"I worry about how hard you're working."

"Can you believe we're opening a factory?"

"Your grandfather's dream."

"I didn't know that."

"We never got ahead in the shop, we always hoped we'd reach a point where we could expand, but we never did. But he would be thrilled. Gianluca is supportive?"

"I think so."

"When Gianluca talks to his father, he confides that he really wishes you could live here."

"Well, maybe someday, but not now. I want the baby to be born at NYU Hospital. I mean, what if he or she wants to be president of the United States someday? And I love my doctor, Alicia DeBrady."

"I understand about the doctors." A look of concern crossed over Gram's face.

"Are you all right, Gram?" I panicked.

"I'm good. But Dominic . . ."

"What's the matter?"

"He's going to tell Gianluca, but he's been having some trouble breathing."

"Oh no."

"No, no, it's nothing to worry about. But he does have a diminished capacity from the chemicals he was around all of his life. They did some damage to his lungs."

"Is there anything they can do?"

"He has to rest, but of course, he doesn't."

"Make him."

"Not easy. We're old dogs, Valentine. We have our ways. I knew when I married him that he had a mind of his own. He's so stubborn."

"So is Gianluca. Is that Italian, or is it their Vechiarelli genes?"

"I don't know. But it's a challenge."

"Do you want to bring him to New York to see a doctor?" I offered.

"No, he likes his doctor. He wants to be home."

"Who doesn't?"

"We've talked about the possibility . . . the inevitability of one of us passing before the other, and what we would do." Gram fixed me a sandwich. "Look, let's forget about all this and have our lunch. You're a young bride, you don't have to think about all of this!"

"I always think about you. I miss you. So tell me, what's your plan?"

"Well, if Dominic goes first, I'll return to New York."

"You can live with us!"

"I don't know. Your mother offered to have me, but I'd die early from the fumes of the wallpaper glue."

"She just redid the hallway. If redecorating was crack, she'd be in rehab."

"I know. She's a fixer. Anyway, the alternative is for me to stay here. And I like the idea of that."

"Okay, I get it. If we moved back, you would have family here."

"I don't want you to do it for that reason, but there's a big house, and the town is wonderful. We love the people."

"Hey, in a hundred years, by the time anything happens, who knows?" How cavalier I was, but I couldn't see past the moment. And the truth was, I didn't want to. "Let's just enjoy the summer."

Gram smiled. "Of course."

Gianluca and Dominic joined us. Gianluca's face was flushed with color, and the tension in his jaw was gone. This was the face that had captivated me when I came here on my first visit.

The warm breeze ruffled the cloth of the canopy over the table, as well as Gianluca's hair. He looked like a kid to me, with nothing ahead but days of summer vacation to fill.

Gianluca guided me up the mountain path outside Assisi, where Saint Francis and Saint Clare lived, she with the nuns, he with the priests, surrounded by a forest sanctuary filled with woodland creatures and the music of birds. He took my hand on the path.

"How many prayer cards did you buy?" Gianluca wanted to know.

"I wiped out the gift shop."

"That can't be good."

"We have so much to do that I doubt we'll get back here. Do the math. Do you know how many First Communions and confirmations we have ahead of us? Including our own kid? Nothing like a prayer card tucked in the card with the check. Or the iTunes card."

"Very spiritual."

"I'm doing my best."

"I think it's this way." Gianluca pointed to a divergence in the path. I was hoping he would choose the path heading downhill instead of the one going up.

The Umbrian hills were carpeted in the palest green while the olive trees' gnarled branches were golden brown in the sun. The pungent scent of palm nettles and sweet honeysuckle filled the air.

Gianluca put his arm around my waist and guided me down the path. Soon we stood at the edge of a large field filled with sunflowers. Beyond the sunflowers was a Tuscan palazzo, its beige stucco pitted and cracked. Its clay roof, baked by the sun to a soft orange, looked like frosting on a cake.

"She lives there," Gianluca said.

"Who?"

"Alma. My mother's first cousin. She's the last living member of my mother's family."

"Besides you."

"Besides me—and our baby." Gianluca smiled.

As we walked the path through the sunflowers, I reminded myself to plant these on the roof of Perry Street. Every year I meant to do it, and every spring, I chose the tomatoes over the sunflowers. There is something about their brown faces offset by the bright yellow petals that make them look like a choir.

Gianluca pulled his cell phone from his pocket and made a call. He spoke Italian and motioned to me as he talked into the phone.

"She's waiting for us," he explained.

"Does she speak English?"

"Your Italian is fine. It's actually getting better."

"Do you think I'll master it between here and her front door?"

"I am filled with hope."

We laughed as we climbed the steps into a simple marble foyer. The high ceilings and windows let in lots of light. Beyond the main hall I saw the living room full of overstuffed old furniture draped in colorful cloth.

Gianluca called out to his cousin, who appeared in the doorway. Alma was around eighty years old, striking and tall. Her white hair was piled high on her head. She wore simple black pants and a flowing pink blouse, with jeweled gold mules on her feet. Her lipstick was hot pink. Gianluca rushed to her, and they embraced. As they had an urgent, warm conversation in Italian, I took in the grand proportions of the old house.

"Come, Valentina." Gianluca motioned for me.

I hugged Cousin Alma, seeing that she had set up a tray with coffee in a French press and biscotti in the living room.

"What a beautiful home you have," I said.

"Grazie, grazie," she said as she put a pillow behind me on the chair.

"I'm fine," I told her.

"Alma was my mother's best friend and her favorite cousin," Gianluca explained.

"Magdalena's mother and my father were brother and sister," Alma said as she poured a cup of lemonade for me, an espresso for Gianluca.

"I'd love to know about Gianluca's mother." My husband spoke of his mother only occasionally, but I knew he was devoted to her memory. He had a small framed photograph of her holding him when he was a baby that he placed on the nightstand when we married. The photo of mother and son is in vivid 1960 Ektachrome. Her blue eyes and his look like sparkling agates. As much as my husband looks like his father, he has the soul of his mother. He will mention her and something she said or wore offhandedly, as though his mother is in the forefront of his thoughts and some small thing will trigger a memory of her. He also carried a photograph of her in his wallet, along with the memorial card from her funeral. The small card had an illustration of Mary Magdalene at the tomb of Jesus on Easter morning. It is traditional to have a person's patron saint on their memorial card, but my mother-in-law's was particularly lovely.

"She was very shy. But she was a strong woman. Dominic was good to her."

"They make good husbands in the Vechiarelli family."

Alma did the strangest thing. Instead of agreeing with me, she shrugged. I shot Gianluca a look.

"It's been hard for Alma since my father remarried."

"Oh." Gram never mentioned Cousin Alma. "Has Alma met Gram?"

"No," Gianluca said. "And she hasn't wanted to."

I had very little experience in the etiquette of remarriage and blended families, even late in life, so I took the British approach. I ignored the topic entirely.

"Cousin Alma, did you grow up with Magdalena?"

"Oh, yes, we went to school together. She came here most days and played. We swam in the lake."

"You have a lake?"

"A very small one."

"I'll take you there," Gianluca promised.

"This home belonged to my parents. And I moved in with my husband to take care of them."

"Did you have children?"

"No." She shook her head. "A married woman without children in Italy has to find a purpose. It fell to me to take care of my parents and my husband's parents. They all lived to be very old." She looked at my stomach and smiled. "But I wanted children. They just never came to me."

Alma showed us around the main floor of the house. We went outside onto a lovely portico where she had set up rattan furniture. Her reading glasses were perched on top of a stack of books on a side table, next to a chaise longue. The pillows were arranged for Alma's comfort.

"Do you spend a lot of time here?" I asked.

"Every day."

"No television?"

"No. I listen to music." She smiled.

We followed her back into the house. As I stepped up to

enter, I saw a mezuzah anchored to the door. I got up on tiptoe and touched the inlaid work on the brass.

"That was my father's," Alma said.

"Did he travel somewhere and bring it home?"

"No, he was Jewish."

"Gianluca, your mom was Jewish?"

"Yes." He smiled.

"Why didn't you tell me we were Jewish?"

"I don't know. I'm not very religious."

"We would have had the blintz cart at Leonard's had we known."

"We had enough at Leonard's."

"I hear you. That's not a cocktail hour over there, it's a food court." I explained the concept of Leonard's as best I could to Cousin Alma. She seemed entertained. "So you see, I wished I was Jewish, at least partly, and now my baby will be!"

"I had no idea you wished you were Jewish," Gianluca said.

"Every kid that grows up Catholic in New York wants to be Jewish."

"And why is that?"

"We wanted Sundays off. Well, that and the latkes."

Cousin Alma takes her siesta every day at three, so we left her and headed down the path to the lake. We invited her to join us, but she has a routine, and that was that.

Gianluca began to run ahead as soon as the palazzo disappeared in the woods behind us. I didn't even try to keep up, lumbering carefully through the brush. Gianluca disappeared on the path ahead. I stopped and looked around.

The golden sunlight came through the trees like wide satin ribbons, illuminating the path. I followed it past a grove of thick trees. Ahead, I could see the clearing where Alma's lake must be. I climbed over a small hill to find the lake of Gianluca's youth in the distance, shimmering like a pool of blue sapphires, softly hemmed by long green grass. Gianluca was already in the water by the time I got to the shore.

"You couldn't wait, could you?" I laughed.

"Come in. It's beautiful."

"I'm not swimming in the buff," I told him as I neatly folded the pants that he left on the ground.

"No one can see you."

"Are you kidding? Even chipmunks have phone cameras these days."

"Come on," he pleaded.

"I don't look good."

Gianluca swam over to the edge of the lake. "Don't ever say that again."

"I was joking." Then I fessed up. "No, actually I mean it. I've felt ugly since I got pregnant."

"What is wrong with you?"

"I've gained twenty pounds."

"Of baby."

"Well, I think we know about six of it is baby, the rest is unaccounted for. Actually, I think I'm sitting on it."

"Valentina, do you understand that if you feel this way, our baby knows it?"

"Oh, honey, this baby is protected by so much fat, he thinks he's in a vat of cannoli filling."

"That's not funny."

My husband rarely called me on my self-deprecating humor. This time he was not letting go.

"You're beautiful," he said. "Don't I tell you every morning?"

"Yes."

"Because I promised."

"Because you promised. And I even let it count when you say it during REM sleep when your eyes are still closed."

"My eyes are never closed. I mean what I say. You have to make me a promise," he said as he came out of the water and helped me with my clothes.

"Okay, okay, I'll swim. Orca had a career, why not me?"

"No, I'm serious, you have to make me a promise."

"What is it?"

"That when I tell you you're beautiful every morning, you'll believe me."

I kissed my husband. "I believe everything you say."

He led me into the water. It was as warm as a bath. As he held me in the water, it was just the three of us.

I wondered how many times I would think of this moment in the years to come. The sun was hot, his skin was warm, and the water pooled around us like fine silk. If I ever had a moment of bliss, this was the one.

I don't know who invented *la passeggiata*, but I'll bet she was pregnant. I was finding, as my pregnancy unfolded, that walking was the only physical activity I could still attempt and feel like a normal human being.

I had tried Mommy Yoga at Tess's suggestion and Mama Zumba at Pamela's. Neither was for me, and frankly, seeing any pregnant woman huff and puff and sweat only reminded me of the marathon to come.

But walking after dinner in Arezzo, as the cool night breezes bathed the town on the hill, was a tonic. We stopped and talked to people that Gianluca had known all of his life, some who sold him leather, others who were new to town and had heard the story of *Vechiarelli et Figlio*.

"You know, if we have a boy, and I think we're gonna, we can finally put an S on *Vechiarelli et Figlio*. It has always bugged me."

"But the sign is true. My father only had one son."

"Then you call it the Vechiarelli Tanning Company, or V and V, or something, anything but Son without an S."

Gianluca waved ahead to a man and woman who sat on the steps of the piazza, having a cup of gelato. Gianluca and the man, around his age, embraced, laughing.

"Valentina, this is my best friend from childhood. Piero Greco."

"The Greek!" Piero said. "This is my wife, Alice."

"I love the way your name sounds in Italian. Ah-lee-chay. So beautiful."

"Name your baby Alice," Piero said.

"It's going on the list." I smiled.

"This man knows all my secrets," Gianluca said.

"There weren't so many. Only one was named Monica."

"Monica Spadoni." Gianluca made the international sign of voluptuousness with his hands. "She was a goddess."

In my current physical condition, I wasn't a goddess, I was the size of a temple, and the last thing I wanted to hear was about some beauty in Gianluca's past who evidently still burns in his memory.

"So where did Signora Spadoni go? Back to Mount Olympus?" Alice said.

"I like your sense of humor," I told her.

"I will tell you one thing about Gianluca. He never loved any woman more than his 1979 Renault convertible. *Bellissima!* He used to ride it around these hills like a crazy man. He took the curves like a whip," Piero said.

"You were lucky you weren't killed," Alice said.

"Almost," Piero admitted.

"What?" I couldn't help it. I was pregnant, and any thought of living one day without my husband scared me.

"I was driving on the old Viterbo above Arezzo." He pointed. "I was going very fast when I turned a corner, and there was the priest on a Vespa. He was coming up the mountain to give last rites."

"He might have done the favor twice . . . ," Piero interrupted.

"Except that I veered off the road and went up the hill, over and past him, and then spun off the side of the mountain. Luckily I landed in a ravine, upside down, but I walked away without a scratch. I climbed back up onto the road, and the priest was waiting for me. Instead of administering last rites, he condemned me to hell on the spot."

Piero and Gianluca laughed. I looked at Alice, who rolled her eyes. She had probably heard that story a hundred times. I made a vow that no matter how many times Gianluca told the story of the priest and the Vespa, I would laugh the loudest and the longest, because had the story ended differently, we never would have met.

We went for a drink before walking home. Gianluca had a limoncello, while Piero had two. Alice had a fizzy drink of bitters. I drank a gallon and a half of plain water.

Gianluca nuzzled me as we walked home to find Gram waiting on the porch. "Orsola's husband just called. She had the baby!"

"Is she all right?"

Gram nodded.

"And the baby?"

"Healthy and perfect. A boy!"

Gianluca dialed his son-in-law. They spoke Italian to one another, their tone operatic. I heard the pride both of them had in the news that the baby was a boy, their machismo instantly thrown into high gear. A son is a name legacy and camaraderie. My husband was giddy.

He hung up the phone. "I'm going to drive to Florence tonight."

"Give me a minute to pack."

"No, no, you stay. You need your rest."

"We're going in the morning, Valentine. You can come with us."

"Okay. Are you sure?" I asked Gianluca.

"Mirella and her husband are there," Gianluca explained. "You come tomorrow."

"I understand." When it came to his daughter, I did not question anything. He made those calls, and I did whatever was asked of me. I had put it out of my mind that I might actually meet the ex-wife, and now that it was going to happen, I wanted to lie down.

Gianluca gathered a few things and kissed me good-bye. He planned to stay with Matteo and help him with whatever he needed. I walked Gianluca to the car.

"What did they name him?"

"Francesco."

"Like Saint Francis of Assisi," I thought aloud. Was this coincidence or a message from the next world? I had a stack of prayer cards of the saint in my suitcase. I should have Gianluca bring a card to the new baby. But my husband was in a hurry.

He kissed me again and jumped into the car.

"Be careful!" I called after him.

Gianluca sped around the corner. I remembered that he'd had a cocktail. I had a terrible feeling as I watched him turn the corner and disappear from sight.

Gram had woken Dominic up to tell him that he was a great-grandfather. Elated, he promptly fell back asleep.

I followed Gram back to their kitchen. As she put a pot of espresso on the stove, I remembered her doing the same in her kitchen on Perry Street. There are times when memory is as potent as the moment. This was one of them. I sat down at the kitchen table and put my feet up on a chair. I leaned back and felt the full weight of my pregnancy.

"Gram, I have feelings of doom."

"That's just pregnancy."

"All the time."

"Those are the mother hormones kicking in."

"I thought those hormones would make me happy."

"They will come when the baby is in your arms."

"I believe you." But I didn't believe her.

"What are you afraid of? Go ahead and say it out loud—that will take away all its power over you."

"You think so?"

"I promise."

"Okay, here goes. I don't think my husband thought things through. A younger wife is a kind of baggage. He's had the life we're starting now."

"He had a few years of being alone."

"I know. I guess I wouldn't expect him to want to be alone all of his life. We found each other."

"And you're good for each other."

"I don't think he wants me to meet Mirella."

"He has his reasons," Gram admitted.

"Why? Besides the awkward nature of number one meeting number two, what's the problem? *She* left *him*."

"I can only tell you what Dominic told me. When Mirella asked Gianluca for a divorce, it's true, she and Gianluca had been living separate lives for a few years. But the reason they were living separate lives is that Mirella was turning forty, and she wanted another baby. Gianluca tried to talk her out of it, but she wanted that second baby. And it caused a rift that eventually ended the marriage."

"Why wouldn't he have another baby with her?"

"He thought Orsola was enough. And at the time, he had big ambitions for the tannery. He was thinking of going to Sicily and opening one there. There was talk of buying a tannery on the Amalfi Coast. When he was young, Gianluca was very ambitious."

My head was spinning. "Why wouldn't he have told me this?"

"Obviously he wanted to have a baby with you."

"Um, I don't know that for sure because this baby is a surprise."

Gram rested her face in her hands. "Oh, boy."

"No kidding. I trapped the guy. Not before I married him, but shortly thereafter. I can't believe it. Sharon Testa, the hottest girl at Holy Agony, was the trap-setting queen of our high school, and I make her look like an amateur."

"Don't say that."

"Well, what else would you call it? We go to New Orleans, have a giant doozy of a fight that I think is going to end the whole marriage, and I find out later that I'm pregnant."

"Then everything is fine."

"He looks after me. He makes sure I take my folic acid. He's good, Gram. Very good. But he didn't have a choice in the matter."

"Why are you worried? What's at the root of all this?"

"Gram, you're talking to a pregnant woman. I worry about everything. Oh, let's face it, it's not just the pregnancy. I'm a worrier."

"Yes, you are."

"Well, tomorrow we'll see what's going on behind the curtain. I'll meet my new grandson, dear God help me, and his grandmother. I should get a jump on my beauty sleep. What time will we leave for Florence?"

"First thing."

When I got up to my room and slipped out of my shoes, I looked down at my swollen feet, feeling worse. I called my mother with the news of Orsola's baby boy.

"Honey, wonderful news. How much did he weigh?"

"Nine pounds."

"Now that's a canned ham!"

"I'm sure he's adorable."

"I'll bet. Now. What is he to me again?"

When I married Gianluca, it was so confusing to my mother that she had yet to sort out her relationships in this new, extended family. Gianluca was her stepbrother, which made me her niece. Orsola would be her niece also, so baby Francesco was her great-nephew. The whole thing gave me a headache, but my mother had to know because she was sending a gift and a card and had to know how to sign it.

"Ma, just sign the card 'Mike and Dutch.' "

"Will they know who we are?"

"Yes."

"It seems so informal."

"It should be!"

"All right. Whatever you say."

"Ma, I need your advice."

"I'm listening."

"I'm going to meet the ex tomorrow."

"Who?"

"Mirella. Gianluca's first wife."

"Uh-oh."

"I know. I'm meeting the first wife, and I can't fit in my pants."

"We can't have that!"

"No, we can't. But we do." I looked down at my stomach. My pants weren't buttoned, and the zipper only went halfway up. "I'm the opposite of a trophy wife. I'm a booby prize."

"Don't you have a dress?"

"Yeah, I guess."

"You need something flowing."

"I have that sleeveless sundress."

"That's the ticket. And I don't care if you have to cram your feet into them, you put on a high heel. Three inches up equals five pounds of weight loss across."

"Oh no. I didn't pack my stilts."

"Honey, you're pregnant. You're not supposed to be rail-thin."

"That's good to know. Because I'm *not*."

"You shouldn't make a big deal out of this. I mean, she kicked him to the curb, didn't she?"

"That's the story." I cannot possibly tell my mother the rest of the story. She'll get on a plane and come over here in fear of a sequel to Sally Field in *Not Without My Daughter*, the Italian version.

"So, clearly, what you're saying and what I'm hearing is that Mirella is not interested in Gianluca anymore."

"She might be after she sees me in pants."

"We've already settled the fashion question. You're wearing the dress."

"Right, right."

"Oh dear, Valentine. You've got short-term memory loss."

"Yeah, and I'm going for full-out dementia. I can't remember anything. My face looks like a satellite dish. I'm running out of base foundation, there's so much more skin to cover. My eyes look like raisins floating in a bowl of puffy cereal."

"Even if it's hot, you have to wear mascara and use an eyelash curler."

"Okay."

"That doesn't sound like a yes."

"Ma, I'll do everything you're telling me to do. What do I say to the woman?"

"Say congratulations."

"Always a good opener," I agree.

"And tell her that Orsola is fabulous. Mothers always like to hear nice things about their children. You'll find *that* out soon enough."

"Before you go, I have some more news."

"Spill, honey."

"We're Jewish."

"Of course we are. Jesus was Jewish."

"No, I mean we really *are* Jewish. Gianluca's mother was Jewish."

"Honey, since we found out we had black people in the family, nothing surprises me."

"I hear that."

"Wait until I call Iris Feldman. She'll be thrilled when I tell her. She'll insist I buy an entire table for the UJA fund-raiser. Usually I buy a pair of tickets, but with Jews in the family, I'm going to have to put out for a table of ten."

"Ma, spring for the table. Come winter, we'll be able to fill it."

The ride to Florence from Arezzo through the Tuscan hills looked like a patchwork quilt stitched in summer colors. The fields were covered in sunflowers, spindles of olive trees were loaded with ripening black beads, and nestled in the folds of the valley were stucco farmhouses painted yellow, peach, and coral. But I observed most of it in a blur from Dominic's car because I was strapped in the backseat like a paratrooper, with a pillow under my knees for safe landing. The hot summer had shifted the weight in my body. I was puffy with fluid, where there was a joint, there was swelling. It was a wonder I could even dress myself.

We arrived at Santa Maria Battista Hospital right after lunch. Gianluca was waiting outside Orsola's room. I saw him on his cell phone at the end of the hallway. I had a notion to turn around and run back to Arezzo on foot. I really didn't want to meet this Mirella person.

I tried to stand tall in my strappy sandals, throwing back my shoulders, knowing that I already looked big, so I might as well go for Big and Tall. Gram and Dominic walked ahead of me at a clip, filled with joyful anticipation. When Gianluca saw them, he motioned them into the room.

"How is she?" I asked Gianluca. He kissed me on the lips.

"She's fine, and the baby . . . *che bello.*"

I entered the dark hospital room. Gram and Dominic were cooing over the baby in Orsola's arms. I was about to join them when I saw a petite blonde in her mid-fifties with a layered haircut standing by the empty crib. She looked up at me.

How odd to see the face that I had only seen in pictures, photographs I searched for at Dominic's house. I was insecure about the first wife, and now I was facing my worst fears.

I turned to my husband to introduce me to his ex-wife, but he wasn't there. I'd make an appointment to kill him later.

Gram and Dominic were busy with the baby, and Orsola was giving them the high points of the birth. So, like the good Yankee I am, I pulled my version of the Marshall Plan and extended the warm hand of friendship to Mirella.

"I'm Valentine," I introduced myself.

"I'm Mirella." Up close, her smile was clenched and tense.

Her white teeth were small and straight. Great. I had cornered a declawed cat.

I don't always do what my mother says, but this time I reached into the Mike Roncalli Sack of Good Manners and pulled out the big gun.

"You have raised a beautiful daughter who will be a wonderful mother," I told Mirella.

This cracked the veneer of wife number one ever so slightly.

"I had a lot of help. Her father . . . ," she said and stopped.

"Oh, no, Orsola is just like you. In fact, I feel I know you already."

And with that, I turned to ogle the beautiful baby boy and his happy mother.

Gianluca joined us. He looked at Mirella as he placed a hand on my shoulder. "Have you met?" he asked her.

She nodded as I kept my eyes on the baby.

"Stop asking me questions, I'm not going to tell you another thing," Gianluca said to me as he loaded the car with our suitcases. "I'm taking you somewhere so wonderful, I can't describe it."

"I just don't know whether to pack my pants or my bigger pants. Are we going to Lake Como?"

"Maybe."

"Well, I'm not Clooney ready."

"What is that?"

"George Clooney has a house on Lake Como, or haven't you heard?"

"I wouldn't know."

"Clooney ready is Gabriel's concept. When you're working out and you've dieted and gotten the right haircut and the best job, and you feel gorgeous, you're Clooney ready. When you're not, you go to Miami, put on your swim dress, and hide in a cabana with a can of frosting and a big spoon. You only go to Lake Como if you look good enough to snag George Clooney."

"This is why Gabriel is alone."

"I know. He admits that he overreaches, but what's wrong with high standards, honey? I have them."

It soon became apparent that we were traveling west, not south to Rome, not north to the mountains of Lombardy, but farther west, to the shores of the Mediterranean Sea. When we pulled into the seacoast village of Santa Margherita Ligure, I remembered Gram telling me that Gianluca had spent a lot of time there.

I hadn't had the nerve to bring up the new Mirella information that Gram had shared with me. After I met Gianluca's first wife, he really didn't want to talk about her. It was as if I'd seen her, and that was it, we were done. Besides, what good would it do to discuss whether Gianluca wanted to have a baby when we already had one on the way?

I was in the beginning stages of mastering the art of communication with Gianluca. He seemed to be pretty open to any subject, unless it was about his past choices and romantic history. I figured there was a room somewhere in Arezzo filled with memorabilia of all the women he'd loved before (let's call it the Willie Nelson room), but I didn't want to know the location and I certainly didn't want to visit. Yet a conversation about Mirella was different. Her mistakes needed to be understood. I could walk down my choice of paths in this marriage, but I wanted to avoid the one that ended in failure.

The last thing Gianluca wanted to do was examine his first marriage at the beginning of his second. There wasn't going to be any soul searching. I would have to put aside my curiosity until he was ready to talk—if he ever did.

He pulled the car up in front of a beautiful salmon-colored house with ornate white trim. A series of balconies faced the sea. Planted boxes overflowing with purple blossoms spilled over the sides like festoons of silk.

I loved Perry Street, but this was something else entirely.

"Is this a hotel?"

"No."

"Oh, is it one of those bed-and-breakfasts? If it is, please let's find another place to stay. I don't want to sleep with the house cat, and there's always a cat in a B&B."

"It's not a bed-and-breakfast, and there's no cat," he said as he climbed out of the car to unload our suitcases. "Do you like it?"

"Honey. It's a palazzo."

Gianluca took a key from his pocket and opened the door. A sweet breeze blew through the house, from the windows in the front and on the sides.

The house was furnished with comfortable couches and chairs slipcovered in white linen. The terrazzo floors were buffed to a high polish. The simple decor was the backdrop for a few paintings of the sea and objects like old urns in shades of turquoise with small cracks in the resin. I felt inspired there, and very much at home.

Gianluca held me close.

"Where's our bedroom?" I asked.

"You need to rest."

"Not exactly."

Gianluca took me by the hand and led me up the stairs past a floor with a suite of two bedrooms to the third floor, the master, an enormous room that took up the whole floor with a king-size bed and a suite of a sofa, two deep armchairs, and a chaise, all covered in linen. We had landed in a sumptuous, white cloud, floating over a blue ocean.

Gianluca pulled the drapes aside to reveal a set of French doors to the balcony. He opened them and invited me outside. The view of the Mediterranean Sea was breathtaking, an expanse of the deepest turquoise blue as far as we could see. Everything was blue, except the sun that shimmered like a gold ring. The scent of the ocean, both salty and sweet, sailed over us like musical notes.

The port below was cluttered with sailboats that knocked against one another like ice cubes in a fizzy cocktail. I rested my head on my husband's shoulder and closed my eyes. I opened them to his kiss. Before we turned to go back inside, I touched the plants, full with ripe tomatoes. "Gianluca, just like my roof."

"Is the Hudson River this blue?"

"No, it isn't. But God only made one Italy," I told him. "We get Staten Island in the distance like Bali Hai. Which is not without its charms, by the way."

Gianluca plucked ripe tomatoes off the fragrant green branches. He handed me a few, then gathered some of his own.

Sometimes I forgot that we were still newlyweds. Honeymooners. When I hit the wall in New Orleans, I hadn't surrendered to marriage yet. Slowly and surely, I felt we were getting there. A marriage is for life, so what are a few quibbles here and there, and a couple of mysteries that don't get solved right off the bat? My husband didn't volunteer a lot of information.

My mother said I needed to go on a fishing trip with Gianluca. You bait the hook, make him bite, and reel him in for the interrogation. Besides, we had all the time in the world—or maybe it just seems that way when you're in Italy.

I was finding out so much about him, and as much as he fascinated me in general, the specificities of who he was, what he used to do, and what he cared about before he met me were all of interest to me. I just had to wait as he slowly revealed what he wanted me to know in his own time. A woman knows when there's a mystery. After all, we invented it.

As we made love, I remembered all the things I treasured about him, and how someday soon we would have a baby who would remind me of those things. I was beginning to understand the phrase "the miracle of life."

Gianluca held me close.

"Where are we?" I asked him.

"Santa Marga—"

"I know where—I mean this house. I want to meet your rich friends. Who are they?"

"No friends. I wanted to buy this house when I was married to Mirella."

"What happened?"

"She didn't want it."

"Why?"

"She wanted to live in Firenze. She likes the Adriatic. Venice. Rimini."

"And you like the Mediterranean side. Of course she liked the white beaches of Rimini and the cool waters of the Adriatic. The Mediterranean Sea is as warm as a bath, and the sun bakes everything like sweet bread."

"I like the heat."

"So you didn't buy the house because she wouldn't live here."

"I didn't say that."

"What are you saying?"

"I bought this house after the divorce."

"It's yours?"

"And yours. This is your house now."

"Mine?"

"I own it, and so do you."

I sat up. "Are you serious?"

"Do you like it?"

"Like it? It's a Barbie dream house."

"Who is Barbie?"

"The doll. She had a dream house. But I had to share it with my sisters. This is better. Believe me. Much better."

"You don't have to share this house with anyone. Though your family is always welcome, of course."

"If we tell my mother you have a house on the Mediterranean Sea, she'll plotz! Why didn't you tell me?"

Gianluca shrugged. "You don't want to live in Italy."

"It's not that I don't want to—"

"I know, the shop, the shop."

"Yes. The shop. I held on to the shop through near bankruptcy, Gram leaving, Alfred joining. But can't I love Santa Margherita too?"

"Of course."

"Then let me."

I got up and gathered the tomatoes on the dresser. "I'm starving."

"I'll cook for you."

"In *our* kitchen!" If I had the pep to shout, I would have. "Oh my God, we have a kitchen on the Mediterranean Sea."

Gianluca helped me carry the tomatoes down the stairs. I took in the house in a different way, knowing now that it belonged to us. The stairs built from terra-cotta tiles trimmed in black marble were stunning. The windows outfitted with graceful white shutters let in the ocean breeze. I adored the details of the place. Our baby would come here and know this village as his own. I couldn't quite believe my luck.

Gianluca put a pan on the stove. He diced up some garlic and drizzled olive oil in the pan. He wielded the knife gracefully, just as he did when he cut leather in the shop. He chopped the tomatoes and added them to the mixture sizzling in the pan. He stirred in a tablespoon of fresh butter. Soon the air filled with the glorious scent of fresh tomatoes cooking slowly. Gianluca lowered the flame on the stove and put a lid on the pot. He filled another pot with water, sprinkled salt into it, and put the flame on high. As we waited for the water to boil to cook the pasta, Gianluca chopped up some basil and grated fresh parmesan cheese into a bowl.

"How do you feel about being a grandfather?"

Gianluca looked at me. "Thrilled. But odd."

"Too young?"

"No, I'm exactly the right age. But I'm about to be a father again, so it's strange."

"I'm sorry."

"I didn't mean it like it sounded."

"I'm going to hold you to that."

"You may." He smiled.

I was feeling a lot like a first wife because now we owned a

house I didn't know we had before. I also felt that Santa Margherita was a place that was important to my husband, and he
had never shared it with anyone but me, so it made us even
closer. Emboldened by this new knowledge, I wanted to know
more about Gianluca's past.

"What was it like to see Mirella at the hospital?"

Gianluca chopped parsley for a moment without answering.
He put down the knife. "It's difficult."

"Do you still have feelings for her?" We had just made love,
and he had just shared this house with me, and yet I had to ask.

"Of course I respect her. But she left me, so I didn't have a
choice in the matter."

"So you never stopped loving her?"

"I love you—that's all that matters."

"I'm secure, Gianluca. You don't have to convince me that
you love me. I get it. And your first marriage doesn't hurt my
feelings. Life is complicated. And you're Italian. This is a country of dogs hanging on to bones. Stubborn is the name of a
chromosome in the Etruscan line. I don't think you're a man
who could stop loving anyone, including me."

"You're very intelligent."

"Thank you. That's always a plus when physical beauty is
temporarily off the table."

I went to the terrace outside the dining room. I peered over
the railing. There was a terrace on every level of the house.
They were filled with pots of plants and vines loaded with bou-
gainvillea. There was vivid purple and the deepest green like
a frame against the blue panorama of the Mediterranean Sea.
I wondered if I would become a different person entirely if
I could take in this view every day. Would I just give in to the

beauty and never leave? To own this view and live in the scope of its magnificence might quell my desire to create beauty with leather and nails.

Even more tomatoes grew on this terrace. There were small trees in ceramic pots loaded with ripe lemons, and another with figs. I picked a few as Gianluca brought me a plate of Parmesan cheese and prosciutto.

"Look, honey. Figs. We need a fig tree on our roof."

"They won't grow in New York."

Gianluca had never been to Brooklyn, where fig trees were as common as fire hydrants. But I didn't want to fight, so I said, "Well, we have the tomatoes."

"That's true."

"They grow beautifully on Perry Street. But I remember one year when they didn't grow at all. I was around six years old. And I was devastated."

"Why?"

"I helped Grandpop pot the tomato plants and water them, and had done everything in my power to make them grow, but when I went up to the roof, week after week, no tomatoes.

"We had Sunday dinners on Perry Street then with the whole family—the cousins, Aunt Feen, her weird husband. We'd go to church, and then we'd have dinner, homemade manicotti, meatballs and sausage, a big salad. Somebody made a cake or picked up a sleeve—that's what we called them, a sleeve—of cannolis at Caffe Roma, and we'd feast. We'd laugh and catch up on the week's news. And the kids, we played on the roof.

"So after dinner, I'd go up there and check on the progress of my tomatoes. One week, there weren't any buds, not a sign of a tomato. They must have been bum plants or worse. I cried to my

grandfather and then forgot about it until the following Sunday.
When I went up to the roof, they were loaded with tomatoes—
but not real tomatoes, magic tomatoes, my grandfather called
them. He had made tomatoes out of velvet in the shop and hung
them on the branches like Christmas ornaments. A vine of
velvet tomatoes."

"That will be my bedtime story to our baby. I'll tell him that
story every night."

"Don't leave out the part where his mother has a nervous
breakdown. Let's condition this kid early."

I sat down on a chaise and watched the sun melt into the ho-
rizon like a pat of butter. Soon Gianluca came with our dinner.
He set the table, then placed the bowl of pasta in the center.
He grated fresh cheese onto the macaroni. I had never been
so hungry in my life—of course, this was something I said six
times a day since becoming pregnant.

My husband pulled out my chair. I placed my napkin on my
lap, and he on his. I twirled the pasta on my fork, then tasted
it. The linguini was al dente, smothered in the sweet tomatoes,
buttery cheese, and fragrant olive oil.

"You got me," I told my husband.

"What do you mean?"

"I surrender. I will live with you by the sea for the rest of our
lives. Our son can learn to read at home. I have no desire to go
anywhere else or do anything else ever again."

"If only you meant that."

"I do mean it."

"Until your American ambition comes rushing back like a
fever."

"You think my ambition is a disease."

"No, I'm proud of you. But sometimes it overtakes you."

"Not when I'm looking at the Mediterranean Sea."

"How about we pour everything into your career and make you a world-class shoe designer, and then you have your fill, and it's you and me and our baby right here with the tomatoes."

"I'm going to have a son, you know."

"I love my daughter, and I'd love another girl."

"Nah, you're Italian. You want a boy. The only reason Italian families used to be so big was because they'd have girls and have to keep going until the son was born. I'm ashamed to even repeat it, but Aunt Feen told me that when I was five, and it stuck."

He shook his head. "Whatever God sends, and as long as he's healthy."

"Gianluca, is there anything else you're keeping from me?"

"What do you mean?"

"This place is awfully clean. Do you have a girlfriend, a sexy one that looks like Sophia Loren when she came out of the water in *Boy on a Dolphin*? Does she come over here and take care of the place when you're gone?"

"I cannot answer that."

"Oh, man, there's more than one? I knew it. I'm going to find negligees in the closet and tap pants in the bureau."

"They're very nice ladies."

"I bet they are."

"Yes. Three sisters."

"Ugh. Sisters."

"They're very capable."

"Sure they are."

"They clean the marble, they tend the tomatoes, they wash the windows."

"I can imagine what they do for an encore."

"You'd be surprised. They're very flexible."

"They'd have to be."

"Especially at their ages, seventy-four, seventy-five . . . seventy-eight."

"*Now* I find out you like older women?"

"I'm sorry, *cara*. I had to tell you the truth eventually. It's best you hear it on a full stomach."

"It's full. And now that you have a full stomach, tell me. How many children do you want?"

"Let's start with one."

"Why did you only have Orsola?"

"The marriage wasn't strong enough for a second baby."

"Okay."

"It wasn't."

"Our little one is a surprise. Is that okay with you?"

Gianluca got up and kissed me. On his way back to the kitchen he pulled two figs off the tree; then he thought better of it, and took two more. Then he turned to me. "I like surprises. I live for them."

<h1 style="text-align:center">⤜ 10 ⤛</h1>

Gianluca decided to take a ride down to Sestri Levante. An old friend of his had just acquired a small textile mill, and he wanted Gianluca's advice about how to run the operation. I had the day to myself in the pink house by the deep blue sea.

The only problem with Casa Vechiarelli was that I couldn't decide which room I liked the best. The rooms that faced the sea, including the master bedroom, were filled with luscious ocean breezes, but there was something wonderful about the back of the house and the garden with its stone pizza oven, chaise longues, and awnings. I loved it all, and I had to tell someone all about it.

"Gabriel, this house."

"I got your text. And the pictures. Seriously? It's gorgeous! What do you mean, he owns a house? Is the man rich? Should I put my feet up?"

"I have no idea if he's rich. I think he just bought this because he loved it. His ex-wife wouldn't live here."

"Idiot!"

"I know. What's wrong with people? Of course, I should send her a thank-you note for leaving him. I would've never had a chance with him if she had held on to him."

"Are you sure she left him?"

"That's what he tells me. And Gram says that's what Dominic told her."

"I don't know. Who would leave that guy? I mean, it sounds like a smart woman would stay with him just for the house."

"That only happens on nighttime soaps."

"And in my family."

"How's it going in the shop?"

"We got a couple of orders for winter weddings. I took measurements."

"I'll get started on them as soon as I'm back."

"You are having a baby. Take a break."

"You're crazy."

"Val. Get real."

"I'm not going to change my life because I'm having a baby."

"You won't have to—the baby is going to change it."

"No. He's coming to live with us, we aren't going to live with him."

"Are you drinking over there? Everything is going to change. Your father was over here baby-proofing, and he rigged the toilet. I took a wee, and the thing snapped shut on my Junior like the mouth of a mighty alligator."

"We don't need childproofing."

"Not yet, but Val, the baby is coming. We're going to have

gates everywhere in the shop. Can you imagine a baby near the steam press? We can't have that. Upstairs is your problem."

"How's your new apartment?"

"It ain't One Sixty-Six Perry."

"Why don't you live with us?"

"Val, there was a TV show about it when I was a kid, *Three's a Crowd*, and it got canceled."

"I miss you. We're coming home."

"I wouldn't miss me if I had a view of the Mediterranean Sea. Enjoy it."

"I am."

"No, you're not."

"No, I really am. I just miss New York."

"Why? You have a man and a house, and he can cook. And I'm assuming he can cook in every room . . ."

"He can, and he does."

"So forget work, forget New York. The Hudson River is a gray stream of mystery moisture in a dank, stinking heat compared to the Mediterranean Sea. Stay in the moment. Be with your husband."

Mom and Dad picked us up at the airport when we landed. The expression on my mother's face when she took in the size of me reminded me of the time we went to Sarasota and visited the tank of the Mighty Manatee. The expression was one of awe and then horror.

"Honey, you look . . . amazing."

"Code for gigantic?"

"Oh, I'm not biting on that one. I had four babies, and I know exactly where you are hormonally."

"Yeah, I remember that crazy place," my father said. "You were there so often, we took a rental."

"Now, Dutch. Watch it."

Gianluca carried our bags to the car and put them in the trunk. As soon as we were in the car, my phone rang.

"We have a situation," Gabriel said urgently.

"What's the problem?" I looked at Gianluca, whose jaw had returned to its clenched position upon landing at JFK.

"We need a press release."

"For what?"

"Let's put it to you this way. All your vendors are nervous. They've heard about the factory, and now they're wondering if you're going to deliver your specialty lines to their stores."

"Oh for Godsakes, of course I am."

"I held them off at the pass. Look, I am many things, but I am a lousy writer."

"Hold on. I know a writer."

"Don't tell me. Salman Rushdie is hiding in the leather closet."

"Not him. Pamela."

"She can write?"

"Really well. Call her and ask her to spin this thing into a press release. Something like . . . Angelini Shoes, in the spirit of their founders over a hundred years ago, are breaking ground on a new American factory to produce a retail line of fabulous American shoes in the Italian tradition."

"Got it."

I hung up the phone and tried to join in on the conversation between Gianluca and my parents. My mother was quizzing Gianluca about the house in Santa Margherita, while my dad did his best to avoid orange highway cones and bad cabdrivers as we made our way into Manhattan.

I put my hand on Gianluca's. "Did I do all right?"

"What do you mean?"

"I'm hiring Pamela to be our press agent."

"Whatever you want to do, *cara*."

"You think it's a bad idea?"

"This is not a good time to ask me. You already hired her."

My heart sank. I always figured out how to consult my husband after I'd made a decision instead of before. No wonder he felt excluded. "I'm sorry."

"There's nothing to apologize for. Pamela is a smart hire."

"I mean, she's in school, but she's got plenty of time to take care of our press."

"Good." Gianluca smiled, but it was lacking warmth and kindness, which were on tap in abundance in Italy. I felt terrible, but the baby kicked, and I took that as a sign that he was happy to be home, just like his mother.

There is a tricky moment in the making of a shoe when the sole is sewn to the upper. The shoemaker almost has to imagine a foot inside the shoe as she sews, providing enough give in the leather to hold the shoe's shape, but not so much as to have the sides spill over the sole once the shoe is in it.

In custom shoemaking, we do several fittings. Gram taught me that human beings, made mostly of water, have shifts in their weight. Not just losing and gaining fat but shifts in water weight, which occur daily and come from external factors like the weather, or internal ones, like a long run in sneakers that temporarily spreads the bones of the foot.

I was on the last stitch of a closed satin boot for a November bride when I felt a rumbling deep within me. I felt the baby kick, but this kick was followed by a low, hollow pain that spread through my stomach and around to my lower back.

I changed position in my chair. The pain passed. I stood next to the table to get a better view of the shoe. The cramping returned. This time, I draped my body over the table to steady myself.

Gabriel came in from lunch and saw my position. He rushed to my side. "Are you all right?"

"Go and get Gianluca. He's on the roof." Gianluca had decided to clean out the gutters since fall was upon us.

The pain subsided, and I knew I had a few seconds, so I went to my phone. I was about to call my mother. Instead, I put the phone down and waited for Gianluca.

The thought of him going through this process with me calmed me down considerably. After all, he had seen it all before. When you're embarking on a new journey, it's always best to go with the sherpa who's already climbed the mountain.

"Valentina!" he said when he came into the room.

"They're coming a few minutes apart."

"Gabriel, call her mother."

"No!" I bellowed.

"What do you mean? You wanted her there, remember?"

"I changed my mind. I want it just to be us."

"Are you sure?" Gabriel said. "She has experience. Four times."

"When the baby is born, we'll call her," I said softly.

Gianluca drove us to NYU Medical Center slowly, as if we were in a parade. Gabriel sat next to Gianluca in the front seat, and to be honest, he was reacting as though he was the one about to give birth. We had to drive about a mile and a half, across the village and up First Avenue to Thirtieth Street. Gianluca was careful around the potholes, and not so patient with people who crossed without obeying the signals. He laid on the horn and gave one poor jaywalker a diatribe in Italian.

When Gianluca helped me out of the car in front of the hospital, Gabriel jumped in the driver's seat and drove off to park the car. The sidewalk was crowded with people going to lunch. The lobby of the hospital was a mob scene, and no one noticed the pregnant woman in labor. Gianluca guided me through the crowd. The whole time I was thinking, I'm about to add one more soul to this circus.

When we arrived on the birthing floor, it was a madhouse. Evidently, there was a drop in the barometric pressure from an oncoming storm, and when the baby dropped inside my body, babies all over the city who were at term dropped too. There were gurneys in the hallway with ladies curled up in labor and one who was not so far along, who sat up and hugged her enormous belly like she was holding a beach ball.

I was taken into a small room with a divider curtain. On the other side of the curtain was a woman I couldn't see but could hear. She was chanting "Om" as loudly as the law would allow. Great, I got a chanter.

A petite nurse came in and helped me into position on the bed. My water broke as she shifted me. The fun began. I remember thinking that the nurse looked like a cricket in a cartoon: all eyes, and so tiny, she could fit in my hand. She handled me skillfully and asked Gianluca to wait outside.

My sisters had told me to ask for an epidural, so I did. A Filipino doctor came in and gave me the shot, telling me if I moved, I could be paralyzed. I said a soft Hail Mary as he did his job. When he was done, he said, "Hail Marys always do the trick."

I was wheeled into a birthing room. Gianluca took a CD from my duffel and put the music on. I was going to give birth to the music of Frank Sinatra, B. B. King, or Lady Gaga. It was anyone's guess.

My husband sat down on a rolling stool next to me and took my hand. I focused on his hand, the shape of his fingers, the clean, square nails, and the strength of his grip.

My doctor, Alicia DeBrady, a beautiful African American dynamo, came in, took a look, and said, "Sooner than later, hon."

"What does that mean?"

"It means you're about to have this baby."

"Wait!" I said. I thought I had hours of labor ahead of me, based on waiting for Tess's girls and Alfred's sons. I remembered in some instances, I left and came back in the morning and the baby still hadn't been born.

"Call my mother!" I shouted.

"You said you didn't want her," Gianluca said calmly.

"Just do it! Please!"

In an instant, I needed my tribe. I didn't want my baby to enter the world without the family around her. I'd been there for all the nieces and nephews, and they should be there for their cousins.

Gianluca left the room to make the call.

"Girl, you made fast work of this baby," Dr. DeBrady said.

"Are you kidding? This was the longest nine months of my life."

"Well, you're about to have him in the shortest nine minutes of your life."

"It's a he?" I whispered.

"No, I didn't say that. I call all the babies he so I don't get caught spilling the beans."

"But what if it's a boy?"

"Coincidence, Valentine. Coincidence."

As Gianluca came back into the room, he was followed by a team of students. NYU Medical Center was a teaching hospital. Of course I'd forgotten this and agreed that I could be observed. Now I was sorry because a pack of students from Illinois, not my mother, were going to see my child born.

Every feeling I had during labor was magnified . . . love, guilt, insecurity, anxiety, and anticipation. I wanted to meet my child, and I wanted him to enter this life with all he needed.

"Did you get a hold of the family?" I asked Gianluca.

"They're on their way, darling."

"I hope they have wings," Dr. DeBrady said. "Push, Valentine."

As the students shouted their support, I pushed. The baby slithered out of me and into the light. I heard a student say, "Awesome," and I thought, The first word my child heard was *awesome*.

Gianluca kissed me as the baby was whisked away.

"Where is he going?" I shouted.

"It's not a he—you had a beautiful baby girl," Dr. DeBrady said. "We're just going to check her to make sure she's perfect."

"A girl!" I was thrilled. "We didn't want to know what we were having, and I would have been happy either way, but a girl!"

"She's beautiful, Valentina," Gianluca said to me as he watched them weigh her, sponge her, and swaddle her.

The nurse brought the baby to me. She had a full head of black hair and tiny rosebud lips. She was warm from me, and I pulled her close.

"*Che bella,*" my husband said. He often spoke Italian when he was happy.

"What should we call her?" I asked.

"Whatever you want."

"May we name her after my dad? Do you like Alfreda?"

"Yes, I like it."

"We'll call her Alfie."

"Alfie?" Gianluca smiled. "*Mi da tanto piacere di finalmente conoscerti.*"

"Alfie." I kissed my daughter's head.

I couldn't take my eyes off her. I couldn't compare how consumed I was by the reality of her to anything else in my life.

I'd been able to work on one piece of suede for hours on end and was known for my undivided attention to detail, but all of it, anything I had ever known or done, just fell away in comparison to my total, instant, and primal devotion to this baby. She fascinated me unconditionally.

As in every life-changing event, there was no way to prepare. You don't know what you're going to think in advance, or how you'll react in the moment. I had observed mothers, and loved my own, and certainly knew a good one on the street, but this was an altogether different sensation. My life had changed in a matter of seconds. And the shocker: I wouldn't have it any other way.

"Honey, get the iPad out."

My husband fished in the duffel again.

"Let's Skype Gram and your dad."

"It's the middle of the night there."

"They won't care."

Gianluca smiled. "You're right."

At first, it rang and rang, so Gianluca called separately on the phone. He told his father about Alfie, and instructed him to pick up the Skype.

The next face we saw was my grandmother's. Gianluca moved the iPad to show Alfie.

"Oh, Valentine, she's gorgeous!" Gram said. "Was it a long labor?"

"No, it was so quick, I'm stunned!"

"Oh, isn't that wonderful! You dodged a bullet!"

"I know! How lucky am I?"

"Kiss her for us."

"That's not a problem!"

My mother burst into the room. She was dressed head to toe in white, with a hot pink pashmina thrown over the ensemble. The ball fringe on the cape swayed as she moved. Leave it to my mother to wear a white pantsuit in a birthing room.

She was followed by my dad, who was rattled. His hair was askew, and he was dressed to clean out the garage.

"Oh, Ma, it happened so fast."

"I'm sick I missed it."

"You didn't miss anything. She's here now."

I handed my baby delicately, like a precious teacup, to my

mother. She took the baby skillfully and held her close, as she had in the first few hours of the lives of all of her grandchildren.

"So you and Gianluca did this alone?" my mother asked.

Gianluca looked at me and smiled.

When I married Gianluca, he joined this massive family who are around all the time. We call each other every day, sometimes more than once. When we don't get a return call or text quickly, we assume the person is dead. When we have a spat, we hang up on one another and Gianluca shoots me a look that says, "Call your sister back." He had become brother-in-law, mediator, and olive oil on the troubled waters.

We spent many Sunday dinners with my family. Holidays. There was a social life around sacraments. First Communions gave way to Confirmations, then marriage, and on your way out, Last Rites with a funeral Mass followed by a buffet. There was always a school play or a recital or a game that required our attendance. It never mattered whether anyone else showed up. We made up for any last-minute cancellations. The Roncallis filled the seats, pews, or bleachers, no matter the occasion.

Gianluca moved to Perry Street and took on the Roncallis, Angelinis, Fazzanis, and McAdoos as his own. Yes, it could be a pleasure, and sometimes it was wonderful and fun, but there was something great about it just being the two of us for the birth of our baby. We were exhilarated. We did this. Alfie was *ours*. And our daughter would be forever our own.

So on that day, I figured Gianluca needed to be the only voice in the room. I wanted my husband to navigate the birth coach, the doctor, and the nurses. I wanted him to make decisions on behalf of the baby's welfare. I wanted him to have the knowledge that we were his family now, and that Orsola and Matteo were part of it. It seemed crazy that Alfie would have a twenty-seven-year-old sister, but looking down the line, I trusted it would be a gift to our daughter. I couldn't see how, but hoped it would be true. We would make it so.

"What's her name?" Mom asked.

"Dad?"

My father had put on his reading glasses and was studying his latest grandchild as though she was a delightful bit of news he was reading in the newspaper.

"As long as you don't name her after a street or a state, I'm happy," he said. "Enough with the Paris Dakotas."

"No problem. That's a good thing. Because we named her after you. Her name is Alfreda."

"Valentine. Really?" My dad's eyes filled with tears.

"I want her to be just like you."

"She'll need a coach for the vocabulary section on the SATs," my mother said.

"She'll have one." I laughed.

"Her middle name is Magdalena, for Gianluca's mother," I added.

"It is?" Gianluca beamed.

"You'll have to tell our daughter all about your mother."

Gianluca kissed me on the forehead.

"There are a lot of stories in this family. The good, the bad, and the ugly." Mom sighed. "But we never repeat the ugly. Denial is a good thing."

She opened a small gift box and removed a gold pin. Dangling from it was a small cross and a Star of David. She pinned it to the blanket swaddling Alfie.

"A pin?" Gianluca said.

"It's an Italian tradition," Mom said. "What, you never heard of it?"

"We pin a saint's medal to the crib."

"Don't worry. I have that covered. I have Saint Rose of Lima in my purse for the bassinette."

"I'll bet you do."

My mother held her new granddaughter close. "I had to cover both religions. Doris Gluck sent the Star of David. I had a Capuchin monk bless them."

"Thanks, Ma. You might as well go ahead and book Leonard's for the bat mitzvah."

"Are we going that far?"

"You never know."

"Good point. We can always cancel. Carol Kall is nothing if not flexible."

"May I?" Dad said to Mom.

She gently handed him the baby.

"Hello, Junior," Dad said to his namesake.

"Honestly, Dutch. We have a little princess here, and you're calling her *Junior*?"

"This one is all mine," he said.

"You say that every time we have a grandchild."

"Yeah? Well, this time I mean it."

Alfie was sleeping in her car seat on the worktable when I showed the staff of the Angelini Shoe Company our new line.

Gianluca and Gabriel leaned against the cutting table. Tess had a notebook open to jot down ideas, while Charlie helped himself to a doughnut and a cup of coffee. Pamela had her laptop open with several new designs of the new logo. Jaclyn and Tom sat on the worktable, eager to see what new designs I had come up with.

"Okay, I want your honest feedback," I announced. I noticed that Gabriel and Gianluca shot one another a look.

Evidently I had been a little less than cooperative in the shop in my postpartum state. "In honor of our new venture, I based the new designs on macaroni."

"Made of macaroni?" Tom blurted.

"No, brother, *inspired* by macaroni." I was glad I had Tom working in shipping and not creative.

I held up the first sketch. "This is the *Orecchiette* sandal. I took silver discs like *orecchiette* pasta, and strung them on silver mesh with a flat buckle."

"Nice," said Tess. "I'd wear those."

"Me too," said Jaclyn.

"I love them," Pam said as she typed into her laptop.

"Here's the *Pastina,* a simple beige or plum pump with a square heel embellished with tiny beads à la *pastina*."

"You'll sell those like cannolis in Brooklyn," Gabriel said. "Those girls like glitz."

"And this is the *Rigatoni,* a bouclé vamp and a block heel shaped like—"

"*Rigatoni,*" Charlie finished.

"Right. And here's the *Fusilli.* A leather mule in vivid blue, black, and red, with a spring heel—"

"The Fush-heel." Gabriel helped my presentation along.

"Yes. And here's the *Linguini.* A neutral calfskin golf shoe accented with bright laces of rolled leather—"

"I'm rolling the leather." Gianluca smiled.

"And you do it so well, honey. Well, what do you think?"

"I think we're going to have a ball marketing these," Pamela said. "They're kitschy, but they're beautiful. They're functional and whimsical. We can do a whole campaign with the shoes in the kitchen, in pasta pots, that sort of thing. Hip for your feet."

"Go wild," I told Pam.

"I'd like to thank my staff for helping me pull this presentation together."

"Staff of one," Gabriel said.

"This was a family business from the beginning, and it will remain that way forever. You've all made Gram very happy. She loves that we're all under one roof."

"And let's face it, since you had Alfie, you need us." Tess smiled.

"And that too."

Alfie's birth had given me a whole new perspective on family. I had been the guest for years at my nieces' and nephews' milestones and passages. Now they would be there for Alfie. And if we were going to have them around all the time, why not put them to work? Why shouldn't they benefit from the business? After all, it was their family business too.

My mom became built-in child care. Tess and Jaclyn and Pamela brought their children to the shop, and just like when we were kids, they had full run of the house and the roof. Our childhood wonderland had become theirs.

My sisters had thrown themselves into the work. It was like the old days when Gram called Feen to help with a shipping deadline. Mom would drop everything to come into the city to wrap the shoes in chamois sleeves and box them. It was natural for us to help one another in business because we had seen this sort of teamwork all our lives. Tess and Jaclyn had worked as temps or did odd jobs here and there after they became mothers. Now they had a place to go; each had her own desk on Perry Street.

The couture line paid our salaries, and once Youngstown took off, we'd be able to plow more money back into the business. Eventually, I hoped to offer retirement and shares in the company to my family.

The business was going great, but I was torn. For me, motherhood and work was a terrible combination. The only way to make shoes and maintain a family was to have a husband so supportive, I could jump from one high wire to the other with ease. I had a net, after all. The net was Gianluca.

"Do you really like the line?" I asked Gabriel after everyone had left.

"It's adorable and doable. God, I sound like Pamela. She's a walking advertisement. The new factory should be able to handle these."

"Charlie says the equipment should arrive in Youngstown by the end of the month."

"You realize that you've hired every Roncalli in the family except for the goldfish in your mother's koi pond."

"Can you imagine?"

"Family: the gift that keeps on taking," Gabriel reminded me.

Gianluca was rocking Alfie when I came up from the meeting. He was looking out the window, and for a moment, memories of my own dad rocking Jaclyn when she was a baby came rushing back.

"That was a great meeting," I said as I poured myself a glass of water.

"Alfie is hungry."

"She has my appetite," I said as I took the baby. I took her to the kitchen and prepared her a bottle.

"You're not going to nurse her?"

"I'm weaning her."

"So soon?"

"It's been six months. My doctor said it was fine. She got all the nutrients up front."

"That's part of breast feeding, but the more important aspect of it is the bonding."

"That's judgmental."

"It's not a judgment. It happens to be true."

"Look, they're my breasts, and I'm done with it."

Gianluca looked perplexed and then fixed his gaze on the baby.

"Is something wrong?" I asked him.

"Your staff is unhappy."

"Gabriel?"

"The upstairs staff. Me."

"What are you talking about?" All I could think was, Nice, buddy. I carry the baby, I have the baby, I nurse the baby, I am up all night with the baby, and it's not enough. Gianluca had some idealized, old-fashioned notion of the Italian mama who wraps the baby in her apron, does her chores, nurses the baby on her breaks, and then tends the husband with any leftover time she has. I was furious. "I know I don't multitask like a perfect mother in Italy, but I'm doing my best."

"Why do you always have to denigrate my country and my people when we get in an argument?"

"Because you judge me."

"When did I judge you?"

"I came upstairs, and you're all cold and weird."

Alfie began to cry. She spat the formula out. Gianluca jumped up and grabbed the bottle. He tested it on his arm. "It's cold, Valentina."

I grabbed the bottle from his hand. "I know what I'm doing."

"Now we get to the truth. You know everything."

"I know a lot, and frankly, more than you."

"It's a contest."

"You're making it one!"

"Well, guess what, Valentina? You're losing. You can't do everything you want to do and do it well. You rush down to your meeting as though it's more important than Alfie and me, and then you rush back up the stairs and feed her cold formula. My daughter deserves better than this!"

"Are you kidding? She is surrounded by love!"

"That's very loving. Screaming at the top of your lungs. Let me raise my voice, so perhaps you will hear me. I asked you to take time off with the baby, but you insisted on working through the first weeks of her life. We will not get these moments back."

"I am so tired of you being the expert."

"You asked me to help you through this process. I am only telling you what I know. But you ignore every suggestion. You glared at me at the hospital when I took away your phone when you were having contractions."

"That's extreme."

"It's true!"

"Here's my truth, Gianluca. I'm angry."

"And that's what I wake up to!"

"Poor Gianluca! You're not getting enough attention, so you lash out at me?"

"I don't need your attention, but your daughter does."

"How dare you? You see what I have to do in a day."

"I watched you sketch an entire line of shoes in Italy, and you never once lost patience or became angry."

"We were on vacation!"

"Life can be that easy every day in Italy."

"Oh, my God. You and Italy. Italy is the solution to every problem!"

"It's a start. Don't you see? You're like a tense piano wire. You are pulled as far and as tightly as you can be by obligations and commitments, so tight that when the hammer hits the wire, it makes no sound. Listen to me, the shoes aren't important. Your business is not the thing you will remember when you're older—"

"Oh, now I'm going to take advice from the man who had big dreams to put a tannery on the Amalfi Coast and it didn't happen, so now I'm going down in flames too!"

I saw rage rise deep within my husband. "You are not only selfish, you're cruel. Who told you about my business?"

"Your father, through my grandmother, told me what happened."

"And you bring it up now?"

"I should be asking the same thing of you. You shut me out, and then you're hurt when I keep things from you. Well, here's what I've been keeping from you—I have no intention of moving to Italy. It's fine for vacations, but here's the deal. I plan to stay right here on this block, in this house, with this view, forever."

"Good to know," he said.

Gianluca turned to go down the stairs.

"Where are you going?" I demanded.

"The baby needs diaper cream."

Gianluca went down the stairs. I realized that I had no idea that my baby was out of diaper cream—but give me a break, I had presented the new line of shoes today and had other things on my mind. Was it too much to ask that I could rely on my partner to do the shopping? Why should I feel badly about that for a second? Why have a husband if he's not going to participate in the day-to-day raising of our child?

Alfie was dressed in her traveling ensemble, pink pants and a jacket with duck buttons made from a vintage chenille bedspread, when she went on her first car trip.

The Supreme Macaroni Company was set to open in Youngstown, and the entire family would be there for the ribbon cutting on the new factory.

We pulled up to the building on the main drag of Smokey Hollow. The facade of the building had been painted red, white, and green, in blocks, like the Italian flag. I loved it already. The building stood out against its drab, industrial neighbors like a giant Popsicle. Our logo was in a circle in the center of the wall. The r's in Supreme Macaroni Company were upside-down boots. This was Pamela's idea, and we ran with it. There was a bright red ribbon across the entrance door.

I turned to Gianluca. "The Italian flag is for you, honey."

Gianluca smiled.

My brother and sisters were waiting for me by the entrance. My parents were standing back, taking in the exterior renovation. Their kids were running up and down the sidewalk. They were dressed up for the ceremony, just like Alfie.

My parents were beaming, so they must like it. Gianluca helped me out of the car and took the baby. Charlie and Don came around the side of the business and joined us.

"I'm going to take you all on a tour before the official ribbon cutting," Charlie said. "Are you ready?"

Charlie held the ribbon to the side as Don propped the door open. My family filed into the vestibule.

This day had been months in the making. When Charlie returned from Argentina, he waited for the equipment to be shipped to Youngstown. He came out for a couple of months, bunked with Cousin Don, and put the whole thing together.

My brother-in-law was the best hire. He poured himself into the factory, and now we were seeing the fruition of his months of hard work. While Charlie was working with the mechanics, Bret and Alfred were working over the local banks with Don. Alfred carved up some crazy deal with Carl McAfee that helped us get a loan from the bank. Hopefully, when we started turning a profit, we'd be able to pay off our loans quickly. My husband kept reminding me that this was the price of doing business.

My family stood in the vestibule, which was repainted and well lit, with a new clock to punch.

"Hey, this is like when we went in the Haunted House at Great Adventure. Remember how they crammed us in?" Tom laughed.

"This time the floor won't fall out from under you," Charlie said. "I poured the concrete myself."

"Is everybody ready?" Don wanted to know.

"Yes!" we shouted.

Cousin Don pushed the door open; we filed into the main room of the factory. The Supreme Macaroni Company had been restored to its former glory, but instead of ravioli presses and pasta machines, the enormous and glorious equipment used by our great-grandfather and his brother, protected and maintained by our cousin Roberta, was back home in the United States of America.

The presser, with its new steel rollers, glistened at the center of the room. The cutting table, with a state-of-the-art automatic motor and blade, was lit by a series of tin-capped lamps painted red, white, and green.

The buffer, with a ramp and conveyor belt that would deliver the shoes to finishing, took up the entire back wall. The finishing department consisted of four long worktables, stools lined up underneath on either side, where fifty employees would snip threads, polish heels, and glue embellishments on the shoes on their way to shipping. I felt as if I were inside the gears of a Swiss watch. Each operation was dependent upon the one before it.

Charlie had taken one of my sketches and, with Pamela's help, framed a series of operations in the factory, from the impulse to design a shoe to the creative end, when the shoe is worn by the customer. To see the steps dramatized on the wall, in order, and with such reverence, brought tears to my eyes.

Gabriel joined me as I looked up at them. "These are the

stations of the cross for anyone who has accepted shoes as their religion."

"What do you think?" Charlie asked me.

I threw my arms around him. "You weren't just a guy who sold alarms, you're an artist."

"Nah. You're the artist. I'm just a pretty good mechanic."

My brother Alfred joined us. "And thank you, Alfred!" I gave my brother a hug.

"Let's thank the money gods."

"Carl McAfee?"

"For one. We got lucky. When we needed an infusion of cash, it showed up. That's how we do it."

"Hey, everybody! They want us outside for the ribbon cutting. Mayor Ungaro is out there! And we got Monsignor Cariglio to bless the joint!"

My family joined the mayor and the monsignor outside the factory. A small crowd had gathered on this special day, and we were happy to have them.

"You like it?" Gianluca put his arms around me and the baby.

"It's a miracle. I can't believe it all came together. And that you and I didn't fall apart in the process."

"You have angels all around you, Valentina."

"Yeah, well, I like the tall one with the blue eyes." I kissed my husband.

As the mayor cut the ribbon, I leaned over and whispered to Cousin Don, "Where's Carl?"

"He doesn't do spectacle," Cousin Don said. "He's a behind-the-scenes guy."

Don turned toward the camera and beamed. That's the shot that made it into the *Youngstown Vindicator*.

That night Don threw us a big party at the Lake Club. There was an Italian spread that would put the best restaurant in Little Italy to shame. Lou Fusillo went in the kitchen and whipped up a polenta appetizer that had the crowd begging for more. The night began with antipasto and ended with chocolate soufflés and Napoleons.

My mother walked the grounds, marveling at the gorgeous view behind the dining room. I have decided that my mother loves catering halls as much as double-point days at Saks Fifth Avenue.

My husband, father, and brother were enjoying a cigar on the veranda. I loved seeing my husband relax with my family.

Cousin Chrissy had found a fabulous team of local girls to babysit the kids. Alfie would sleep through the fun, but she was safe and happy. For the first time, the new parents were free. We decided to make a real party of the opening of the Supreme Macaroni Company.

I handed Gabriel a glass of wine by the lake.

"What the hell are we doing here?" Gabriel asked.

"In our small way we are revitalizing manufacturing in the United States."

"You never think small, do you?"

"What's the point?"

"I never thought I'd set foot in Youngstown, Ohio," Gabriel said. "Steubenville, yes. I'm a Dean Martin fan. But Youngstown? Never."

"So, what do you think?"

"Well, they're our people, aren't they? You got more Italians here than you do at the soccer finals in Calabria. I feel at home here."

"Good. Because we'll be spending a lot of time here."

"Yes, we will. We have to take care of the Cathedral of the Shoe."

"Let's pray for good profits." Don Pipino laughed as he passed us on the way to the bar. "Because, let's face it, I'm not in this for my health. I'm in it for the green. Or should I say, the red, white, and green."

Gianluca and I stayed in the same room at the Marriott we'd stayed in when we first visited Youngstown, except this time, in addition to extra towels, we requested a crib. Alfie was fast asleep when I poured my husband a glass of wine in a plastic cup and then one for myself.

I toasted him. We sipped and kissed.

"Thank God that's over."

"Val, it's just beginning."

"I know. But it's built, and it's going to run."

"You should be very proud."

"Thank you for everything you did for me. For us. For Alfie."

"I learned some things along the way. I want this to work."

"The factory will make it."

"No, I mean us. Our marriage."

"It's going great, Gianluca. You know what I dream about?" I asked him.

"Tell me."

"Our house on the ocean. Once the factory is in full operation, let's take time to go and enjoy it with Alfie."

"When do you want to go?"

"Soon."

"But you love springtime in New York."

"I do. But I love our house in Santa Margherita."

"It's just a house."

"It's a palazzo on the Mediterranean Sea!"

"It's just an ocean."

"The most beautiful ocean in the world."

"When did you fall in love with Italy?"

"When I saw it with you. Besides, Alfie's going to start talking, and you know she's going to be speaking Italian too, so when we go, she can practice. And so can I."

"We'll see, Valentina."

"Hey, I'm telling you I want to go to Italy."

"Alfie's little, we should stick close to home. You love her pediatrician."

"Good point. Dr. Papadeas is the best anywhere."

"See? Italy isn't going anywhere."

"And how about you?" I asked.

"Me? Where am I going? I love you and Alfie. If you wanted to live in a cave, I'd find one."

"You really want me to be happy, don't you?"

"I do."

"Everything changed when you stopped putting pressure on me."

"Was that it?"

"That, and the postpartum hormones cleared out."

"Don't forget the hormones."

"I couldn't."

Gianluca kissed me and pulled me close. He fell asleep quickly, as men do when they have clear consciences. Even in small ways, I learned from him. He might exasperate me sometimes, but the truth was, there was always something to learn from him. He had wisdom, and of all the things I thought I would treasure in my husband, that had not been high on the list. But now I know it might be the most important thing, because it's exactly what saved us.

11

"*Gianluca!*" I called out from the kitchen. He often took the baby to the Hudson River Park, but usually he left a note.

"We're down in the shop!" he called up the stairs.

"I thought you went to the park."

"Not yet."

Gianluca was pressing a sheet of white leather while Alfie chewed on a plastic serving spoon and jumped up and down in a bouncy chair. Occasionally she would laugh, then go back to her chewing.

"What are you making?" I asked.

"Alfie's first shoes. She's going to be walking soon."

"The tanner makes shoes now?"

"I always have." He shrugged.

"Why didn't I know this?"

"You make all the shoes around here."

"Show me what you got."

If I had to go back and pinpoint the moment I fell in love with Gianluca Vechiarelli, I know it was for sure when I saw him press leather for the first time. His hands smooth and drape leather skillfully. He has a command of the delicate—he can do the smallest detail work—and yet he can lift and cut and press and roll with strength of purpose.

When he holds our daughter with his hands, I feel no harm will ever come to her.

"Why are you watching me?" he asked.

"I'm falling in love with you all over again."

"Someday when Alfie is older, you have to show her how to roll leather."

"You can show her."

"What if she's forty when she asks?"

"Neither of us will be here to show her."

"You more likely than me." Gianluca smiled.

"Why do you do that?"

"Do what?"

"Imagine all the things she won't have."

"It's my job. I'm the father. I have to be practical. I'm building her shoes, aren't I?"

"That's practical," I admitted.

"Maybe I worry about Alfie because I want her to have everything that I had, and there's no way to be two places at once. Our lives are here, and yet I want her to know Italy."

"When the new line is complete, we'll go," I promised him.

"It's all right, Valentina. We'll go when we can."

"You're okay with it?"

"You're happy here."

"And how about you?"

"I can't lie. I miss the light and the quiet and the long after-noon naps in Italy. I've traded them for the setting sun over New Jersey, the noise of the trucks, and the naps interrupted by our baby when she wakes up. But no place gives me what you and Alfie provide. We're a family, and wherever you are, I am home. That's all I need. I really don't need a country. I just need you."

"But we can have both!"

"Valentina, you have your life with us and your work. Italy doesn't need to be in the top three." He kisses me.

"Oh, you two with the romance." Gabriel placed his mes-senger bag in the cubby. "Still in love, what's it been? Almost a year?"

"Two in February," I corrected him.

"What do we have here? Don't tell me. Baby shoes?"

"Papa is making his daughter her first pair of shoes," I ex-plained.

"How lovely. What's next? We cut our own hair?"

"Done it," I admitted.

"Gianluca, do you need my help?" Gabriel asked.

"Do you want to help?" He smiled.

"Of course. I am always looking to work a little harder around here."

"Then cut the soles for me."

Gabriel traced the sole on the pattern paper. He took a pen-knife out of his pocket and carved the soles perfectly. Two little soles for our little girl.

"You know, someday we'll be sitting around and I'll be able to tell your daughter about her first pair of shoes."

"Oh, Gabriel, will you please remember everything? Gian-luca is really good at it, but my brain holds no new information."

I took Alfie out of her swing and held her as her father fitted the shoe to her foot. There's an old expression, "The shoemaker's child always goes barefoot." Not this time, not in this house, not this child. Her father has seen to it that she'll have everything she needs.

My cell phone rang which caused Alfie to jump up and down in her bouncy seat. "Val, are you planning to go to Italy anytime soon?" my mother asked when I picked up her call.

"I don't know. I'd like to, but Gianluca doesn't think it's a good time."

"Oh, Lord, we've Americanized him!"

"We have the factory to think about," I reasoned.

"Cousin Don has it under control."

"I have a feeling if we left the country, something would go wrong."

"Well, trust your instincts then."

"I do."

"I'm trusting mine! We've got to go and see my mother."

"Does Dad want to go?"

"Are you kidding? He doesn't even like a day trip to Coney Island. No, it'll be me solo unless I can twist your arm."

"I dream of our house in Santa Margherita. Ma, why don't you take Gram and Dominic and go and stay there?"

"I'll ask them."

I hung up the phone and turned to Gianluca. "Honey, we have to make a plan. Let's buy our tickets right now. New Year's Eve in Italy."

"You want to go?"

"We need to go."

"I'll book the travel, then." Gianluca took out his phone.

"Oh, honey, on second thought, let's not buy the tickets just yet. It's cold on the coast that time of year. Summer would be better."

Gianluca switched off his phone and put it in his pocket. "Good point."

I stopped on Jane Street and picked out our Christmas tree. I would have liked to make this a family outing, but it looked like the good trees were going fast, and I didn't want to take the time to go home and come back out, fearing I'd miss the best tree for our home. I paid Mr. Romp and gave him my address for delivery.

"Honey!" I called out, throwing my keys on the counter. Gianluca came out of the nursery and put his finger to his lips.

I tiptoed back to him. Alfie was lying in her crib. Her big blue eyes were wide open, staring at me. She reached for me, and I picked her up.

"I almost had her down," Gianluca said. "We were seconds away from Dreamland."

"I'm sorry." I kissed him and then kissed our baby.

"What are you reading?"

"*Pinocchio.*"

"Do you think she understands it?"

"Every word," he promised me.

"Just so you know—I studied Goldoni in college. And it was a challenge." I gently laid Alfie back in the crib. She fought to keep her eyes open, but soon she was fast asleep.

We went into the kitchen. I unwrapped a pair of steaks that I'd picked up at the Chelsea Market, threw some olive oil into the skillet, diced up mushrooms and onions, and added them in with a little butter. I drizzled cream on top until there was a gravy. I put the steaks in the pan and covered them with a lid.

Gianluca brought his laptop over to the counter. "Look at Francesco," he said as he brought up pictures of his grandson. He had the same black hair and blue eyes as our Alfie.

"What a beautiful baby."

"I wish he lived next door."

"Gianluca, we'll get there."

"Let's see where life takes us." Gianluca smiled.

"We're going to do the Feast of the Seven Fishes here this year. Is that okay with you?"

"I'll order the fish."

"And get the sausage at Faicco's for Christmas Day."

"Absolutely." Gianluca opened a bottle of wine and poured us each a glass.

I made a salad of baby spinach, artichoke hearts, and slices of fig, drizzled with olive oil and salt and a little fresh lemon juice, exactly as Gianluca liked it, set the table, and lit the candles.

Gianluca went to check on the baby. When he came back, he gave me a thumbs-up and sat down at the table. I served him steak and mushrooms and his favorite salad.

"How's your steak?" I asked.

"Perfetta!"

The doorbell rang. "Oh, that's the Christmas tree."

"You bought it without us?"

"Sorry. They were getting picked over."

Gianluca went down the stairs and let in the deliveryman. He tipped him, then carried the tree up himself.

"You'll hurt your back."

"Too late."

"We keep the tree stand in the spare room," I told him. "It's in the bottom of the closet."

I cleared the dishes and loaded them into the dishwasher. Gianluca returned with the tree stand while I looked through a stack of bills from the day's mail. "Do you need my help?"

"No, it's all right," he said as he wrangled the six-foot tree into the metal stand. I went and stood by him and the big tree anyway.

The doorbell rang. It was almost eight o'clock. I pressed the intercom.

"UPS," the voice said.

"I'll get it." Gianluca went down the stairs.

A few moments later, he appeared in the living room, hauling a big, heavy box. "What the hell did you order?"

"That's your Christmas present."

"Did you buy me a box of rocks?"

"That's funny. I did."

Gianluca put the box near the undecorated tree. I grabbed the scissors to open the box.

"You're going to open it?"

"Why not?"

"It's bad luck," Gianluca said.

"I also got you a tie."

Gianluca laughed. "You can't keep a secret, can you?"

"Not as well as you."

"You think I have secrets?" He laughed.

"I don't know." I ripped into the box. Gianluca lifted out a simple bluestone carved with inlaid words:

PALAZZO VECHIARELLI

"Do you like it? American stone, Italian carving."

"It's beautiful."

"Now, don't go out and buy me a rock for Christmas unless that rock comes in a small blue box from Tiffany's."

"Got it," he said. "Where are we going to put this?"

"For now, let's put it on the roof, and when we go to Italy, we'll bring it to the house in Santa Margherita."

Gianluca smiled. *"Va bene."*

"Alfie and I start ABC Music and Me tomorrow at the Chelsea Day School."

"You think I'm too advanced with the reading, and you have her learning music?"

"Don't get too excited. It's banging on boxes and shaking maracas."

"I love you," he said, pulling me close.

"You'd better," I told him.

We tiptoed past the nursery where Alfie slept and into our bedroom. When Gabriel moved out, I'd taken the master bedroom and redecorated it for Gianluca and me. I gave Tess Gram's old bedroom suite and replaced it with a king-size bed and a chaise. As we undressed, I remembered that I owed Cousin Don an e-mail about a shipment to Neiman's.

"I forgot to e-mail Don," I began.

"Forget it. He's at the club having a scotch. It can wait until the morning."

Gianluca's tone told me not to push it, so I dropped the idea of running to answer the e-mail. He kissed me. The kisses trailed down my neck.

It was hours until morning, and Alfie slept through the night. As Gianluca kissed me, I surrendered and closed my eyes, remembering the room in Santa Margherita and how blue the sea was in the sunlight. I pictured our house every night before I went to sleep. I wonder if Gianluca did the same.

The place held such sweet memories. We made love to the music of church bells and the early-morning whistles of the fishermen as they loaded their boats. It was a time I would never forget. I wanted to go back to our home by the sea, with Alfie, with my new family.

At three a.m., Gianluca was fast asleep. I went and checked on the baby. I stopped in the bathroom and was on my way back to bed. I knew I had the class in the morning. Gabriel had some leather to cut for a prototype, so the shop schedule was set. Alfred had a conference call with Don and a shipping meeting with Tom.

I didn't want to spend the class on my phone answering e-mails, so I grabbed the laptop, sat down at the kitchen counter, and commenced answering e-mails. I was lost in my work when Gianluca appeared in the doorway.

"You're impossible," Gianluca said.

"Sorry." I snapped the lid of the laptop shut as though I had been caught in a lie.

Later I thought about this small interaction. Had I gone back to bed, or had I kept answering e-mails? I would look back at this moment, and I wouldn't be able to remember. I even went back through the e-mails of that morning to see. All I know is that when I finally went back to bed, Gianluca was fast asleep.

Later, I felt the warmth of my baby as she crawled over me.

Gianluca lay down in the bed with the baby between us. "What a great way to wake up in the morning," I told him.

"Come on, Alfie." I wiggled her legs into pink tights with red hearts on them, pulled a soft red chenille jumper over her head, and brought her into the kitchen. "How do we look?"

Gianluca looked at the baby and me. "I don't know who is more beautiful. So I choose . . . *me*."

"You would." I gave him a quick kiss on the cheek. "We'll be back for lunch. Unless of course, there's some young, hunky daddy yum yum at ABC Music and Me."

"Where is this class?"

"Chelsea. Oh, right, good point. He'll be gay. A my-two-daddies situation."

"It is always wise to lower your expectations."

"I'll keep that in mind. Here, hon. Hold the baby for a second."

Gianluca took Alfie into his arms and kissed her. Her jet-black curls and blue eyes were a killer. I knew I was biased, but she photographed like Elizabeth Taylor in *National Velvet*. I tried not to get too excited, because she also had my Roncalli nose.

"Say cheese," I told them.

I took a snap with my camera and checked it. "It's not the Christmas card, but it's cute."

Gianluca kissed Alfie and handed her to me.

I loaded Alfie into the stroller in the foyer. There was still some snow on the ground from the last storm. I navigated around the sheets of ice on the sidewalk and the melted mud at the corners. Alfie, under a curtain of clear plastic, was playing with a yellow plastic monkey that spun on the handlebar.

As I pushed the stroller, a million things I had to do before Christmas swirled through my head.

Do I have enough silverware for the Feast of the Seven Fishes?

Do I need to borrow Mom's tureen for the cioppino?

Still have to send Christmas gifts to Gram and Dominic in Italy.

Christmas cards? I'll skip them this year. No, can't. Alfie turned one. That's a crime, to withhold baby pictures.

Call Tess to make arrangements to pick up Aunt Feen.

Alfie and I took our place in the circle at Music and Me. The teacher, who had more rings than Saturn in her nose and ears, dumped a bunch of toys into the middle of the floor.

The babies crawled to the toys, grabbing them out of each other's hands. One little boy hit another over the head with a maraca. The mother of the hitter grabbed her baby. The other one was on her phone, so there would be no repercussions.

It was so loud in class for the hour, I didn't hear my phone. But when class was over, I saw several messages from my brother Alfred.

I loaded Alfie into the stroller and made my way back to Perry Street. I stuck a bud in my ear and listened to the messages.

The first message: "Val, it's Alfred. Look, don't worry. But I've taken Gianluca to NYU Med Center. Mom is on her way to the house. You can leave Alfie with her, and come over as soon as you can."

A second message: "Val, we're here at the hospital. Call me when you get this."

A third message: "Val, call me."

I began to run, pushing the stroller in front of me. Alfie thought it was fun. She was flying, and she giggled, looking up at me through the clear plastic.

A slew of thoughts entered my mind. *It's nothing, maybe he fell. Alfred would tell me that. He has no health issues. What could this be? He has a cigar once a year, if that.*

Then I began to panic. My heart raced. I crossed Washington Street with the stroller and heard the blare of a car horn.

A cab stopped dead a few feet in front of me. I kept going. When I reached the shop, I called out, "Gabriel? Gabriel!"

He came out of the shop and took Alfie. "Go. They're at NYU Medical Center."

I didn't even ask Gabriel if he knew anything. I didn't think to ask. I just had to get to Gianluca.

Crossing the west side to the east in midmorning is impossible. The cab stopped and started. Finally I threw open the partition and screamed at the driver, "You have to get me there!"

I called Alfred's phone. No answer.

I called my mother's phone.

"Mom, where are you?"

"I'm almost at the shop."

"Have you heard from Alfred?"

"He doesn't know anything. He found Gianluca in the kitchen on the floor. He and Gabriel were in the shop, and they heard something fall. They called for Gianluca, and when he didn't answer, Alfred went looking."

I began to cry. "Mom, this isn't good."

"Valentine. Stop it. You don't know anything. Pull it together. He's a young man. He'll be fine."

I hung up the phone, and instead of calling Alfred, I held

the phone in my hand and waited. Every awful scenario and worst outcome played through in my head. Why do I always jump to the worst possible conclusion? Maybe it was nothing. Maybe he'd just fallen and hit his head.

I paid the cabbie quickly and jumped out of the car. I ran into the hospital, going around the corner to the check-in desk, which I remembered from the day when I delivered Alfie.

They sent me to the fifth floor. I pounded the numbers in the elevator, willing it to move faster. I pushed through the crowd when the doors finally opened on the fifth floor.

Everywhere there were signs that read, "Cardiac Care." My chest tightened with anxiety as I processed what those words meant, and what they might mean regarding my husband.

As I turned the corner to go to the nurses' station, I saw Gianluca on a gurney. Alfred was with him, doing that double-step walk to keep up with the wheels as the orderly pushed Gianluca.

"Stop!" I shouted.

Alfred put his hand on the shoulder of the orderly.

I ran to my husband's side. "What happened, honey?"

"I don't remember."

"The ambulance brought him here. I called 911," Alfred explained.

I looked down at my husband's feet. He was wearing one black sock and one navy blue one. I covered his feet with the sheet to keep them warm.

"He needs emergency surgery, Val. I'll explain. Let him go. He needs to go," Alfred said gently.

I took my husband's face in my hands. "I love you."

"*Ti amo*," he said. "Where's Alfie?"

"Mom is with her."

"Don't worry," Gianluca said with a weak smile. "I'm not going anywhere."

The orderly guided Gianluca through the doors to emergency surgery. Alfred signed the paperwork. There was nothing for me to do.

Alfred guided me into the visitors' lounge. I sat down in the chair and began to shake. This is what it is like to be in an earthquake, I thought. The earth is rupturing and swallowing me whole.

Alfred handed me a cup of water. He put his arm around me. "Val, let me tell you what happened."

"Mom told me how you found him."

"He was unconscious. I called 911, and they were there within three minutes. And it was a good thing they got there quickly."

"What happened to him?"

"His aorta ruptured."

"He's going to die, isn't he?"

"No, we got here in time."

"Are you sure?"

"It's not anything you see coming. He's had this condition since he was born. That's what they told me, anyhow."

"Is this even a good hospital for cardiac surgery?"

"They're terrific. Don't worry about that."

"Oh, God, Alfred. The Christmas tree." I shot out of my chair. Alfred followed me.

"What happened?"

"He hauled it up the stairs, and he put it in the stand. That's what did it."

"No, Val, you're not listening."

"And I gave him this stone sign, and he hauled it up the stairs too. Oh my God, that put the stress on his heart."

"Val, they said it was congenital."

"But something had to trigger it."

"Don't do this."

"Alfred?"

"Yeah?"

"Don't leave me."

Alfred sat with his arm around me for an hour. Tess arrived with Jaclyn. Moments after they arrived, my father came. They sat vigil with me as Gianluca was in surgery.

Every hour or so a nurse came out and told us how it was going. I didn't press her, because I felt if I did, she wouldn't be nice to my husband and somehow something would go wrong and he would die. He couldn't die.

We had a life.

We had a baby to raise.

We had dreams.

I wanted to pray, but I couldn't remember any words. As the surgery moved into the fourth hour, when I thought I was beginning to get a grip on what was happening, I was summoned into a conference room next to the waiting room.

I turned and saw that my sisters and brother and father were with me. Dad took the seat next to me at the conference table, placing his hand on mine. My dad doesn't do things like that, but it didn't dawn on me that the gesture meant anything either. I was now focused only on a happy outcome, how soon I could get my husband home, how we could plan Christmas and put up the tree and have our normal holiday.

I was convinced as I sat in the chair that everything would be absolutely fine. I saw Tess and Jaclyn look at one another nervously. Pamela was dabbing her eyes with a tissue, but she has allergies.

Alfred kept his hand on my shoulder. I looked up at him, and he stared at a point on the far wall, as though he was boring a hole into it. No one said a word. In my family, there has never been a gathering where there wasn't constant noise and continuous conversation. Small arguments flare up like those paper wrappers lit with a match on confetti cookies, blowing out into a giant orange flame and then floating off like loose ash.

If I was going to worry, there was no point to it then. Whatever happened had already happened. I chose to believe that Gianluca was going to be fine. I clenched my fists so tightly, the nails broke through the skin on my palms. I didn't know it then, but I was trying to hold on for dear life.

A doctor pushed the conference door open in his scrubs. His face held a particular intensity, but I didn't read it as doom. He sat down at the table.

"Who is Valentine?" he asked.

"I am."

"I'm Ed Jansen, and I was your husband's surgeon."

"How is he?"

"I'm so sorry. We did everything we could—"

I held up my hand. "Please, Dr. Jansen, don't say anything. Please. Just take me to him."

My sisters protested. My brother tried to reason with me. My father kept saying, "Valentine, Valentine," over and over again. Pamela began to sob.

"I want to see him now, Doctor. Right now."

"Come with me."

Dr. Jansen took me down a long hallway. The fluorescent

light overhead was blinking. It was spitting out the smallest sputters of light and then dimming, only to charge back. It was like the rewind of a movie reel. The light came and went, and with it, any understanding of what could be seen.

My legs were only holding me up because I was determined to be with my husband. I thought of Alfie. She was with my mother. She was safe. I was not. My husband had died, but I would not say the words.

"If you'll wait here, I'll bring you in."

The doctor went into a room, leaving me alone in the hallway. I looked down at my hand. I had forgotten to put my wedding ring on that morning. I couldn't work wearing a ring, and, in a rush to get Alfie to her music class, I'd forgotten to put it on.

It was an ongoing joke in our house. My husband never took his ring off, and I never had mine on.

Did I doubt sometimes that I should be married? Is that why I wore the ring here and there and not always? I loved him, but did I really believe he was mine and I was his?

I'd been so busy trying not to surrender to true love, I'd pushed it away. I'd pushed *him* away. But now he was gone, and there would be no proving it any longer. I wasn't given the gift of time, but I wouldn't have known what to do with it had it been mine.

I remembered Orsola. Dominic. Gram. I would have to call them. But I wouldn't until after I saw my husband.

Dr. Jansen came out of the room with a nurse.

"This is Elizabeth Beverly, my surgical nurse. This is Valentine, the wife of our patient."

"I'm so sorry," she said.

"May I see him?"

She handed me my husband's file.

When someone dies in a hospital, they are pushed through a process similar to the one they have when they are born. One year ago, Alfie was weighed and measured, named and filed, on the third floor. She was tested and swaddled and delivered to me.

Today, on the fifth floor, my husband's moment of death was noted: 11:03 a.m.

Cause of death: Aortic embolism. Age: Fifty-four. Married: Yes. There were lots of other lines filled with information, but I saw all I needed to see. I needed to see the *yes*. Proof that we loved each other. Proof that we'd decided to share our lives. Proof that we were married and that we were happy.

I looked at the married *yes*.

Nurse Beverly brought me into the room. Gianluca lay on a gurney, covered with a clean white sheet. There was a threefold blanket covering his calves and feet. I began to weep and placed my face against his, encircling my arm around his head. I ran my hands through his thick hair.

His body was still warm. I nestled into him. I decided to look at his chest, which was bandaged only where they'd entered his body. His stomach, his arms, his hands, and his neck were just as they were when I left him that morning.

I am someone who has to see it to believe. I have to understand why, and if there is no answer, I want a spiritual reason. Something told me, as I kissed my husband's neck and hands and face for the last time, that I would never know.

The nurse let me stay a long time, until she couldn't. She helped me to the door, and in my hand placed a bag with my husband's wedding ring, his clothes, and his socks, one blue and one black. She pushed the door open to the hallway, and there, under the light that wouldn't stay on, were my father and my brother. The men of our family. They waited for me like two good soldiers. They honored my husband with their concern for me. I didn't have to be strong around them.

My father took one arm, and my brother the other. They walked me down the hallway, and I swear they carried me, as I could not feel anything. I wept the kind of tears that make no sound. But when I hung my head, I saw them hit the ground.

Before we pushed through the doors, I stopped and fished for my phone. I called my grandmother and Dominic. Alfred had let them know that Gianluca was having surgery.

"Dominic?"

"How is he, Valentine?"

"I'm so sorry. He didn't make it."

"Why? What happened?"

"His heart stopped, and they couldn't save him."

Dominic began to weep, and I could hear Gram encouraging him to be strong.

"Nessun padre ha mai voluto bene a un figlio tanto quanto io ho voluto bene a lui," Dominic said to me.

"He knew, Dominic. He knew you loved him."

I called Orsola. Alfred had also called her to let her know that Gianluca was in surgery.

"Orsola, it's Valentine."

"Oh no."

"I'm sorry, honey. Your father loved you with all his heart." As I mentioned her father's heart, I broke down again. Gianluca Vechiarelli had been all heart to anyone who was lucky enough to be loved by him.

Orsola was bereft and could not speak. Mirella got on the phone. "Valentina, it's Mirella. What happened?"

"He had a heart condition since he was born. And the worst happened."

"I'm very sorry, Valentina." Mirella's voice broke. "I loved him too."

Gianluca had liked to go to mass at St. Patrick's Old Cathedral on Mott Street. Italians from the other side, and those of us from this one, find our deepest similarities in church. The mass is the same everywhere, as is the authority of the priests and the structure of the hierarchy. You feel the same sense of peace in Old St. Pat's that you do in the pews of Santa Maria Gloria in Arezzo. Same candles to light, same kneelers, the same statues. The son of a Jewish mother had looked to Mary, another Jewish mother, for strength.

There was so much to do quickly, it was overwhelming. Gabriel was a lifesaver. He figured out how to get the family here from Italy. He made the beds and filled the refrigerator and watched Alfie.

My mother and sisters took care of the rest. They apply the same care to everything they do. They helped plan travel, lodging, and food. They printed up the programs and made runs to the airport. They did everything they could do for me, and didn't feel like they could do enough.

I was two people the week Gianluca died. I got on the floor and played with our baby, and then I would turn away and cry for this little girl who would never have her father.

I slept in his T-shirt. I slipped my feet into his giant shoes. I held his wedding ring. I wore it on my thumb until, afraid of losing it, I wore it around my neck. I read every e-mail he'd sent and every one he'd received. I took a check that he had signed in his checkbook and put his signature next to his photograph on the mirror.

I went into the bathroom and put his toothbrush and razor in a ziplock bag and put it in my dresser. I sniffed the cologne in the bottle but did not dare spray it. It would have to last the rest of my life.

I went into the kitchen and examined the receipt of the last things he'd purchased at the grocery store. What good would it do me to know that he'd bought a bar of dark chocolate and three oranges? But I had to know. I had to know everything.

I went through pictures and pictures. I listened to his phone messages. I went through his phone and printed out all the pictures he had taken of Alfie and me. I printed out the last photo he took with Alfie the morning he died.

I was keeping busy, finding proof that we had loved each other and that what we had was real. I had to know where every wedding picture was. I demanded that my sisters go to their houses and print out every photo they ever took of him and me and the baby. I was bossy and insufferable and miserable. I was learning how to be a widow.

Gianluca's funeral took place on December 20, 2012, at St. Patrick's Old Cathedral on Mott Street. It was five days before Christmas. There was a Christmas pageant and a concert. In the midst of all this celebration, my husband needed a proper funeral.

The crèche outside the church had been set in straw and lit in the manger. Lifelike Mary and Joseph, the sheep, and the Gloria angel, but no baby Jesus, because that was placed in the crèche on Christmas Day. There was a gaping hole in the scene, and it bothered me that the baby was not there. I wanted the holy family in full, all three of them, for the funeral. Alfred arranged it with the priest.

Inside, Old St. Pat's had the scent of evergreen and blue spruce. It was decorated for Christmas, but the Advent wreath remained. My husband's casket was set amid the anticipation of Christmas. There was something right about that, but it did nothing to make me feel redeemed. My daughter wriggled in my arms through the mass. I wanted her to be there, so someday, when she asked, I could tell her she was present.

Chiara and Charisma read the Prayer of Saint Francis aloud. All those devotional cards I had bought up on our last trip to Assisi had been distributed through the family and had some meaning for us now. The girls took turns reading from the cards we had brought from our vacation.

Lord, make me an instrument of your peace.
Where there is hatred, let me sow love;
where there is injury, pardon;
where there is doubt, faith;
where there is despair, hope;
where there is darkness, light;
and where there is sadness, joy.

O Divine Master, grant that I may not so much seek
to be consoled as to console;
to be understood as to understand;
to be loved as to love.
For it is in giving that we receive;
it is in pardoning that we are pardoned;
and it is in dying that we are born to eternal life

At the end of the mass, the priest asked anyone who wanted to speak to come forward. My brother gave a eulogy. Cousin Don spoke. Orsola chose not to, but I decided to say something. I didn't think I could, but when I thought of Alfie, I thought she deserved to have her mother speak about her father. So, I told this story.

"One day, Gianluca was cutting leather in the shop. And we got in an argument.

"I was building a pair of shoes, and we began to speak about where art comes from. And he told me the story of the shoemaker and the elves, the Italian version.

"It turns out, he told me, that elves were not real. It was the shoemaker who, when he laid out the leather and lay down to dream, was actually dreaming the shoe, and he built the shoe from the picture he had in his mind. It wasn't magic. It was knowing what you needed to do and finding the will within yourself to create it.

"I believed in the elves. I believed that when you were most weary, most down on your luck, the poorest you could possibly be, you couldn't do it on your own. You needed help. And today I am right.

"Dominic, you gave me the gift of your son. He loved you so much. The thought of losing you was so terrible he couldn't think about it.

"Mirella, thank you for taking such good care of Orsola. The loss of her father is terrible, and you are always there for her.

"My family. Without you, I don't know how I would have gotten through the events of the past few days. You carried me and Alfie. Thank you.

"The man we love, Orsola and Alfie's father, Matteo's father-in-law, and Francesco's Nonno, is in heaven. Now, I know this for sure, because a better man never lived. He was kind, he was funny, he was talented, and he could make things with his hands.

"He loved everyone in this room, even when we didn't love him.

"I leave you with the words of my husband, which he wrote to our daughter on the day she was born, one year ago tomorrow. He wrote:

Alfie, you are a miracle. I have a baby girl. I am so happy! I had one before, you know, Orsola. You will love her very much. You are named for your grandfather, your mother's father, and my mother. I still cannot speak about my mother. I miss her too much. But I will be sure and make an exception when it comes to you. I will tell you all about her, Alfreda Magdalena, because it is a mother you can't live without. A mother who will sustain you. And a mother who knows your heart better than you will ever know it yourself.

Ti Amo,
Your Papa

12

I was thinking of June Lawton as I put out the silver coffee urn on the server in our dining room. We'd had her funeral luncheon here, and the mourners were a ragtag bunch of Village eccentrics offset by the health nuts that she met at Integral Yoga.

Aunt Feen came charging toward me in her funeral/wedding/Sunday black suit. She smelled like mothballs and Aqua Net.

"I can't believe this happened to you," she said. "I'm sorry."

"Thank you."

"You know, I was reminiscing as I was sitting in church. And I remembered that wonderful car ride when Gianluca drove me home from Jersey that Christmas. He was so handsome and tall. He had to push the seat so far back with those long legs of his. I had a crick in my neck from turning to talk to him. But I'll remember it forever. He was so chatty that night."

"Yes, he was, Aunt Feen."

"Came into my house. It was the only time he was in it."

"Yep."

"Hey, you need anything, you tell me."

"Just pray for me."

"I never miss a novena."

The house was beginning to fill with mourners. I'd done enough of these, and attended enough, to know that it would become loud, there would be laughter, and people would try and forget their sadness with food and conversation. Alfie would know it as another day when her family was over for dinner. She sat on Dominic's lap. Her grandfather was very familiar to her. She kept grabbing his nose, just as she had Gianluca's. After a while, Dominic gave her to me with a quick kiss.

Dominic got up and went into the hallway that led to the stairs to the roof. When I saw him go, I handed the baby to Gram and followed him.

He had pushed the door open and walked across the roof. There were about two inches of snow on the roof. It looked like a white carpet. Dominic went to the edge, buried his face in his hands, and wept.

"Dominic? I'm so sorry."

"I don't know what I will do."

"You will hold on to Gram. And Orsola, and Francesco, and Alfie and me. That's what you'll do."

"We spoke every day."

"I know."

"He was such a good son."

"He wanted to move us home to Italy, you know."

"Yes, yes, but you had the factory."

"I'm sorry we didn't just live in your house with you for this year."

"Nothing could have saved him."

"I don't know. That air in Arezzo is a pretty good healer."

"It is."

"Dominic, is there anything you need from me?"

"No, nothing."

"There must be something."

"I would like to have a funeral in Arezzo."

"That's beautiful. We'll be there."

"A mass."

"Of course."

Dominic was trying to tell me something, but he couldn't seem to ask me for what he needed.

"Dominic, do you want me to bring Gianluca home?"

He began to cry. He nodded that he did. "I didn't want to ask," he said.

"But he's your son. He belongs with you. He belongs at home."

"Thank you."

When it comes to the Vechiarelli men, a woman has to be a mind reader. They will never come out with what they want. You have to guess until you hit it. And when you hit it, it is so completely worth it.

"Gianluca told me so much about you. And he loved his mother so much. Will you do something for me?"

"Of course."

"Will you write down the story of how you met Magdalena? What she looked like, why you chose her, why she chose you?"

"Yes, I will do it."

"Gianluca and she were very close."

"Very close."

"Come on. It's cold out here. The last thing you need is the flu. Gram will kill me."

Dominic kicked the dusting of snow off his shoes before going back down the steps. I had turned to pull the door shut when I saw a shard of blue peeking through the snow by the fountain of Saint Francis. I went to it and brushed my hand across the stone.

PALAZZO VECHIARELLI was revealed beneath it. I leaned against the wall for a moment, trying to regain my composure. I had to fight my instinct not to blame myself for everything that had gone wrong, every argument we had up to the moment he died. I was ashamed that I was not wise, and angry that I had not given him every small thing he wanted. He deserved that and so much more.

The house was overflowing with mourners. I saw Orsola and her husband standing against the wall by the windows. Orsola was bereft. She watched as her son ran around the room. Matteo chased Francesco through the crowd.

When I saw that Mirella had been pulled away by Aunt Feen, I seized my moment and invited Orsola back to the bedroom.

"How are you doing?" I asked her.

"Terrible. And you?"

"You know how it is. We have babies to take care of."

"It helps."

"Orsola, you know, I still have my dad, so I don't know how you feel. But I worry about losing my father, and I understand how awful the thought of it is."

"There is nothing to be done."

"We did everything we could."

"I know."

"Your dad loved you so much, and he thought about you every day."

"I wish he could have been in Italy with us, but he wanted to be here with you."

"I'm sorry." I felt the stab of regret anew, and had a feeling that it would be the first of many.

"Nobody gets everything they want, Valentina."

"I can't say that. I had everything."

"You know, he was so nervous that we might not get along. My father came to ask me if it would be all right to ask you to marry him."

"You must've said yes."

"He said something very wise. He said a man should not be alone. I was so happy when you married him because I knew he'd never be alone."

"I did everything I could. I wasn't perfect. But I loved him. And I married him for many reasons but mostly because of you. I saw how you turned out and I said, this must be one special person who could raise a daughter like you."

"Thank you, Valentine."

Orsola's eyes fell on the nightstand and the framed photograph of Gianluca and his mother.

I handed it to her. "Here, you take this. Your father loved this photograph. It's your grandmother."

Orsola closed the stand on the frame and held the picture tightly to her chest.

I opened Gianluca's closet. "Come here, Orsola. You take whatever you want. However much you want." I pulled a new duffel from the floor of Gianluca's closet. "Here, you fill it. And if you need another, it's right here."

"Anything I want?"

"Anything." I handed her a jewelry case. "I kept a pair of cuff links for Alfie. But you take the rest. You have a husband and a son, and they will need to remember your father."

Orsola's eyes brimmed with tears. "You're too kind. I wanted something of my father's, but I was afraid to ask."

"Here's the deal. If you leave here without something tonight and you want it, I'll bring it to you. I made copies of all the photographs he took. There are many of you through the years."

"I thought they were lost." She wiped away her tears.

"I put them all on a disc for you. I had to do something. And so I collected everything I could."

Orsola put her arms around me. "I love you, Valentine."

"No matter what, you will always have us. And I want Alfie to grow up with Francesco, and all the many babies you'll have down the line. We have to stay close. We're family."

There was a soft rap on the door. Mirella opened it.

"May I come in?" she asked.

Mirella came into the bedroom I'd shared with her ex-husband. It had to be strange for her to be there, because it was strange for me. She didn't sit on the bed with Orsola and me. She perched instead on the end of the chaise.

"Mama, Valentine gave me all of Papa's jewelry. And she told me to take whatever I wanted."

Mirella looked at me gratefully. "Thank you, Valentine."

"I'm going to check on Francesco," Orsola said. For the first time, I was alone with Mirella.

"The funeral was lovely," Mirella said, looking at her hands.

"I'm sorry your husband couldn't make it, but I understand. It's difficult." Then it was my turn to look at my hands.

"They never really liked one another."

"That's understandable."

"Massimo is a very rigid person, and he drew a very sharp line. He didn't want to be at any event where Gianluca was in attendance."

"That's too bad."

"No, it's fine. Orsola had her parents together, and that's what mattered."

"I have a couple of questions for you."

"Of course."

"Did you know that Gianluca had a heart problem?"

She nodded that she did. "The doctors said it might not ever be an issue. But Gianluca was not one to go to doctors. He thought he knew best about his health."

"I couldn't get him to go for a physical. I really didn't want to marry an Italian."

"So stubborn."

"I knew what I was in for, but he proved to be a very good husband and father."

"Alfie is a beautiful little girl."

"He loved her."

"I wanted to have a second baby with him. It just didn't happen for us. Sometimes I think if the baby would have come, it might have changed the end of the story. But it wasn't my story to change. You see, you were meant to have your baby, and the plan unfolded exactly as it should have."

"Do you have any regrets?" I asked her.

"Too many. But you don't think your ex-husband will ever

die. If you did, you'd never divorce him." Mirella's eyes filled with tears. I gave her a tissue. I understood what it was to make a baby with someone. Of course she loved him, and she always would.

Divorce and separation are just labels. There is no finality in a divorce in an Italian family. The connection remains. Just as we believe in the afterlife, an eternity of time where souls never die, so we believe the bonds we share with one another here sustain us through everlasting life.

Once family, always family. And once a wife, forever one, even in divorce. I had to share Gianluca with Mirella. It was the Italian way.

I wandered through the reception, trying to get my bearings, but I was numb. My mind raced as people expressed their sympathy. As they spoke, I did not hear them. I was planning to pack quickly and take Alfie and go to Santa Margherita Ligure and find him there. I believed that he was there waiting for me. I wanted to believe this was all a misunderstanding. It couldn't be true.

Don Pipino put his arms around me. "I'm so sorry, Valentine."

"Thank you, cousin."

"Gianluca was a great man. He wanted to give you everything you wanted. Including our factory."

"He worked hard on it." I didn't want to talk about the factory. I didn't want to talk about work. I just wanted my husband back.

"You know, Carl cut us a deal on the building, but the bank wouldn't give us the money to transport the machinery from Argentina. And that cost more than the building."

"Don, I'm sorry. I can't talk about this right now."

"But I'm trying to tell you something. Gianluca had a house in Italy somewhere. He sold it to finance the move of the equipment."

"He did what?"

"He sold a house."

"Don, how do you know this?"

"I knew. Your brother knew. Bret knew."

"Why didn't you tell me? Why didn't they?" My mind raced. Would this have made a difference? Did selling the house break his heart? Did my refusal to move to Italy cause him to give up any hope of returning? Had I denied him the breadth of his dreams, when he had made all of mine come true? "Oh my God." I collapsed into a chair.

Don kneeled next to me. "Hey, hey, he wanted to make it happen for you. He told me that anytime he could make you happy, it was double happiness for him."

"I'd do anything to have him back. Anything to be in Santa Margherita with him right now with Alfie. If only one of you would've told me the truth."

"Would it have made any difference, Valentine?" Don looked at me.

"Well, yes—I would've done everything differently."

"And if his fate was to die young, you now control fate?"

"No, of course not."

"Hey, I lost my wife too. The worst part of being a widower is going over all the things you would've done to make them happy, to make them stay. But I learned one thing in the process. If I had died first, she would have tortured herself with the same thoughts. So stop it. Appreciate what he did for you.

Don't be angry at the people who put the factory together so you could have your dream. Besides, Gianluca swore us to secrecy. He said by the time he had to tell you that he'd sold the house, you wouldn't care anymore. You'd have your factory, and that was your real dream."

I couldn't speak.

"He was a special guy. He didn't want to burden you. He wanted to make your life easier. He knew your plate was full, and he wanted you to enjoy the meal, not be overwhelmed by it. I'm so sorry, kid."

Jaclyn and Tess moved across the room. I must have looked like I needed shoring up. "Get me out of here," I said to them softly. The next thing I remember is Gabriel coming into our room, holding a cup of tea, with my sisters draped on the bed beside me.

"I'm going to kill Aunt Feen," Gabriel said as he handed me the tea. "I saw her put a place setting of your silver in her purse."

"She's stealing from her own niece?" Jaclyn sat up, mortified.

"On this day of all days?" Tess was horrified.

"It gets worse. She told me there was twenty in it for me if I didn't say anything."

The thought of that made me smile. "Did you take the twenty?"

"Damn right."

Gabriel made me an appointment with K. Cazana, a world-renowned psychic. He did this not because he believed in psychics, but because he was trying to find some way to help me. I'd become a shell of a person in the first few weeks after Gianluca died. I wandered through my days tethered to the world by a shaky thread of complete and utter disbelief.

I felt I had no purpose. Alfie provided a reprieve from my haunted days and nights. Luckily, she was surrounded by family. She was so used to being with my parents, or with Tess and Jaclyn and their children, that not much in her life had changed. I dreaded the day I would have to explain where her father had gone.

She must have wondered where the tall man with the blue eyes who took such good care of her went, but a one-year-old wouldn't be able to understand it, even though she buried her face in her father's pillow. I think she remembered his scent.

I agreed to go to the psychic because I felt that she might know something, some small piece of information. I wanted to know why he'd died suddenly, and if he'd chosen it. Had taking him away from Italy been the root cause of his death?

I believed that sometimes people chose death. But the last thing he said to me was, "I'm not going anywhere."

When I sat down in Ms. Cazana's office on Twelfth Street, I studied the room for clues. But there wasn't a photo of a guru, no tarot cards, just a plain sofa and chair. It was more a therapist's office than a medium's.

As soon as she entered the room, I began to cry. The thought of communicating with the man that I'd lost had seemed like a good idea when I was home missing him, but in the moment, I was afraid.

What if I had done something to make him leave? I told her about the house.

Why hadn't I seen the physical signs? I explained every argument I ever had with my husband.

He'd mentioned something about his heart in Buenos

Aires, and I had forgotten it. Roberta reminded me of it, because she remembered it. I was the guardian of my husband's health. How had I let that slip through the cracks?

Ms. Cazana gave me a tissue.

"I understand what happened with your husband, but why are you here?"

"I want to talk to him."

She closed her eyes. "Where is the lake?"

My mind raced. "In Italy."

"He almost died there once. Almost drowned. There's a castle."

"I know it."

"This man almost died three times. Once in the lake. Once in a car. And a third time of a broken heart."

"What broken heart?"

"He loved a girl and she left him."

"Why?"

"He wanted a child with her but was afraid that she would take the baby from him."

"What?" I was stunned. I remembered asking Gianluca about Mirella and the end of their marriage.

"He wanted a child with her."

"He had one."

"A second child. The relationship was over." She sighed and then repeated herself. "He was afraid to lose the child because he was certain she would take the child from him."

I leaned back in the chair and had a revelation. My husband wanted the second baby with Mirella but didn't think the marriage was strong enough. That's why he waited so long to remarry. Orsola came first, just as Alfie had in the last year of his life. I shuddered when I thought about our arguments about nursing the baby, and my working hours. "Did he know he was going to die?"

"It doesn't matter."

"It does to me."

"It shouldn't."

"Why?"

"Because he had to go."

"Why?" I pressed her.

"He was part of your life, but there is more for you."

"I don't want it."

"That's not your choice. Do you want to know what I see for you?"

"I don't care."

"When the grief goes, and it will, you will be surrounded by loved ones. I see nothing but family, loving family, around you. Your dreams have no limit. None."

She continued to speak. She spoke of my parents, and a land far away, and said that my baby girl would grow up and become a doctor. She said all of it with such conviction that had I not been so sad, I might have believed her.

What she told me that stuck with me was that Gianluca was only part of my story. But isn't that true of everyone that you love and who loves you? Why wasn't I dreaming of my husband? Where had he gone? And why couldn't he reach through to find some way of communicating with me? He'd said he wasn't going anywhere. I held him to his word.

Did Gianluca know he was going to die?

Who goes about doing ordinary things like making a pot of gravy and folding the laundry minutes before the worst happens?

Who showers and gets dressed and puts on one black sock and one blue one?

Or does a man who knows he is going to die rise early, feed his baby, and bring her into bed, where the mother rolls over to awaken to father and daughter with matching blue eyes, looking at her? Was everything I had with Gianluca for the sole purpose of leaving me with that moment—the three of us, a family? A perfect family.

Was this the meaning in our grief? Was our ordinary routine each morning the point? The mother and father encircled the baby, taking in the scent of her new skin, the soft tufts of black hair, the long, slender fingers with sharp nails that needed a trim, the grip of the small foot in a soft white sock that wriggled out of her mother's grasp as the baby rolled over and onto her father's chest.

He couldn't have known that this was the day he would leave this life. This is not the picture of a dying man, but of one who is wholly and completely alive. Gianluca knew what was important and tried to show me so I might know joy. This is the man I had come to count on, to lean on, the one who protected us. We were safe in our small circle. I would never know that security again.

"Val?"

I heard my father's voice from the other side of the bedroom door. I was so tired, I did not answer him.

"Val?"

I shut my eyes so he'd think I was asleep. He pushed the door open.

"Valentine?"

I opened my eyes. My father came and sat on the side of the bed. Though it was daytime outside, I had the shade pulled down, so the room was dark. My father flipped the switch on the bedside lamp.

"Honey, you can't keep doing this."

A few days after the funeral, I thought I was okay. I was answering letters sent to me about Gianluca, and Alfie was taking a nap. The pen in my hand became very heavy. So heavy, I couldn't lift it. The room began to feel oppressive, as though I couldn't breathe.

I couldn't feel my body or hear my breath.

I called my mother. She came immediately. I asked her to take Alfie home with her, that something was wrong with me. They called my doctor, who came to see me. I was physically okay, he said, but I was grieving, and everybody grieves in a different way. I took to my room and stayed there. I couldn't face anyone. I couldn't face myself.

Mom called Gabriel, and he came back to live at 166 Perry Street. I still hadn't left the bedroom.

After three weeks of solitude, I still had no desire to leave the room. Now my father was angry, though he tried not to show it.

"You're hiding," my father said.

"I don't want to see anyone."

"Alfie is asking for you."

"Bring her home."

"It's okay. She's with her cousins. With your mom."

"I don't know how to pretend to be okay, like all of this didn't happen."

"Val, we can't change it. But you have to get out of this bed."

"Why?"

"Because it's been almost a month. Because you have responsibilities."

"I don't want them."

"It's too late. You have them."

"I want him back." I began to cry. My father lay down beside me in bed.

"I can't bring him back."

"He promised he was going to be all right. His last words were, 'I'm not going anywhere.' Shouldn't that count for something?"

"It should," Dad said helplessly.

"He promised."

"Maybe he meant that he would always be with you. Even in death. No matter what. Is that a possibility?"

"I keep trying to look for clues and signs and some warning that this was going to happen, and I can't find a single one. I want to know *why* this happened."

"I don't know. There must be a reason."

"What is it?"

"I wish I knew. But you know, even if you had the answer, what good would it do? How would that information help you, Val? Really, what good would it be to know the grand scheme?"

"What am I going to do?"

"You have to figure that out. You have to make a plan with where you are right now and what you have. You can't plan the future based on what you don't have anymore."

"I can't think. It's all just doom." I rolled over in the bed, away from my father. We didn't talk for a long while. My father was present with me, and that's all he could do. And I couldn't offer him anything. I couldn't assuage his worry, I couldn't make him feel better, not even for a second. Finally, Dad said:

"Alfie ate blueberries today."

"She's never had them." I turned to face him.

"She liked them."

"She did?"

"Loved 'em."

"How did she have them?"

"One by one. What do you mean?"

"Did Mom freeze them?"

"Who eats frozen blueberries?"

"It's a new thing."

"It's a stupid idea."

The way my dad said this made me laugh. My laugh sounded strange to me, as though it was new. It was the first time I'd laughed since Gianluca died.

"Is that all it took? Frozen blueberries?"

"I guess."

"Wait till she eats an artichoke. We'll have a laugh riot." My dad smiled at me. "I want you to get up and come up to the roof with me."

"It's too cold."

"It's New York in January. Of course it's cold. Every person from here to the Rockaways is freezing their ass off. Why should we be exiled?"

"You mean *exempt.*"

"Right, right, whatever left out means. What am I now, King of Synonyms?"

"You are not to make Alfie's flash cards."

"Forget it. Your mother already started. She's putting words on wallpaper samples."

"She found a use for them."

"How many decoupage coasters does this family need?" Dad took my hand. "Come with me. Please. You need air. You need to see the sky again."

"Go and tell me what it's like."

"I'm not your errand boy, Missy." Dad went around to the side of the bed and helped me up. "Come on. You're not dying, Valentine. You're heartbroken."

"There's a difference?"

"There's a difference."

"Dad, I did everything wrong."

"What are you talking about?"

"He wanted to raise Alfie in Italy. I worked too much. I didn't pay enough attention to him. I was a terrible wife."

"So what?"

"I blew it! That's what."

"He chose you, didn't he?"

I nodded.

"So he got what he wanted. He had his dream. A man who gets his dream in this life has everything."

My dad helped me walk across the snowy roof. It was freezing cold, but I didn't mind. The air felt good. When I inhaled deeply, it made me cough. I realized that I'd barely been breathing since Gianluca died.

The Hudson River was frozen except for a strip of water flowing in the center. I'd never seen this configuration on the river before. It was odd to me, but it was also intriguing.

Why didn't the river freeze completely over? And how was there one small strip that did not freeze? What did it mean?

I pondered this as my father held my hand.

"You have a daughter, Val," he said. "She's your gift and your miracle. You know, a gift isn't owed you. You don't get a healthy baby just like that. But you did. And she loves you. She needs her mother. I want you to get your life back on track so you can bring her home."

"I want her to come home."

"Then show us that you want to get better."

"Can you and Mom come and stay for a while?"

"Here? Sure, sure. Whatever it takes."

My parents moved in. I didn't invite them as a daughter. I needed them as grandparents. I needed to surround Alfie with chatter and noise, gatherings and meals. With family. I had to make her feel a part of something now that we were all alone. I would look back on my parents' generosity and understand it one day. There isn't anything a parent won't do for her child. There is no limit on love.

My mother was thumbing through a magazine late one night when I went into the kitchen to get a glass of water.

"Are you okay, Val?" she asked.

"Mom, please stop asking me that."

"Come here."

I sat next to my mother with the glass of water. "What is it?"

"What are you thinking?"

"That I did everything wrong. Every decision I made was wrong. I never compromised. I insisted. I ruined my husband's life. I didn't change my name. He wanted me to change it, and I wouldn't. Why wouldn't I do it? I want every piece of him I could possibly have now."

"You didn't know he was going to die."

"I should have lived knowing that he would. I should have

been aware. No, I was too busy defending my turf, climbing the ladder—to what? There's nothing but air up there. There's nothing to hang on to. There's no Gianluca."

"You made him happy."

"Did I? I thought nothing would change when I married him or had his baby. But whenever one person takes on caring for another, all lives change. Those who provide the care and those who receive it. And I acted like that wasn't true. I acted like I could handle all of it. What made me think for one second that opening a factory would fill me up?"

"I am not going to let you sit here and denigrate yourself like this. You're an artist. You have talent. A lot of people put a lot of effort into you, not the least of whom was me. I know you. I'm your mother. And you didn't do anything wrong. You were strong and assertive and ambitious. Since when is *that* a crime? And if your work was such a nothing, then why did Gianluca spend so much of his time helping you realize your dreams? If you're an idiot, then he was a bigger one. But I don't think he was an idiot. I think he was marvelous and kind and he loved you. Why won't you think of that?"

"Because when I do, my heart breaks a little more."

"Valentine, I am going to say something that will shock you. It's time for you to go back to work. Enough weeping and wailing—you can do it over the leather, but not the suede."

"Ma . . ."

"I am giving you a gift with this advice. Do you ever wonder why I am constantly redecorating?"

"I think Dad wants to know more than me."

"I redecorate when my artistic spirit needs to take flight to lift me up in my life. Every time I change the wallpaper or redo the yard, it's when I don't have control of the world around me. When your dad got the prostate cancer, I went English country. When he left me for that spell, I did the house in Louis Quatorze. You see, we all run. We all hide. When we're disappointed or heartbroken or grief-stricken, we all bury ourselves in our version of living. We want to outrun the pain. But honey, it's one wily bastard. You can't catch up with it to stop it. So you have to live. *That's* how you beat it. You have a business to run and art to share. You need to go back and do that again. It's the only thing that will heal you."

I gave my mother a hug and went back upstairs. I checked on the baby, then crawled into bed. I stayed safely on my side, where I could pretend that nothing had changed. And that's how I went to sleep that night, and for many weeks following it.

$\sim$ **13** $\sim$

Gianluca's death happens all over again, every day. There's an e-mail or a letter or a piece of mail from a cousin or a tool company that arrives, and I see his name and my heart stops.

I'm not far from his passing yet. Six months later, the pain is fresh. The only passage of time that uses months as markers is when you have a baby—*She's sixteen months old*, or *She's twenty-three months old*—or when you're a widow—*It's been two months, it's been eleven months*. How bizarre that I am both new mother and widow.

Caring for a baby is happy exhaustion; grief is debilitating. The ache and sadness dulls over time, but it hasn't left me. Sometimes real life intercedes, and for a moment I forget the story that led me to this day. As soon as I'm reminded he's not coming back, I remember the moment I lost him.

The ache returns, and I let it.

The only time I really let go of the pain is when I'm creating.

Creation is the opposite of destruction. The first lesson I learned in Catholic school still applies.

Somehow, sketching, drawing, drafting, cutting, sewing, buffing, and measuring lift me out of the moment and into the sacred place of imagination, where all that is required of me is to feel the textures of the leather, observe the drape of the fabric, and imagine a finished shoe.

The grief is like unwieldy fabric, familiar in my hands now. Sometimes it lies flat. Other times, I cannot for the life of me manage it into the desired shape.

I am most bereft when I can't sleep in the middle of the night, when panic and fear join me in bed. It's as if there's no room for me there. No one ever told me that grief moves in and becomes a permanent resident in your life. And no one told me that you have no choice in the matter. It's there.

And it's not going anywhere.

I get up when this chain of thought rattles loudly in my head. I go into Alfie's room and watch her as she sleeps, something my husband no longer has the luxury of doing.

I know then that happiness is not getting what I want or missing what I had, but in being useful, in being her mother. I must carry the story of her father forward in her life. That thread must not be dropped. Not his intent, not his aim, not his acumen, not his leatherworks or his point of view, but the essence of him, the love he had for her. That living love must be nurtured and kept alive and real so she might turn to it and know him as if he were still here.

My happiness will not come in the nourishment of the appetites I have fed all my life, but in *meaning*. I didn't get a long life with my husband, but that wasn't promised to me. I haven't been cheated out of anything, I just didn't get the big prize.

"Valentine. You didn't hit the chalk mark." Gabriel interrupts my thoughts, reaching across the cutting table and taking the sheet of leather from me. "Here, I'll do it. You don't have your mind on the game."

"Sorry."

My mother is wrapping an order under the windows. Her gold bangle bracelets jingle merrily as she tapes the box shut. Jaclyn and Tess are hunched over a laptop studying an ad our competitor has placed in the *New York Times*.

Outside the window, Charlie, Tom, and Dad are loading a truck with an order for Picardy Shoe Parlor in Mequon, Wisconsin.

Bret and Alfred sit at the desk and figure out a loan restructure. The factory in Youngstown is coming up on its first anniversary. Payroll is met, loans are being paid back, and we've added a third vendor to the order pool. The Supreme Macaroni Company is working, and I can't help but think that my husband willed it so.

I have everything I'll ever need in this room right now.

My family is all around me—my father and mother, my daughter, my sisters and their husbands, my brother and his wife, cousins in five states, Gram and Dominic in Italy—I have everything and everybody within reach with the press of a button on my phone, everyone except Gianluca. He built this life for me, as if he'd sat down at the table with a fresh sheet of butcher paper and sketched a life in a world that I could live in without him.

Gianluca took my vision for the shop and went about

building the dream. He made the deal with Cousin Don, found the space, and opened the factory in Youngstown. He gave me Alfie, and made sure that my family was close by to help me raise her.

The only way I can thank him is to raise Alfie to be a woman he would be proud to know and surround her with people who remember him, who can tell her the stories that came before her, before Gianluca and I met, before all of this was imagined.

I will probably always cry myself to sleep, but knowing this, someday the tears won't be sad, or filled with regret. Maybe they will be joyful, as the aspects of Gianluca Vechiarelli fill my own final days with the memory of what we had. Without him, life wouldn't have been so rich, nor our hearts so full. Memories, it turns out, take up as much space in the human heart as feelings.

All we have, all of this—a sturdy life filled with hard work, deadlines to honor, and my family, united under one roof with a common purpose—was Gianluca's idea. It was as if he chose the musicians, handed out the instruments, and let them play. The Italian way of life thrives on Perry Street. My dream is no longer to be the best and turn the biggest profit, but to enjoy my daughter and the family that loves her as much as I do, and as much as her father did.

Any happiness we enjoy—any feelings of security and this newfound treasure, our solidarity as a family, all of this and so much more—is because of him. My Gianluca.

What I remember is not what we ate for dinner, or what we were wearing, but what was *said*—the conversations, the words, the intent and the meaning. These make life full, and the memory of them will carry me through the rest of my life.

"Alfie is calling for you on the roof," Tess says from the doorway.

Pamela stops me to look at an ad campaign she designed for the web. She placed our winter line on a sea of emerald velvet. I swear since she came to work here, she's made this business as it's perceived in the world so much more elegant.

Clickety-Click has become the Muckety-Muck.

"I think it's dazzling," I tell her.

"Could use another tinker," she says. "I'm on it."

I take the stairs two at a time until I'm up to the roof. I push the door open. My nieces and nephews are showing Alfie and Bret's girls how to plant tomatoes.

All Alfie wants to do is water the dirt, so she stands over a pot without a plant in it and sprinkles water on the black earth.

Bret guides his daughter Piper to put a stake in the pot. He shows her how to tie the strings to the plant so it will grow straight in the sun. He is patient as she grapples with the stem, the stick, and the string. When she completes the task, he compliments her. He drags the pot to the side of the roof, where he lines it up in the sun with the others.

Alfie tugs Bret on the sleeve. She takes him by the hand and puts a stick in the pot. She digs in the black earth with her hands. He drops the plant into the well in the dirt. He pats the dirt to demonstrate. She follows suit. She puts her entire body into the patting down of the dirt until it is smooth.

Bret quickly ties the string up the stalk while Alfie holds it in place. Bret shows her how to rinse her hands in the clean water in the bucket. My daughter takes the watering can and pours it over the plant. She looks up at Bret, who smiles his approval. He lets her help him haul the plant over to the side of the roof.

A chill runs through me as I watch them. I remember when I was a girl and my grandfather and I planted tomatoes on this roof. I see how determined she is, how serious, how invested she is in doing a good job, how pleased she is that Bret approves of her hard work.

"Mama—" She turns to me and runs into my arms. "Tomato!"

"I see."

"He helped!" She points to Bret.

"Aunt Val, can we plant some flowers up here?" Chiara asks.

"You know, I was thinking sunflowers."

"Cool. Those grow really tall."

"Who wants cupcakes?" Tess says from the door.

A small stampede of her kids, Alfred's, Bret's, and my daughter make it to the door, whooping and hollering as they follow Tess down to the kitchen.

I stand and watch as Bret turns off the hose and winds it around the storage wheel. He adjusts the pots to tilt out a bit so they get the most sun. He places the chairs back around the table.

I watch him straighten the roof. I don't know why, but I can't help him. I just stand and watch, a bystander, frozen in the moment like one of those butterflies that lives for eternity in a resin paperweight.

Bret crosses the roof and joins me. "Are you okay?"

"I really miss him. A flyer came in the mail. I saw his name, and here I go." And out of nowhere, I begin to cry just like a new widow.

Bret takes me in his arms. I collapse in the strength of his grip and weep.

I cry for everything Alfie won't have, everything I will miss, and the terrible helplessness that comes from the interminable mourning that comes from sudden loss. Gianluca's death is final, and therefore it controls everything. I am rendered weak and useless by the finality of it all. The only thing I know, the only thing I believe, is that only Gianluca could make all of this better. There's my reprieve and I can never have it.

My heart is so broken, there is no hope of ever mending it without him.

My father thinks that when he willed me out of bed, I began the slow walk to acceptance of Gianluca's death. But really, I just got up for Alfie. She was my excuse to live. What kind of mother am I? I can't show her how to navigate sadness because I haven't figured out my own.

She is a girl who will never know her father, and I feel I have to be everything to her to make up for that loss.

If I was going to turn to anyone when the worst thing happened, it would have been my husband. But he was gone. In life, there is always a shot at a do-over. Only death doesn't allow one.

"You know, Val"—Bret digs in his pocket and hands me his handkerchief—"there's nothing sad about loving someone so much that nothing makes sense without him. It's the definition of joy."

"I don't feel joy anymore."

"You will."

"How do you know?"

"Because everything is a grace."

"Everything?"

"Everything," Bret says with such certainty that for a moment it's as real as anything I've ever known. "Come on. Let's check on the kids."

"What do they want for dinner?"

"What do you think? Macaroni."

Bret pushes the screen door open and goes down the stairs.

I dry my tears on Bret's handkerchief and take a deep breath. The scent of the earth, the spicy green of the new tomato plants, and the feeling of the warm sun on my face bring me back to my childhood, when I knew grace, but didn't have a name for it.

I remember the day my grandfather filled the barren plants with velvet tomatoes so I wouldn't lose hope. If Gianluca were here, he'd have me tell the story again. I don't want to forget it, so I race down the steps to tell Alfie.

Alfie and I took a pass on the feast of the Seven Fishes at Jaclyn's. Evidently, so did Aunt Feen, who decided that she'd rather not miss the *Country Christmas Special* starring Martina McBride and the Band Perry on TBS. It had come to that with Aunt Feen. She refused to get TiVo, so she had to be home so as not to miss her favorite programs. It might as well be 1955.

I hosted Christmas Day on Perry Street with Gabriel's help. He works in the shop, helps with Alfie, and as often as he can, makes me laugh.

I pulled all of Gram's silver out of the closet, spending a week polishing the heirlooms. Gram and Dominic had taken the guest room, and would be with us through the new year. They would head down to Florida to our cousins for the month of January. I saw Gram slowing down for the first time on this trip. Dominic had never used a redcap in his life, but now they needed one, and he coughed up the tip.

My sisters set the dining room table, built by my great-grandfather. They loaded the candelabra with red candles and festooned it with fresh holly. They placed the starched napkins on the plates and filled the crystal goblets with water. Alfie was keeping busy under the tree, moving ornaments gently from one lower branch to another. Gabriel bit his hand every time she touched one.

My father was hand-cranking ice cream on the roof. We could hear a spat in full force through the open window in the kitchen. My sisters, my brother, and I got a kick out of our parents. They still didn't know exactly how to get along, but it didn't matter. Neither of them could live without the other.

Pamela had designed our company Christmas cards this year. We gave her every task that involved words—whether on a gift basket or in an ad on Huff Post. She had blossomed in the glorious garden of self-reliance. Alfred and Pamela seemed to be getting along well, but a lot of that had to do with the fact that he gave her everything she wanted.

Gram called me from upstairs as Chiara put a roll on each bread plate on the table. I climbed the stairs quickly and joined her in the guest room.

"Your mother and father are having a brawl on the roof."

"Gram, that makes it Christmas."

"Dominic and Alfred went to pick up Feen."

I sat down on the bed and remembered when Gianluca and I drove Feen home that Christmas Eve. It was a night that lasted a year. She hadn't changed a bit in the interim. In fact, it seems we'd all changed, everyone but Aunt Feen.

"How are you holding up?" Gram asked.

"I'm okay," I told her honestly. "I had to assemble so much plastic crap for Alfie that to tell the truth, my mind was occupied."

"Good. I was worried when you didn't come to the feast at Jaclyn's."

"Gram, I know my limits. You get one meal out of me per holiday. I don't have the energy."

"I understand. There's something I wanted to talk to you about."

"Is it bad news?"

"No—Dominic told me something, and I thought it was important."

"What is it?"

"He remembered something that Gianluca said to him."

"Was it about Alfie?"

"No."

"Me?"

"No. The house in Santa Margherita."

When I heard the name of the town, it was a stab to my heart. It represented my husband's greatest sacrifice, and frankly, even with visits to grief counselors and psychics and pouring my heart out to Gabriel, I hadn't cracked that one yet. It still haunted me.

"Oh, I didn't mean to upset you all over again," Gram said.

"What did you want to tell me?"

"Gianluca had Dominic cash out an account in Arezzo when you bought the factory. And when Gianluca sold the house, Dominic did the transfer. And Dominic knew how much Gianluca loved that house. And he also knew how much Gianluca loved Italy. So he was worried that his son was cutting ties where he shouldn't. So he expressed his fears to his son. And Gianluca told him, 'You know, Papa, I have this house that was mine before I met Valentina. And we live in a house in Greenwich Village that belongs to the family, and neither of these belong to us. Someday, when Valentina is ready, we'll buy a house together, one that will be ours.' "

"But I didn't care about a house! I wanted him!"

"Don't you see? He didn't care either. He was happy with you. So stop mourning all these things that you think brought him sadness, because the fact is, you only brought him joy, even when you thought you weren't."

"Did I? I really didn't understand what it meant to be married. He brought me to the house, and I didn't feel it was mine. I was still drawing lines in the relationship like angles on pattern paper. But the whole time, we were one."

"Yes, you were."

"But I didn't know it. He knew it. And I didn't."

I began to cry, and Gram put her arms around me. "Do you think he would've ever told me about the house?"

Gram smiled. "He knew he would have to someday, but he wasn't worried. He knew you'd understand."

Gram and I went down the stairs to join the Christmas Day party. It was like walking into FAO Schwarz with a killer Italian buffet. Aunt Feen was guzzling a Fuzzy Navel while Alfred brought the pork roast to the table and my mother gathered the troops to sit. We took our places as Gabriel hoisted Alfie into her high chair.

Aunt Feen unfolded her napkin and placed it on her lap. "I hate when Christmas falls on a weekday. They do a schlock episode of *General Hospital* where they sing Christmas carols. I like blood and guts on my soaps, not warm and fuzzies."

Mom handed out the devotion cards, and we recited the prayer of Saint Francis. It's my mother's way of remembering Gianluca without saying his name.

"Jaclyn, go get that package I brought."

Jaclyn, busy wrangling the kids, shot Aunt Feen a look to kill.

"It's a gift for the entire family," Feen barked.

Jaclyn brought a large, square package wrapped in brown paper to the table.

"I had something made for you, Valentine."

"Oh, Aunt Feen, you shouldn't have."

"But I already did, so say thank you."

I ripped into the package. It was a painting. A painting of my family from Christmas Eve, the night Gianluca asked me to marry him. It was in a gold-leaf frame, very ornate, museum-quality even.

"I was at the beauty shop, and I was reading about these people in Denmark who make paintings from photographs. So I sent off for it." Aunt Feen lifted her bifocals and squinted at the painting. "I think it's pretty good."

"Not since John Singer Sargent . . . ," Gabriel said.

"I don't know about him. I just sent the family picture." Feen shrugged.

I picked Gianluca out in the middle of the family. My head was resting on his shoulder, and instead of dark brown hair, for whatever reason my hair was red, and it looked like I was wearing a wig. But it didn't matter. They had captured Gianluca perfectly. He was laughing with that wide-open smile of his.

"We don't look like ourselves—are you sure this is our family?" Mom asked.

"What the hell are you talking about? Don't you listen? I said I sent the photo."

"Then why do I look like Tony Bennett?" my father wanted to know.

"I don't know. Maybe you look like him."

"That's not me," my father insisted.

"Mom looks like Cher," Jaclyn said.

"When she was with Sonny, or now?" Mom wondered, as she squinted at the painting.

"We look like Destiny's Child, Tess. Look at us. They painted them over our faces."

"I'm telling you, somebody was pulling your leg with this thing, Auntie," Dad insisted.

"I like it," Feen said defensively. "What do you want from a bunch of Swedes?"

"I thought you said the artist was from Denmark," Tom piped up.

"It's one of those cold salmon-eating countries. The artist interpreted our family, and this is what he saw," Feen said defensively.

"I look like Yogi Bear," Charlie said.

"What the hell do you want? You look like him in real life."

Gram began to laugh at the absurdity of the bad painting. She couldn't stop. Soon, we were all laughing until we cried. Everyone of course, except Aunt Feen, who stood by the artist's vision, no matter how flawed it had been.

I don't know exactly when I began to sleep on Gianluca's side of the bed. Like any routine I fell into after my husband died, it seemed to happen naturally. The two years we were married seem like twenty on some days, and two seconds on others. The dreams that come when I sleep happen in and around water, they fold into my memories seamlessly. Sometimes I wake up and feel that I traveled through the night. I remember being pregnant with Alfie and swimming in the lake, just the three of us. I can't wait for Alfie to grow up so I can tell her the story and take her to the place where her father held me.

A widow relives her time with her husband over and over again, searching for clues and hoping to find some small proof that the love they shared here on earth was eternal. I haven't had much luck with that, but what I do have, the things I do remember, those moments, have a funny way of stringing together and sustaining me.

In my mind, I swim with Gianluca in the Blue Grotto. This was long before I loved him and he loved me. It was when we were new friends and had just met. It's like I'm there again. I feel the veins of coral on the cold rock walls and the warm blue water. I see the beams of pure white light as they cut through the rocks and dance on the surface of the water. I shiver at the touch of Gianluca's arms around me as we float in the deep. I even remember being afraid of the depths and then suddenly courageous and brazen as long as he stayed close.

I have decided that love is only real and true when it makes you feel safe. I am alone now, and without him, everything seems uncertain. It is then that I put on the necklace he gave me on our wedding day, and I look in the mirror and face our family history as it shimmers in the glass. It feels substantial, not just because the coral and the pearls are real, but because Gianluca gave it to me. The family heirloom connects me to the memory of him. I can touch it. It is proof that we married, that he loved me, and that for twenty-two months, he was mine.

Gianluca left me with coral and pearls and diamonds, but they were the least of his gifts to me. I have him in Alfie, who has his humor and blue eyes. I have the factory, which he bought and paid for with a house he loved but not as much as he loved me. He gave it up so I might have the Supreme Macaroni Company.

But it's the dream that keeps me connected to him.

I imagine returning to swim in the Blue Grotto, and somehow, I know that when I do, I'll find him there.

Acknowledgments

This book is dedicated to the memory of Violet Stampone Peters Ruggiero, my beloved cousin. Violet was born on May 18, 1926, at home on Garibaldi Avenue in Roseto, Pennsylvania, eventually marrying and moving across the street where she raised her family. She married Joseph Peters in 1951, had their daughter, Ann Carol, and was expecting their son, Joe, when her husband died suddenly of a heart attack. They had been married a little over a year. Eight years later she married Dominic "Bake" Ruggiero, and had Dominic, Connie Rose, and Phillip. Her highest dream was for the children from her first marriage to feel as one with the children of her second. She blended the families beautifully.

Violet worked as a button sewer in a blouse mill that was walking distance from her house. She loved her job, family, weekly Bingo, cleaning her house, and a stiff Manhattan cocktail before dinner. When I think of the people I most admire, Violet tops the list. She worked hard, laughed a lot, and made a big dish of macaroni every Sunday. She was an Italian girl who loved to be home. She once told me she didn't understand people who traveled. "Everything you need is right here," she said.

I am grateful to the brilliant team at HarperCollins, led by Brian Murray and Michael Morrison. Jonathan Burnham, my editor and publisher, has exquisite taste, a big heart, and a keen eye for detail. I believe every word he says because he says them with a British accent. Maya Ziv is his excellent right arm, and a treasure.

The marketing and publicity teams are amazing, thank you Kathy Schneider, Tina Andreadis, Kate D'Esmond, Leah Wasielewski, and Mark Ferguson. The novels are artfully designed by Leah Carlson-Stanisic, Robin Bilardello, and Eric Levy. Virginia Stanley, the queen of libraries is one in a million. Our sales reps are the best: Michael Morris, Josh Marwell, Andrea Rosen, Mary Beth Thomas, Doug Jones, Kathryn Walker, Kristin Bowers, Brian Grogan, Erin Gorham, Lillie Walsh, Rachel Levenberg, and Diane Jackson. Love our paperback team: Amy Baker, Mary Sasso, and Kathryn Ratcliffe-Lee.

Much heavy lifting at Harper's is done by the great Laura Brown, Katie O'Callaghan, Mary Ann Petyak, Stephanie Selah, Tom Hopke Jr., Kathryn Noonan, Annie Mazes, Milan Bozic, Feeza Mumtaz, Douglas Johnson, Eric Lovaas, Frank Albanese, Megan Hodnett, David Wolfson, and Earlene Thomas. You're a constellation of stars!

At William Morris Endeavor, I am indebted to Suzanne Gluck, Tracy Fisher, Cathryn Summerhayes, Nancy Josephson, Laurie Pozmantier, Michelle Feehan, Eve Attermann, Samantha Frank, Anna DeRoy, Becky Thomas, Alicia Gordon, Anna Graham Taylor, James Munro, Ellen Sushko, and Claudia Webb. Look no further for excellence.

In movieland, thank you Donna Gigliotti, Richard Thompson, Michael Pitt, and Lou Pitt. Larry Sanitsky at the Sanitsky Company gets the call at 2:00 A.M., always answers, and is forever wise, funny, and brilliant. At Simon & Schuster UK, my love and thanks to Ian Chapman, Suzanne Baboneau, and Nigel Stoneman.

At the Glory of Everything Company, the fabulous team led by Allison Van Groesbeck and Laura Corrigan, our amazing interns: Joie Giordano, Kathryn Haemmerle, Jillian Fata, Michelle March, Diana Vlavianos, Jodi Imperato, Samantha Rowe (with extra love to Judith Gold!), Bri Kennedy, Dana Walsh, Kelly Meehan Doig, Emily Morrow, Amanda Rodrigues, Eleanor Fisher, Katie James, Emily Homonoff, Michelle March, Diana E. Vlavianos, Hannah Spratt, Erin Brady, and Daniela Cardinale. Thank you Antonia Trigiani for the gift shop and Mary Trigiani for your digital expertise. The translations from English to Italian were done by Professor Dorina Cerghino-Hewitt of San Jose State University's Italian Department. Thank you Gina Casella and Nikki Padilla, who make our walking tours and tours abroad the best in the world!

My evermore love and thanks to Chris and Ed Muransky, the best team—anywhere they are, I want to be.

Gratitude and love to Doris Gluck, Mary Pipino, Tom Dyja, Liz Travis, Eamonn McChrystal, Diane and Dr. Armand Rigaux, Phil and Cindy Timp, Karen and Emmett Towey, Caz and Alex Rubin, Dagmara Domincyzk and Patrick Wilson, Dan and Robin Napoli, Sharon Ewing, Adina Pitt, Robin Kall Homonoff, Jennifer Kall D'Angelo, Eugenie Furniss, Philip Grenz, Christina Geist, Joyce Sharkey, Jack Hodgins, Jake and Jean Morrissey, Mary Murphy, Gail Berman, Debra McGuire,

Cate Magennis Wyatt, Ian, Ryan and Nancy Bolmeier Fisher, Carol and Dominic Vechiarelli, Gloria Zalaznick, Jim and Mary Deese Hampton, Suzanne and Peter Walsh, Heather and Peter Rooney, and Aaron Hill and Susan Fales-Hill, Mary K. and John Wilson, Kate Benton Doughan and Jim Doughan, Ruth Pomerance, Joanna Patton and Bill Persky, Angelina Fiordellisi and Matt Williams, Michael La Hart and F. Todd Johnson, Richard and Dana Kirshenbaum, Hugh and Jody Friedman O'Neill, Nelle and John Fortenberry, Val Thomas and Henry Reisch (newlyweds), Karen Kehela and Ben Sherwood, Cara Stein and Barry Rosenfeld, Laura Monardo and Mario Natarelli, Rosalie Ciardullo, Dolores and Dr. Emil Pascarelli, Eleanor "Fitz" King and daughters Eileen, Ellen, and Patti, Sharon Hall and Todd Kessler, Aimee Bell and David Kamp, Mary Ellen Gallagher Gavin, Rosanne Cash and John Leventhal, Liz Welch Tirell, Rachel Cohen DeSario, Charles Randolph Wright, Constance Marks, Mario Cantone, Jerry Dixon, Marolyn and Hank Senay.

Nancy Ringham Smith, Sharon Watroba Burns, Dee Emmerson, Elaine Martinelli, Kitty Martinelli (Vi and the girls), Sally Davies, Michael "Mickey" Morrison, Sister Karol Jackowski, Jane Cline Higgins, Beth Vechiarelli Cooper (my Youngstown boss), Max and Robyn Westler, John Searles, Gina Vechiarelli (my Brooklyn boss), Barbara and Tom Sullivan, Brownie and Connie Polly, Catherine and John Brennan, Greg D'Alessandro, Jena and Charlie Corsello, Karen Fink, Beáta and Steven (the Warrior) Baker, Todd Doughty and Randy Losapio, Craig Fissé, Anemone and Steve Kaplan, Christina Avis Krauss and her Sonny, Joanne Curley Kerner, Veronica Kilcullen, Lisa Rykoski, Tara Fogarty, Eleanor Jones, Mary Ellinger, and Iva Lou Johnson.

There's a special place in heaven for Michael Patrick King and a table at Bergdorf's for Cynthia Rutledge Olson, Mary Testa, Wendy Luck, Elena Nachmanoff, and Dianne Festa.

My great-aunt Lavinia Stella Perin Spadoni, "Ziwinnia," turned ninety-one this year. She deserves a parade, as she has always been a beautiful example for all of us who are lucky enough to be her grand-nieces and -nephews. Ziwinnia's example has made me a better aunt to my nieces and nephews, all of whom I adore.

Thank you to my brothers and sisters, their husbands and wives, and the mighty Stephensons.

I will be forever grateful to Ann Godoff for opening the door to my literary career, and for the gift of Lee Boudreaux, who made me a better writer.

Pat and Paul Vogelsang generously provided shelter during the storm as I finished this novel. I can never thank them enough for their love, generosity, and electricity. Thank you James Horvath and Fran Minnarik, as you were the key.

So many happy customers ate at the Legendary Guido's Supreme Macaroni Company on Ninth Avenue in New York City. The Scarola family made good food and great memories, and inspired this title.

As I wrote this book, I lost some dear friends and family I would like to honor here. The world is not as beautiful without Carol Williams Wilson, Dolly Farino, Liane Revsin, Sue Pence, Marion Gigliotti LeDonne, Carmelina "Tiny" Roma Perin, and Mary Loyola Culhane Shaughnessy (mother of eight who made time for her book club and me). There are roses in heaven now, for sure.

Dr. Sidney Wallace was a healer, a painter, an amazing husband, father, and grandfather.

My lifelong friend Joe O'Brien, first of Scranton and then Manhattan, was the best brother and friend, and a fine actor who lit up the stage and screen with originality and passion.

Rafael Prieto was a gentle soul and as fine and loyal a friend as I have ever known.

Thank you Lucia and Tim for making our home the best place on earth. Finally, what nice Italian girl doesn't thank her mother? Thank you, Mom, for everything you are and everything you taught me. I am so lucky fate sent me your way.

About the Author

Adriana Trigiani is an award-winning playwright, television writer, and documentary filmmaker. Her books include the *New York Times* best seller *The Shoemaker's Wife*; the Big Stone Gap series; *Very Valentine*; *Brava, Valentine*; *Lucia, Lucia*; and the best-selling memoir *Don't Sing at the Table*, as well as the young adult novels *Viola in Reel Life* and *Viola in the Spotlight*. She has written the screenplay for *Big Stone Gap*, which she will also direct. She lives in New York City with her husband and daughter.

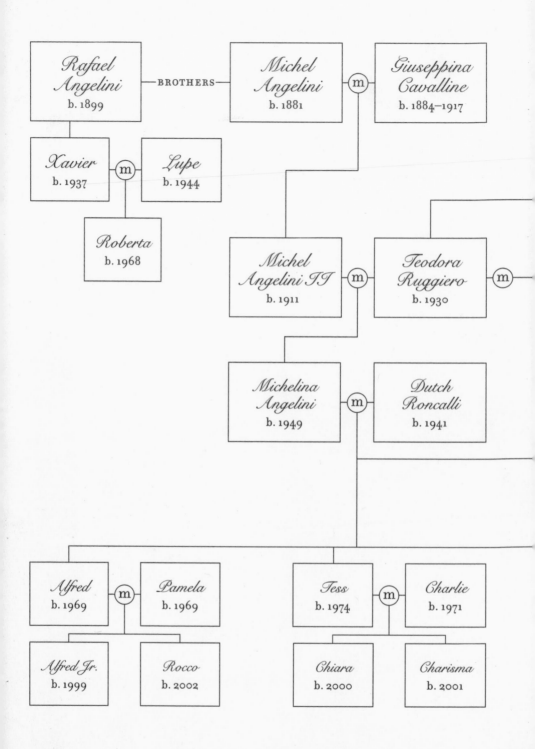